'This haunting supernatural thriller is full of hidden treasure that will delight you long after you've turned the last page'

Sarah Pinborough

'A K Benedict is snapping at the heels of Ben Aaronovitch as one of the new stars of the sub-genre of crime with a supernatural twist . . . A sparkling authorial voice and sassy dialogue keep the weird story grounded but ultimately the novel is, as it should be, haunting'

Sunday Express

'An absolutely glorious crime/fantasy/ghost story mash-up. Beautifully written, darkly funny, constantly surprising . . . my find of the year so far'

Sharon Bolton

'A K Benedict can write beautifully and has imaginative flair'

Guardian

'Wonderful! The work of an exquisitely twisted imagination'

David Mark

'Written in sinuous, elegant prose with characters that linger in the mind . . . one of the more interesting debuts this year'   *Daily Mail*

'A stunning read. I cannot recommend this book highly enough'

Crime Thriller Girl

'Thought-provoking and haunting. Gorgeous speculative story-telling'   *Liz Loves Books*

'The best kind of novel. It's witty, tense, intriguing, brimful of great ideas and so compelling that you have to fight the urge to turn the pages almost faster than you can read it just to find out what happens next.'   Mark Morris

A K Benedict read English at Cambridge and studied creative writing at Sussex. She composed film and television soundtracks, as well as performing as a musician before becoming a full-time writer in 2012. She now writes novels, drama, poetry and short stories, and lives in St Leonards-on-Sea with her dog, Dame Margaret Rutherford. Find out more at www.akbenedict.com or follow her on Twitter @ak_benedict

Also by A K Benedict

The Beauty of Murder

THE EVIDENCE OF GHOSTS

A K BENEDICT

An Orion paperback

First published as *Jonathan Dark or The Evidence Of Ghosts*
in Great Britain in 2016
by Orion Books
This paperback edition published in 2017
by Orion Books,
an imprint of The Orion Publishing Group Ltd,
Carmelite House, 50 Victoria Embankment
London EC4Y 0DZ

An Hachette UK company

1 3 5 7 9 10 8 6 4 2

A CIP catalogue record for this book
is available from the British Library.

ISBN 978 1 4091 0393 6

Typeset by Input Data Services Ltd, Somerset

Printed and bound in Great Britain by Clays Ltd, St Ives plc

www.orionbooks.co.uk

For David
My wonderful brother

In Memory of Mumrah and Liono
Keyboard guardians and the best of companions
1995–2014

Prologue

The prostitutes on the flyers stir as he enters the phone box, whispering like a naked jury. Finnegan scans the street. Soho flows around him in a high tide of tourists and commuters. Sunglasses turn faces into one-way mirrors. He checks his watch. One o'clock. They're coming for him, ready or not.

He dials her number, finger trembling. 'Pick up, baby,' he says.

'You have reached Rosa Finch. I'm busy at the moment but please call back . . .' Answerphone – they've got her already. He closes his eyes on images of Rosa with a hand clamped over her mouth, her hands tied behind her back. This is the game they play when people disobey.

Getting out of London will be nearly impossible. No one has outrun them. Yet. They took everything except his Oyster card, watch, a cigarette, the coins in his pocket and an hour's head start. Any journey he makes using the card will be clocked within seconds and, when the hour is up, they'll swoop like the pigeons in Trafalgar Square.

Delaney is his only chance. He'll be in the Doggett's Coat, watching the match. The last of Finnegan's coins clunks down. 'All right, mate?' Delaney answers. In the background, a partisan crowd roars.

'Pick-up point,' Finnegan says. 'Fifteen minutes.' He drops the receiver and barges through the door. A flyer floats down to the pavement, turning her back on him. He runs: down Greek Street, up Dean Street, through an island of tourists outside the Dominion, by a reclining Oscar Wilde, across the Strand, between cars and along Villiers Street into Embankment Station.

At the machines, a bloke in a baseball cap feeds a fiver to his Oyster card. Chest tight, Finnegan walks up to him. 'I'll swap you,' he says, holding out his own card. He wipes his forehead – sweat makes you look guilty. 'There's fifty quid on it.'

'I've got less than a tenner on mine,' the man says. He grips his card tighter.

'That's plenty for me. All I ask is that you move around the city for an hour: hop from one line to another, double back on yourself, get on a bus if you can.'

'I don't know, mate,' he says, slipping his hand into his pocket.

Finnegan presses his card against the yellow circle: £50 available.

A seed of greed shows in the man's eyes. Finnegan recognises it: he sees it in the mirror every day.

They exchange the cards and, for one moment, Finnegan wants to reach out and ask for help. But what would he say? That he's a murderer and doesn't want to be any more? The moment goes. 'Don't suppose I could have your cap as well?' Finnegan asks.

Finnegan sprints through the station and up the steps to the bridge, pulling on the baseball cap. In ten minutes he'll be in Delaney's car, headed for Ramsgate and the ferry. He'll find out where Rosa is and send for her, somehow. If she's still alive. Rosa. She's the one he's let down. He looks at the yellow diamond ring on his right hand. He fought, killed and lied for that ring. He valued it above the one she gave him.

He tugs at the ring. He'll get rid of it, throw it in the river and leave it to the tide. The ring doesn't budge. He has grown fat around it and it has sunk into the skin. The diamond glints.

Above him, the London Eye takes everything in. He prays to it – wishing on the capsules like rosary beads: 'Don't let them find me,' 'Keep Rosa safe and I'll, I'll . . .' He'll what? The promises he makes are as empty as some of the coffins he burns.

The South Bank bustles. Skateboarders roll, drinkers clink in the sun as if nothing is chasing them. He's never wished to be anyone else before, now he'd do anything to swap lives with the man on the bench with the *Evening Standard*: he looks as if he's going to stay alive for the next few days. Finnegan had thought he'd be the sort to face death with a wry smile, to drink his way through a bottle till he lay on the floor like a mescal worm, then, as the gun was cocked, grin at his killers and swig the last drop. But he's not. Sweat betrays him, kissing his back.

Landmarks pass on either side: St Paul's over the river, the Oxo Tower ahead. His lungs blaze, his legs feel as heavy as if they're already in the concrete cast they'll give him if he's found.

The Tate Modern comes into view. He never thought he'd be glad to see it. Slipping round the back to the delivery point, Finnegan collapses on the low wall. Delaney will be here in minutes. He tries a deep breath. It comes out as a rasp. He digs in his pocket for the cigarette. It has a kink in the middle but who doesn't?

He pats his pockets. Shit. They took his lighter, the bastards, those are the arseholes he's been working with – people who give a man a cigarette and steal his fire. A woman walks out of the corner shop. She is thin, busy-looking. 'You got a light?' he asks.

She rootles through her handbag, pulls out a box of matches.

'You're a lifesaver,' he says. She walks over and strikes the match. He leans in, cigarette to his lips. She cups her hand round the flame. It lights up the yellow diamond on her ring finger.

As he turns, something hits his head. Hard. His knees sink. His vision fades. He feels sound leave his mouth but never hears it.

In the basement of a house in Hackney, a man swipes through his photo gallery. He stops on his favourite picture. There she is, there's his girl, the one who will make up for all the bitches. He captured her on the way out of the hospital, her hand pressed against her blindfold. Her other hand fixes a hairgrip in place. Two shots later and the lock of hair is free again, bouncing in an auburn curl.

Something falls in the kitchen. He places his tablet on the table and walks through to the back of the flat. The kitchen is chilly throughout the year, even with the underfloor heating, but it is even colder than usual, as if an iced hand grips his neck. A mug has tumbled from the draining board to the floor and rolled against the fridge. It is cracked down one side. How did it get there? The window is gummed shut so it can't be a breeze and, anyway, there was a glass and a bowl on the board and they haven't fallen. It's not the first time this has happened; things keep falling or moving. He was woken last night by a splintering crash and stumbled out of bed, heart held in

3

a frozen fist, to find the Venetian blind on the floor. Its slats were broken like his last girlfriend's bones.

It will be better when he has her with him, when Maria is his. He will see the incidents for the nonsense they are: buses passing, road works, the rumbling of the Overground. There will be some logical explanation. There are no such things as ghosts.

1

Day One

Three girls giggle as they pass Maria. She must look a sight, groping her way along Jamaica Street in waders, wellies and blindfold. A bucket is hardly the latest in handbags. 'You'll all be dressed like this next week,' she calls after them.

Fingertips trailing along the railings in King's Stairs Gardens, she finds the place where 'I ♥ M' is scraped into the paint. Lucky M. Unlucky I. Grasping the handrail, she climbs down the steps. Her feet crunch onto Bermondsey's foreshore; gulls scatter and squawk. 'Hello?' she calls out. No reply. The stretch of beach is hers.

Sitting down on her rock, she scans the sand with her fingers. Pebbles; old clay pipes; bottle tops. The Thames has pulled back its covers to tell the tales of nights before. Soon the beach will be tucked back in again but she'll hear when the tide has turned by the way the river strokes the stones. She feels for regular shapes, squares and circles – nature does not make things perfect.

Touching something smooth and cool, she eases it out of the mud with her trowel. A fragment of porcelain. Very thin, curved at the edges. Part of a plate? She places it in the bucket and breathes deeply. This is the only time she is at peace, when teasing out mysteries from the earth.

Clank of metal against stone. Someone is coming down the steps. Slow and heavy, unsteady as they move onto the beach, breathing laboured.

'Morning, Martin,' she says. The smell of his aftershave, pine cones and patchouli, barrels down the beach towards her.

His metal detector whirs, sweeping for coins. 'No Billy today?' he asks.

'He hurt his leg down here the other day,' she replies. 'I left him pawing at the front door. Haven't seen you since the conference.'

'I've been around,' he says. Martin is trying to be enigmatic and failing. 'Didn't the doctor tell you to remove the blindfold while mudlarking? It would be less dangerous. I wouldn't have to worry about you as much.'

Maria hopes he can't see her flushing. Before she lost her blindness, she never thought about people looking at her, now she feels eyes on her at all times. The city is full of windows and people looking out of them. The blindfold is her idea. Iain, the psychologist assigned to help her 'cope' with becoming sighted, told her to remove it for at least a few hours a day. She refuses. Her world is complete, she doesn't need to see: her city gleams like the notes on a glockenspiel; her Thames is the colour of the way plums taste and she wants it to stay that way. She'll take the blindfold off and see the river one day. Not today. 'The only person who need worry about me, is me,' she says.

Martin murmurs, shuffles on the stones. She's embarrassed him. She should say something, make him feel better, but it will only make him ask her out and then she'll have to say no, again. His metal detector beeps as if trying to fill the silence.

Maria settles further back on the rock and, crossing her legs, knocks something onto the sand. Reaching down, her fingers flit, pickpocket-quick, and find a long rectangular box. Opening the lid, she touches a large gemstone, cold and faceted, on a metal band. The ring rests on a cushion. The stories float up – it's dropped out of someone's pocket, and they won't be able to propose, both parties going through life not knowing what the other would have said; or perhaps the proposal was turned down and the night ended with an overarm throw from the riverside.

Maria freezes. The ring isn't embedded in a cushion. A cushion wouldn't be so hard. Or cold. Or have a fingernail.

She cries out.

'What is it?' Martin says, worry creasing his voice. He takes the box and makes a noise as if being punched in the stomach. 'I'll call the police,' he says. Maria reaches for his arm as he searches his coat pockets. He's trembling. 'There's something in Braille in the lid,'

Martin says. He places a small piece of card in her hand. He once asked her, completely pissed in the union bar, to touch him the way that she strokes the raised dots. She laughed but locked her door that night. Stupid to think of that now.

She reads the writing: 'MARRY ME, MARIA,' it says.

Across the river, in the 24-hour café, his cappuccino cools in its cup. The mudlarks look like monkeys, picking at and grooming the beach. Replacing the binoculars in his bag, he holds up his phone and films through the open window. Maria and her mate are flotsam on the screen. He does not need to see her in detail. He could paint her face from memory. No, it's enough to have seen her holding the ring, knowing that she knows she is loved. Soon she will realise that he has been watching over her all this time, that he has left love notes to her all over London. She will understand the engagement gift and understand him as has no other woman. And she will love him. It won't be like the other times, the other ones. He has learned.

But he won't reveal himself. Not yet.

Maria's yellow pixel moves out of sight. The screen goes black, battery dead. He slams the phone down on the table. The cup jumps.

The waitress glances over from the counter. Brown make-up smudges circle her eyes. It is nearly the end of her shift, she has been serving burgers to clubbers and lattes to losers all night. Swiping at the cappuccino foam, he slips his finger into his mouth and sucks, staring at her. She blushes, turns away and concentrates on the ketchup bottles that she is arranging in lines. Coy bitch. There are stains on her apron where she wipes her hands on her hips. He follows her, sometimes, back to her shabby flat in Pimlico. But no more than that. His girl is Maria. And she is perfect. At least she will be soon enough.

Jonathan raises his head from the floor. The alarm shrills: six a.m. Ten minutes before the cleaners arrive and pretend he hasn't been here, again. Stepping out of his sleeping bag, he reaches into his filing cabinet for a fresh shirt while licking the end of the toothpaste tube. A hangover hammers at his temples.

His phone buzzes the arrival of a message. He grabs at it, hoping it's Natalie and that she's remembered. But it isn't her. Of course it isn't. It's the front desk. If he's in luck then they are about to give him a case to take his mind away from the significance of the day.

'DI Dark,' he says.

The river looks lived-in. Some days it is fresh and blue, brand new. This morning it is the brown of history teachers' trousers. Jonathan sweeps back his coat and climbs down the steps in plastic-covered boots. There was a time when he would have been embarrassed at looking like this. Not now – heartbreak gives perspective. But so does a holiday and he'd much prefer that.

SOCOs are already searching the cordoned-off beach. DS Keisha Baxter waves then runs towards a cormorant pecking at a Coke can. 'Bugger off,' she shouts. 'That could be evidence.'

Tony Rogers from Southwark CID sits on a rock with his hands in his pockets. He stares at the river lapping metres from his feet. Jonathan walks over and crouches by him. Tony has aged ten years in the last six months. He has lost weight from his face and gained it on his stomach. 'I hope this isn't a waste of your time,' Tony says.

'I'm hoping it is a huge waste of both time and resources,' Jonathan replies. 'Otherwise—'

'I just meant . . .' Tony trails off. He picks up a stone and turns it over. 'As soon as I heard I thought of Tanya. I didn't want to take any risks.' The unspoken words 'this time' hang in the air like gulls. The soundtrack of cranes and trains gets louder.

'We could be worrying about nothing.'

Tony nods the nod of a man who doesn't believe.

'Tanya wasn't your fault,' Jonathan says. 'Your hands were tied.' Their silence acknowledges the inappropriateness of the remark.

'Wasn't your fault either,' Tony says. 'At that point, the stalking laws had no teeth.'

'I could have listened to you earlier.'

Tony rubs his forehead. 'Lesson learned, eh?' He shuffles away with hunched shoulders.

Keisha walks over. 'You should see the ring before it's taken away,' she says, gesturing to the SOCO. He steps over with care, holding the jewellery box.

Gloves snapped on, Jonathan looks down at the contents of the box. The ring is on a slim, long finger with chipped red nail varnish. Desiccated skin clings to the bone.

'And this says "Marry me, Maria"?' he asks.

Keisha nods. They need not say any more. Eleven months ago, Tanya Baker had received a yellow ring on her doorstep. The message on the box said 'MARRY ME, TANYA'. She reported this and accounts of being followed but the police had no powers unless she had reason to believe her life was in danger. One month later she was dead, her red-nailed ring finger removed.

'Get it to Richard Agnarsson immediately. We need to know if that's Tanya's,' Jonathan says. Panning across the river to Westminster and down to Wapping, Jonathan knows that behind a winking window – on a balcony; on a bridge – the person who placed the ring will be watching. If it *is* Tanya's murderer, then he'll be watching with pleasure. Rising pleasure. He wouldn't want to miss out. An image floats up, like a body that's been weighted down and then freed: Tanya, on her bed, her hand on the knife thrust up into her ribcage, her eyes already blank. His doubt and lack of clarity clouded her case and has got worse since. If he could he would send teams out to sweep the banks of the Thames for a man with binoculars in one hand and his cock in the other. In this city, watching goes unwatched. Every day people are caught as blurs on camera, moving jerkily through the streets. Thousands of glass eyes help him catch criminals but they still unnerve him. It should make you feel less lonely, being watched over. It doesn't.

Jonathan holds up his middle finger in the air and turns in a slow circle. The fucker should catch that, wherever he is.

Keisha points to the top of the stairs. His officers are speaking to mud-covered people and taking notes. 'All potential witnesses are up there,' she says. 'Mostly mudlarks, the odd dog walker.'

Jonathan has seen mudlarks on his early morning call-outs and stake-outs and nights out that turn into mornings out: it's a strange kind of person that chooses to leave a warm bed and wade in Weil's disease. 'Which one is Maria King?' he asks.

'The one at the end in the yellow waterproofs, talking to Amanda. There is a complicating factor . . .'

The woman is wearing a blindfold. It takes up a third of her face. She is slight, with shoulder length red hair and pale skin. No physical resemblance to Tanya. 'Was she wearing the—'

'Blindfold at the time? Yes. She was born blind,' Keisha interrupts, 'but recently had an operation to gain her sight. For some reason she still wears the blindfold. All the time.'

So she wouldn't easily know if she *was* being stalked. Jonathan watches as Maria walks over to the railings. Why doesn't she want to see? Or should that be *who* doesn't she want to see?

'She says we've got an hour and counting till the tide takes over.'

'Better get on with it then.' Jonathan climbs onto a rock. Stretching his arms over his head, he shouts: 'We have sixty minutes before the Thames stashes the evidence. I want every part of the shore searched and every pebble placed back where you found it – we don't want to piss off the Port of London Authority. We don't leave this beach, however, till the river is at the steps. If your socks aren't soaked then you're walking home.' He starts to step down, then turns back. 'And if any of you contaminate the evidence I will take great delight in killing you and I will make sure every detail is written down for the CPS. Any questions? No? Excellent.'

*

The Angel looks out to the north of the river like a lover it will never meet. Jonathan sits on the old pub's narrow balcony, facing Tower Bridge and a sky lit in pink and orange. He can see why Turner painted *The Fighting Temeraire* here. The smell of bacon comes from the pub kitchen. His stomach rumbles. He hasn't eaten anything in twenty-four hours but he doesn't feel hungry, just empty.

The air is damp, the deceptive September sun no longer touches the mornings or evenings. Late commuters are still hurrying, jostling and bumping till they settle like autumn leaves in their offices. On the foreshore, the water reaches for the wall. The chance of finding further evidence is ebbing.

Jonathan fans out the initial statements on the table. Of the five mudlarks interviewed, all of them knew that Maria searched in the same place every day. Each of them denied knowledge of the ring and of seeing anyone who could have placed it on the rock. The two CCTV cameras that cover the area should be more helpful.

He lingers on Martin Crow's statement. He was the only one who pointed to a potential suspect – Hugh Foister, Maria's boss at the Museum of London. 'He's not right for her,' Martin had said to Keisha, an interestingly proprietorial response. Martin and Maria have been friends since university and 'it's a running joke between us' that Martin asks her out every few years. Maybe so, or maybe he doesn't see it as a joke any more. He *was* with her when she found it, which would have been convenient for leaving the jewellery box for her to find.

Jonathan rolls a cigarette – teasing damp cherry tobacco onto the paper. The ritual soothes him and helps him think. He tucks the rollie into his cigarette case. These aren't for smoking. Engraved into the silver case is a message: 'Happy 5th Anniversary, Darling. Now give up!' He hasn't smoked since. Turns out that she didn't mean he should give up smoking: his wife always was good at mixed messages. And she *is* still his wife, not his ex. Not yet. Everything hangs in the balance.

His phone goes. Unknown number – it could be her, calling from work.

'Have I got you out of bed, you lazy bastard?' It's Neil, Jonathan's cousin from the corner of the family with all the money and none of the courtesy. Neil is in Spain on a recce for a new bar. Which means recceing for one-night stands.

'I'm working, Neil, can I ring you—'

'No, you can't. I've got a favour to ask.' Here we go. 'You know the house I bought in Spitalfields last year?' Neil continues.

'No.' Jonathan can't keep track of Neil's burgeoning business as a bad landlord.

'Well it needs a lot of work. I've contracted three different firms and they've all cried off with bullshit reasons. I need someone to chase up new contractors and be on site at night so I don't get squatters. If you can chuck some paint at it then all to the good.'

'You want me to live there?'

'You'd be doing me a favour.'

Neil is never this straightforward. Suspicion kicks in. 'What have you heard? Who's been talking?'

'Don't know what you mean, mate.'

Jonathan watches as Maria walks along the waterfront, followed by Keisha. He hopes that the ring is just a prank, a false alarm. He doubts it. 'I'll think about it.'

'Got a better offer, have you? Get in there. Never liked Natalie – cold, manipulative. You can do better, mate.'

Anger pulses in Jonathan's neck. 'You'll have to find someone else to babysit your house.'

'You just carry on living in your sleeping bag in the office, then, cuz.'

Who told him? Does Jonathan's mum know? No – she would have insisted that he came to her in Cardiff. He has always kept difficult things from her, especially since Dad died two years ago, in case this will be the time her stent stops working. She doesn't want to know about death or bad news. He didn't tell her when his best mate and meticulous sergeant, Jacob Coleman, died in the line last year. She doesn't even know that Natalie, having taken his heart and folded it over and over into a paper aeroplane, has torn it down the fuselage. And what about Natalie? Does she know? The uncertainty makes his stomach clench. He had told her he was staying at a friend's house, hoping she would feel the same jealousy he experiences when seeing her lover's car outside his old house. Maybe a Spitalfields address will make her think he's moving on. That he's over her. And that will bring her back.

From the other end of the line comes the sound of a straw at the bottom of an empty glass. Neil's drained his first cocktail of the day already. 'I'll send a bike round with the key, shall I?' he says.

Jonathan says nothing.

'It'll be with you in an hour or so. I'll raise a glass to your new home. Maybe you'll last longer than all those foremen. Who'd have thought builders would be superstitious?'

Jonathan takes out one of the cigarettes from the case and lights it. He holds the rollie, letting it burn itself out. Smoke gathers around his finger like a phantom ring.

Maria walks away from The Angel, dancing her fingers along the wall. There used to be three bronze statues here: Dr Salter, waving from the bench metres away; his daughter, leaning against the wall; and his cat, slinking on the bricks. Dr Salter's statue had possessed the presence of a living man. She had talked to him sometimes, other times they had sat in happy silence. She often chats with statuary: the gardener in Brewers' Hall; the Young Dancer of Broad Court; Mr George Peabody. They are London's confessors, sculpted in metal and stone; only the river keeps more secrets. She still talks to Dr Salter, even though he was stolen years ago. It's as if he's still there. She walks over to his old bench and sits down. 'What should I do, Dr Salter?' she whispers.

DS Baxter follows with quick, snapping steps. Maria pictures her with a swishing tail and padded paws. She wishes Billy were here, to lean against her and make her foot go numb under his weight, to place his big head on her lap and harrumph: he'd take her mind off the idea that somewhere in her city, someone is stalking her.

DS Baxter sits down next to her on the bench. It feels crowded.

'I need to ask you some more questions,' DS Baxter says. The pages of her notebook rustle as they're turned. 'Has anything gone missing from your home recently?'

Maria shakes her head.

'Can you describe your relationship with any ex-partners?'

'Non-existent.' It's weird if you're friends with an ex: either you're fooling yourselves or you weren't crazy about each other in the first place.

'Who was your last boyfriend?'

'Carl. Although I don't think he's worth going after.'

'What is his surname?'

'Janus. Simon calls him Janus the Anus.'

'And Simon is?'

'My friend. We've been mates for years. We used to go on double dates – me and Carl, Simon and Will.'

'Would Simon have any reason to leave you the ring?'

'No – for obvious reasons.'

'Don't discount someone just because they're gay,' DS Baxter says.

'I didn't mean *that*. He loves me, it wouldn't be him.'

'Mmm,' DS Baxter says. Her pen scratches out some words. 'And is Carl an anus, would you say?'

Maria sighs. 'Not really. He just wasn't that into me. Which is probably why I was into him.'

'Could *he* have left you the ring?'

Maria laughs. 'The only thing he left me was a kettle. Carl doesn't even believe in marriage, thinks it's a defunct capitalist and patriarchal construct.' Maria leans towards DS Baxter. 'But given that he used my credit card to subscribe to porn sites, I'm not sure how far he can be believed.'

DS Baxter's pen grazes the page. 'Anyone else that could be responsible?' she says.

'Not Martin, if you're thinking that. Too squeamish. He wouldn't even touch the dead dog that washed up last week.' Maria opens a packet of chewing gum. Who would leave her something like that? Hugh Foister, her boss, 'joked' about being her secret admirer last Valentine's Day when he gave everyone in the office a limp garage-bought rose, but she can't see him being a stalker. He's far too lazy. She takes out a strip and chews. 'The problem is that anyone who has seen my blog will know that I always arrive ninety minutes before low tide,' she says. 'And that I usually go to the same stretch of the shoreline, for an hour or so, most days.' Different shoes are approaching. An even walk, determined. 'Isn't this a bit much? Couldn't it just be a sick joke?'

'It's possible,' a man's voice says from a metre away. Maria had heard him on the beach. The river had gone quiet for him. 'But unlikely. I'm Detective Inspector Dark.' He touches her hand and she shakes his. 'I hope DS Baxter here has been looking after you. Is there anyone we can call to come and be with you? A friend? Family member?'

'My friend, Simon,' Maria says. 'He'll be working, though.' She hears him tapping onto a tablet or phone.

'We'll want a word with him anyway,' DI Dark says. 'As to whether this is over the top, we are investigating in connection with another case, one in which a young woman was murdered,' he says simply.

Maria grips the seat.

'She was proposed to in a similar way. If you *are* being stalked by the same person then we need to protect you while using any new information on finding him.'

'It doesn't help that . . .' DS Baxter trails off.

'You can say it, you know,' Maria says. 'That I'm blind.' She smiles at them and taps the blindfold.

'But you're not blind, are you? Not any more,' says DS Baxter. Her voice has an edge to it.

'I had corrective surgery six months ago for the visual impairment I've had since birth. It was a complete success and a huge mistake. I knew straight away that I should have stayed the way I was and covered my eyes. My surgeon and therapist both think that I'll come round. Either they don't know me very well or they do not understand how I feel about sight.'

'Or both,' DI Dark says.

'If I had been through that,' DS Baxter says, 'I'd be off around the world. Imagine how amazing it would be to see Ibiza for the first time. The sea, the beach, a whole club jumping. I envy you.'

Maria raises her eyebrows.

'I suspect that Maria has been imagining since she was born,' DI Dark says. 'And that her head is full of images that wouldn't match up.'

Maria nods and turns towards him. 'It's Pelmanism with no matching pairs.'

'But wouldn't it be better to see, especially if you are being stalked?

It would help us to help you, at least.' DS Baxter's voice is high, taut-ened by exasperation.

'From what I've heard,' Maria says, 'stalkers enjoy making an impact. I'm not going to give him that victory over me. I've travelled across India, Thailand and the US with only a guide dog to help. I'm not going to alter my life for a coward.'

DI Dark steps forward. 'Have we got the name of your doctor? The one who did your operation?'

DS Baxter shudders next to her.

'Don't you like doctors?' Maria says.

'Keisha abseils, scuba dives and has a pet tarantula but get her in a room with a medic and she'll jump on a chair and thwack them with a slipper.'

'I don't mind MDs as long as they don't come near me,' Baxter says in a vulnerable voice that makes Maria want to hug her.

'They're more scared of you than you are of them, Keisha. Maria, we're going to send you home, with another team to look over your flat,' DI Dark says. 'They will be searching for anything you may have missed.'

'You're not coming with me?' Maria asks, standing up. She sounds pathetic, she knows.

'Your flat could be a crime scene,' DI Dark replies. 'We keep teams separate so that we don't compromise evidence. Don't worry, you'll be fine. If you remember anything that could help then tell one of my team or phone me.' He slips his card into her hand, then retrieves it, tutting at himself. 'Sorry. I didn't think. Please consider having someone with you at all times and stay away from social media. And that's advice for life, not only because of stalkers.' He touches her hand briefly. He is cold. She would give him her gloves but one of them has gone missing.

This should not be happening. The proposal was supposed to be be-tween him and Maria, a private moment that they would remember forever. He has given her a valuable gift and she spoiled it by letting Dark touch her. Why did she let that fool with the metal detector call the police? Her faithlessness will be punished in due course and DI Dark will discover that, just as last time, he is not the one in control.

'Sorry to interrupt your thoughts. Are you a twitcher?'

'What?'

An old man in a clerical collar sits at the table behind him. He raises his coffee cup to his lips slowly as if it were a sacrament. He repeats the question.

'I am, yes,' he replies. He adheres a smile. 'Although I call myself a birder.'

'Don't you ever get bored, just watching birds?' the priest asks.

'Do you ever get bored, just listening to sinners? No? Well, I'm the same. I can sit and watch a target for hours. Without sleeping or eating, sometimes. Here. You have a go.' He hands over the binoculars. 'There's a cormorant on the nearest post.' The old man turns the binoculars over in his hands. 'Heavy, aren't they?'

Standing up, he twists his head till he has the bird in sight. 'I can see every feather!' he says, grinning. He then goes quiet, watching. Minutes pass.

'What do you think?' he asks the old man. He is bored of this now. He is missing out on Maria.

The cleric's forehead wrinkles as he passes the bins back. 'It's soothing,' he says. 'Like praying.'

'Yes,' he replies. 'In a way it is very much like worship. And we all kill our gods in the end.'

His phone bleeps. It is work – time to leave. He raises the binoculars again. Maria is being taken to a police car with one of the detectives. Her head is turned in the direction of DI Dark, listening to him walking away.

3

'Come on through, love,' Frank McNally says, walking into the mourning room and turning on the lamps.

Mrs Winters follows, staring at everything she passes. He pulls the curtains on the Spitalfields street. The last thing she'll want to see is the world carrying on as if nothing has changed.

She settles into the armchair, pale against the red cushions.

'Tea?'

She nods.

Frank puts on the kettle and prepares the pot. She won't drink it, they never do, but it is an anchor. It's calming, the ritual of the thing. He places a box of tissues next to her. She reaches out a hand but does not take one. She stares at her palm as if it is new to her, when it has never been so old.

'Take your time, love,' he says. He keeps his tone low and reassuring. Solid as an oak casket.

She opens her mouth but no words come out. She can understand him, though – that's a good sign, considering what she's been through. Sometimes the bereaved are so thrown that it can be months, years even, before they are really present.

She wriggles in the chair and seems at once a child, a young woman and an ancient one. She is waiting for him to speak.

'You've had a shock,' he says, taking off his top hat. 'The biggest shock of all. Give yourself the time and space to filter what is happening to you. It's overwhelming, and all you will be able to think about and feel is your loss but as you go through the grieving process you'll begin to remember what you had, and what you have now. As the undertaker here, my job is to guide you as best I can.'

She looks through him. She's in the land of those who have lost.

'Let me take you through your options.' Frank reaches for his folder. 'You don't have to make any decisions now. Take your time. You can come back when you're ready. But, just to give you an idea, here's a run down of our services. After death we—'

The door opens. Barbara, Frank's wife, stands in the doorway, clutching her hands, her fingers chasing each other. 'There's someone for you, Frank. He won't talk with me. He ran upstairs.'

A crash comes from the landing. 'Please excuse me, Mrs Winters, I will be back as soon as I can. Could you please help her, Barbara? I'm taking her through her options.'

Mutterings and murmurings echo against the wooden panels of the hallway upstairs. Mrs Winters turns her head towards the noise. Another good sign. She'll be OK, given tea, time and attention.

Frank dashes into the hall. A vase smashes down the stairs. 'I'm coming up,' he shouts, sprinting up two steps at a time. 'No need to fret, we can sort anything out. Nothing a couple of pints can't solve.'

Frank stands, panting, at the top of the stairs. His outsized heart pounds. 'Hello?' He checks in the bathroom and then under the bed in the main bedroom, in the wardrobe, behind the curtains. No one is there, only the telling smell of burning candles. 'You have come to the right place. I can help you.'

'You'd better, Frank,' says a voice behind him. A sharp knife jabs against Frank's spine.

Frank raises his arms, slowly, and turns.

A man stands shivering in front of him, a knife in his hand. He is pale and thin and looks very much like . . . 'Finnegan?'

'Where is she? Where's Rosa?' Finnegan Finch asks. His voice is weaker than before, like tea that's barely seen the bag.

'At the crematorium, as far as I know. I spoke to her earlier today. She's arranging a cremation for me.'

'She was OK?' Finnegan says. His hand is shaking. He looks hardly strong enough to hold the knife.

19

'She seemed fine but it's hard to tell on the phone. I haven't seen her since last week, of course. At the funeral. But I'd say, considering everything, she's doing well. Bearing up is what we say.'

'You're lying.' He presses the tip of the knife to Frank's chest.

'I never lie, Finnegan, you know that. I deal out truth in small doses.'

'Homeopathic doses.'

Frank takes a small step forward, holding his arms up, palms forward. 'Tell me what's going on and we'll work it out together.'

Finnegan's face contorts, passing from hope into rage. 'For all I know you're in on it. One of them. Somebody I knew told them that I wanted to leave. It could have been you. Your wife has probably already called—' He stops, confusion creasing his forehead. 'Barbara was downstairs. I saw her. But I can't have . . .'

Frank waits. It's coming.

Finnegan stares at Frank. 'It can't be Barbara. Her service was at my crematorium . . . what the fuck is going on?' His hand shakes; the knife nicks Frank's chest. Blood spots through his shirt. Finnegan whimpers.

'I'm here,' Frank says. 'I'll help in every way I can.'

Finnegan crumples like a coat without a hanger. The knife clatters to the floor. He sobs and rocks on his heels. Last time Frank saw him was at a night out in Soho, an evening of loose living for death professionals. Finnegan had been flat on the floor in the corner of a restaurant, flushed with booze, snoring an arpeggio of whistles and snorts. Dim sum were balanced on his forehead and bets taken on when they would fall. Frank was told that Finnegan was in trouble, in over his head with a dodgy crowd. Now he is dead and shaking. As transparent as rice paper.

Finnegan takes a lungless breath. He stares with horror at his hand. It is fading.

'We can only hold on to so much at once,' Frank says gently.

Finnegan looks up at him. He opens his mouth to speak then closes it. Tries again. 'You said you saw Rosa at a funeral.'

Frank nods. Here it comes.

'Whose was it?' Finnegan's voice comes out as a whisper.

Frank kneels next to him, knees and floorboards creaking. 'Well, there was an incident in—'

'The truth, Frank. Lethal dose.'

'It was your funeral, Finnegan,' Frank says.

4

Two male officers are waiting outside when Maria gets home. They are discussing last night's episode of a crime show. Billy joins in, barking and pawing on the other side of the door. All Maria wants is to curl up on her bed with him, and feel her way into a book.

'Whoever they've got as an advisor is bollocks,' one of the men says. 'You'd never get it past the CPS.' His voice is strident. He sounds young, in his twenties, possibly trying to make up for inexperience. Being in your twenties is already young to Maria, and she's only just stepped out of them. Not that she'd be twenty again. Not for anything.

'But that superintendent is fit, eh?' he says. 'Did you see the heels she was wearing? Do you reckon Allen would ever wear those? She'd look all right, I reckon.'

'I didn't know that the high heel was such a well-known way to fight crime,' Maria says.

Neither of the men replies. Maybe they'd thought she couldn't hear: some people believe that since her sight is out of action, her other senses are as well; others that alternative senses compensate. Disability is a city of myths.

'Sorry about that,' the man says, coming up the path towards her. 'The first syllable of "Constable", was made for the likes of me.' He smells of generic body spray. 'I'm DS Peter Rider, part of DI Dark's team. This is Mike Reynolds, Scene of Crime Officer. He'll be under-taking an initial search of your flat. Hopefully he won't find anything. I know we must be blending into one officer by now. If it helps, Mike is an ugly sod and I've got black hair and a nose that a pug would be jealous of.'

'Of which a pug would be jealous,' Mike Reynolds says. 'He's a better officer than he is a grammarian, you'll be relieved to know. We'll be as quick as we can, don't worry.' His voice is Paisley-raised, his 'r's sound like the flicking pages of a paperback.

She takes the long chain around her neck and fishes the key out from under her jumper. They are watching her, she can feel it, checking out her competency. Soon they'll be poking around her flat wearing squeaky gloves. Her kitchen hasn't seen a pair of rubber gloves in years.

'Are you OK, Maria?' Mr Amello calls down from his balcony.

She can smell wet geraniums. A blob of water hits her head. He must be watering the hanging baskets – at this time of year he normally only waters them before he goes to bed. He's using it as an excuse to check up on her. She'd love to go up to the Amellos' humid front room filled with plants and the chatter of parrots. 'I'll be up later. Save me some cake,' Maria says.

'You know I don't eat cake, Maria,' Mr Amello says.

Mrs Amello's cackle of derision cascades from their flat. Mr Amello is diabetic but can't stop buying and eating family packs of biscuits.

'Any trouble from these people and I'll send Mrs Amello down,' he says.

'You don't want to mess with Donatella Amello,' Maria says, wagging her finger towards Rider.

She opens the door. 'After you,' Reynolds says. His hand brushes the small of her back as she walks into the hallway.

Billy bounds up. His tail thumps against the carpet as he nuzzles at Reynolds' hands. 'He's a wonderful guide dog, not so great a guard dog,' Maria says, before they can. Bending down, she wraps her arms around his thick middle and lays her cheek into his fur. He wriggles round to lick her.

'You don't need a guide dog, though, do you?' Reynolds says. There is an edge to his voice. 'You're taking a trained dog from someone else.'

Maria fights the urge to snap at him. Sometimes she'd like to be able to bark. 'Billy is nearly eleven. At his age he wouldn't be placed with anyone else.'

'So you're an old man, then?' Reynolds says to Billy.

Billy huffs. Would Reynolds say that to a human? Probably.

As soon as the officers enter the hallway, their movements become swift and officious. 'Stay here, please,' Rider says. They search her flat, shoes moving from the laminate in the lounge to the lino in her small kitchen and the tiles in the bathroom.

Returning to the hallway, Reynolds opens the door to her bedroom and closes it behind him. She has an impulse to follow and kick yesterday's knickers under the bed. And the day before's. Has she left anything embarrassing on the bedside table? Billy ate her vibrator so he can't find that. Shit – did she take that teenth from her sock drawer?

'Could you please check if anything is missing or has been moved?' Rider asks, handing her a pair of gloves. 'Try not to disturb anything more than necessary.'

Maria reaches for the shelf above the radiator. She whispers her fingers over the books, all are in the right place.

'Are they in Braille?' Rider asks.

Maria shakes her head. 'They're old, either first editions or the nearest I have been able to afford. Braille copies don't have the same smell. It's the age of the paper. Anyway, I know them so well I don't need to read them.' Maria feels her face flare. They're probably imagining her with her nose in the crevice of the book and they're not far off. Her copy of *Great Expectations* smells of the marshes she grew up on, of Romney salt, of sitting on sinking beaches and digging for treasure. A thought is uncovered. 'I didn't think of it before. A few days ago I noticed that this statue had been moved.' She walks over to the bookcase opposite the front door, stands on tiptoe and feels for the tiny clay goddess on the top. It teeters.

'Careful,' Rider says, sharply.

Maria snaps her hand back. An odd sense of shame shivers through her. 'Sorry.'

'Don't worry, keep talking.'

'I always keep her up there but she had moved to the next shelf down. I put it down to being absent-minded.'

'Anything else that you put down to forgetfulness or being distracted?'

'I lose things all the time so it's hard to tell. I drop them on the foreshore – I like to think I'm providing finds for future mudlarks. I'm missing a glove, a bracelet and I'm sure that I'm lacking an earring. I wore a pair last week and I was convinced I had taken them both off and put them in the jewellery box on my dresser. Either I was drunk and remembered wrongly or it went missing overnight.' She swallows. Someone could have been in her bedroom at night. Watching her. In those private moments when she thinks she is completely alone, and acts so. She would know though, wouldn't she? If someone was in the room with her? She always thought she'd be able to sense it, like when she knows if a television is on by the fizz of electricity. What if she couldn't? Fear slinks between her shoulder-blades.

'You'll need to list specific personal items that are missing,' Rider says. His matter-of-factness is reassuring. He moves closer and takes the icon from her. 'What is it?' His tone gives the impression of not being impressed.

'A divinity. I was on an excavation in Greece a couple of years ago and we found hundreds of them. The organisers of the dig gave it to me when I left. This one is Theia, a Titan. The goddess of sight.' She's over-explaining. She does that when she's nervous.

'Right.' Rider clearly doesn't care. Behind him, Reynolds opens the bedroom door. 'And you put it back?'

'That's where she lives,' Maria says. She sounds ridiculous and doesn't care.

Rider takes photos of the bookcase. It sounds as if her flat is being snapped at. 'We'll need to take the statue away and examine it.'

Maria fights back the urge to grab Theia back. She walks into the lounge and by touch surveys the ornaments on the mantelpiece. Did she leave that bow-shaped driftwood slightly more to the left? What about the Bellarmine jars lined up like an identity parade of bearded assailants? If she could see then maybe it would be more obvious. What if she's just being stubborn? She lifts the corner of her blindfold. Black images swim against brightness like inverse ghosts. She slips the blindfold back in place.

'Maria,' Rider calls out.

She walks towards the sound of his voice.

He's in her tiny spare room. 'What is all this?' he asks. His voice is angled upwards – he must be looking up to the shelves and boxes that pile up to the ceiling.

'This is my mudlarking room. I keep my finds in here,' she says. She moves her hand to touch the box closest to her. There is not enough room for the two of them in here. She feels exposed.

Rider pulls a box nearer to him on the shelf. 'Are those rubies?'

'Garnets,' Maria says. 'There's a place on the foreshore that, when the tide goes and twilight arrives, apparently glows red with garnets. It's near a flow pipe so they could have been dumped, stolen goods maybe. You can't move for them. When I heard about it I made a special trip.'

'Where is it?' Rider asks, digging into the garnets with his fingers and letting them fall and chink into each other.

'I can't tell you that,' Maria says. 'Larkers' secret.' She winks, not that Rider can see behind her blindfold.

'Have you checked your collection recently?' he asks. He's flicking through Maria's catalogue. She records everything she finds in that book, and then online at the Foreshore Records Observation Group database.

'Not for a few months, not the ones up high, anyway. I make sure my favourite items are easy to grab.'

The metal rungs doink as he climbs. Boxes slide out, shushing against the shelf.

She'd give up her first coffee of the day for them to go away. 'Is this necessary?' she says. 'I can't see how this can help you locate a stalker.'

'I'm making sure he hasn't left you anything else,' Rider says. 'There could be a note, a present . . . look at all these pipes! You must have hundreds here.'

'Those are just the complete ones. Please don't move them,' she says. 'Some of them are more than three hundred years old.' She blushes again. When Rider and Reynolds eventually go, she will sit down with clay pipes and cradle her 1650s specimen in her palm. She discovered it in the dark layer of ash and smoked stones that lies in every cross-section of the foreshore – the Great Fire still present and turned up by the Thames. When she holds it, she feels connected with history and a sense that nothing matters, nothing changes and nothing is lost. She's learned more from the foreshore than from six months in therapy.

'Who else has access to your flat?' Rider says, stepping down.

Her chest burns like pipe smoke in the trachea at the thought of someone taking her finds. She tries to hide it. 'The Amellos,' she says, 'and my landlord. Carl, my ex, had a key but he gave it, well, threw it back.' She touches her temple, remembering the cold strike of the metal against her head. 'I have friends round, of course. Sometimes I have a boyfriend, but not for months.'

Billy huffs up next to her and sits on her foot. She places a hand on his big head. His eyes close under her palm.

'I'll need a list of everyone who has been here in the last six months to a year,' Rider says.

'You're joking. How am I supposed to remember that?'

Rider's phone bleeps. He exhales, heavily. 'Shit,' he says.

'What is it?' Reynolds says from across the room.

'Did you check the bedroom for cameras?' Rider asks him.

'Of course I did. There was nothing I—'

Rider runs out of the room. Maria follows. 'Tell me what's going on,' she says.

Rider moves into her bedroom, muttering about angles. He stops. 'Did you have two smoke detectors installed?' he asks. His voice is directed to the ceiling.

'Why would I do that?' she says. She hasn't touched a smoke alarm since changing the battery last year.

'*Someone* did.' He drags her chair across from the dressing table. It creaks as he steps on it. Something scrapes on the ceiling. He jumps back to the floor. 'You can't stay here tonight,' he says.

'I'm not going anywhere,' she replies.

'Listen.' He presses a button on his phone.

She can't identify what she's hearing at first. A woman's voice. Then it hits. It's her voice. 'Are you ready for bed, Billy? I've got to get up at five tomorrow. Early tide. You can sleep in if you like . . . fuck . . . I should get new ones . . . remind me to . . .' Maria backs away, into her dressing table.

'Someone has been filming you from your smoke detector and now they've sent us excerpts of the footage,' Rider says.

'What can you see?' Maria asks.

Rider hesitates. 'I don't think you should—'

'You're getting ready for bed,' Reynolds interrupts. 'There is night vision footage of you taking off your clothes. You put cream on your legs then trip as you get into your pyjamas—'

Behind the mask she closes her eyes. 'I can picture the rest,' she says. Maria crosses her arms over her chest, imagining the sight of her hunched over in her underwear, stomach bunched as she moisturises her scaly legs, falling into scuzzy old cosy pyjamas that gape round her breasts, bag round the bum and have a hole in the left armpit. The ones she wears when no one is watching.

5

This can't be happening. Last thing Finnegan remembers is lighting a fag on the South Bank and then – nothing. Nothing at all, right up to the point when he was driven here in a cab. The memory of him dying is as opaque as the Thames. He sits down at Frank's kitchen table, trembling. But how can he be? Sitting and trembling both require a body, and his has been burnt in his own crematorium. A sob throbs through him.

'Take your time,' Frank says, big hands flat on the table.

Every time Finnegan gets close to getting a grip on the situation, more of it floats away. He reaches for the mug of orange tea. His hand passes straight through.

'Don't worry,' Frank says, gently. 'It takes practice and a lot of control to affect the physical world. You are learning everything all over again.'

Finnegan tries again. The mug does not budge. 'I don't understand. I threw that vase.'

'And held a knife to me.' Blood dries on the pocket of Frank's shirt.

'Sorry. I don't know who to trust any more.'

'Forget it. You were full of fear. It galvanised you, let you become solid enough to grasp the handle.'

Finnegan shakes his head. This makes no sense.

'Strong emotions such as fear and hate, and love, of course,' Frank continues, 'help to pull a ghost through from the Gloaming into this world and make its spectral body more present. It takes a lot of energy just to sustain consciousness, let alone move physical items. You'll learn how to control things, in time.'

'And that's the same for all . . .'

Frank lifts his eyebrows, waits for the end of the sentence. Finnegan can't – he gags on the word 'ghosts'.

Frank, thank God, takes over. 'Some may struggle to even surface from the Gloaming, some never manage and give up, others take to it no problem. You'll be OK though – you've come through quickly and that bodes well. It takes years for some spirits to take the form you have now.'

'How come you can see and hear me? And how could that woman?'

'Barbara?'

'That old taxi driver who picked me up. Laugh like Babs Windsor in a storm drain.'

Frank laughs. 'That was Margery. She's an old friend of mine.'

Finnegan reaches into his pocket and takes out a small coin. It is see-through in his transparent hand. He places it on the table. It is now as solid as any coin. On picking it up again, it becomes translucent. 'She said to give you this,' he says, holding it out.

'Gratefully received,' Frank says, bowing his head once.

'What is it?'

'An obol.'

'What kind of a word is that?'

'It's an ancient Greek coin, traditionally used to pay Charon when he ferried the dead across the River Styx.'

'She gave me two, then took one back again and told me to give the other one to you.'

'Your payment,' Frank says. 'To us, for your crossing. Margery has been bringing me newly surfaced spirits to guide through the process since before she was dead.'

'Why you?'

'I have been able to see and communicate with ghosts since I was a kid, same as Margery. My first word was "dada", which isn't unusual, only my dad died before I was born, and my mum never mentioned him. That confused me because I saw him all the time: rocking my cradle, telling me a bedtime story, pushing me on a swing . . . whenever I cried, he'd be there. I was the only one in the family with Sight. I learned not to mention it to anyone – mum either cried or gave me a wallop for lying. Teachers just went for the cane.' He shrugs. 'Some people don't want to know the truth, even if deep down they know all too well. We could all see ghosts if we could handle it.'

Finnegan rocks backwards and forwards. He grew up in a family where the only ghost spoken of was the Holy one. 'Is this some kind of purgatory?' he asks.

Frank's forehead creases in pity. Finnegan has seen that look on Frank's face before, when he talked to mourners. 'I'm sorry, Finnegan. This is all there is. There is no heaven, no hell, just a world where the living live with the dead.'

'That's a lot of dead people.'

'One hundred billion odd,' Frank says. 'The majority of those are in the Gloaming but, even so, the world is crowded with spirits.'

Finnegan walks over to the window and looks down into Frank's yard. Hearses lurk like shiny black horses. In the garden next door, a tall, thin ghost turns and stares at him. Finnegan lurches back. If his heart hadn't been unhooked it would have stopped.

'Did you see one?' Frank asks.

Finnegan nods. 'Are they everywhere?'

'Most houses have a ghost, most streets have one on its corner; most people have one or more spirits behind their backs. There are more people-shaped shadows in the world than there are people to cast them.'

This is all too much. 'Can you take me to Rosa?' Finnegan asks. His voice is so quiet that Frank has to lean forward. He must see her. He needs to see that she is OK. That one thing remains the same. And that she misses him.

'We'll go later,' Frank says. 'I promise. I want to make sure that you have absorbed some of this first.'

'So tell me,' Finnegan says, in an attempt to change the subject. He walks back to Frank. The air seems thicker now, like pressing into the skin of a balloon. 'How was my funeral? Can't have been enough booze for a decent party: you didn't wake me.' He tries to laugh but all he can think of is Rosa in black, standing by a coffin containing another man.

'It was a very moving ceremony.'

'How did I . . .' He pauses. He has to say it. He must know. 'How did I die?' The edge of another memory is forming. Of him falling and then . . .

'It was an accident, Finnegan. You were the worse for wear and stumbled into traffic. By the time the ambulance arrived, you'd died.'

'No, that's not right.'

'It is usual not to remember dying. It's too much for the mind to take.'

The memory slides into place. Finnegan slams his fist down onto the edge of the table. It judders under the force. 'The fuckers killed me.'

Frank jolts in his seat. 'What do you mean? Who killed you?'

Finnegan paces the kitchen. Anger flows through him and it feels good. 'They knocked me out and then, when I came round in a dark warehouse, beat me round the head until I was dead.' He won't tell Frank about begging on that cold floor, about promising the world to the masked men.

'Memories can be sketchy when they come back. Maybe when you've had a bit more time to—'

'Don't patronise me, Frank. I know what happened. Back off if you're not going to help me. So much for the fucking ferry man.'

Frank holds his hands out, palms up. 'What can I do?'

'Persuade Rosa to sell up and get out of London. Michael too. The further away from those people they are, the better.' Finnegan's thoughts spin faster and faster. 'They're probably trying to move in on her – maybe they've forced her to comply already, that's why she's still alive. What will they make her do? God – what if they've gone for Michael instead and, wait, what if they've told them what I did?'

'Slow down,' Frank says. 'You lost me there. I can't help if you don't give me details. Who murdered you?'

Finnegan stares at Frank. Frank's eyes do not waver. Thinking clearly now, Finnegan knows that there has never been a reason to distrust Frank. He is as straight as a grave. It is why Frank would never be invited into any criminal enterprise – the good are not to be trusted with grey areas. This is one of the consequences of being in the Ring – you think everyone is on the take. Finnegan takes what would have been a deep breath. 'I don't know where to start.'

'Begin at the end,' Frank says, resting his big, benign face on his hand.

'Stupidity caught up with me. Two years ago I was recruited into a, well, a *networking* organisation. It works right across London: politicians, celebrities, entrepreneurs, all *helping* each other. I was promised low interest loans, decisions going my way, major clients, investment opportunities, you name it. I lapped it up.'

'In return for?' Frank asks.

Finnegan turns away from Frank. 'I helped them out, put business their way, covered up their "activities", among other things. I went a certain way but wouldn't go any further. I wouldn't do what they wanted. They came after me.' They didn't even give him the full hour to escape. It's a game weighted so that they win.

'And that was?'

'They ask that you kill someone. Someone within your friendship or family circle. I didn't want to do that. They also wanted me to involve my son.' Finnegan looks past Frank to the photos on the fridge. In one, Barbara is about twenty, wearing a furred hood at their winter wedding. In the next, their two sons grin at a family picnic. He can't tell Frank what he's really done. He needs his help for one, and the shame would be too much.

Silence. Frank's jaw works as if he's chewing. 'I shouldn't be surprised,' he says. 'But I am.' His chair scrapes back against the linoleum. 'Right. Let's get you to Rosa—' he breaks off.

Finnegan turns. Barbara, Frank's late wife, stands in the doorway. The chequered floor shows through her feet. She is pulsing, one second solid, then waning. Frank moves over to her. She leans towards him, seeming to rest her head on his chest without touching him.

'Good to see you, Finnegan,' she says, smiling. Everyone looks younger when they smile but Barbara appears twenty-five years younger than when Finnegan first met her, closer to her age in the photo. And then she stops smiling, and she looks ten years older than during her illness. 'How are you adjusting?' she asks.

Finnegan tries to grin. 'It's like a new pair of shoes, only I've got no feet.'

'You'll get used to it,' she says. 'Enjoy it, even. There are so many spirits to meet, friends and family to get back in touch with.'

Finnegan shakes his head. There aren't many of the dead that he would want to be reacquainted with, and none that would want to be reacquainted with him.

'How is Mrs Winters?' Frank asks her.

'She's beginning to understand. It's a relief, I think. She's thinking about returning to the Gloaming and waiting for her husband. Says she was too tired by the end of her life to keep active during death.' ·

'Maybe that's for the best.'

'What's the Gloaming?' Finnegan asks. 'You keep mentioning it.'

'It's where your spirit first goes when shrugged from the body,' Barbara says. 'It has a strong pull. It is like when your alarm goes off in the morning: some people leap out of bed and embrace the day; some press snooze every ten minutes for an hour; some sleep right through the alarm. It is the same with the Gloaming. It is warm and safe and enveloping. Just as some people get up, make themselves a cup of tea and go back to bed, some ghosts can't resist going back to sleep in the Gloaming.'

'Sounds attractive right now,' says Finnegan.

'It takes a lot of willpower and energy to keep living when you're dead,' Barbara says quietly.

'It's worth it though, isn't it, love,' Frank says. His tone is overly bright.

Barbara nods, once. 'I've left her to think, for a while. She wants to know if she can come back again for special occasions. She says she loves weddings and funerals. She even managed to laugh at "funerals".'

'Did you tell her that she could, if she had consciousness enough to know what was happening in the present, and will enough to pull herself back?'

'Are people ever lost forever?' Finnegan asks.

'Some don't want to leave or don't have the energy, but some have been fed on by spectres until nothing is left. A ghost can send another ghost into the Gloaming and there is no way back.'

Finnegan has never felt so cold.

'You're scaring him, love,' Barbara says, reaching for Finnegan's arm. Her touch feels like soft water on his skin.

'It's not just ghosts,' Frank says. 'They come after the living too.'

Barbara rolls her eyes. 'Very reassuring. Anyway, I told Mrs Winters that we can perform the Gloaming ceremony for her, if she wants one, after her funeral.'

'You're an angel,' Frank says.

'Don't confuse him,' Barbara says, smiling and young again. 'Angels aren't real. He's only just getting used to being a ghost.' The word hangs in the air. It's out there now. Naming him more fully than baptism.

'I'm going to lay down for a while,' Barbara says.

'Are you all right, love?' Frank asks, sitting down.

She laughs. 'I'll come clean – I want to read my book. I've got to a juicy bit.' She kisses Frank on the top of his bald head and walks slowly down the landing, moving like someone desperate to show they're not drunk. Can ghosts get drunk? Finnegan eyes the bottle of Jack Daniel's on the shelf.

Frank gazes down the hall to the bedroom door. 'Something's wrong with her,' he says.

Finnegan laughs and finds he can't stop laughing. At last he says, 'What's worse than being a ghost?'

Barbara sinks onto the bed. She hasn't felt this tired since dying. Frank won't notice if she can keep pushing all her energy into staying present. He'll worry his heart attack back if he finds out.

The room is chilly. She pulls the cover over her. The blanket lies barely an inch above the bed.

All she needs is a long sleep. That's what her mum used to say when she was exhausted, crochet hooks ticking as the hot milk cooled. A long sleep and a—

Ss-cutt.

Barbara's eyes jolt open.

Ss-cutt.

Something is moving across the room.

Sss-cut.   *Sss-cutt.*   *Sss-cutt.*

The sound drags nearer. Barbara struggles to sit up and look around but her spectral body is locked and cold.

A hiss slithers towards the bed.

She fights to stay above blackout but the only thing to hold onto is a scuttling whisper – *he's lying*, it says.

6

M aria turns over in her sleep. She settles on her side, partially covered by a duvet. Her mask is on the bedside table. It feels wrong to watch her sleeping eyes, her eyeballs darting beneath their lids as she dreams of things they've never seen.

Jonathan looks away from the footage. Judging from the number of nanny cameras found in Maria's lounge, bedroom, bathroom and store room, the stalker has hours of her daily life to watch at will. All memory cards have been removed from them. He has been in to collect them today, possibly while she was out this morning. Or still asleep.

Compensatory real smoke alarms were put up in the hallways, in case there was an actual fire. What a caring and considerate stalker. He wants to see what she is up to but doesn't want her to die – only deaths of his own making are permitted. He'd know that she wouldn't notice another smoke alarm, and anybody else would think she was being ultra-cautious. If it is the same stalker then this is an escalation. Two hidden cameras were found at Tanya's flat but no recordings were sent to the police. Why would he start now? Is it a warning, telling them to back off? Or is he taunting them, and perhaps Jonathan in particular? Maybe he didn't appreciate Jonathan's middle-finger salute. Surely he would know that his voyeuristic fun would be over once the footage was sent. Unless he thinks he will soon have the real thing.

Picking up the phone, adrenaline giving him the jolt that coffee can only dream of, Jonathan calls down to IT.

Denver Brown, head of the Metropolitan Police IT Investigation Department, answers. He has a smooth, suede voice. He is far from the cliché of a computer geek. He wears a different designer suit every day and shaves so closely that Jonathan once wondered if he waxed. He drives a Jaguar and regularly gets tickets for leaving it outside the station. 'Jonathan, I was about to come up and see you.'

'Any luck?' Jonathan asks.

'The email address used to send the recording was fake – made at a site that sets up false accounts and deletes them within sixty minutes, just like the one used to contact Tanya. The address itself is – iseeyou@—'

'Compared to iknowyou@, the one sent to Tanya.' That information was never released to the press.

'The IP address was routed through a series of proxies. It's a challenge,' Denver says. 'But no one gets away from me for long. At least with the footage there's more to go on. It's easier to fight something with a form.' Denver signs off and hangs up. He will now spend the whole day, and probably night knowing him, combing through code, checking the edits on the recording. He'll have to spend almost as many hours with Maria as her stalker.

Jonathan sorts through the envelopes. The top one is a jiffy bag containing a key for the Spitalfields house, the next is an invitation to an event he'll never go to and . . . he stops on a yellow letter, addressed in his wife's handwriting. His heart turns over. She has remembered. Twelve years ago they had stood together in a registry office in Stockwell and he had cried his way through the ceremony. He carried her over the road to an evening with friends and family in the back room of the Hanged, Drawn and Quartered. He wore her veil and celebrated with ale that left him with a mouth tasting of bin day.

He drops the card into the wastebasket without opening it.

On his way down to the interview room, Jonathan is stopped by DCI Alannah Allen. Usually she glides through the corridors with a smile faked to her face but today she is out of breath and frowning. A strand of hair has dared to plummet from her bun.

'Good morning, Jonathan,' she says. She folds her arms and stares at him. Still no smile. 'DS Baxter has been getting me up to speed on the beach find this morning.'

Jonathan has to get in fast. Allen was brought in to sort out, among other things, financial problems within the division. She has her hand tight round the throat of the budget and is not keen on budging. 'I know you'll have cost concerns,' Jonathan says, speaking quickly. 'But the evidence is pointing to a genuine threat to Maria King's life. Simply reporting the stalking caused the aggressive behaviour against Tanya to escalate. It would be dangerous not to—'

'I completely agree, Jonathan. It strikes me that Miss King is in considerable danger. I will squeeze the budget for a surveillance team, although I don't think it can stretch to twenty-four seven. Anything that can connect this to Tanya Baker's case will help when I go further up the chain. Have you had any leads yet on the ring she was wearing?'

'Not yet. Richard Agnarsson has it, along with the finger.'

She nods once and turns. Her boots spit down the corridor as she talks urgently into her phone.

Martin Crow is in the interview room already when Jonathan arrives. He reads through his statement, folding the corner over. He doesn't look up when Jonathan and Keisha sit down.

Jonathan switches on the recorder. 'I'm DI Dark. With me is DS Keisha Baxter and we shall be recording this follow-up interview with Martin Crow. Thank you so much for your co-operation with my team in obtaining your DNA and fingerprints, Mr Crow, it will be of great help.'

Crow has a tanned face and sun-bleached hair, suggesting a summer of digging archaeological trenches. He reminds Jonathan of a golden retriever. 'I'm trying to work out if I saw who left it,' he says, staring at the page. 'There must be a way I can help Maria.'

'Why do you want to help her so much?'

Martin looks at Jonathan as if he is mad. 'She's my friend, I want to protect her. If I had found it first, I would have thrown it away and she would have been spared all this.'

'But then she wouldn't know she was the object of a stalker's attention. That is hardly the best way of protecting someone,' Jonathan replies.

'I didn't think of that,' Crow says. He is either playing a clever game or he is naive. Instinct says the latter but instinct can be his downfall.

Crow was in the station when the email and attached footage arrived but it could have been set up to send while he was away. Or was sent by an accomplice. The possibilities tumble. An accomplished stalker would love giving such a performance. Tanya's murderer managed to stay ahead of them every step. It won't happen again.

'Humour me by going over your trip to the beach this morning,' Jonathan says. 'No detail is irrelevant.'

Crow takes Jonathan at his word. An hour later and Jonathan has learned how Crow's new shoes give him blisters on his heel but not his toes, about the journey from Peckham to Rotherhithe by bus and how he sat next to a woman who had once been to a garden party at Buckingham Palace. It was of some use, though. As Crow was describing his walk along the river, he remembered that a young girl had been walking away from the steps. He'd been distracted at the time as he'd burnt his tongue on his coffee. The woman was young, late teens, with short blonde hair. She had headphones on and a bag slung over her shoulder.

'You didn't think of mentioning her before,' Keisha says.

'I thought you'd be looking for a man,' Crow replies.

'That'll be it for now,' Jonathan says. 'We'll need to take your computer and any hard drives, tablets, your phone.'

'Anything to help,' he says with clear eyes.

Keisha shakes her head as they leave the room. 'If I didn't suspect him before, I do now,' she says. 'Anyone who isn't worried about what the police would find on their laptop is definitely guilty.'

'Oh, really? Maybe I should arrange a raid on you. Organise the collection of his hardware, would you?' Jonathan says.

Keisha walks away quickly, her fists balled. She's fired up about this one. Tanya's case was one of her first as DS. She has yet to accept that cases go cold as quickly as corpses.

Jonathan takes the stairs instead of the lift up to the CCTV team. Their office is perched at the top of the building, looking down on the streets like the cameras that take up their days. It takes a certain sort of officer to work in CCTV, picking through time codes, watching people move like stick figures in a flick-book. Celeste Francis leads the team of two. She sits in front of a bank of screens, pale and focused. Ed Castor sits behind her. He nods to Jonathan and raises the West Ham mug Jonathan bought him for his birthday.

'Have you found anything yet?' Jonathan asks.

Both shake their heads. Their eyes never leave their screens.

'Can you look out for a young woman, a teenager probably, leaving the scene shortly before Maria King arrives?' He pulls over a chair and sits down next to Celeste.

'It'll take a couple of days,' she replies, pausing the video. 'We've got even more on our plates than usual.'

'Funny,' Jonathan says. 'You always say that.'

'I wouldn't get my hopes up,' she says. 'That's all I'm saying.'

'You always say that as well.' He is leaning towards her, and she towards him.

'There's no point in you flirting to get further up the list,' she says, smiling. 'You're more committed to your wife than anyone I know.'

'I didn't know I was so transparent.'

'Well now you do. You might be out of luck with the cameras. One of them is too high and another is broken. Only one is promising. I'll come to you later.'

'I bet you will.'

'I told you, your heart isn't in it.'

His heart. He'd rather not think about his heart.

Back in the office, he reaches into the bin and pulls out the card. He tucks it into his pocket for later.

Finnegan's former home stands at the end of a shingle drive. Two bay trees, shaped into spheres, guard the front door. Frank thumps the door knocker; Finnegan shuffles from foot to foot, staring around the barbered garden. The flower beds look freshly turned over, with new soil sitting at the base of a flowering agapanthus. He bends over a bush, tries to catch the smell of the last roses of summer. Frank can barely see him, partly due to the sunlight shining through him but mostly because the journey has taken most of his energy. He didn't speak for most of the car ride out to Greenwich, just sat, turning his head back and forth, pointing at spectres as they passed.

'What if she's not in?' Finnegan asks. 'Her car isn't in the driveway.'

'Then we'll come back tomorrow,' Frank replies.

'What should I do?' Finnegan asks. 'When I see her?'

'Be near her, people often sense a presence and feel comforted, even if they don't truly realise you are there. You could speak to her. She may hear you on some level. It is like what you're encouraged to do with coma patients – let them know you're there, thinking about them and loving them. It can't hurt, anyway. Be careful, though, not to move anything by mistake. That could really scare her.'

Finnegan traces the brass number plate on the door. 'I put that up,' he says. 'I hit my finger with the hammer and chipped a bone. Bitched about it for weeks.'

Frank knocks again and pats Finnegan on what would be his back.

Finnegan looks through the half moon of glass near the top of the door.

'You could pass through the door, if you wanted,' Frank says quietly. 'To greet her by yourself.'

Finnegan shakes his head. He can't meet Frank's eye, as if ashamed. He steps back. 'She's coming,' he says.

'We won't stay long,' Frank says. It's what people say when they're visiting sick people. Mourning brings about the most feverish dis-ease.

The door opens. Rosa stands there, smoothing down her hair with one hand, holding her mobile in the other. 'So sorry to keep you, Frank, I was on the phone.' Her eyes are shadowed underneath.

Finnegan shivers next to him. 'Hello, baby,' he says. His voice cracks down the middle.

'Come in. You've timed it well – I've been baking. They're sup-posed to be healthy, even though they have three types of sugar and enough fat to harden the arteries of an elephant. Apparently if you throw linseeds in then the rest doesn't matter.' She is talking too fast, covering her emotion. She walks back down the hallway, turning round to beckon for Frank to follow.

Finnegan hesitates in the doorway. Poor bloke.

Rosa goes through into a huge kitchen that smells of golden syrup and butter and into an orangery that spans the length of the house. Finnegan must have been doing well out of this networking ring, the last time Frank visited his house it was a one-bed flat in Battersea. He knew that Finnegan had expanded his crematoria business rapidly but assumed it was achieved with a wish, a prayer and keeping one step in front of the receivers.

Rosa pulls over a wicker armchair and places her phone on the seat opposite. Frank picks up the tall, straight-backed chair near the door and moves it next to her. 'I'll sit here, if that's all right. My back's bad at the moment.' He nods for Finnegan to take the armchair.

'Tea?' Rosa asks. She doesn't wait for Frank to answer before stepping back into the kitchen. She knows he likes his tea.

Finnegan settles into the chair. His eyes are fixed on Rosa as she goes back and forth, putting the kettle on and arranging flapjacks on a plate.

'What brings you here, Frank?' Rosa asks when the cups are filled with tea and their mouths with sticky oats.

'I needed to see you, Squidge. Check that you're OK,' Finnegan says. His voice is so soft and loving that Frank feels he should leave, but Finnegan is too volatile to be left alone at the moment, his emotions could give him the strength to turn over that table, smash the teapot or grab that dream catcher from the ceiling and give her nightmares for life.

'Did you want to add something to Mrs Winters' cremation arrangements?' Rosa continues, turning to face Frank.

'How are you doing, Rosa? Truthfully? Aside from the "taking each day as it comes" and "bearing up" platitudes,' Frank says. The chair creaks as he leans forward.

'You know better than anyone, Frank.'

'I do. And when Barbara died I could have done with talking to someone who understood. Finnegan told me that you used to be an actor – you don't have to pretend with me.'

'I don't know where to start. It's only three years since my brother, Seamus, died and I'm only just beginning to get over it. Now this. I can't take it in. Opening up might finish me.'

'I know that it feels impossible. Anything you want to say is fine,' Frank says.

'Tell me how you feel, baby,' Finnegan says, standing up and moving next to her. He is agitated, nervous.

Rosa's eyes become teary. 'I feel as if someone has taken out my heart like an avocado stone. Is that what you were after? To know that I'm wandering around empty in the centre?'

'I'm the same, baby.' Finnegan is crying ghost tears. 'I'm not going anywhere again, you'll be able to see me in time.'

'I didn't mean to upset you, love,' Frank says. He hands her his handkerchief.

'You're not the one who upset me. He did. My stupid husband. Getting pissed and then getting himself run over. Leaving me with the business to run.'

Finnegan steps back at the force of Rosa's fury.

'I can call around, find people to help you and Michael cope while you get used to running it yourselves. You're not alone in this,' Frank says.

'Oh, I've already had people offer to step in and take over.'

'Who?' Finnegan tries to grab her shoulders. He misses. 'Who has been in contact? It's them, the ones who murdered me.'

Frank tries to keep his eyes from sliding over to Finnegan. 'When was this?' he says to her.

'Three men came to the crematorium last week. They looked the part, I must say. Expensive suits. They were from a big company in the US. They said they'd been in negotiations with Finnegan to buy him out.'

'Do you remember their names?' Frank asks. 'Or the name of the company? I may have heard about them.'

Rosa shakes her head. 'They left a card, though.' She goes to the kitchen island and searches through her handbag, returning with a dog-eared business card for Simmons Crematoria.

'It was the first I heard that the business was in trouble,' Rosa says. The shadows under her eyes seem even darker. 'If he had only told me, I could have helped. It doesn't matter now. I was shown some initial paperwork with his signature—'

'There have been no fucking negotiations. No signature. They're lying, baby. Dirty lying fuckers.' Finnegan's original County Clare cadence overtakes his South London tones.

'Calm down,' Frank says to Finnegan.

Rosa's eyebrows rise. '*You* asked me what I was feeling.'

Frank rubs a hand across his head. He is never normally this clumsy when visiting mourners with the one who is mourned. 'I'm sorry, Rosa. I was talking to myself, something I do when stressed. When I'm *really* stressed I do it out loud, like just now.'

Rosa stands and turns to the kitchen. Probably to hide her tears. 'I don't understand what's going on, Frank, but I'm not stupid. Finnegan always tried to protect me and ended up underestimating me. Don't do the same thing.'

'I didn't mean to, baby. I wanted to make everything OK. Give you a good life. I'm sorry.' As he reaches for her, Finnegan becomes more solid, knocking over the milk jug.

She turns, pulling back her hand to her chest as if scalded.

Frank rights the jug, mops up the milk with his discarded hankie. 'Sorry about that,' he says. 'You're right. I'll level with you,' Frank says. 'Finnegan warned me some time ago about people sniffing round the business. He said they were dangerous.'

'He shouldn't have got himself killed, then, should he?' Rosa says. The tears are streaming now. She doesn't care if he sees.

Finnegan is trying to shush her, comfort her.

'I'll leave you now,' Frank says, walking to the kitchen door. 'I'm so sorry to have upset you. Please, if you need anything then call me, any time. We are worried about you.'

'We?' she says, forehead creased.

He swallows and smiles. 'That's how I know what you're going through,' he says. 'I can't get used to being alone. And I don't want to.'

7

M argery turns up Heart FM. It's in the code of the taxi driver, to play songs of love and its loss for those who seem in need. One of her customers today seemed in more need than most, poor love. Frank will help him, if anyone can.

Switching her orange light back on, she turns onto Hatton Gardens. A young couple flag her down outside a coffee shop. They pile in, never letting go of each other's hands as they drag suitcases into the back. In her mirror, she sees them kissing and giggling. When she swerves to avoid a cyclist, they don't even notice. She likes to see life used right.

They get out at St Pancras, paying by card and not once looking her way. It's a grand system. Especially now people are so used to everything being automated – checkouts, bank machines, phone calls. The taxi reaches the destination, the price pops up, a card is swiped or inserted and the punters go on their way assuming the figure on the other side of the grille is as alive as they are.

A woman stumbles up to the couple and reaches out. They move out of the way without seeing her. She screams after them. Other people walk around her without knowing why, changing direction without thinking, heartbeats increasing for no apparent reason.

Margery presses the button that opens the side door. 'Come here, love,' she calls out.

The woman is in her early twenties by the looks of her, so she probably died not much later. You can't be prepared at that point in life. The young woman turns, snarling. She spits towards Margery.

A wraith – a ghost made up of fear and anger. New to death.

'Come on, sweetheart, I can get you help. You don't have to feel this way. I know you're afraid.' Margery holds out her big arms.

The wraith screams at the car.

'I've had the windows reinforced, love,' Margery says. 'Get in and you can screech all you want.'

She screams again. A sparrow copies her cries. A passing ghost tuts and shakes his head. 'Amateurs,' he says.

Slowly, the girl drifts into the cab. She is not realised enough to walk. She could go either way at this point, find a sub-physical form that she can learn to control or stay as she is: malice manifest. Wraiths are one of the types of ghosts that really scare the living.

Margery moves off into the traffic. People wonder why taxis turn off the sign when there are no customers inside. This is why.

The girl pulses in the back. Versions of her flash like a slideshow across her face – a little smiling blonde girl; the old woman she would have been.

Margery turns round. 'What's your name, love?'

The girl tries to speak. She is summoning all that she once was. Margery wills her on. She knows the pain.

'Tanya,' she says at last. She seeks out Margery's eyes in the mirror.

'Well done, sweetheart,' Margery says. 'That must have been difficult.'

The girl is coalescing, becoming more solid with every memory that returns. More versions of her run past. The baby; a teenager; the young woman holding the knife in her chest, trying to pull it out.

A wave of hate rocks the car.

Margery swerves and pulls into a bus stop.

Tanya is gone, passed through the car and away. Margery will see her again, she hopes. She switches the orange sign back on and moves off. As she turns down Gower Street, a young man flags her from the other end. She squints at him, not sure if he's a body or a ghost. It is edging into twilight, her favourite time of day, when ghosts and people look most alike, especially if the living are lost and the dead have found themselves. The boy is alive but, and on this she hopes she is wrong, not for long.

The radio is playing 'Together in Electric Dreams'. He starts to cry. It is those lyrics. If the living knew that when they listened to songs about love, they were listening to songs about death, then they would know why it hurt.

Garry Harding clings to the edge of the scaffolding. He is attached to it with two ropes but he doesn't trust ropes. Or scaffolding. Or the health and safety people who strapped him in. The only things he trusts in life are the ground beneath his feet and the money in his safe.

'As you can see, from the top floor you'll look out on the Pinnacle one way and the Can of Ham the other.' The engineer points but Garry does not look. He has seen the blueprint and the map. There is no need to trigger his vertigo by peering down. At least the wind is blowing his hair over his eyes.

Hélène from PR steps forward. 'Of course, we need to call it something,' she says. Her hard hat is too small for her head. He happens to know that she's added the 'e' at the end of her name, and the acute, grave and Estuary accents. Not to mention the breasts.

'Why does every building need a nickname?' Garry asks. 'London's become a boarding school.'

'We need something that fits. We've got the Napkin, the Cheesegrater, the Gherkin . . .'

Garry stops listening. He commissioned the building so that his firm has a prestigious base in the city. He is not interested in how the skyline is turning into a seventies kitchen.

'The Champagne Bottle, that's what we're thinking,' Hélène continues. 'It's the right shape. If you half-close your eyes.'

'If we get the money to complete.' And that's the dour voice of William Flag, project manager and pain in the arse. He wouldn't know how to have fun if it lay on its back and begged. 'I hate to remind you all, but we're still several million short. *Many* several million.'

Garry clears his throat. He catches a glimpse of the drop down and his stomach threatens to jump into his hands. 'I'm dealing with that,' he says. 'I'm in negotiations with some very big investors. We will have the money.' He turns to face the others. 'You're all doing a great job. Couldn't be happier. Can I get down now?'

Back in his ground floor office in Clarence Street, Garry opens his mail. First on the pile is an invitation to a party at some fashion house. God knows how he got that invite, probably through Carole, his wife. He knows nothing about clothes. She lays them out for him every morning like dead versions of him on the bed. The next envelope contains a letter from the cot death charity he supports. He smooths it down and the memories away, and pins it to the board.

The next is a padded envelope, containing a box. No stamp, no address. There is something inside, straining at the jiffy bag.

He tears open the top of the envelope and tips out the contents. It's a jewellery box. The lid creaks as it opens. Inside is a photo of a yellow diamond ring and a printed note. 'You want in? Earn the ring.'

Simon opens his door and envelops Maria in a hug. 'I'm so sorry,' he says. She can hear in his voice that his face is missing its smile. She buries her head in his thick woollen jumper.

He's left work early. It's enough to make a sob balloon in her chest. She didn't cry in front of the police, she's proud of that. Aside from Billy, Simon is the one to whom she always turns. They have been friends for twenty years and have helped each other through everything, from partners coming and going to deaths in their families. He holds her by the shoulders. 'Right,' he says. 'I prescribe wine and *Downton Abbey*. Will is picking up a Thai takeaway on his way home. As for you, my friend,' his voice becomes muffled in Billy's fur. 'Marrow bone and *Morse*.'

Billy ruffs his assent.

'I tried to call you to say I'd pick you up,' he says.

'They've taken my mobile.' She holds out a new, clunky one. 'And given me this. I think they reckon that if they give me a phone from the nineties then I can pretend I'm back in the days when I wasn't being proposed to with a sawn-off finger.'

'Sound logic,' Simon says. His smile is back now, she can hear it.

'Did they interview you?' she asks.

'A woman came to the office. A DS Baxter. Very polite. Seemed protective of you, of which I approved.'

'I'm sure she approved of you too.'

Rider coughs. Maria jumps.

'Are you coming in as well?' Simon asks. 'The more the merrier.'

'I'll be outside for a while,' Rider says, placing Maria's small suit-case inside the hallway.

'Thank you. As for anyone else watching,' Simon says, 'you can FUCK OFF and leave us alone.' His shout echoes down Morris Street.

8

He shuts the front door, muting the hassle of Hackney, and walks through into the kitchen. He removes the gold cage from the top of the champagne bottle and waits for the cork, battling with unseen pressure, to pop of its own accord. He smiles and means it for once. Today he got engaged. That doesn't happen every day. He has been engaged before, of course. Three times, which just goes to show what a romantic he is, whatever his first fiancée said. She lied about everything, anyway. He feels carbonated rage rushing up inside him and breathes out slowly. He has seen Maria do this. She helps him in so many ways. Everything will be right this time. If he had paid such attention to detail before, then maybe things . . . but this is no time to dwell.

Celebrating. That is the order of the evening. The cork has not budged. He can wait. He has the patience of tens of men. It will give in to force in the end.

He slots last night's plate into the dishwasher, next to five days' worth of solitary eating. It will be good to eat and live with a woman again. He smells his sleeve. He spritzed it with her perfume this morning and a faint vanilla sweetness remains. She will be a welcome companion. He will allow her to bring six or seven items of her own so that she will really feel at home. Of course it is his apartment first and foremost, she will have to respect that: he has worked too hard to afford it, done too many unpleasant things to have someone else take control. Not that she will. At the moment she does not fold her clothes over a chair before she goes to bed or floss nearly enough, but this is how he can help her improve and develop, along with getting rid of that blindfold. He will be the first thing she sees when she willingly peels it from her pretty face.

He carries the champagne through to the living room. How has it not popped? He retrieves everything else he needs for his celebration. Sweating bottles of beer are positioned on the table next to the sofa; salted peanuts poured into the bowl; champagne flutes taken from the cabinet; a bowl of water and fresh folded hand towel placed by the peanuts so that he can rid his fingers of salt whenever he touches the keyboard.

The laptop screen is as blank as her blindfold. It tempts him. He knows he should wait, he hasn't even shaved after all, but he can't resist. There is new footage on there. He kept it from himself, as a little test, a tease. It is the footage that follows the excerpts he sent to the police to warn them not to interfere. DI Dark knows what happens when he is not happy.

He wakes up the laptop and opens up her smallest, most intimate, hours. She lies curled up on her bed, hugging the pillow. She is so lonely without him. At 03.13 she turns over onto her left side. Her lips move as if talking. Locating the audio file, he can only pick up murmurs. Perhaps she is kissing him in her sleep. Now that Dark has removed the cameras from her flat – some of them, anyway, the smallest ones remain – he will not get such a clear view. He has enough footage from the last few months, though, and soon they will be together without the need for cameras.

Enough. He is spoiling their celebration. Off to the bathroom. She deserves for him to look his best on their engagement day. He has been told, several times, that he is attractive in this suit. He had it dry cleaned for this very occasion. It is sentimental but she will love it when he tells her, shyly, all the details, all the effort he went to without her even knowing. They will mark the day in the same way every year and he will be so loved. A woman who touches the ground with such gentleness and precision will appreciate him all the more.

He is nervous. He can admit that, to her at least. She knows the real him, the one that hides behind the everyday mask. *She* would laugh at how nervous he is. She will be nervous too. He has seen her vulnerability. Last month she was so worried about an article that she had to get in to some archaeology magazine that she had paced the flat, stomped from camera to camera, occasionally frustratingly out of view, but finally she wrote it, right on the bed so he could share her success. She celebrated sending it off with a large glass of Baileys. Maybe that is how she is celebrating today. He hopes not. He should have sent champagne to that man's flat, that Simon, her supposed friend, to show him how she should be treated, but it does not matter. She will be only thinking about him and their engagement, just as he is thinking about her. Imagine what they will be like before his wedding day, so wrapped up in each other that they can hardly think or work. His colleagues will hardly recognise him as the man who is normally so calm, sophisticated and determined. He is sweating more than when he ran his last marathon. She should have seen him then, at peak fitness, with a six pack that she would admire, judging from the number of times she looks at pictures at Hugh Jackman. He will have to talk to her about that.

The takeaway will be here in eight minutes. He has tested them on three other occasions so that he can rely on them today. Everything has to be right. Just like the ring. He hopes that she is wearing it now, that the police did not crush her by taking it away. He does not think she could be easily crushed. That is very attractive. It is good that he knows what she thinks are attractive traits in men so he can be a better man for her. His mother always said that the right woman would make him want to be a better man. And if he found her then he should keep her for good. He will keep her for good. Not like before. He can hardly bear to think of Tanya and her treachery. But he will not be a better man if he allows himself to get too caught up. He will only enjoy this if he has clarity. Control.

The razor blade scrapes at his face. He feels a shove to his shoulder. Turning round, there is no one there. He is imagining things. The nick on his neck gives him the momentary pain needed to zip together. He looks at himself in the mirror. He could be better looking. He could be richer. But she will not find a man who loves her more. She has only just realised that he loves her, she hasn't even kissed him and he adores her. Who could compete with that? No one. And if they tried he would destroy them.

He takes the new cologne out of the cupboard. It is a brand that she has mentioned she liked on another boyfriend. He agonised over that, over whether it was the right thing to wear an aftershave that she knew from someone else's neck, especially as he knew she was sensitive to scents, but what can he say? He's a slave to her wants and needs.

The cologne stings. His skin reddens. The thought of her exploring his face with her fingers, seeing him with her hands, makes him hard. The doorbell rings. Eight minutes exactly. It's a sign. Everything will be perfect.

As he walks back into the living room, the cork launches out of the bottle. The champagne does not bubble over – it dare not touch the lip of the bottle without his hand. He picks up a flute and pours. The pale fizz tastes of peaches and he raises his glass. 'To my future wife,' he says. Behind his back, the other glass shatters on the table.

Jonathan looks up from Tanya's file. It's ten o'clock – over twelve hours into the case already. Two slices of pizza remain in the box. He picks one up, sees that the cheese has congealed, puts it down again.

The anniversary card stands on his desk in a wide stance. If it had hands they would be on its hips. There are no hearts and flowers on the front, it is not addressed to 'My darling Husband', just the plain kind that you would give a couple you vaguely know. He rubs his eyes.

Keisha walks over.

'Rider's off, Guv, and so am I. Caz is convinced I died sometime in my probation year. I'll go home one day and find her doing the downward-dog with her yoga instructor. Oh, sorry, Guv.' She slams her hand against her head. 'I have less tact than Bernard Manning.'

'I wouldn't worry, Keisha.' He taps her shoulder and shunts away the thoughts of coming home to Natalie for the last time. And finding she was not alone. 'You should go and get some sleep.'

He may have been able to cope if his wife *had* left him for the yoga teacher. Maybe then he would've been able to rationalise it in some way – that it was the job that got in the way, that few marriages survive the unsocial hours, let alone the monomania that accompanies some cases. But no. She couldn't even give him the solace of that. She went off with another policeman. Sergeant Justin Masters from Traffic. *Traffic.* And Jonathan didn't even suspect.

Jonathan stands and takes the keys to his cousin's place out of his pocket: 'Pedlar Cottage, Spitalfields.'

He emerges onto the street. Walking through London at night used to make him feel better, whatever the situation. He's been strolling through the dark city since he was a teenager, walking from Wandsworth to the Wapping streets he grew up on, taking an alleyway rather than a brightly lit street, searching out a road he's never gone down before and drifting along it, one side then the other, taking in its walls and highs and lows, reciting road names like poetry. It used to feel that he was having an affair with the Night City, the one that lets slip a shoulder of moon through the clouds to see him through, that held his hand from the South Bank to Camberwell to Nunhead and back, that made him want to learn its every line and dimple and for it to know him. Now he feels London breathing him in like a whale that takes in plankton while it trawls the sea. He's nothing to it, it is a ridiculous thought that it could know him or love him back.

Christ Church rises against the grey-violet sky, as pale and pointed as a cuspid tooth. Jonathan has always liked Spitalfields, even now, with its gentrified market and Ten Bells pub full of hipsters not Rippers, he can feel the leper colony underneath its streets, see the fruit and veg men who have not sold here in years. Jonathan stops for chips in a place that was not here last week and, feeling the heat through the paper, heads for Folgate Street.

Pedlar Cottage sits squat and skew-whiff in the middle of the street. It leans to one side as if pissed. Tall, blackened-brick houses tower over it like stern Victorian spinsters. Jonathan reaches out and touches its Tudor-striped walls. 'I'll look after you,' he says. 'If you look after me.'

The cottage creaks.

'I'll take that as a yes.'

The front door opens into a small sitting room. The smell of damp and air freshener hits him and he steps back. He reaches for a light switch. No electricity. Holding out the torch on his key ring, Jonathan steps onto a floor covered in dustsheets. The wall is pockmarked with bad plastering. Wiring hangs from the ceiling. He eases his rucksack from his shoulder and leaves it in the corner. A floorboard shifts, and settles.

Walking through to the kitchen, Jonathan ducks beneath a beam and shines light around the room. A freestanding sink, wall shelves and a table are the only intact furnishings: the cupboards have been partially torn down and left in a pile by the back door. Flat packs of new units lean against uneven walls. The place is clean, though. Jonathan wipes a finger across a shelf lined up with candles and cleaning fluids. Not even a centimetre of dust. He can smell lemon furniture polish. Neil must have hired a cleaner.

This will be his home for the next three months, fewer if he's lucky. It would be good to have somewhere permanent, if only for a while. Maria will be in another place tonight as well. Jonathan hopes that her friends will treat her well, fuss her up, and that Keisha is right in that they can be trusted. Telling himself there is nothing more he can do for now and almost believing it, Jonathan picks two pillar candles, lights them and carries them up the narrow stairs. He has to duck again as he emerges onto the thin carpet tacked down the centre of the floorboards. Opening the first door, he finds a small bedroom overlooking the back of the cottage. Next door is a tiny bathroom. He tries the taps – no water. His face looks grey in the grubby mirror, distorted and flickering. The flames make it appear as if there are two Jonathans, each one as tired as the other. He could do with two of him. They could be alone together.

The larger bedroom, at the end of the hall, is swathed in floral wallpaper. It has an old wardrobe and a double bed at one end. The mattress dips in the middle as if someone is already sleeping there. It seems colder than outside here, although that's not possible. He places one candle on the chest of drawers, the other next to old-fashioned shaving equipment on the dressing table. The razor, brush, soap and mirror are laid out equidistant from each other. Again – no dust. A sense of unease rises. He shifts the cut-throat razor so that it breaks the perfect line.

Head brushing the low ceiling, he moves over to the window and looks down onto Folgate Street. Two young men walk along, hand in hand, laughing. The happy sound slips through the single glazing. He closes the floral curtains.

Jonathan takes off his coat and shoes and sits on the bed. What will Natalie be feeling right now? Perhaps she sent the anniversary card as a sign that she wants to continue the marriage. Maybe they can retake their vows one day. He'll try one more time – she'll have her phone switched off if it's too late to ring.

Natalie's phone rings twice, then switches to voicemail.

He sits with the phone in his hand.

Another laugh blasts from outside. He places the mobile on the floor and yawns. The candlelight is making him drowsy – he's used to the flicker of station fluorescence. He should go downstairs and get his rucksack, put his clothes in the old wardrobe, but tiredness is tiding in. It's been a very long day.

Throwing his coat over him, Jonathan lies out on the mattress. His toes touch the end poles of the bedstead. It'll probably take ages to go to sleep. He should put some music on his phone and—

The man under the greatcoat turns in his sleep. He mutters. Whimpers.

It tastes the air. Heartbreak radiates out of the sleeping man.

Ss-cut.

Digging its nails into the floorboards, it jerks forward.

At the foot of the bed, it stops and tastes again. His anguish is delicious. A living one has leached from him but there is plenty left. His dreams will be full of deep unease. It'll make sure of that.

Ss-cut.   Ss-cut.   Ss-cut.
Sss-

it claws into the bedpost

cutt –

drags itself up

The Whisperer begins whispering, inches from his head. *You are not to be loved.*

The man stirs, turns, and is hauled into sleep.

9

Day Two

Billy paws at the front door and whines. 'Quiet,' Maria whispers, clipping on his lead. 'Don't wake up Simon and Will.'

She had promised them last night that she wouldn't go mudlarking alone, that she would wait until tomorrow when the surveillance team was in place and she could be safe on the beach. 'It's isolated,' Simon had said. 'If you cried out, anyone would think it was a bloody seagull. Promise me you won't go alone.' So she had, and meant it, too – last night. After most of a bottle. This morning she had woken up with the need to forget everything in the turn of a trowel. This way she got to be alone before going off to her counselling session.

'We'll go to a different part of the foreshore,' she says to Billy. 'The stalker won't be expecting that.' That's a compromise Simon might just agree to, if she told him. Which she won't.

Closing the front door carefully, Maria breathes in the morning. It has the crispness of oncoming Christmas. God – Mum will freak when she finds out about the stalker and Maria will have to spend hours on the phone reassuring her. Best not tell her yet.

Maria has only been down to this part of the foreshore twice before, both times with Simon, both times hung-over. She stops walking and Billy takes over, remembering the way, still limping. He hesitates at the entry to the narrow alley by the Town of Ramsgate pub then leads her along it to Wapping Old Stairs.

At the bottom of the dishevelled steps, she listens. No one is around. If anyone approaches, she'll hear them on the shingle. Calm washes over her as she settles by the wall. The city is creeping about on its tiptoes, trying not to wake everyone up and she is by herself, picking up secrets and keeping most of them to herself. She tells the city her secrets in return, whispers as she moves its stones one by one, placing them back where she found them so that the mysteries can live there like insects.

The sand smells different this side of the river, more earth in it. She can't imagine not living by smell, the world would be so flat.

Billy sniffs at a rock like it's laced with cocaine.

'Exactly,' she says.

She feels out something cool, with a rounded edge. A key. There's a story behind every key. It was a key that sent her on the way to becoming an archaeologist and mudlark. One morning, when she was seven, her mum was going on about Tupperware to a group of women in the kitchen. Maria couldn't see any point in plastic boxes, especially if it meant that she couldn't have the fresh scones her mum had made until after the ladies had gone. The women smelled of perfume that made her throat raw and made jokes they thought she didn't understand.

She had found her way to the beach with her sticks, knocking back cowslips and reeds, and felt her way down to where the rocks squatted, briny as a bag of chips. Squashy things clung to the stones and one anemone grabbed her finger like a teething toddler. She clung to the rock too, picking up things that people had left nearby – a button, three coins, a key. She put them in her mouth and turned them round with her tongue. The key tasted of her knee when she fell over and made it bleed. Keys were magic. They let you in and, if you didn't know the right lock, kept you out. This key had a story, and she wanted to read it.

She didn't hear the roar of the tide coming home or notice the wave sweeping away her bag. It was only when she realised that her rockpool was no longer a pool but the sea that she fumbled her way to the highest rock and waved. Her arm ached with the waving and she wondered if this was how starfish felt. She waved with the other arm, holding the key tight in her palm. She then realised that if someone else blind were on the rocks nearby then they wouldn't be able to see her. So she shouted as well.

Just as she was wondering how to grow another starfish arm, the blast of the lifeboat worried the waves around her. They lapped over her and her rock but her rock and her stayed where they were. A man called Jim caught her in his arm like a fish and brought her into the boat. It skimmed the surface like one of Dad's stones, its rubber skirt skipping back to the harbour.

A whole group of people were waiting for her when they pulled in. Mum rushed up, shouting. She was so angry she was shaking and sent Maria to bed, although she did give her two scones to take up in a Tupperware box. She ate them on her bed, her lips made them savoury with flakes of seasalt. She placed her key in the box and hid it under the bed.

It wasn't long after that that Mum decided to move away to live with her new husband, Nigel. She denied that the reason she didn't want Maria to live with her was that she ran away and got rescued by big man called Jim, but Maria knew it was.

That was twenty-five years ago and she can still feel the salt on her skin, crinkling it up like crisps, the joy of finding secrets and keeping them. Now she has boxes and boxes of keys; keys of all kinds, from all the centuries that London keeps hidden. Taking her new Braille phone out of her bag, she holds the key out in front of it and Instagrams, hoping she hasn't taken a picture of a pile of stones.

The sun is coming out. She can feel it on her face and skin. Long may it last. Winter will whip at her larking time, the short days and high tides will throw blankets over the Thames. She normally doesn't mind, it needs its hibernation time, but today she hates the thought of it not being by her side. She'll need it in the coming months. Picking treasure from the beach helps her order her thoughts and, whatever she said to the police, she knows that she holds the identity of the stalker in her memory, just as the Thames stows everything away for later. The Thames makes the best witness and she'll be fucked if she's going to run away from this stalker.

Billy sits and scratches as she squats down on the heels of her wellies by the Wapping steps. As she reaches for the unfamiliar stones, she lets her mind mudskip across memories, reaching for areas that feel too man-made, too much like a stalker.

She removes stones carefully as she works but will always place them back again. In theory, as a holder of the Port of London Authority licence, she could dig down three inches but she hates the thought of disturbing the strata of the earth. There are others who can go deeper – 'the fifty-one'. These are mudlarks given special dispensation to dig deeper but this elite group is a closed shop. You can only join if selected, and only then if someone leaves, or dies. There always have to be fifty-one. She'd like to be the one.

As her fingers feel out a brooch; a coin; the nub of a burnt candle; a partial plate, her memories are turned over: the anonymous flowers sent on Valentine's Day; silent phone calls; the way Carl turned on her when she dug up his lies; the man on the night bus with the Collie breath.

Each item goes in her notebook, plastic bags and into her rucksack. Each memory will be stored. It could be treasure, it could be worthless, she won't know till she gets it home and cleans it up. None of them feels quite right, though. Nothing excites her. She's the Goldilocks of mudlarks.

The sun passes over. Its weak eyesight touches the top of her head.

She'll have to leave soon, but not yet. Give it five minutes. Her fingers glance over something sharp, slicing the side of her forefinger. Broken glass? There's lots of that – the result of centuries of cirrhosis. This is why many mudlarks wear gloves but it would stop her contact with the beach and the city. Resisting the urge to pop her finger in her mouth, she splodges anti-bacterial gel onto the cut. She slowly lowers her left hand to pick up the glass and wrap it. It is not a bottle, though – it is thin, square and smooth-edged. Only half of it is above the mud.

Using the thinner trowel, she scraps away the mud, releasing the item bit by bit. The mud gives in, the foreshore offers up its history like a drunk telling a stranger their secrets.

She plays her fingers across the find. It is a comb, with teeth as fine and spindlesome as icicles. Something is etched into it. A manufacturer? A name? Whose hair has this been through? Who has it caught in its teeth?

Hair. The last time she was at her hairdresser's, Kim said that a clump was missing from the back. Maria had dismissed it then, thought that maybe Kim was covering up a mistake. But Kim doesn't make mistakes. Unlike Maria.

Billy barks at a boat, dashing in and back to her side, shaking himself into a fur-scented fountain. Now the waves are only metres away, she loses time as easily as gloves. Standing up, she stretches till her back goes crack.

Footsteps sound out in the alleyway. She can't tell which ones are echo and which ones are real. Either way, she knows who is inside the shoes.

'DI Dark,' she says, turning to face him.

Jonathan sits on the bottom step. He is so tired that he could go to sleep right here. He'd had nightmares throughout the night and woken clutching his coat and sweating. Things didn't improve when he got up and found that the razor had been placed back in line with the other items on the dressing table. And his mobile phone had joined them. 'Having a good morning, Maria?' he asks. 'Because I'm not.'

Maria folds her arms across her chest. 'How did you find me?'

'Did you forget our instructions to stay away from social media?'

Her hand goes up to her face but it doesn't cover the blush. 'I didn't say where I was.' She lifts up her chin. Defiant.

'Your phone did.'

'You're tracking me?' Her hands are in fists as she paces the short space between shingle and waves.

'What would you rather: the police track your new phone or an unknown killer tracks you on your old one? Because that's what happened. Our IT guy found spyware on every one of your devices and that's not counting the apps that give open access – your iPhone, AirDrop, Facebook.'

'You have no right to trace me. I already have one stalker.'

'Would you rather be traced as a chalk outline in a murder scene?' he says.

She steps back. Her mouth opens, then closes.

Jonathan wishes he didn't have to do this.

Maria's head tilts to one side. 'That sounds very much like victim blaming,' she says, her words slow and weighted. 'I have done nothing wrong.'

'I never said you had,' Jonathan replies. This is slipping away from him. Like the words Natalie had said in his nightmare.

'I can see that you're trying to protect me, but I will not make huge changes for a man too scared to show himself. Besides, have you thought that me altering my routine might anger him more?'

Jonathan nods slowly. 'It's possible. Anything could anger him.'

'So why would I do anything differently?' Her voice sounds more scared now than angry. 'But I am taking this seriously. This is someone who already cut off a hank of my hair.' She lifts her hair up at the back. A slice of it is missing.

Look at you, with your hair tangled by the wind. Your bright clothes that make you look like a clown. When you find a new item, like that comb in your hand, the rest of you becomes motionless, the nerve endings in your fingertips telling you everything you need to know. You look like a harlequin scarecrow. You can't see and don't care. Do not change.

So many apologies, my love. Sorry that *that* man is hounding you: that is twice in two days that you have had to be in contact with him, and he has bugged your phone – Dark is the *real* stalker; a stalker does not love. Sorry too that they have made you move away from your favourite place. Can you see now what happens when people intervene? It will be one of the things to talk about when you live with me: how we do not need anybody else. That friends and colleagues will do you harm if you give them the opportunity. We will also have to talk about your security – it is not right that you are out alone, nor that you broke your promise. It will not be allowed when we are together. Of course, you are not really alone. No one ever is.

Give over your trust. Detective Dark will be dealt with – a process has been put in place that will see him gasping for air like a line-caught pike. He is not the one to trust – he had to check your phone to know which beach you would go to. Only one person knows you from the freckles on your neck to your choice of karaoke songs. Who else knows you like a river knows its stones? No one.

You had better leave. It is time for your therapy. The quack's clock ticks. Don't be scared, Maria. You are in safe hands.

10

Jonathan walks to the nearest coffee shop and stands in line. His hands still shake with a rage that started in his chest and moved outwards. He doesn't know why he feels this angry; it was Maria's choice and, to some extent, not that he would tell her, he admires her attitude. It is not her fault that she is being stalked and she shouldn't have to be a prisoner in order to be safe. But the fury is there, churning. Her counsellor would probably call it projection. He is angry with himself for giving in and phoning Natalie, for the chill he felt this morning when he found that someone had been in during the night and it scared him. He'd rather project – it's better than dread.

He picks up his coffee at the counter and is about to leave the coffee shop when his phone goes.

'I've managed to remove the ring without damaging the finger any further,' says Richard Agnarsson, a Met pathologist.

'Have you been home yet?' Jonathan asks.

'This one was important.' Richard's voice is uncharacteristically quiet. Every case is important to Richard these days. His sister was killed last year and he has not stopped since.

'What came up?'

'We'll get DNA results back today, but I think it will confirm the partial print I managed to take from the skin on the finger.'

'And?'

'It's Tanya Baker. You were right.'

Jonathan breathes out slowly. 'I wish I wasn't.'

'No – this way we get another chance to find the murderer, that can only be good. First step – we were lucky with the ring. It had a hallmark on it and some letters – DMD.'

'What could that be, someone's initials?' Maybe it was someone else's ring before Tanya's. She'd mentioned that he spoke of another fiancée.

'I did some detective work of my own – don't worry, your job is perfectly safe. It only took a Google. DMD stands for Dearest Memory Diamonds. It's an outer-London based company that takes a corpse and, forgive my vernacular, turns it into bling.'

'I've heard of these,' Jonathan says. 'You can get the ashes of your relative or pet made into a necklace.'

'Or a ring. Anything you want. Although you'd be hard pushed to get enough ashes out of a hamster for a tiara.'

'It would be more honest to call it Dead Made into Diamonds,' Jonathan says. He thinks of all the loved ones that he has lost and how it would feel to send them away to sparkle. 'How is it done?'

'We're all carbon life forms: diamonds-in-waiting,' Richard says. 'Intense pressure and stress will do it, and time.'

'Tell me about it,' Jonathan replies. One day Keisha will come in and find a diamond buried in his overcoat.

Maria hurries out of Greenwich Station and down the ramp. '0956 and twenty-two seconds,' says her talking watch. She's early, amazingly, for her session. Nine therapeutic hours and she has yet to be 'cured', or even want to be.

The houses on Straightsmouth nestle against each other; she imagines them dressed in pastel shades like a fifties girl group. All of the window boxes are filled with new season flowers. She slows to stroke the velvet beard of a pansy. She wouldn't mind moving to Greenwich. There have been some great finds on the foreshore here – someone found an apostle spoon last week, at least they said so. Mudlarks are notorious for giving out misleading information.

Iain Parker answers the door on her first knock, as if he had been standing waiting. 'I thought you might not be coming,' he says, opening the door into his therapy room. The air freshener smells of feel-ups in boys' bedrooms.

'Why would you think that?' Maria says, settling in the armchair. Billy flomps down next to her.

'A Detective Baxter has been in contact, requesting an interview in connection with something that has happened to you. She didn't give details but sounded concerned.'

Silence. He should know that the trick of leaving so much quiet doesn't work on her. If he wants to know, he's going to have to ask.

'Would you like to tell me what's happened?' Iain says. Emotional warmth steams off him. She imagines the look in his eyes to be like the dippy centre of a soft boiled egg.

'It'll be good to talk it through,' she says. It's a lie but he won't know that.

'That's a lie, isn't it?' Iain says.

She grins. 'I'm all talked out. They examined my flat and behaviour for most of the day yesterday.'

'And why was that?'

'Someone proposed to me using a dead woman's finger.'

'What?' His voice snaps out of its counselling lull.

'I'm being stalked. I have a stalker. I'm a stalkee. Yippee.'

'Could you be using sarcasm as a way to distance yourself from events, do you think?'

'I think that is entirely possible.'

Another silence. Maria senses the ultimate therapy question being hooked and flung into the sea. 'How do you feel about being stalked?' he says.

Maria inhales slowly. She's being adversarial, she knows that. Talking may just help. 'I'm angry. And confused. But most of all I feel stupid – I had no idea at all that someone was following me. He was in my house,' she says. Her voice sounds small in the small room.

'Tell me more.' His voice is nearer, he's moved the chair forward without her hearing.

Panic rises through her layers. If she digs underneath she doesn't know what will be there. 'I have no idea why someone would follow me. I'm not interesting in any way.'

'You have had a fascinating life,' Iain says softly.

'Everyone has,' she replies.

'*You* are special. You are unique.'

Uneasy, Maria leans back into the armchair and doesn't reply. That's the kind of language a stalker would use. And wouldn't this be a job a stalker would love? She shakes her head out of paranoia. That is what inhuman acts bring on – humans stop trusting other humans.

'Do you feel that you're endangering yourself by wearing the blindfold?'

'No. Next question.'

Silence.

'I'm not responsible for another person's behaviour. Only mine,' she says.

'You could look at this situation as a catalyst for personal growth. In your own time, I would like you to take off your blindfold in front of me. That's all. You don't have to open your eyes for more than a second.'

'I don't see how this helps.'

'Trust me,' he says.

Maria's heart is beating so loudly she's sure Iain can hear. She raises her fingers to the front of the blindfold and eases it over her head. The light on her closed eyelids changes the quality of the dark inside them. She can see streaks of not-black. 'I don't like it,' she says, 'it's not right.' She doesn't even know if she's talking aloud. She holds the cushion tighter.

'Can you open your eyes?' Iain asks.

Her eyelids flutter with the strain of clamping them shut. She can feel him there, watching. Her hands tremble, her neck sweats. The nausea that comes before fainting sweeps over her. Billy stands against her legs, puts his head on her lap and whimpers.

'That's enough,' Iain says. There is worry in his voice. 'I'd like to take you through a guided meditation for the rest of the session, with an emphasis on calming down and feeling strong.'

'I don't think I'm going to calm down,' she says.

He counts down. 'Five, four, three, two, one . . .'

Sounds drift back – the road outside, the clock in the hall, the mutters of others.

Iain shifts on the sofa.

'I hadn't realised I'd gone under,' she says. She wishes she could go back and get that feeling all the time. The only time she has felt similar is when she was on morphine when her appendix burst at her cousin's wedding. She can't remember much of what happened then, either.

Something is nagging at her, though, something she feels she shouldn't forget from the visualisation. Something that could help.

'Could you hypnotise me into remembering more details about someone?' she asks.

'What are you asking?' Iain says. She can feel his puzzlement. It crackles through the air between them. He is trying to work out her angles.

'There must be a time where I've been in contact with him.'

'Your stalker?'

'The person who is stalking me,' she corrects him. 'Yes. If I was in a relaxed state I could bring back details that could help the police.'

Iain pauses. 'I feel uncomfortable about that,' he says at last.

'Why?'

'Visualisation is a therapeutic tool. I don't feel it's right to use it for possibly traumatic purposes. There are others who will take you back in your life to other times but I don't subscribe to it.'

'I want to do something,' says Maria, thumping her hand on the arm of the chair. Her relaxed state is ebbing. Fast.

'Maybe next time. Meanwhile, consider opening your eyes when you go to bed. Just for one minute. You can time yourself if it helps. Count it down. You will be in the dark so it won't be a confrontation, but there will be information for your eyes to adjust to. You could see it as a great achievement.'

'Or giving in to a criminal. It's like telling me that I'm at fault for wearing a short skirt if I was raped. I won't.'

'Even if he's enjoying the power he has over you?'

'You can't possibly know what he's enjoying or feeling.'

'I can take a guess,' Iain says.

Keisha paces outside Dr Parker's house, looking through her notes for the third time. She's not usually this nervous. What if she misses some detail in this or another interview? At least she's doing this one alone. Rider threatened to come with her but the Guv has sent him off to talk to Maria's boss. If anyone is used to talking with counsellors, it's her.

The door opens and Maria emerges, red-eyed and looking as if she needs several days' sleep. 'Who's that?' she asks, reaching for the door joist.

'DC Baxter has come to ask me some questions, Maria. Remember? To see if I can assist her with her enquiries.' There is a hint of irony in his answer, only slightly, but discernible, like the colour of milk with a drop of blood in it.

'I don't see how he can,' Maria says, frowning. She turns to Iain. He places a hand on her shoulder. There is something proprietorial in his action that Keisha doesn't like.

Maria walks off down the path, talking to Billy. Iain Parker watches them walk up the slope to the station.

'Come in,' he says. 'I've got half an hour before I need to leave.'

'Where do you have to go?' Keisha asks.

'I have errands to run,' he says. Maria is now out of view. He turns to Keisha. 'You have thirty minutes maximum, I'm afraid.'

'As I explained, sir, it may take longer than that.'

Iain shrugs. He leads her through the hallway with its posh purple wallpaper and a writing desk that has no sign of ever having been used. A clock ticks down the hour for all of the therapists behind the doors. Photographs of Greenwich and the foreshore line the walls.

Keisha walks into the room ahead of Parker. Judging from the indentation on one side of the sofa and the textbooks on the other, he sits there whereas his clients sit opposite in the low-slung armchair. She sits on the sofa and gestures to the chair. Parker already looks confused.

'So tell me,' she says, placing her hands on her lap, palms open. 'How do you feel about Maria's stalker?'

His mouth opens and closes. He doesn't like the tables turned. Counselling is about power for him, perhaps. Keisha has known a few of those. 'It is shocking,' he stammers, 'shocking. And to find out in such a macabre way.'

'Is it your impression from your sessions that Maria may have known about the stalker, even if unconsciously?'

He crosses his legs, shifts position. 'My conversations with Maria are entirely confidential.'

'It would be a betrayal of her trust for you to do otherwise,' Keisha says. 'We need to know as much as possible without breaking those therapeutic boundaries.'

'You have some experience of therapy,' he says, leaning forward. His eyes have the twinkled, crinkled look of a lecturer about to make a move.

'I studied Psychology and Criminology.'

'No, you've been through it,' he says. 'The whole deal. I can see it.'

'A psychic as well as a therapist? You're bad at both.' She stops herself shifting and showing her discomfort.

'Why do you feel the need to get the upper hand?' he asks, smiling. He's enjoying this.

'Why do you think a stalker would announce him or herself in that way?' she asks. Flattery will be the way in for him, make him think she needs his expertise.

He rubs his ear. 'It has a lot more impact than your usual love letter written in cut-out newspaper print. And it's personalised, to her. He might think that she would feel singled out, special. I have much less specialised knowledge of stalkers than you do . . .'

Cheeky. He's trying to flatter *her*.

'. . . but I would say that he's trying to show her how much he loves her. He is showing her that he would do anything for her, maybe even kill for her.'

She looks up from her notes. 'What would make a suitable victim to show her his love?'

Iain shrugs and leans to one corner of the armchair. Keisha has the urge to slap him. 'Someone for whom she has expressed a dislike. Or an old boyfriend. Or someone who didn't revere her to the extent that a stalker thinks she should be.' He stands up now and walks round the room, hands pressed together, tips of his fingers to his chin. 'I assume you have thought of all of this,' he says, picking up a china clown from the shelf. It is holding balloons in its hand. He smiles at it and very gently positions it in the same place.

'Without breaking confidentiality, can you say why Maria will not remove her blindfold, even when in danger?'

'I don't think there is any way I can answer that,' he says, sitting down. He clenches his fist as if holding onto her secrets as tightly as balloons.

'Where were you early yesterday morning?' she asks. 'Around six a.m.' He takes a sip of water from the glass next to him. 'The day before had been particularly trying,' he says, standing up again. Keisha wishes she had something to suspect him of and then she could take him in and insist he fucking stayed in the chair for five minutes. 'I arranged to meet a mate for a drink, Dave . . .'

Every case has a deluge of Daves.

'. . . and he turned up at nine. We then went all around Soho till one when he went home – lightweight. I stayed in town and chatted up a girl. She suggested that we went back to mine. I don't think I need say any more than that about what happened.'

'What time did she leave?'

'It was after six, as that was when I went to sleep. The problem is,' he says, smiling, 'that I didn't get her name. What's your first name by the way?'

'You don't need to know.'

'That's what she said. I must say that I agree. If I don't know her name, I can't get it wrong.' He winks at Keisha. 'I'm sure you've been in the same situation.'

She has. But he won't find out from her.

Maria gets off at Old Street, feeling as if she's left her brain running all night and it is out of all thoughts. Counselling always leaves her empty. Will says it shouldn't be like that, but then Will pretends he knows a lot about everything.

She decides to takes the longer route to work, getting Billy to take her through Provost Street and Cropley Street, with a diversion via Bletchley and Wenlock because she likes the names. The smell of the river leads her as much as Billy. Mortimer Wheeler House sits with the river at its feet. It has a lot of stories to tell, does Mortimer Wheeler. It contains the London Archaeological Archive and Research Centre, or LAARC for short, apposite for her as an acronym.

It is the largest archaeological archive in the world and she gets to work there, documenting site records and writing summaries. Most of these are the only records of a site – digging up the past also destroys it. There was once a Roman London house that only survives now as an archive and, as the Museum itself says, in the memory of the archaeologists who found it. Her job is to make sure London's past is not lost.

Maria walks down the stairs to her basement office. It is small, secure and Billy has his own beanbag by the door. He sniffs at it and climbs on, beans shifting like tiny pebbles.

'I hope you have a good reason for being late,' Hugh Foister says.

'I'm sorry, Hugh,' Maria says, standing up. Braille papers flutter to the floor. 'I thought somebody would have—'

Hugh laughs a laugh too big for the room. It makes it seem like he is taking up even more space. He can brush his fingers on the ceiling when he stretches up. 'I'm joking, Maria. I'm surprised to see you here at all. Shouldn't you be at home, not your home, of course, I mean, what with the, you know . . .' He trails off into humphs.

'What do you mean?' Maria asks. She's not going to tell him anything if she can help it.

'Your friend Simon called and talked to Sasha. He told her what had happened. We're really sorry. If that stalker tries anything I'll . . . well, I'll do something.' He humphs again and nods. 'Just say if you need time off to, well, not be here.'

Hugh means well. At least she thinks he means well. Maybe that time he brought her flowers in hospital after her operation meant something else. That's the effect of all this, thinking that everyone has an agenda. Distrust imbedded in a day.

'I want to be at work, Hugh,' Maria says. 'I want to get lost in old London, not think about anything else.'

'Well I commend that entirely. Don't let the bastards get near your mind, even if they're in your home. That's what I say.' She's been told that he has a red-brown tan from yet another holiday and imagines him the colour of how Shiraz tastes. 'We're not going to let any pervert get near our little Maria.'

Maria flinches.

'Patronising means speaking down to people,' Rider says from the doorway. Now there's definitely no room. She's never felt claustrophobic in here until now. That's the effect this is having on her. She'd love to get away. Somewhere open. London has never seemed like a prison before.

Billy gives a little bark. The beanbag rustles as he stands up.

'Too late, Billy,' Maria says. 'He's already here.'

'Better late than not all,' Rider says. 'Now, you must be Maria's boss, Mr Foister.' She hears the soft shunting sound of a handshake. 'I'm Detective Sergeant Rider. I'd like to ask you a few questions about security if you don't mind. Let's go in your office, shall we. It's cramped in here.'

Their voices retreat down the hallway, Hugh's boom reducing the further away they go. Sasha, the department intern, clacks down the corridor. Her heels are so high that the day that Sasha sprained her ankle and came in wearing flats, Maria thought she must be sitting down as her voice was located so much nearer the ground. 'Who was that?' she says.

'Who?'

'The bloke going into the main office. He was hot as a phaal in a heatwave.'

'That was sergeant Rider. And no, I have no idea of his marital status, shoe size or anything else.' This is one of the reasons she is glad she can't see as others do. People are confusing enough as it is without adding looks or beauty into it. Rider doesn't *sound* attractive. His voice has a bite to it, as if he punches words at people. DI Dark's voice, on the other hand, is low and smooth.

'Mate, if getting stalked brings you into contact with cops like that then it can't be all bad.'

'Other than the invasion of privacy, threat to safety and general terror at not knowing what is happening, no, it's fine.'

'Exactly my point. Do you reckon you could get him to interview me? I'll give him a thorough—'

'Sasha, could you find me the post-excavation reports for JAC96 please?' Maria says, putting her head in her hands. Sasha clicks away, still talking. Setting VoiceOver to work on selected field records,

Maria stands on a chair to open the high window so that she can hear gulls and helicopters and other things that fly while listening to data on prehistoric peat and alluvial finds. She will bury herself in the past.

'Please,' says Hugh Foister, 'take a seat.'

'There isn't one,' Rider replies. Foister's office is sweltering. Two heaters pump out heat, turning jerkily on their plinths like twin R2-D2s.

Foister looks round, appearing genuinely surprised. 'Terribly sorry, they must've all been moved upstairs. We've got the Thames Discovery people in this morning. I think the plan is to use them to stop the banks of the Thames being eroded.' He waits for Rider to laugh. Rider doesn't laugh. 'Erosion is up four hundred per cent year on year. There will be many losses to archaeology that we will never know about.' He shakes his head. His hair flops onto his forehead like a fish tail. Rider tries not to look at it.

'I'm glad you're here,' Foister says, leaning in conspiratorially. 'I've been racking my mind since I found out about the stalking.'

'So you have information that could help our enquiries?' Rider says.

'My brain is not what it used to be – you should have seen it twenty years ago.' His laugh blasts out like one of the heaters. 'But I came up with something.'

It is so hot. Rider wipes his forehead.

'A couple of months ago, Maria's hard drive went down. Had a virus that attacked all the records and turned them into some hooly-flip computer language. An IT guy arrived, said he was from the suppliers. He was in there for a good hour while Maria was down in the archives. When she came back, it was all fixed but she noticed that things had been changed around in her office. She is very particular about where everything is kept, you see. She phoned up to complain and was told that no one had been sent – they had replied to her email offering online or phone support but she never got back to them.'

'So this IT guy could have been the stalker, you think, or hired by him, at least?' Rider asks. 'Did you report the intruder?'

Foister shifts in his seat. 'I changed the security protocol so that all visitors must be thoroughly checked.'

'But you didn't phone the police.'

'No.' Foister looks out of the window, humming.

Rider's patience ebbs. 'Do you have a description of the man?'

Foister rubs his clammy hands. 'Let's see. He was average height, I'd say. Came up to about here.' He points to his shoulder. 'Lean, not like me, as if he goes running. He was wearing a woolly hat, one of those black fisherman hats. He was white and, well, that's about all I can recall.'

'Eye colour? Hair colour or style? Distinguishing marks? Did he give you his name?'

Foister shrugs. 'Sorry. I remember thinking that I liked the hat. I feel the cold, you see.'

Rider wrote down the description. It might be worth getting a photo artist in, although it would probably resemble any number of London joggers. 'Can you think of anyone who would have a reason to stalk Maria? And that can mean holding a grudge or indeed having a crush. Anything at all.'

Foister looks baffled. 'Why would anyone want to hurt Maria?' he says.

The wind speeds round the business park like a boy racer, pushing the diamond-shaped sign into a frantic swing. Jonathan sits on the bench outside DMD. Stretching his legs out, sun on his face, he watches people enter the shop. A young woman walks in, a canvas bag held to her chest. She comes out five minutes later without the bag and with make-up streaks on her cheeks.

Mozart's 'Requiem in D Minor' is playing as he enters DMD. Everything is shining white, from the walls to the floors to the metre-high gem turning on a plinth on the counter. The motto below the gem says 'everlasting love'.

A woman with careful curls and pink lipstick appears. 'How can I help you?' she asks. She scans him, checking his suit and fingers. She lingers on the wedding band.

'Can I speak to Amyris Church?' Jonathan asks. She bristles, as if he should know who she is. He does. She is featured on every page of the DMD website and in the brochures, sitting down with her hand on her cheek to show that she is listening and that she cares, her face photo shopped into softness.

'That's me,' she says. 'Call me Amyris.' Her smile is silver-plated.

'I'm DI Dark from the Metropolitan Police, Homicide Division. Tell me about this ring,' Jonathan says, placing the photograph in front of her on the counter. You can see the gap where it was sawn away from the flesh.

She leans in.

He shows her the scan sent to his phone. On the inner part of the ring, DMD is printed inside a diamond shape. Next to it is a scratched smudge, the close-up shows an obliterated area.

'That's where the reference number should be,' Amyris says, frowning. 'We make sure that we keep every one logged in case they want to convert more cremains into treasure.'

'Cremains?'

'The cremated remains of the deceased.'

'Ah.' Jonathan's Mum, Millie, keeps a box filled with Dad's ashes on the window sill in her kitchen. She wouldn't like them being called 'cremains' – 'ashes' has more of a biblical ring to it. He should visit her in Cardiff. He should call.

'You said you were from Homicide?' Amyris says. She does not appear disturbed by this but Botox may have smoothed her concern.

'Is there any way of tracing a ring, other than the reference number?'

She puts on her glasses to get a closer look and is suddenly more attractive. Natalie bought a plain glass pair of specs for 'Secretary' moments. He should have known something was wrong when he saw the glasses in her handbag and two marks on either side of her nose. She said they were from her sunglasses. On a dull day in December. He'd put it down to her being pretentious, turns out she was adulterous.

The shop door swings open. An elderly woman walks in, hair wind-shaken, holding a wooden box with a faded print of a tin soldier on the lid. She places it on the counter, keeping her hand on top, stroking the box as if it were a loved one's face.

Snapping into efficient empathy, Amyris's head tilts and the space between her eyebrows puckers. 'Mrs Kane? My colleague told me you'd be in early. I'm so sorry for your loss. Please be assured that we will treat your husband with the reverence and respect he so deserves.' She plucks a form from the shelf below. 'Please fill this out as best you can. We will then place your box in a safe bearing your name.'

Amyris reaches for the box but Mrs Kane holds on, flattening her palm against the top. 'He played soldiers with our son and then our granddaughter. She's in the Royal Logistic Corps now. He was so proud.' Her jaw muscles move to say the words that can't be said. 'I will have him, my Lion, my Lionel, back soon, though?' she says. 'I don't like to go to bed without him.' Her voice is accompanied by a wheeze that is just how his grandmother sounded towards the end, as Gargie's smoke-blown lungs tried to expand despite the tumour taking over.

'Your Lion will be more magnificent than ever,' Amyris says, smiling as she bags up the box.

Mrs Kane stares at Amyris until she looks up. Her eyes are steely. The smile simpers away. 'You would not say that if you had known him,' Mrs Kane says. She nods at Jonathan and leaves, her steps even slower.

Amyris waits until the door has closed behind Mrs Kane before she speaks. 'As you can see, this is a sensitive business. Dealing with cremains is nothing compared to dealing with customers. It must be the same for you – dead bodies are easier than criminals, I suspect.' She looks at him for back-up. He says nothing. 'I thought when I set up the business that I would be doing people a service. I didn't know I'd have to be holding their paws and handing out hankies.' She shakes her head as if it is unbelievable that she should have to put up with this. She is leaning over the counter towards him, confiding with added cleavage.

'Part of both of our jobs is dealing with death, Ms Church. Emotion tends to come with it.'

'Shame, isn't it?' Amyris says, as if he had agreed with her. Sarcasm is as lost on her as her wrist is in that sparkling bracelet. How many died for those dust diamonds?

'There must be a way of narrowing down the buyer of this diamond.'

'I would love to help you,' she says, her nose wrinkling. 'But until you get the serial number then I can't. And even then we take confidentiality very seriously.'

'I am entitled to search your records if I suspect that a crime has taken place. And I do.' This was stretching the point and the law. 'I am sure you would rather that it were not generally known that you were at the centre of a murder enquiry.'

She glances at her mobile phone. Several thoughts seem to squirm across her face. She sighs. 'Our insignia changed to this one at the beginning of this year so that would make it one of the yellow diamonds made in the last nine months, I suppose.'

'I would very much appreciate access to those.'

She taps on her iPad, swipes through a database until she finds what she wants. The printer makes a surprised sound behind her.

She smiles. 'Detective Dark, was it? That's a name I find fascinating. What did that come from?' Her eyelash inserts flick against her skin.

'I have no idea.' He does, of course. His aunt, Neil's mother, traced the Darks, or Darkes as they were then, back to fourteenth-century Cornwall, named in the Anglo-Saxon tradition of a nickname for someone with dark hair like Jonathan. His dad, though, always said they were named Dark for another reason but mum would always shut him up before he could tell Jonathan. And now he's gone. 'How many yellow diamonds were sold?'

'A fair few, although yellow isn't popular this year.'

'What is a fashionable colour in the memory diamond market this year?' Sometimes his job causes him to ask questions that he would never have imagined. This is one of those times.

'Black is in. It's our new range. We've had a number of black Labrador owners wanting that. And the odd Goth bringing in their grandmas.' She smirks. Jonathan doesn't. He was once a goth and has the shirts and straps at the back of the wardrobe to prove it.

'Do yellow diamonds signify anything in particular?' he asks.

'Not that I know of,' she says, taking the list from the printer. She holds out the warm sheets. 'I don't suppose I need to tell you that this is very sensitive information.'

'And yet you just did.' He folds and pockets them. 'I will be very careful. Take me through the process of turning the dead into diamonds,' Jonathan asks, picking up their glossy brochure.

Amyris glances at the clock above the counter. She looks nothing like as serene as her photo.

'Am I keeping you from something?' Jonathan asks.

She takes Mrs Kane's box of soldiers and carefully eases off the lid. 'There are two ways we go about converting the remains. We have a contract with a number of crematoriums and undertakers in the country, mainly in London. They have been trained to cremate the body, take the best sample of the remains and send it off for diamond processing. Other clients, like Mrs Kane, come to us with the cremains of loved ones that can be decades old. We then perform the same process. Spouse or mouse, we'll deal with it.' She laughs at her little joke then takes out a clear plastic bag, tied with a blue ribbon, filled with what looks like cat litter.

Jonathan found out some time ago that 'ashes' is a euphemism. Gargie had requested in her will that Jonathan scatter her ashes at specified locations around London. They were not the kind of ashes left after a wood fire, they are the size of small pebbles. Hers were black. The cancer drugs had caused a chemical reaction in the cremation process. It didn't seem right – she left express wishes that no one should wear black to her funeral, not even socks, and there she was, a box of dark ash. She would have had a big laugh at that. Everyone was to wear something 'bright and shiny. I'll be buggered if you're going to be grumpy bastards at my party', she had said in the video played on a tiny telly on the lectern. The sermon she gave, about enjoying your body while you had it, should be on YouTube.

He had taken her motorbike, her remains stowed in a tea caddy in the sidecar, and set off. He had often sat in that sidecar as she took him round London, showing off its strangest streets, and now he was taking her on her final ride, shaking her out in Brydges Place and other alleys and at the gates of the old Londinium Wall. He placed the last few pieces of her cremains on the crumbling parts of the wall that still stand near the Museum of London. Two teenage girls, passing a cigarette between their varnished fingertips, watched him as he muttered his goodbyes and cried. One of them stood up and asked what he was doing. She picked up a piece and tried to draw on the wall. He told her what it was. She dropped it as if it were still hot. He decided that day he would be buried.

'Am I boring you?' Amyris says, snapping her fingers in front of his face. Something Natalie used to do.

'Please,' he says, resisting the urge to snap back. 'Carry on.'

'The cremains are given a unique identity number and sent off. Carbon is extracted, converted to graphite and then sent to a diamond press in Holland. A contaminant is added to give the desired colour – we offer a wide range of colours now that the process has been refined – red, white, green, blue, black and, of course, yellow.'

'And the contaminant for a yellow diamond . . .'

'Nitrogen.'

'Does DNA remain testable in the diamond?' he asks.

She shakes her head. 'People always want to know that. They wish to know that the essence of their relative is still intact.' She keeps looking at her phone and tapping her fingers on the table. She rubs her hand over her face as if to wipe away the emotions threatening to split through her skin.

'So can you?'

'Can you what?'

'Identify DNA.'

'No. It's broken down in the process. You won't be able to tell who or what makes up that diamond, I'm afraid.'

Jonathan looks through the brochure. Turning her Lion into a diamond is going to cost Mrs Kane at least two thousand pounds. He would be worried about losing a loved one all over again.

Amyris places her pale painted fingertips on the top of the model diamond and presses down so that it can't move. She lets it go again and watches it turn.

Jonathan drives off feeling more positive: the accounts team and IT will get to work on that list of buyers and maybe they can trace the ring back to the stalker.

He has been to this industrial estate before, on visits to the outlet centre with his wife. She had been great with him then, encouraging him to be himself. Last time they went, it must be five years ago now, around their anniversary, she had picked matching halterneck dresses in different sizes and brought them to him, giggling. He had shushed her but loved her excitement, her face flushed. The amber flecks in her green eyes looked like gold leaf. She led him into the changing rooms and, tangled together in the small cubicle, they clambered into the close-fitting dresses and stood next to each other in the mirror. 'I've never felt closer to you,' she said, drew his chin down to her and kissed him. He will never get that again. Not from someone else.

The traffic in Wembley is horrendous but it's worth the diversion. Jonathan turns the corner into Emsdale Drive. Last time he was here, Natalie argued with her father and stormed out. Everything was tempestuous with Natalie and her family. He's learned never to discuss politics, religion or even the relative merits of biscuits in a Family Circle Variety Pack.

Jonathan feels the familiar escalation in anxiety as he walks up the drive. Their house is big. Very big. They have plenty of money to spend on their darling daughter, much more than he does.

Nadia Plymouth opens the door wearing a black skin tight tracksuit. 'Darling!' she says, opening her arms wide but not hugging him. 'How wonderful to see you.' She shoos him into the front room. 'You must excuse what I'm wearing. I'm off to the gym in half an hour. I'm waiting till Mary gets here.' Mary is the cleaner/housekeeper/cook/confidante/anything Nadia wants her to be on any given day. 'I'd offer you tea,' Nadia says, 'but we don't have any biscuits.'

'Right,' says Jonathan, settling into their sofa. There are so many cushions on it that he is forced to sit on the edge of the seat. 'I know this must be awkward for you, Nadia—'

'Not at all, darling! It's wonderful to see you. And you're looking very well,' she says, eyeing him up and down. Mainly down. 'You've lost weight. It's the benefit of heartbreak, isn't it? No appetite and a flat stomach. I think it's nature's way of making us more attractive for the next one.'

'There won't be a next one, Nadia,' Jonathan says, staring at his shoes sinking into the plush white carpet. There's no sign of the red wine stain caused by him flinging up his arms in an argument, causing a spatter pattern that he dabbed at with kitchen roll on his hands and knees. He knows that all this gushing love from Nadia is just for show – he could be just as easily steam-cleaned from the Plymouths' lives.

'I came here,' he says, noticing that their wedding picture is still on the mantelpiece although now it is hiding behind a large photo of Natalie's sister playing the bassoon in the London Symphony Orchestra, 'because I'd like you to talk to Natalie for me. I think there's still a chance. All of this was a mistake. She needed time, that's all, and so did I.' Nadia blinks at him. 'She's sent me this card.' He takes it out of his pocket. He has opened and closed it so many times. His hands shake, either from humiliation, nerves or the extra shot in his coffee at the services. 'Please talk to her. She'll listen to you.' The words 'more than me' aren't necessary.

'I really don't think I should interfere, dear,' Nadia says.

Jonathan has to stop himself shouting: *You were only too happy before, when the house wasn't big enough or holidays long enough for your little girl.*

Nadia tuts when she opens the card. 'It's good that she remembered your anniversary. I brought her up to be a good, polite girl.'

What's he doing here, begging? 'Maybe you could have brought her up not to have an affair.'

'We've told her that we don't approve of that, Jonathan. We're not keen on Jeremy or whatever his name is, although he makes very good roast dinners.'

It is as if one of the glass pendants from the chandelier above him dropped and lodged in his breastbone. They've been to dinner. At Jonathan's house with Jonathan's wife and Jonathan's wife's boyfriend. He stands up and brushes non-existent crumbs from the missing biscuits from his trousers. 'Lovely to see you again, Nadia. I hope you fall off the cross-trainer.'

He doesn't stay to look at her.

On the way down their drive, his phone goes.

'Where are you, Guv?' Rider says. He is outside somewhere – there's the sound of gulls.

'On my way,' says Jonathan.

'Marine squad called. I'm leaving now . . . a body's been found.'
The wind lifts his words away.

'It's not . . .' Not Maria. Say it isn't Maria.

'Not Maria, no. A bloke.'

'Can another team deal with it? We've got too much on.'

'DCI Allen has claimed it for us. It's wearing a yellow diamond ring.'

11

V auxhall. The Thames, again. Jonathan walks down Riverside
View, watching the water. Gargie told him that, within minutes
of his birth, she had held him up to the window so that the Thames
could see its newest son. He had seen the river and smiled, she said,
but Jonathan knew that Gargie often lied and that no newborn
smiles. And definitely not at a river.

He makes his way through the police divers and waiting SOCOs.
Rider is standing with Mike Reynolds. 'The woman over there found
it, sir,' Rider says, pointing to a woman sitting on a bench, arms
wrapped round herself. 'She was out for a run and saw it on the thin
strip of beach, partially out of the water. That's the bag the body was
found in, that's not one of ours.'

Mike Reynolds comes over, zipping up his SOCO suit. He seems
excited. 'You shouldn't be here, Mike,' Jonathan says.

'The DCI asked for me especially,' Mike replies, stepping back.

'You know my rule – no SOCOs at more than one potential site.
I am trying to keep cross-contamination to a minimum. If there *is*
any connection with Maria King or Tanya Baker then I don't want
the defence querying the chain of evidence and putting doubts in the
jury's minds. I know I might be being paranoid, but you know what
they say about paranoia.'

'"It's not paranoia if they're really out to get you?"'

'That's the one. Sorry to waste your time, mate. Take the rest of the
day off, if you like.'

Mike's face falls. Why would he want to be there? This job does
strange things to you.

The corpse is in a body bag on the river bank. The zip is partially open, reminding Jonathan of a pupa. The wrinkled skin is shrugging off the flesh – it must have been in the Thames for at least a week or two. It appears to be a male of between forty and fifty although the bloat and skin slippage make it hard to age accurately. The body bag smells of fish. What would Maria make of this? Maybe she's better off without her eyesight. Unless the imagination is worse. Jonathan pulls his focus back to the right hand that slumps out of the bag. On the ring finger is a yellow diamond ring, the colour of infection.

Richard Agnarsson strides over. 'Good to see you, Jonathan,' he says. 'You're looking—' He stops. 'I was going to say you're looking well, but you know I'd be lying. You're looking only slightly less cadaverous than my patient.'

'I don't know how you manage to make an insult come across as a compliment.'

'It is a skill. My accent helps. The Swedish are innately charming.' Richard bends down over the unknown body. The open jacket of his suit flaps open. His mentee, Debbie, walks over. She is small and round, her head moving as quick as an owl's as she scrutinises the sides of the bag, all the time talking under her breath. Richard nods and prompts her. He is telegraph-pole tall, maybe that's how he's able to pick up her words.

'Any initial thoughts?' Jonathan asks.

'We can't yet tell how he came to die,' Richard says. 'He may have drowned so we'll check for water in the lungs. However, there are two signs of head trauma with bruising suggesting it was shortly before, or a cause of, death. The weights in the bag were enough to keep the body down but not to stop it being dragged along the river.'

'Not a very professional job,' Jonathan replies.

'Will I see you at the examination, as usual?' Richard asks.

Jonathan nods.

'This will be a nasty one, I'm afraid.'

'Those retrieved from the river always are.'

Garry Harding puts down the phone and paces back and forth in his office of the new building. The body has been found and, worse, so has the ring. Through the window, the crane looks like a waiting gibbet.

'You failed to deliver on our very simple demands,' the woman had said over the phone. 'How can we trust you with any further stages of the qualification process?' She used a voice like the one his mum employed when he had done something wrong. With his mother it usually meant a couple of hours in his room followed by an austere tea of toast and water; in this context, it could mean the quick way down from the tallest building in London.

He goes over to the filing cabinet and takes out the brandy.

What would happen if he went to the police and confessed? It wasn't like he killed Finnegan Finch – his task was to bring the van, then collect, deliver and dispose of the body. This was somebody else's murder job. Everyone had to do it if they wanted to join the Ring. And if he gave himself up then he would have to tell that to the police; either way he'd be dead by the end of the day.

It hadn't been real before. He doesn't even know her real name as it changes as frequently as her hair colour. She introduced herself to him six months ago at a networking lunch in Hammersmith to raise finance for the building but, when he Googled her, she didn't exist. She showed up at a dinner a few weeks later, sitting next to him with a black bob instead of long blonde hair, a different nametag in front of her. It was obviously a wig, but maybe the last one was as well. She explained about the Ring but told him that, for his own safety, he would never know much, only that there was a matrix of people in the city who looked out for each other. Even in the midst of the champagne and flattery, he knew that his ignorance was only ever for their safety, not his.

Still, those first meetings had been exhilarating. They'd given him ancient single malts, cigars and the feeling that anything could happen for him and his company. That he would be depression-proof – couldn't he see that even in the depths of a recession, London thrived? There was a reason for that, she said.

Names were dropped like coffins into graves: celebrities and en-trepreneurs, judges, media moguls, high level politicians and high ranking police. All benefiting in some way, backs and blind eyes turned in the name of the Ring. All helping each other along this difficult road. He made the mistake once, a bottle of gin into the night, of referring to his excitement at joining London's underworld.

'This is no underworld,' she had said, anger blazing in her eyes but the rest of her face smiling for any observers. Her voice came out as a hiss. 'We do not operate below people's gaze; or above: they simply look through us, never expecting us to be operating right in front of them.' She sat back in her chair, serenity in place. 'Another bottle?' she said, clicking her fingers.

All they asked was that he prove his commitment in a series of escalating crimes, all to the good of the organisation. If everyone has incriminating knowledge on each other, then nobody would step out of the Ring. Finnegan Finch showed what happened to those that got cold feet. Literally now, in his case. It had seemed so simple: wait for a call then take the body to Finch's crematorium. They had the key and the security codes. Remove the ring, then incinerate his body. 'Let him burn,' she had said. She had even arranged for Finnegan himself to show him how to use the oven at the crematorium a week before his demise. She'd laughed at the irony and efficiency.

Now she was coming over to find out what had gone wrong.

How could he possibly explain what happened? Weeks later, it still doesn't make sense. Still chills him.

He had received the call on Saturday. Leaving his wife watching a film, he had taken the keys to one of the firm's vans and driven to a warehouse on the South Bank. As Garry backed in, the loading door lifted. The van doors clanked open: Garry peered through the mesh into the back of the van but it was too dark to see anything other than lumbering shadows. The sounds of dragging, scuffling and swearing continued for what seemed like forever then the doors were locked and the side of the van knocked on twice: the sign for him to drive away.

He tried not to think of the body in the back.

It didn't work. A man had died and he was going to be burned at Garry's hand. Except for the ring. He had to remember the ring.

Garry switched on the radio and tried to sing over the scene playing in his head: him shaking hands with the man who ended up dead in the van, envying his yellow diamond. He tapped his fingers on the dashboard. The sooner this was over, the better.

After a series of agonising jams, the traffic eased off as the road turned into the A13. He'd be at the Sustainable Industries Park in ten minutes if he was lucky.

As Garry drove onto River Road, something crashed into the side of the van. He jerked forward, seat belt jamming.

He checked his wing mirror. No sign of an animal in the road.

Another impact, from the other side this time, jolted right through the van. Must be kids on the wasteland, throwing rocks. He checked again. Nothing in the rear mirror.

He passed building sites and industrial plants, street lamps getting further apart. Nearly there. As he leaned across to change the radio station, he was slammed forwards into the steering wheel. His neck whipped back.

It was as if someone was throwing themselves against the van. From the inside.

Fear pulled itself up by his spinal column, seized his heart and lungs and squeezed. What if Finnegan was still alive? He could have come round and was attempting to break out.

The grate between the back and the front cabin rattled. Finnegan must be shaking it. Garry craned round but could not see him. The radio jumped from station to station as if following his frenetic thoughts.

Breath rasping, Garry turned down a narrow road, looking for somewhere to stop. Somewhere to run.

There was a surge in the air, like before a storm. The hairs on his arms stood; the radio shouted louder.

Something rocked the van. The engine stopped.

No headlights, no power at all, only enough time and momentum to aim the vehicle as best he could in the dark.

Garry came round to the smell of fried electrics. The van was dead. The spark plugs had overloaded– they had melted and now resembled blackened flat mushrooms. Garry shone the torch around the scrubland that backed onto the shore. It was dark. The nearest light came from a warehouse at the top of the road. What could he do now? If he involved anyone else, he would fail. The body in the back showed what happen when initiates failed.

There was no longer any sound coming from the back of the van.

Maybe the crash finished Finnegan off. Part of him hoped that it had. But what if he was still alive – would they expect Garry to kill him? That would gain him respect. Maybe this was a test. An initiation of sorts.

Garry walked slowly round, right hand clamping his painful neck. No movement from inside the van. He picked up a brick from a nearby skip. He opened the back doors.

Nothing seemed out of place. The body bag lay, zipped most of the way up, towards the back of the van. A tuft of Finnegan's hair and his nose was visible. Everything else was secured – ladders strapped horizontally, building materials harnessed on the walls and floor. It was as if whatever just happened never happened. The only thing that struck him as strange was the smell of burning candles.

Garry went to shut the doors. For one moment, maybe less, a face appeared, inches from his own. The face, mouth wide as if screaming, was Finnegan's. The body bag had not moved.

Garry panicked. Disgust running through him, he scrambled into the back of the van, zipped the body bag till it was completely closed and dragged it, feeling Finnegan's stiffening feet through the fabric, till it hung out of the van. Pain tearing through his chest and neck, he looped his arms around the body and tried to pick it up. Adrenalin sparked, giving him strength. He half-dragged, half-carried the bag across the scrub, stumbling and nearly dropping it twice. He had to get rid of it. Get it out of his sight.

Lungs burning, he placed the bag by the river's edge. All he could think about was sinking it to the bottom of the Thames. Small, heavy stones would help, and there were lug wrenches and other tools in the van. Unzipping the bag, he placed the improvised weights to the sides of the body like funerary offerings. With a last look around, he rolled the clanking bag into the Thames and vomited.

Garry walked back to the main road. His mind and stomach were clear and quiet: the freak was gone and with it that face. The Ring never need know that he hadn't cremated Finnegan. He grinned. He'd got away with it. Garry was supposed to send off the ashes to be made into the ring, the murderer's spoils, but any pile of white ash would do. Maybe murder wouldn't be so bad. This was like extra-marital sex without the regret.

He was near the road when he realised. The yellow ring. It was still on the body. Sinking to the bottom of the river.

The buzzer goes on his desk phone. Garry opens his eyes and tries to dislodge the memories. Jenna, his secretary, says, 'I have your one o'clock to see you, Mr Harding.'

If they're going to punish him, he may as well protect himself. Garry takes his mobile out of his pocket, presses record, and slides it inside a lever arch file, microphone pointing towards him. If he gets in deep water, he may as well drown in company.

12

Frank closes the lid on Mrs Winters' body. He stands for his customary minute of silence, hands clasped behind his back, eyes shut. After days of being the guardian of her body and ghost, tomorrow he will ferry her to the hearse and carry her up the aisle of the crematorium chapel. He didn't know Mrs Winters before her death but he wishes he had. She's a lovely lady. Fond of horses, brandy and walks in the country. Her husband, Roy, loved her so much. He had needed Frank's help as well. It took Roy hours in the mourning room before he could talk about the mole on the small of her back, the salt-sweet smell of her and the way she would snuggle into the crook of his arm. Frank had cried at that and raised his glass to them both. She cried too. She was there, standing next to Roy – the viewing room is as much for the dead to view the living as it is for the living to acknowledge the dead. It was what she wanted and needed to hear: not a badly pronounced précis of her life by a vicar who didn't know her, and who will send the next coffin to the furnace half an hour after.

Frank tips his hat. Margery will be here soon, to taxi her back. Journey well, Mrs Winters. He locks the door to the viewing room and surveys the hallway. All is as it should be. The floor has been polished to a dark shine and the cushions on the sofa are arranged off centre, to encourage people to forget about perfection.

Frank places his hat on the coffee table. Now that was a morning. Time for his only afternoon off. 'I'm off-duty, love,' he calls out. Barbara's been married to him long enough to leave him to unwind after a viewing. She knows him better than his bed.

Now for his favourite part of the day. He throws his tie into the corner of the room and removes his tailcoat, shirt, trousers and belt until he's sitting in his pants on the sofa. His stiff shirt lies like a spectre. Swivelling round, he stretches out and stares up at the ceiling. It's a four-seater but his feet still dangle over the side.

He switches on the telly. The Hammers' manager is having a rant about yesterday's red card controversy. He should've seen what was going on on the sidelines – three one-time managers, the deceased Syd King, Charlie Paynter and Ted Fenton, arguing about which players to send on in the second half. Not to mention the pitch invasion that no one saw but the Sighted. The local news is next. A missing teenager, the opening of a new gym by an unfit-looking politician and then 'A body has been retrieved from the Thames by Tower Bridge. Police divers removed the body after it was spotted by a woman jogging by the side of the Thames. Police sources have confirmed that it is a male, aged between forty to fifty years old.' They're showing footage of a body bag being lifted onto a gurney. Frank leans forward. What if it is Finnegan's body? 'The circumstances are currently considered suspicious. A post-mortem will take place in the next few days.'

Barbara appears in the doorway, frail as lace.

'You all right, love?' he asks.

She puts her hand to his face. Frank leans forward and kisses the place just above her eyebrow where the scar curves like a bend in the Thames.

'Tough day?' she asks. Her voice is barely there.

'Long. Tiring. I spent a long time with Mr and Mrs Winters. I've given her the initial ceremony. Which reminds me, I need to get more rosemary before the next ritual.'

'I used to love rosemary,' she says. Sadness has sapped her today. He wishes he could reach her, touch her shoulders, rub the knots out of her feet.

She's wearing the blue shift dress she got for their honeymoon. It was their anniversary last week. Maybe she's been thinking about that today. That can be a good sign. Or not. She reaches over to smooth his hair. An old habit.

Barbara moves to the window. She tries to part the curtains but can't. He won't let her fade, not again. 'What are you going to do about Finnegan, darling?' she asks.

'Is he still here?'

Barbara nods. 'He's in the kitchen. He wanted to go back to see Rosa but I persuaded him to talk to you first.'

'They found a body, you know. Washed up on the foreshore.'

'Do you think it's him?'

Frank shrugs. 'If it is then they buried him without a body, or burnt someone else's body, and fabricated the accident.'

'He'll go mad if it is. He's been telling me about his conspiracy theory all day; this will make it worse.'

'Sorry, love, that must have been draining. I'll get him out of your hair.'

'That wasn't what I meant,' she says quickly. Her hands are trembling. 'He keeps me company. That way nobody else comes along. Nothing else.'

'What do you mean? What's scaring you?'

Barbara breathes onto the window. Not even a hint of mist appears on the glass. 'Nothing, sweetheart. I'm being stupid, don't worry about me. Have you seen our new neighbour?'

Frank shakes his head. 'Which way?'

'Pedlar Cottage. He's a thoughtful-looking man. I've been told he's a detective at the Met.'

Finnegan walks through the door. 'Put some trousers on, Frank, for fuck's sake,' he says.

'Put a body on, then I might oblige,' Frank replies.

Finnegan laughs and sits down in the armchair. Frank and Barbara exchange glances. There's that smile. The one that haunted him before they were courting and would haunt him if ever it were lost.

'What have you been doing all day?' Finnegan asks. He is more realised today, stronger.

'I was wondering what you'd like to do with your death, Finnegan,' Frank says.

'I want to be with Rosa. End of.'

'And I completely get that,' Frank replies. 'I'd be the same. Barbara can't help herself – she's staying with me forever, aren't you, love?'

Barbara's smile is now at half-mast.

'The difference is that I am fully cognisant of the ghost world. We can have almost the same relationship, with some notable and much missed exceptions.'

'Then I'll make Rosa see me,' Finnegan replies, crossing his arms. 'We were as close as you two.'

Frank takes a deep breath. 'That may take a while. In the meantime, how about I set you up with somewhere of your own? Your own haunt, as it were. It's all part of the service – finding ghost accommodation while they get established. Gast houses if you like.' He rumbles a laugh at his own joke.

Finnegan glances at Barbara.

Tell you what,' Frank sighs, putting his clothes back on. 'I'll take you now. There's a spot you might like. You do like trains, don't you?'

Barbara watches them walk up the street. She'd love to go with them but she's so tired. She'd never have enough energy for escalators and crowds. It's this place. There's something in it. She looks around the lounge. It's not here, not yet. It only appears when she's in bed, its silverfish eyes looking into hers.

Ss-cut.

The sound of its slithering travels down from the attic. It's the middle of the day – what is it doing here?

Barbara shuts the door and, using her remaining energy, pushes a chair against it. She still does these things, even though they are no match for ghosts.

Long laughter, shrill as scraping fingernails, fills the landing.

Ss-cut. Ss-cut.

A pale long nail protrudes from under the doorframe, followed by a spiny arm. It pulls a caul-like body through. It seems fatter, as if recently fed.

Ss-cut. Ss-cut.

'He doesn't want you here,' it whispers. Its eyes flash at her. 'He never wanted you. You were his second choice. You're everybody's second choice.'

Barbara puts her hands over her ears but whispers, like water, always find a way through.

Garry hangs by the neck from a hitman's hand. His feet reach for the ground but it is not there. He hears the breath squeeze through his windpipe with a hiss.

'Do you understand?' the woman says.

Garry tries to nod.

She tips up her chin and the hand releases its grip. Garry drops to the floor. His trousers are soaked and his throat raw.

'We're trying to help you, Garry,' she says in a low, soft voice that suggests she is utterly reasonable in all of her requests. 'That's why you wanted in, but I'm sure you understand that by fucking up the Finch mission, you have drawn attention to the Ring. Congratulations. Now the police have another of our rings in their pockets. There is a great deal of disquiet about that, I can assure you.' She guides him to the chair and sits him down. She is being gentle now, at her most unnerving. He would normally take a shine to a woman like her, sneak a cheeky peek at her legs, chat her up in the bar. But he can't look at her for long. Her face has barely twitched as she talks, she is so calm.

'If it were up to me you would be thrown out of the highest window and cemented into the foundations. London is built on sacrifices like that. There are no second chances in my book. But it has been decided by those above that you will be given another chance,' she says, shaking her head as if that wasn't her choice but she has to go with the consensus. Her cold-fire eyes look like they'd rather be watching his slow and unnatural demise.

'Thank you,' he says, rubbing at his neck. His voice sounds like a creaking door.

'Don't thank me yet,' she says. She smirks. He feels a chill as she takes an envelope out of her pocket and slips out a picture of his wife, snapped while she was out shopping.

'Any more mistakes and . . .' she leaves the threat unsaid.

The man who had gripped Garry's neck turns on the shredder. He feeds it the picture, collecting the clippings as casually as if mowing the lawn.

'I'll do anything,' Garry says. 'I won't fuck up again.'

She bends down from the hips like a clockwork woman and whispers near his ear. 'No. You won't. The next stage of initiation is simple. You will kill someone close to you or someone we choose for you.' Her voice curls into his ear canal and burrows through into his head.

He has no words. They have gone from him as quickly as the life he thought he was having.

'Everyone in the Ring must be implicated in a kill, that way we can trust each other. We have all done something unconscionable, unmentionable, and therefore we can have faith that no one will buckle under pressure.'

'Like Finnegan,' Garry says, nodding too much, trying to ingratiate in a way he has always hated, but now he doesn't care.

'Finnegan thought he could renegotiate his part of the contract, take more money, keep his family separate. He thought he was pivotal, that he could get away with anything because he now wore the ring. When he discovered that he couldn't, he wanted out. The Ring, however, does not work like that.'

As she speaks, the large man very slowly and carefully opens each one of the drawers and tips them onto the floor. Files fall and papers float. 'Which is it to be – a loved one or our choice?'

Garry hesitates.

'Most people go about their lives not knowing what's going on around them. They drift in and out, pick up their meal deal from Tesco, do their job and go out or go home and watch the television, argue, have disappointing sex with unfaithful spouses and go to bed. They are barely alive and do not matter but you could have everything that you and your family want. It's a very small and simple exchange, if you think about it.'

Garry thinks about it. He had so much ambition. This building was going to be his big statement and then he wanted to do the same in Dubai or China. Maybe both. He had longed to winter somewhere hot, and to be able to say that they were 'wintering' somewhere hot. That would show his mates – they can't wait to tell him where they're wintering. And then there's the lifestyle, the drinks, the meals, the buying of shit for the sake of it. But now he can't see himself caring.

'I can't kill someone I love,' he says. 'You choose.'

She walks round to his other side. He wants to lean away from her, pull right back from her worming words, but can't risk it. 'Stay alert. We'll call on you soon, then you must do your part. Don't try to fool us, we'll know. Then we'll pick up and dispose of the evidence, successfully this time. And provide you with your own ring for your efforts.'

She turns to leave and her hair follows, bouncing expensively. The trail of her perfume makes him retch.

Watching the door in case they return, he slowly stands, sways and grabs at the edge of the desk. Nausea rockets through him. He grabs the grey waste bin from under his desk and vomits for what seems like minutes, his body forcing out what it has heard. The sickness passes at last. There's nothing left in him. His heart is still beating out of time, missing one beat then throwing two at his chest wall.

Jonathan sits down at his desk and closes his eyes. Ten minutes till the end-of-day briefing. Ten minutes of sleep.

'We're ready, Guv,' Keisha says, popping her head round the door.

The team are already in place, standing by their desks, folders clutched to their chests. They are primed – this is what it's all about, solving one crime and preventing another. Jonathan feels pride as he looks at them. They are a young lot, several of them new following a couple of retirements and then the death of Coleman last year. It all started to go wrong after he died. The way Jonathan reacted to that was one of the reasons his wife gave for leaving him. He was preoccupied, morose, withdrawn. He had 'lost his brilliance,' she said. As if that justified her going off with another man.

'Impress me,' Jonathan says.

Rider stands like a choirboy taking on a solo. 'CCTV has come up with this.' He presses play on his computer. The camera is pointed down a narrow street of terraced houses.

'This is near The Angel,' Keisha says, pointing to a street sign. The digital time code on the screen is 05:40.13, not long before Maria would have arrived. A young woman in sports gear walks up the road. She has a rucksack over her shoulder and something in her right hand. Rider zooms in on the item in the woman's hand. It looks like the jewellery box. There is a bounce to her walk that belies what she's holding.

The girl disappears out of view. Rider fast forwards. Ten minutes later she is back again. There is now nothing in her hands.

The girl pauses by a high wall. She sticks her hand in her bag and pulls out a plastic box and a piece of paper. She studies the paper, tucks it in her hoodie pocket then opens the box and takes out a large, pale lump. She squeezes it in her hand. It gives in to her fingers. She rips off a piece and rolls it between her palms. When it's spherical, she places it midway up the wall. She does this again – rolling the modelling material into a small ball and positioning it on the wall – and again until the length of the wall is covered. The dots are difficult to see against the dirty white wall.

'It's Braille,' Jonathan says. 'The stalker has left her another message.'

The team murmurs in agreement. 'We've sent someone down to take pictures,' Rider says. 'Ed checked the street camera just now – some of it has fallen off so it's even harder to read. Should be here in the next ten minutes. Maria is downstairs, she can translate it once we've got it.'

Keisha tuts. 'Mr Sensitive in action.'

'What have I done now?' Rider asks.

'What Keisha means, Rider, is that it is inappropriate to ask the stalkee to interpret the stalker's message,' Jonathan says. Rider is still looking at him blankly. 'It may contain something upsetting.'

The footage plays on. The young woman crouches down and places smaller balls in position near the foot of the wall. She then draws up the rucksack, stands and walks off.

Jonathan pours out a filter coffee. The Braille wall worries him. Is that young woman their stalker? Possible but unlikely. Has someone else paid her to do this? Are they in it together? Right in front of the camera as well, that must be a deliberate choice. She had looked straight at it. This message isn't just for Maria. 'Any progress on the list of yellow diamonds?' he asks.

'We're in the process of talking to every buyer of a yellow diamond. Hands up who's been on the phones today,' says Keisha.

Arms rise across the office.

'So far none has declared their ring missing. Now that there are *two* yellow rings we're also looking for multiple or repeat purchasers.' Keisha points to the table in the centre of the room on which sit two sets of files. 'We're also going over all the information from Tanya's case and, not only attempting to predict the next move from the stalker, but trying to find any special significance to the ring.'

Denver from IT clears his throat. 'I've been trying to get to grips with the virus affecting Maria's work hard-drive. There are traces of it left but it's a tapeworm – every time I draw some of it out, another part is left unseen. It's a high level job – tricky to programme. Whoever went in there had advanced technical knowledge to at once isolate her computer from the system, infect it and then cure it. Impressive. We should get them, whoever it is, to work for us.' He laughs. No one else does.

Ed chips in, his voice and hamster-like face as eager as ever. 'I've been looking at CCTV around Maria's work at that time and hope to come up with something soon.'

'But you haven't yet,' Denver says, smirking.

Ed drops his head.

Jonathan gets into his coat. It is emptier on him than it was a couple of weeks ago. 'Thanks, everyone, and I mean every one. Brilliant work. Get a good night's sleep and be here early – the post-mortem is tomorrow and more interviews. I'll see Maria before I leave, get her up to date. Anyone else wants me, tell them they can't have me.'

'Here it is,' Rider shouts out, pointing out an image on his screen.

The panoramic photo shows every one of the clay dots. He imagines Maria running her hands over it. To the stalker, this would be the ultimate romantic gesture.

Keisha has a Braille translation page open on her phone. She writes down each letter when she works it out. 'YOU,' she says, slowly, 'HAVE. SEVEN DAYS.'

'Who has?' asks Maria, standing in the doorway.

'I'm sorry about that,' Jonathan says, 'this way.' He places his hand lightly on her shoulder. They walk down the corridor and into his office. 'That wasn't meant for your ears.'

'It was meant for my hands,' she says. The thought makes her feel sick.

Jonathan pauses. He doesn't know what to say.

There's a knock at the door. 'Can I get you anything to drink? I make a good cup of tea,' Keisha says.

'I would jump at that. It's the only time I've heard her offer. And we have some serious apologising to do,' says Jonathan.

Maria shakes her head. 'I'm the one who should be sorry,' she says. 'I got bored waiting and came up. I should have stayed in the waiting room.'

'I'll have one, Keisha,' Jonathan says. His voice is less tired now. It sounds like Simon's does after he's taken coke. 'I asked you to come to me with anything that worried you so that you can worry *me* with it. So worry me.'

Maria switches on the tablet. It makes the warm, round sound of a gong, like the one at the temple she visited in India.

'What do you think it means,' she says, as the tablet readies itself. '"YOU HAVE SEVEN DAYS"?' Not a predicted life span, I hope.' She laughs nervously, then covers her mouth.

'As this was the same day you found the ring, I'd say it means that you have seven days to accept or turn down the proposal. This would be Day Two.'

Fear rushes in her chest.

'You don't have to put a brave face on,' he says.

'Don't I?'

'You impress all of us. And drive us mad.'

She laughs, for real this time. 'That's why I came by, to say that I will definitely stay away from all social media. I understand what you said earlier. I got two messages today.'

She shows him the direct message to her Twitter account: 'You look beautiful today. Elegant. Blue is your colour. But your hair is not right. Try again, my love.'

'He's a charmer all right,' Jonathan says. 'We'll trace the account immediately. Is that what made you change your coat since this morning? To defy his approval?' He's noticed then, that when he found her in Wapping she'd been wearing a blue coat.

'Yes. I went back to change when I saw the message. Simon said this was my most garish, inelegant jacket.'

'It'll scare the birds away on the beach, that's for sure.'

'You should try mudlarking one day,' she says. 'It's like being a detective but you get to keep the evidence.'

'I wouldn't want to keep the sort of evidence we get.'

'Add a century to anything and it will end up in a museum.'

'Are you saying I'd have a knack for mudlarking?'

'I'll take you with me, if you like. Give you some tips.'

He steps back. 'I rarely go down to the beach, actually. My wife doesn't have the right shoes, although she has them for most other occasions.'

She feels her face flush. 'I can lend her some,' she says. 'If she wants to come with you.'

'What's the other message?' Jonathan asks.

'On Facebook,' says Maria. She is glad to have something else to concentrate on so that Jonathan does not see her face. VoiceOver fills the room as a woman's computerised voice reads out the words of her stalker. 'You should have gone for marshmallows on top. You are so sweet, Maria. I hope you appreciated the proposal. It is a shame you allowed the police to be involved but I can see it is your part in our game. Very naughty. You want my attention and you have it but this must be the end. Inspector Dark will never know love like ours. He doesn't know how to hold onto love. I do. I never let go.'

Jonathan stands. She can feel his anger building. Keisha returns, walking carefully, probably holding a full cup of tea.

The voice continues, echoing round what must be an almost bare room. It is strange how you can hear emptiness. 'If you involve him in this any further then I will have to take steps, Maria. I know you won't. You value what we have more highly than that. Enough of that, it is ugly to talk about, so please do not make me bring it up again. What is so very important is that we love each other. You will soon get another present, I hope you like it. I know you will! With love that hurts my heart, your fiancé x.'

VoiceOver speaks the kiss as an X. Marking the spot. Maria feels marked. Spoiled.

'Where were you when this happened?' Jonathan asks. His voice is nearer, he must be leaning forwards.

'In Caffè Nero. I was having a late lunch – a hot chocolate and a tuna panini.'

'And do you go there regularly?' he says. It sounds like he is scratching his face. He must have light stubble.

'Yes. Most lunchtimes, occasionally after work.'

'Do you always have the same item?'

'Not really. It's cold today so I fancied a hot chocolate. Sometimes I go for a latte, others a Coke.'

There is a silence. Something is being exchanged between Jonathan and Keisha. Maria can feel it in the same way she can tell when jasmine flowers are about to send out their night-time scents.

Keisha stands. 'We need to take your new tablet in as well, I'm afraid,' she says. 'That will just leave you with the phone we gave you. Keep it with you at all times in case you need to call.' She leaves the room with the device. Maria feels as if part of her is being taken away. Two years ago she didn't even have one, now she carries it around all day.

Jonathan taps a pen against the table. 'What do you normally do in the café?'

'I chat to some of the other regulars; use their Wi-Fi to catch up on personal emails and,' her voice drops, 'my website, Facebook and Twitter.'

Jonathan sighs out a swear word.

Maria's flush floods back. It's got her neck this time, like a hot hand reaching round it. 'I wanted to update my finds. I've got people following me.'

'No shit,' Jonathan says. His voice is low, the words snap shut. 'Stalking has never been more easy. The law is trying to keep up with new developments in social media and IT but there's only so much we can do. People are compromising their privacy with every footprint they leave online. You can't remove that.' He stands and paces the room. 'Your movements will be so much easier to track if you tell people where you are: they will predict your next three moves and be there to block you. We're trying to find a stalker who killed his last victim. And we're trying to stop you being the next. Help us.' He is not far off shouting, his voice in capitals.

Maria feels the hot knot in her stomach and the desire to fight him that means he has a point. And he is not her boyfriend so she can concede that bit more easily. 'OK,' she says. 'I'm closing my accounts. So what do we do next?'

'I want you to tell me, or write down if that's easier, everything that happened when you entered the café, any smell or sound that was unusual, anything that can give us a hint of how this person knew your movements within the café. Relax and settle your way back into the memory. I've put paper and pens in front of you.'

Maria picks up a pen and drops down into her memory of earlier today. Needing to get out, she had walked the short distance from work, down past the squawking foreshore, up the road. There was the sound of wheels and a gurgling child behind her to start with but she was walking slowly and the pushchair overtook her, a woman talked loudly on her phone, asking someone to pick up fish for dinner. A pub door opened, letting out a lager-blast. It was cold, the wind chilling her collarbones so she stuffed her bobble hat down the front of her coat. She had lost her new scarf already. There were at least three voices outside Caffè Nero, smoking and talking about *The X Factor*. Billy snuffled at something on the floor and Maria stooped and found him gobbling down half a blueberry muffin. Inside the shop, coffee fog settled over the tables. The smell made her breathe more easily as if it were the eucalyptus oil that Dad dabbed on the collar of her pyjamas when she had a cold as a child. She reached into the chilled cabinet to feel what they had left in the way of sand-wiches. She can tell the freshness of a BLT with one squeeze.

Standing at the counter, waiting to order, she heard a whoosh of steam bothering the milk; the clank of the coffee machine; chatter from people seated behind her; till beep; receipt rush; packet rustle and reward card swipe. Someone was standing close behind her in the queue, but that was quite usual. Wasn't it?

Her favourite seat – the armchair by the cheese plant – was free and she sat down. Leonie, the shop manager, brought over her toastie and drink along with a piece of Italian ham for Billy. 'It fell out of a sandwich,' she said, with a tone of innocence the equivalent of a blatant wink. They had then talked for a few minutes about Leonie's course at UCL. She wanted to know if Maria would come and talk at her History Society.

On the table to her right, two men in, she'd say, their thirties, one with a voice that made her think that he would disappear if he turned side on, the other with a bass drawl so low it could build its own dungeon. They seemed to both work at a nearby bank, the local branch kind, not merchant, and were talking about a woman who may or may not be a bitch. Maria hadn't been able to resist chipping in. 'I've listened to your arguments. And she's not a bitch,' Maria said, leaning back in her chair.

Three women sat at the table on the other side, by the window. Not that she had any evidence that the third was there apart from the other two talking to and about her, 'Isn't it, Gillian?', 'Can you believe it, Gillian?' and 'Gillian had a dose of that and had to go to a specialist, didn't you, Gillian? And on your birthday too.'

The earth around the cheese plant was coffee-ground dry. She poured water into the plant pot. What else? She couldn't see the rest of the room, it could be anyone in there, or outside looking in, although the windows are probably steamy, there is certainly condensation on the inside. There must be another clue. She tries to lift her awareness of her surroundings to the whole coffee shop. People talking; a glass smashing; a child crying; a tinkling bell; keys jangling; tapping on a laptop behind her – wait – a laptop. A Mac from the gong of it being turned on. And she hears that every time she comes in. Now that really is paranoia – there is always an Apple in a coffee shop – it's one of the rules. But then he would count on that. She shrinks back into her chair. What if her stalker also comes there every day with his laptop, knowing that she'll be there? It could be him tapping away, writing to her, getting off on her not knowing. Rage builds in her chest. How dare he? He could have been staring at her, sitting at a table nearby as she slips in her earphones and listens to Eels. The thought that this maniac, who has the delusion that she has affection for him, could be intruding on her as she hummed along disgusted her. Last week, someone had tapped sharply on the glass and scared her shitless. She had laughed to cover the sound of her heart beating fast but what if that was him? That makes her heart slow to the point she thinks her blood has stopped. He is able to look at her at any time without her knowing or being caught. Will told her that when he catches the eye of someone he fancies, there is a moment in which both of them are caught inside each other's eyes. It is not as easy for Maria but there are other ways to tell if someone has their eye on you. Or so she had thought.

What else? She got the message at about half one, while VoiceOver was reading out an email from Simon about a man in his office who brought in egg sandwiches every day and didn't eat them till four in the afternoon. She was laughing when the other message came through, making her feel more vulnerable. She yanked the earphones off and sat shivering in the too-hot shop. Music was playing – a cover version of a Keane song, syrup enough for all the coffees in the room – but it did not soothe.

'It's all right,' DI Dark says, 'we're here.' He places a hand on hers and she can feel a rough patch on the side of his thumb, the warmth of his palm. Her breath is stuck. Maria gulps at the air. 'I can't think of anything else,' she says. Writing down her thoughts as they fall is like trying to bottle snowflakes.

DI Dark picks up her papers. She can smell mint shower gel and a recently applied deodorant that marketing people describe as linen, but linen doesn't smell like that at all. Linen has a touch of lemon in its crinkles.

He places the paper down and scratches his head. 'We'll check for security footage for any time you've been there in the last month. CCTV usually gets wiped every fortnight or, worse, every week but you never know. Hopefully your stalker is stupid. He is almost certainly more stupid than he thinks. If you could write down the dates you—'

'Can you not call him that?' Maria says.

'What?'

'He isn't *my* stalker. People keep doing that. I have nothing to do with him. He's the one who wants a connection and I refuse to give him what he wants.'

Keisha applauds. Maria senses Dark's stern glance. Keisha stops clapping and coughs.

'He *is* stalking you, though. You are his stalkee, if we're not careful then you will be his murder victim, and he will be your murderer and you won't be alive to argue about semantics.' DI Dark's voice slams at angles against the walls. He sounds angrier than is warranted.

'He's making a claim,' Keisha takes over, 'however rightly you dismiss his delusions.'

'You are being stalked by someone who does not respect or even understand privacy, intimacy or boundaries,' DI Dark says. 'It will enrage him that you've come to us. There's no good pretending otherwise – if you could see then you could help us much more than you have in this statement. You may have seen the person at the coffee shop on repeated occasions and wonder why. You're not helping yourself. You didn't even bring this to us straight away. I hear you're moving out of your friend's house, back to your flat. I don't advise it.' There is the sound of him sucking through his teeth as if there were more words behind them, tapping at the enamel and digging a hole to get out.

Maria stands. 'I brought these messages to you because I thought it would help. Give you a further clue. Taking off my blindfold would not help. It would look like the biggest act of love in the world, beating a box of Milk Tray and a bunch of garage roses. I wish you could understand that I don't need to see in the way you do.'

'Then why have the operation?' Keisha asks. She has probably been dying to ask all this time.

'It's complicated,' Maria says. She did not want to tell DI Dark about the arguments she had gone through with Carl on this subject. They were thinking about having children and Carl could not get why she did not want to see their faces. He called her a monster. She was not sure that she wasn't, and went ahead with surgery.

'There are some things I will never understand,' Dark says. His voice is quiet. There are words behind those words as well.

'Well, how about I show you,' Maria says. As she says it she wonders at herself, trying again. 'I'll show you part of London that you think you know by sight, and put you in a blindfold.' Why is she doing this? She is sweating again. She's doing this to prove to him that she is OK as she is. And maybe to prove it to herself.

DI Dark says nothing for one whole minute. Then, 'You're on.'

*

In his office, looking out into a darkening sky, he feels like crying. That's a good sign. He hasn't cried since Tanya died. He stood over her beautiful body, catching his tears in his sleeve. Such remorse. And Sian, most of all he had wept for Sian. To feel that sorrow, despite what she had put him though, shows what a good, decent person he is. Maria is lucky to have him.

But Maria shows betrayal after betrayal, and after he told her explicitly what she was not to do. She is there now, in Dark's domain. The thought of him sitting near her makes him feel ill.

He won't be angry at her for long, she is too precious, and vulnerable to the voices around her. Still, he must carry out his threats just as much as his promises, that way she will trust him. He will punish her behaviour, not her. She will know this from dog training. Click treat, click treat.

He watches her on his computer. She has a mouth that he wants to kiss so very lightly. Barely touch, to start with. He wants to brush her lips with his eyelashes – he has been told he has long lashes. 'Makes up for other things,' his first fiancée once said, laughing as she applied her fake ones.

This is a good time of year for love. There is so much dark to move around in. This morning he moved his desk so that he is in the corner, one wall behind him, another flanking him like a lieutenant. No one can see his screen from here, they will have no idea what he is working on. Even if someone walks in and turns the corner, he will have enough time to switch windows. Any man knows how to do that. His ex was always walking in at the wrong time, catching him looking at something she thought he shouldn't. What's wrong with looking up old friends, girlfriends, and friends he had wished were girlfriends, on Facebook or LinkedIn or revenge porn sites? If they didn't want to be looked at then they wouldn't be online, would they? People like him intercept hundreds of soft porn selfies a day. Maria doesn't take any of those. He knows her computer as well as he knows her. He moves around her software with care. She has class. Not like the others, wearing short skirts and bras that scoop up their tits yet expecting him not to stare. Everyone stares. It wasn't like his ex-wife wasn't looking up her boyfriends on the few nights she stayed up later than him, she probably did it at work too but he didn't have such easy access to her search history. Her history had always been an issue. She was quick to deny that anyone had any importance other than him, but he knew it, from her eyes. He hated it that anyone had been there before him.

Maria would make everything OK. There she is, frozen. Wavering like an angel. It thrills him to have her there when he wants her. He will get her a smaller blindfold. A forgiveness gift. He wants to see the angle of her cheekbones.

He scrolls through the data to linger on the websites she had searched in the café. Interesting. He smiles, feeling out the tooth in his right upper jaw that has been nagging at his nerves. She first looked at a holiday company, searching through trips to Italy and Spain. She wants to get away – he doesn't blame her. The police are worrying her, making her confused, and her work isn't much better.

She then lingered on a website for a florist who claims to have the most heavily scented bouquets in Britain, stuffing rosemary, thyme, lavender and eucalyptus into each of their products. She listened twice to a page with a large rose bouquet. He has always wanted a really *feminine* girlfriend, someone who will appreciate the work he does, be there for him when he gets home. Maria could do that, with more dresses and a softer haircut that flatters her face.

He clicks on the 'Add to Basket' button and goes through the online checkout process. He nearly uses a credit card in his real name but doesn't, of course. He is too careful. He can get away with anything.

13

All day he was going to resist. All day he promised himself that this would be the night when he would resist. On the walk home he very nearly resisted. There was a point when he was three minutes away when he was absolutely definitely going to resist. But he didn't. He can't. So here Jonathan is, standing by the holly bush outside his house.

It looks exactly the same. He doesn't know if that's a good or bad thing. Everything is as he left it, only someone else has taken his place, a new doll in the doll house. He should have repainted the garage. She was always going on about that. If he had done that, then maybe he would be the one walking past the front window. Justin Masters is wearing Jonathan's dressing gown. Jonathan put up those curtains. He has the scar on his thumb to prove it.

Natalie's car is a street away. He can tell by the diesel hum, as if always clearing its throat before launching into an argument. Jonathan crouches behind next door's car. He rocks back and forth on his heels, clenching his fist so that his nails bite into the skin. This is ridiculous. He has never been more pathetic. He's a ghost in his once-wife's life. He should leave.

He doesn't.

She finds a space down the other end of the road. He can hear her walking, plastic bags rustling up to the door. She puts her key in the lock but Masters has got there first, opening the door and enveloping her in a hug. She laughs her fond, loving laugh that Jonathan hasn't heard for several years. It disappeared about the time she lost her wedding ring. He turns his round and round his finger.

He moves around the car. She will have taken the shopping into the kitchen and poured herself a glass of red wine. Or he'll have poured it for her, ready for her to get back. 'Give her time, she'll be back,' people keep saying. 'She'll realise what she's missing.' Others say, 'If you love them, let them go' – well that's sheer passivity. He will fight in any way he can, even if at this moment in time that means crouching behind a Volvo.

He'll give it two minutes. If she isn't visible within that time then he'll go. What is he hoping to see – Natalie staring wistfully out of the window? Or is this just torturing himself for the sake of it?

She walks through wearing a dress he doesn't recognise. She's had her hair done. It is lighter, shorter, her fringe is off to one side. Jonathan's hair is exactly the same as it was when they married. She walks to the window. Closes the curtains on him.

Jonathan shuts the door to the cottage. The sounds of Spitalfields retreat. He hangs his coat over the rungs of a stepladder and walks in the dark to the kitchen. At least the water's on, if not the electricity. He spent most of the journey to the retail park on the hands-free trying to sort out the utilities. The electricity supplier is saying they can see no faults on the line. An engineer will be here tomorrow, but he won't be able to let them in.

Jonathan lights candles and looks around the shelves. This morning the labels on the tins of soup and peas and mince that must have been there for years all faced the wall. Now they are front-facing and proud, identically spaced. Someone is fucking with him. What if it is the stalker? The first flame of fear sparks up, and he snuffs it out.

He heats a tin of soup on the camping stove and turns them round again. Neil insists that he is not paying for a cleaner so somebody is trespassing. He'll dust for prints tomorrow, although whoever is breaking in is as clean as they are mysterious.

Sitting with his bowl of minestrone on his lap, he looks out of the window. The sky is sparsely clouded tonight and he can even see a star. It's Venus, the goddess of love. Her star shines brightly, despite how frequently she fails. She is like one of those birthday candles that people make you blow out, only for it to flare back up again. And again.

The candle flames dance in the window. His face floats next to them, a white oval, transparent and smudged. He moves his head back and forth, watching it weave in the window. It appears to double up, another head next to his.

As he crosses the kitchen to get more bread, something crashes in the courtyard. A figure moves towards the fence. Jonathan shoulders open the sticking door, slamming into the frame.

Lurching out onto the paving stones, Jonathan scans the area. Next door's emergency light comes on, bathing the back gardens in light. Two flowerpots have been turned over, soil running out of them. The fence post on the other side is wobbling as if someone has just climbed over it.

Standing on a garden chair, Jonathan peers into the next garden. It is about four times the size of his courtyard, unkempt and unkept. Weeds grow to waist height. A cat sits on a tall stone water bowl, its tail writhing.

'Can I help you, mate?' says a man's voice behind him.

Jonathan turns.

A large, bald-headed man is peering over the other fence. He is wearing pyjamas.

Jonathan has a last look in the next-door garden but can see no one. He gets down and walks over. 'I thought I heard someone crashing around out here,' he says, pointing to the flowerpots. 'And I was sure I saw a figure scramble over.'

Close to the fence now, Jonathan realises that the man is BIG. His head could have been mistaken for the moon, were the moon not already hanging like a bright riot shield in the sky.

'I'm Frank McNally,' he says. 'I run the funeral parlour here. We heard something too so I thought I'd investigate. I'm sorry for not introducing myself before. I meant to pop round only we weren't sure whether you were staying. There have been quite a few people coming and going over the past year.'

'Jonathan. I'm looking after it for a relative. Apparently he can't get a builder to stay.'

'We'd heard that,' Frank says. 'Have you worked out why?'

Jonathan thinks of the moved items in the kitchen, bedroom and bathroom. The sense of not being alone. 'No idea. I quite like it.'

'It's a wonderful street to live on,' Frank says. 'Smack in the middle of Spitalfields, in the middle of London, but everything goes quiet on Folgate Street. It feels like you've stepped into the past.'

Jonathan nods. 'Nice garden,' he says, taking in the large backyard. On the one side is a small sitting area with a trellised love seat, a barbecue and a bench. On the other two hearses line up, ready to leave by a back gate onto the road that borders the houses.

Frank rests his head against one shoulder and rolls the other shoulder. Jonathan can hear the cranking of gristly muscles. 'My sons used to help out but they've both moved away,' he says. 'What do you do for a living then?'

'I'm a detective in the Met.'

'Aren't you supposed to add, "For my sins", after that?'

'My sins catch up with me in other ways,' Jonathan replies. He stands on the small bench so he can be eye to eye with Frank.

'Well,' says Frank, looking up to a top window in the funeral parlour. 'I'd better be getting to bed. Let me know if you need anything.' He turns to leave.

'You haven't been having trouble with your electricity, have you?' Jonathan asks.

'Not since a power cut during that storm in August. You have, then?' He doesn't seem surprised.

'I have an electrical engineer coming round tomorrow, could—'

'Surely,' Frank says, flicking his big hand as if waving away a wasp. 'Pop the key through the door when you leave and tell them to call for me. I'll let them in.' He leans forward. 'Make sure they ring first though, would you? We had an issue with a bloke who wandered in off the street who thought we were a pub. He walked in on a viewing and ran out blubbing. So make sure your engineer knows my business.'

'It says "Funeral Directors" outside, that might give it away.'

'True – this was in the days that we had the more discreet "Mc-Nally and Family" sign outside. He thought it was an Irish bar.'

'In the middle of a back street?'

Frank shrugs. 'You could find an Irish bar in a desert if you wiped the sand out of your eyes. Anyway, I think you scared off the intruder, if there was one. Let me know how the electrical work goes.'

'I'll return the favour one day,' Jonathan says.

Frank looks at Jonathan. 'I'll take you up on that,' he says.

Jonathan's soup is cold when he gets back, with a rubbery film on the top. Someone is watching him. Someone is watching Maria. He read about a theory that, under observation, the nature of the thing is changed. London is the most observed city on the planet.

On the work surface, an ant is trying to carry a boulder of bread on its back. He never thought of ants as night workers. Maybe they have shifts and strikes as well.

Upstairs, the candles make the bedroom seem larger, bouncing light into the nooks, the shadows making the walls step back. As he goes to breathe them out, he notices that his wedding ring has moved. He only just took it off, before going to the bathroom to make use of the water. It is now on the other side of the bedside table. The room is cooler, on the verge of damp.

He searches the cottage, checking every cupboard, behind every door. No one is there. Yet this is happening. At least he thinks so. Maybe he just needs sleep. Pressure can do strange things to police officers, he's seen it more than once. He wriggles into the sleeping bag, moving his legs to keep warm. He wishes he had taken the beautiful dreamcatcher from the house when he left. The one he bought in Spain that caught the nightmares by their tails. It also let the good dreams through its woven circles and fanned them with feathers. He could do with one of those now.

SS-cut.

It was you.

SS-cut.

Only you.

You cannot have a relationship with anyone.

You are broken. Why would Natalie want you?

She saw through you

Everyone will see through you

You are empty inside

SSS-cut.

Nobody wants you.

14

Day Three

'Are you all right, Guv?' Rider asks, frowning as they walk into the Home Office building.

'Why do you ask?' Jonathan replies. He knows why. He saw his face in the mottled mirror this morning. It looks as grey as those kept in Agnarsson's fridge. Jonathan is just about holding on, but his grip is slipping.

'You look like you could do with a few days off.' Rider looks as if he has had nine hours' sleep and showered in sunbeams. Bastard. What it is to be young and not yet undone.

'The weekend is coming up,' Jonathan says, trying to pull on professionalism like the socks that had been placed by his shoes when he woke up. 'I'll catch up on sleep then.'

'My weekends aren't for sleeping,' Rider says. His grin is lascivious.

'I don't need to know any more, Sergeant. Is this your first post-mortem?' Jonathan asks.

Rider nods. 'No bother. I've read everything I need to know.'

'Have you now. Then you'll be fine, I'm sure. Although if you want to be sick, don't vomit on the cadaver.' Jonathan presses the buzzer to enter.

Richard Agnarsson's pathology lab looks out onto rooftops that keep a lid on some of the best- and worst-kept secrets of London. Government officials scurry and whisper under those slates, decoding messages windows away from where Agnarsson translates the whispers of the dead.

'Is this a new one of yours, Jonathan?' Richard asks, washing his hands at the long sink.

'DC Rider, this is Richard Agnarsson. Richard is the finest pathologist I have worked with. I met him on sabbatical in Sweden and persuaded him to go for a job when it came up, what – how long ago?'

Richard holds out a hand to Rider. 'Twelve. And why are you flattering me so obviously, Jonathan? What are you after?'

'You're in a cynical mood today.'

'Keeps me sane,' Richard says. He walks over to the sleek grey cupboards in the wall and opens one of the drawers. The covered body is pulled out. 'Photographs have been taken and appear on the large screen behind the table. The evidence sheet is packed up ready to be examined,' he says.

He uncovers the cadaver. It is grey-blue; bloated and blotchy; the face swollen beyond recognition. Bagged paper sacks have been wrapped and taped at the wrists.

'Part of the epidermis gloved off in transit,' Richard explains. He begins his process by poring over the body with a magnifying glass, going over every millimetre, examining the body with the attention and care that only a parent would give a baby. No one will take such care of him again. He picks up a microscopic something and places it in a tiny bag. His labelling is meticulous.

Richard dictates notes into a recorder. 'There are impressions on the skin, possibly from handling on the way out of the water.' He brings forward the trolley of instruments. Rider blanches.

'Is he squeamish?' Richard asks.

Jonathan looks at Rider's face. 'Time to find out.'

Richard squares to the man's torso and makes the Y-incision in the chest.

DCI Allen is waiting in his office when Jonathan gets back to the station. 'Well?' she says.

'We have a positive identification for the body. Actually, we have two.'

'Two?'

'His dental records come up on the system as a Mr Marc Bannister, missing presumed dead since 2011. The estimated age would fit – forty-eight years old.'

'And the other?' She leans forward, places her hands on his desk. He's never seen her so caught by a case.

'That came when he was opened up,' he replied. 'Richard found that he had a replacement kneecap twenty years ago. The serial number is linked to Finnegan Finch, forty-nine. Problem is, Finnegan Finch was cremated at his own crematorium two weeks ago.'

Her eyebrows rise. A flush spreads from her neck to her cheek.

'We'll be looking into both names,' he says.

She paces back and forth in the limited space. 'The likelihood is that it's Finch,' she says. 'If someone was trying to cover a trail they would have changed dental records and DNA. They wouldn't have known about a knee operation.'

'Particularly not one in a comparatively young man,' Jonathan says. 'The time and probable cause of death would fit. Richard thinks that from the state of the adipocere, the fat beneath the skin, the body has been in the Thames for at least twenty-eight days.' Jonathan remembers the soggy sound as Agnarsson cut into the water-logged lungs. 'The lungs had degraded so it was hard to tell if the cause of death was from drowning but it's more likely that it was from one of the contusions to his head.'

'No chance it could have been accidental death followed by a cover-up?' She sounds hopeful.

'Possible, but not likely. Richard tweezered out a splinter of wood in the wound and the indentation of the wound suggests—'

'A baseball bat?'

'Yes, ma'am.'

Frank's office is barely wider than his arm-span. It's like a walk-in coffin. He's said before that, when he dies, they might as well just brick it up and call it a tomb. He's in there all the time at the moment. Since Barbara started losing interest in the business, he's had to do all of the laying out and most of the books as well as counselling ghosts. They can't afford an assistant, and obols don't buy much at market.

The phone rings. Frank considers leaving it to the answerphone, then reaches over, picks up his hat and places it on his head. The feathers tickle his neck.

'McNally's Funeral Directors,' he says.' His voice is six foot deep.

'Frankie, mate. I've got a great deal for you.'

'Don't you ever start conversations like a normal person, Glen?'

'Are you saying I'm not normal? Could be a compliment coming from you.'

'Does it occur to you to ask how I am?'

Glen is quiet. He hasn't mentioned Barbara at all since she died. When people hear about cancer they find their mouths can't say the word. At length, he says, 'You all right, mate?'

'I'm in excellent health, thanks for asking. I had a prostate exam last week which was a shock to my system, I can tell you, but other than that I'm getting on OK.'

'So what's the problem? Geez. Look. I've had a call from Dutch Bob. He's got some quality coming over tomorrow.'

'What's that got to do with me?' Frank stands and stretches his arms over his head.

'Give me the nod and I can get you a bargain off the boat. A parlour load for fifty quid.'

'Skip to the bit where I'm interested, Glen,' Frank says. They do this dance every week.

A weak knock at the door. Barbara comes in. She looks pale as muslin today.

'It's Glen,' he whispers.

She smiles – she's fond of Glen. He came round for dinner a few months after the twins were born. Glen picked up their boys and sat them on his lap like pot plants. They grizzled, then fell into a deep and dribbly sleep. They still have the photo, twenty years later. It comes out of the trunk when the boys visit and girlfriends come round. And there have been a lot of them. Frank didn't know whether to be proud, worried or hand out prophylactics. He misses the lads. They are in Adelaide, setting up a new parlour. The Antipodean dead are in safe, McNally hands.

'You listening, Frank?' Glen is waffling on. 'Tulips, roses, peonies, and two kinds of lilies. Mainly lilies. Don't ask me how I can do it. Green stuff thrown in for free.'

'I've told you before, Glen: no lilies. I don't care what you say. Lilies are bullies and don't merit a place in my parlour.'

Barbara rolls her eyes. Frank swats towards her bottom with a rolled-up *News of the World*.

'I don't scare easy,' Frank continues, using the paper to punctuate his point. 'I've seen things that would chase the eyes out of your head and use them for marbles, but lilies freak me out. I have to cross the road if I see a bunch. On their own they're fine but get them in a gang and it's a different story. Short answer, Glenny: no. I much prefer the peony. Better still, come back when you've got me some nice narcissi. And I'll have five quid on the Hammers to win at the Emirates.'

'No chance.'

Glen slams the phone down. Frank laughs. He'll be phoning back within half an hour with a deal on dodgy phlox.

Barbara laughs. 'How many times have I heard you give the lilies speech?'

'Never enough,' Frank says, standing up. 'I'll still be giving it when we're both dead and stowing away on a Caribbean cruise. They still insist on lilies on cruise liners, you know. That's just inviting disaster.'

She puts her finger to his lips. He feels a sensation of coolness and holds onto it. 'Did you mean that?' she says. 'About us being together then?'

'Of course I did. Why would I not?'

'No reason,' she says. An unwelcome thought crosses her face. Then another one.

'What's wrong, darling?' he asks.

The phone goes again.

'I'll leave it,' he says.

She shakes her head and opens the door on her third try.

'McNally Funeral Directors,' he answers.

'Frank, I've got some news.' It's Glen.

'Got me a bargain off another boat, have you?'

'I've just heard a rumour about Finnegan,' Glen says, all jocularity gone from his voice.

'So have I.'

'All I could think of was that he asked me for money a while back. Said he was in trouble. I should have handed it over.'

'There's nothing any of us could have done.' But there were things he could do now.

Rosa Finch stares at him and shakes her head. Her hands are trembling, tucked in her lap in a ball. Her eyes are raw, her cheeks red and salt-stung from tears that haven't stopped since she arrived. She probably doesn't even know she is crying. 'I'm sorry,' she says. 'I don't understand any of this.' She stares around the interview room as if expecting an explanation to write itself on the walls.

'I'm so sorry, Mrs Finch, this must be a terrible shock.' How could it not be? She thought her husband of twenty-five years had met his death in a car accident and had been cremated. Instead his body is on a slab, after most likely being murdered and then dumped in the Thames. The mourning process had been under way for her, but now it has been torn away.

'Can I see him?' she says, grasping the end of the table.

'I'll arrange that for later, if you're sure.'

'I won't believe it till I've seen him.' She probably won't believe it even then.

'Who identified the man that was in the accident?' he asks her, gently.

'My sister, Lauren. She wanted to spare me the pain, she said. He was in such a bad way after the car crashed into him – but it wasn't him, was it?'

'I'm afraid not.'

'How can something like this happen?' she says. Her eyes are fixed on him.

'I'll do everything I can to find out how this error took place and how your husband died.'

She nods but he can see from her eyes that she can't find her way into his words.

'I have some questions, if I may,' he says.

She sits up straighter.

'Did your husband own a yellow diamond ring?'

Her eyebrows rise. 'Do you have it?'

'It's part of the investigation, for now, although your husband's effects will be returned to you in time.'

Her mouth twitches as if trying to stop a sob from escaping.

'You don't seem very happy about it.'

She flushes. 'We fought about it once. I don't want to think of it every time I see it. There was never normally a cross word between us.'

'Then you'll always have that to remember him by. Can you tell me how he came to possess the ring?'

'He had it made from a lock of my hair. He has an arrangement with a company that takes ashes and hair and makes it into diamonds.'

'Why did you fight about it?'

She shivers. 'I told him it was creepy – I can understand it if someone has died but I was alive.' Her mouth twitches again. 'I could tell there was something he wasn't telling me. He got angry when I pressed him on it. I thought it might be from another woman. I should have left it alone. Appreciated him more.'

'Were there other women?' Jonathan asks.

She pulls her hands back into her lap. Not looking at him, she nods. 'He always came back to me. I was the one he loved. I must have been. Or he wouldn't have made me into a diamond, would he?'

Taking the last lungful of outside breath, Keisha enters Moorfields with all the trepidation of an arachnophobe setting foot in the Australian bush. The DI said it was therapy – prolonged exposure to doctors. She shivers.

Shown to Mrs Pargeter's office, she sits down outside to wait. The memory of the last time she was here slips into her bloodstream like a cannula. Punched in the face while on duty in the drunk van, she had gone in with a scratched cornea. The valium she had taken had worn off too quickly and hadn't taken any of the edge off having her eyes clamped open like she was in *A Clockwork Orange*. Why would you fuck around with people's eyes for a living? Eyes are creepy. They look soft, like egg white, but are tough, as anyone who has had to cut through a bull's eye in biology lessons will know.

She knows she shouldn't be so childish – she looks into people's eyes all day, detecting signs of lies – but she can't help it. But she wouldn't be without her eyes, which is why she hadn't run away screaming when the doctor on call that night touched her eyeball. She has no idea why Maria King would choose otherwise.

'Please come in,' calls Mrs Pargeter from inside.

Keisha collects a cup of cold water from the dispenser and walks in, shoulders back.

'How can I help you?' Mrs Pargeter says, not looking up from her notes.

Do doctors get taught to do that at medical school? Asking how they can help while giving every indication that they would rather you were anywhere other than their office? It's probably in the NHS guidelines to get waiting lists down.

Keisha has the perverse desire to keep her waiting. She shakes it off. 'I'm DS Keisha Baxter. I am here in connection with a murder investigation. One of your patients is thought to be in danger.' That should get her attention.

Mrs Pargeter looks at her with as much interest as if Keisha had announced she was about to read out the entire dictionary. In Latin. 'Miss Maria King. Yes, you explained on the phone. I have her file here. I fail to see how I can assist you, though. The operation was a success, that is about as much as I can tell you.'

Keisha looks Pargeter dead in the eye. 'Was there anything in your consultations with Maria that could help?' This was worse than clutching at straws, there weren't any straws to clutch.

Pargeter flicks through Maria's notes 'One thing I put down was that she was a WFTU.'

Keisha throws words at the acronym to see if any of them fit. Nope.

'Won't Fucking Turn Up,' Pargeter says, growing smilier now she has stumped Keisha. 'A time-waster - the pet hate of all doctors. In private practice I can charge for consultations and cancellations; it's not that simple on the NHS. Yet.'

'The current government will do their best to change that, I'm sure,' Keisha says, smiling as sweetly as a piranha at a pool party.

Mrs Pargeter nods. She may be a very good surgeon but she's not a great listener. 'She came to her first consultation with her boyfriend.'

'Carl Janus?'

'I don't remember his name, just that he was keen and she was conflicted. She couldn't see the point, if you'll pardon the pun. He said it was pre-surgery nerves and that she would come round. It seemed to mean a lot to him that she saw his face.'

Keisha grimaces.

'Precisely. I see this sometimes. I said she shouldn't do anything she regretted. There was a reasonable likelihood that I would be unable to connect the retinas anyway, this was breakthrough, not far beyond experimental, surgery, and probably wouldn't be a complete success. If it was then the results would need a great deal of getting used to.'

'What did she say?'

'I'm dancing a fine line here between helping your enquiries and breaching confidentiality. Maria's operation wasn't standard, by any interpretation of the word, in fact we are a pioneering hospital in the field. I intend to write up her case for a medical journal although it would help if she would . . .'

Keisha assumes she was going to say that it would help if Maria used her new eyes.

'I will tell you, though,' Mrs Pargeter continues, 'that her boy-friend didn't like her answer and left in a hurry, slamming my door so hard that my clock swung backwards and forwards.' She tuts as if the worst thing that he did that day was worry her clock.

A minute ticks by. 'What happened then?' Keisha nudges.

'She wasn't a WFTU after all. I next saw her at the pre-op tests and then on the operating table. When I went on the round to check up, I gave her the number for a counsellor who deals with pre- and post-operative trauma. I've had several patients go to see him after regaining their sight and found him very useful, I thought it might be even more helpful as Maria has *never* seen before.'

'And that would be Mr Iain Parker?'

Mrs Pargeter raises her exactly waxed eyebrows. 'I believe it's *Dr* Iain Parker. Although he of course is a PhD or, as we call those with a non-medical doctorate, an NMGPC.'

'You've lost me,' Keisha says.

'Not Much Good in a Plane Crash,' Mrs Pargeter replies. Her laugh is thin and tinny.

*

Carl Janus isn't at home. Mr Janus Senior, however, is and shows Keisha into the house with a nervous smile. He is wearing the same Cath Kidston apron that she gave her sister last Christmas.

'Come into the lounge where it's warm,' he says. 'Our boiler broke down last night and we've been reduced to huddling round a candle.'

Keisha sits down in the chair next to a halogen heater. 'Will Carl be back soon?' she asks. She doesn't want to accept another cup of tea if she's going to have to come back here in two hours' time.

'He phoned half an hour ago. He'll be back with the new boiler soon. He's Corgi registered.' Mr Janus Senior has the look of blind pride that her father has for everyone in the family except for her. 'Why do you want to talk to him? Is it from when his friend got picked up the other night? Because I heard that it was just a misunderstanding between the lads.'

'It so often is,' Keisha says.

He pats his knees and stares at the clock on the mantel. 'I fixed that last week,' he says, getting up and tapping the glass on the front. The second hand stutters but can't move onwards. She knows how it feels.

'How long has Carl been living with you?' she asks.

'He moved in after the break-up. He couldn't afford a flat by himself so he's living with us till he gets enough for a deposit. All the kids are doing it these days. The older kids, I mean. You know how they never stop being your kids.' His face is eager for her to confirm him.

'I don't have children,' she says.

'Ah well, you'd know if you did. You don't know who you are until you have a kid.'

Keisha bunches out her cheeks and doesn't answer. Better that than a quick slap to his face. The smug adoption of superiority by some parents pisses her off. 'You wouldn't know though, would you,' her sister says. Some of her friends are at it too. Even an ex. 'You don't know love till you've had a kid.' No? Well you said you loved me, are you taking that back?

The front door opens and, after a series of grunts, moans, 'fuck's and 'bollocks', Carl Janus walks in with a combination boiler with a six pack of bio yoghurt on top. His face is red and sweaty. He bends over the sofa, breathing heavily. He must be nearing six foot five.

She'd like to put a long wig on him and have him in her basketball team.

'Got your yoghurt, Dad,' he says.

He turns to Keisha and grins. 'Hello, there.'

'DS Baxter is here to talk about your Maria,' Janus Senior says, taking the yoghurt pots.

'She isn't my Maria, Dad,' Carl says. 'Not right now. I don't even know if she ever was.'

'Were the two of you not that serious, then?' Keisha asks, her tone as light as popcorn.

'Carl was completely committed to Maria, weren't you?' says Janus Senior. 'He was devastated when they broke up. She's a lovely girl, we were so upset. She used to come round here for Sunday roast, didn't she, Carl?'

'Yes, Dad.' Carl glowered.

'Could I have a word with Carl alone, please, Mr Janus?' Keisha tries the wide eyes on him. The ones that suggest sweetness and innocence and all the things that Mr Janus Senior possesses and Keisha definitely does not.

'You can ask me while I install the boiler,' Carl says. He hulks it over his shoulder and up the stairs.

Set up with his toolbox in the room by the bathroom, Carl Janus seems to relax. 'Sorry about that. My dad does my head in. Not his fault, he means no harm. That's what's so annoying.'

'That he means no harm?'

He aims a sharp glance at her. 'I don't mean that I *do* mean harm. He just gets on my tits with all his fussing. Look, I'm thirty-four and living at home. I have to wrestle my boxers off him so I can do my own laundry.'

'I need to ask some questions, sir. Where were you two days ago in the early morning?'

His monobrow jumps. His surprise seems genuine but she's been fooled often enough to know she can be fooled. 'I thought this was about Maria.'

She raises her eyebrows back at him and waits.

His eyes roam to the left. 'I'm always out of here by half six and at work by quarter to eight. There was a delay on the Northern Line, I think, so I was a bit late for the meeting. I'm a clerk at Gray's Inn. But then you probably knew that. I got there at ten past, carrying a tray of muffins to make up for it. Everyone will back me up. They never forget a man bearing muffins.' He smiles then and his face crinkles up like a Shar Pei's, which is surprisingly attractive, on him at least. His warmth shows in his voice. Maybe this is what Maria found attractive.

'How about earlier?' Keisha asks. His assumption about what time she meant may be calculation not innocence.

He frowns. 'I got up before six, beat my youngest brother to the bathroom and made up a protein shake.'

'Have you had any contact at all with Maria King since you broke up?'

He stops fiddling with the boiler altogether. 'What's wrong? Is Maria OK? Is she in trouble? God, she's not—'

'Could you answer the question, Mr Janus?' Keisha says.

He bends his head. 'She asked me not to call or write to her. So I haven't.'

Keisha says nothing. She looks at him as if he is guilty. It nearly always works. Everyone is guilty of something.

'OK, I sent her a bunch of flowers on Valentine's Day. I thought she may have changed her mind – that she only broke up with me because of the stress of the operation. I mean, she said it was because things were going nowhere and she wanted more. I told her that I didn't want to get married yet, but that was only because I don't have any money. From what I could tell, she didn't have anyone else. That was a while ago, though. I've moved on now.'

'How could you tell that she was still single?' Keisha says.

His face is red again. 'I check out her Facebook page sometimes. And we have mutual friends – they let me know about her. Nothing creepy. I try and keep an eye on her, even now. She brings that out in people, even though she doesn't want any help. She'll rebel against you if you try.'

'Please tell me that she is OK?' Carl asks. His eyes are the amber-brown of medicine bottles. 'I may have lost her but I still care.'

Worried that she is about to take pity on a potential suspect, Keisha walks down the hall. 'Can you show me your room, please?' she asks.

He shows her into his room. The double bed is covered by a single blue duvet, probably the same one he's had for twenty years. Boxes cover the floor, leaving only slivers of space in which to step. She goes over to the low desk with a laptop on it.

'I'll need to take your computer, I'm afraid,' she says. 'To eliminate you from our enquiries.'

'Who will see it?' he asks, putting a hand on top.

Keisha forces her mouth not to flip up at the sides. 'Why?' she asks, using the wide eyes again. 'Is there something on there you don't want people to see? I must warn you that you can never really get rid of something on a hard drive, the shadow of it can be seen and brought back.'

He looks like he's been sucker-punched. So much so that she would bet her new bike on the likelihood that all IT will find on there is some medium-strength porn and tepid gambling. They probably see more sin on their phones in one tea break.

She boxes up his laptop and writes him a receipt. 'You'll get this back when we've finished. Now, I've been informed that you were very keen on Maria having the operation to get her sight back. So much so that you argued about it.'

'Sometimes people need pushing in the right direction, for their own good,' he says, sitting down on his bed.

'Even when it's against their wishes?'

'If you love someone, you don't let go,' he says. 'You look out for them, look over them, guide them when they are going wrong. Maria doesn't know how lucky she is to have friends like hers. She needs someone special, though. I know she still loves me, she just doesn't know it herself, yet.' Carl looks up at Keisha. His smile is now lupine.

She is no longer so sure about that bet.

15

Day Four

The foreshore is quiet, the tide on its way out. Gulls squabble in the sky. The traffic noise is light, even for a Saturday. The stalker will be watching. Seeing her with Jonathan is only going to enrage him even more. This is a bad idea. What is he doing? This is technically a day off and he is with a victim. Jonathan looks round for anyone who looks like a stalker, and looks very much like a stalker in the process.

Maria walks up, shoulders high against the cold.

'You're early,' he says.

'So are you,' she replies.

'Where's Billy?' he asks. He doesn't like the idea of her walking here alone.

'At home, probably chewing my only other pair of shoes.'

'Three hundred and twenty-eight clay pipes from the Thames and only two pairs of shoes?'

'You've been reading my inventory. I'm impressed.'

Is that flirtation? He can't tell, it's been so long. He looks at her – no, that's banter, not attraction. He is hardly a catch at the moment. He hasn't been to the gym in months and has caught another rash of grey hairs, not that Maria would see that but failure is a fog around him and surely she can smell it.

'Right,' says Maria, producing something black and silky from her pocket. It is a blindfold like hers, large and deep, covering down to the nose. She reaches for his hand and places the blindfold in his palm.

'I am not wearing that,' he says.

'You want to know why I refuse to take off the mask? You want to know how I can take care of myself without eyes? Then you'll wear the mask and follow my lead.'

Jonathan snaps the blindfold round his head. 'After you,' he says.

Maria takes his hand. It feels right, like he has come home. Guilt trips him up. That'll be the sensory deprivation – finding comfort in even the most recently familiar.

'Crouch down,' she says. 'Hold out your hands and glide them over the surface. Be careful, there are sharp items down here.'

The stones are cold. They are damp but not wet; it is a while since high tide. Some are more like rocks; here is the bulky roughness of concrete. He feels something smooth and curved.

'Ease it out, that's it,' Maria says. She must be able to hear him. Or hear the absence of him searching.

'It feels like a shell,' he says. 'It's big though.' He scrapes out more mud, feeling the contours. It is like an ear, the cold ear of a statue.

'May I?' she says, taking it from him. 'That's probably a shell from the Indian Ocean.'

'What's it doing here?' Jonathan asks.

'It probably came over in a ship. Coral and shells were used as ballast and then thrown out when they got into dock in London. Or it could be an offering. I often find Hindu statues or items that have been given to the river gods.'

'Or someone bought a load of cheap shells for a fish tank and threw them out when the goldfish died,' Jonathan says.

'Or that. I like the mystery. Sometimes it stays that way, you get so far and then can go no further. I like that.'

'I don't,' Jonathan says. 'Mystery is no good to me. It just makes me want to find the answer. I don't like living in limbo.'

'Really? Most people do – between the job they've got and the job they want, between the relationship they've got and the one they desire, between meals, between haircuts. I'm in the middle of a mystery at the moment—'

'Is that what you call it?' Jonathan says, amazed.

'I didn't mean the stalker. I'm trying not to give that too much thought.'

'Admirable, only don't become complacent.' Jonathan searches the ground. He's playing the stones like piano keys. He touches something cool and smooth, with rough edges, like his tongue when he's been drinking. It lifts out of the mud with a sucking sound.

'Wow. It didn't want to let that one go,' says Maria.

'It feels like the sole of a shoe. Like an insole but made of something tough.'

'Leather?'

'I think so,' Jonathan says.

'Do you know, for a long time I thought it was the "soul" of a shoe. I didn't even question it as it seemed right that feet had souls – they take you on your journey from life to death, they are as close to you as anything else. Feel again, there are lots of Victorian leather shoes in the river. Sometimes you can feel the indentation of the owner's foot.'

Jonathan follows the contours on the sole. It's definitely dipped here, and is much thinner on the instep side. His, or her, feet must have rolled inwards. It is strange to be so close to someone's intimate history. 'Do you believe in ghosts?' he asks.

He hears stones shift under Maria's feet. 'I don't know,' she says. 'Sometimes. There are times when I'm cataloguing finds or cleaning an item and it will be as if that person is in the room with me, their presence. It's silly, really.'

'I understand completely,' Jonathan says. And he does.

'I found something the other day that makes me think of ghosts. It's a bone comb, with a name embossed on it. Simon read it to me – Wilhelmina Wallace. Presumably no relation to William. I've traced one Wilhelmina Wallace alive in London in 1850, the estimated date of the comb. I can't help but see her as a ghost, one whose hair keeps growing, flowing like a crinkled river around the room.'

'You have an amazing imagination,' he says.

'Finding items on the shore is about finding out about the people who lost them,' Maria says.

Jonathan nods. 'When I find an unknown victim, I want to trace them as well. I want their story to be known.'

'That's why I keep on looking,' Maria says.

'Me too,' says Jonathan. He sits on his heels, feeling the water soaking up his trousers. He doesn't want this to end. The rest of London doesn't exist for now. THIS is the city. 'What would be your ultimate mudlarking find?' he asks.

She moves a few stones. She sounds shy, like a teenager playing with her hair. How can a sound be shy?

'Do you mean one I've found or want to find?'

'Go for both.'

'I found a Mesolithic tranchet adze a few years ago. It's a flint tool that's thousands of years old. I dug it out and felt connected with the past, as if the person who had used it handed it to me and started talking.'

'Wow. And I was excited by finding this coin.' He holds it out for her.

'Not bad for your first find. It's probably 1930s.'

'What about the find that is yet to be?'

'A pilgrim's badge,' she says. 'I've never found one. One day.'

He has an urge to get her one. 'What's a pilgrim's badge?'

'A mediaeval badge worn by – surprise, surprise – pilgrims. It was made of pewter and was often thrown into rivers for good luck, God knows why. It's not like the river will look after you.' She pauses. 'Actually, the river always looks after me.' She pauses. He can almost feel her thinking. 'Here's a challenge for you – I bet you can't walk to Borough Market by yourself wearing the blindfold.'

'Where will you be?'

'I've got some errands to run.'

He's walking over London Bridge alone wearing a blindfold. This job brings very strange experiences. It is disorientating. He keeps stumbling. If Celeste or Ed go through CCTV next week and see this then they'd play it over and over till his retirement party. She wouldn't say where she was going or why. He feels the beginnings of panic, for both of them, and removes the blindfold – she is nowhere to be seen. He runs.

His heart only starts to climb down when he sees her outside the market, standing against the wall. Her nose is in the air, smelling something. Her hand is by her side, palm spread as if searching for Billy. At her feet is a small bucket. She looks like a Smiths single cover.

'You cheated, didn't you?' she says, coming up to him and lightly tapping his chest.

'How do you do that?' he says. 'And how did you know it was me?'

'Have you not got it yet? Detectives and mudlarks use all the evidence around them. Admit it – you cheated and took off the blindfold.'

Jonathan says nothing.

'I knew it. You never know when you need to find your way round London in the dark.'

'On the other side of the argument – we have footage of a woman creating graffiti about you. If you had been able to see then maybe you—'

'And maybe not,' she interrupts. 'And maybe yes, and maybe I'll find a pilgrim's badge. I'm not going to live my life according to maybes. Right, before we go into the market for your sense education, I'm going to give you this present and then go and get a coffee, the smell is driving me mad. And I'm embarrassed.' She walks over the road to Middle Street and the Monmouth Coffee Company. 'Do you want one?'

'Flat white, no sugar. Thank you.'

She shyly shoves the bucket into his hand and walks away. In the bucket is a trowel, some boxes and little sample bags. His own starter mudlarking kit.

He watches the street while he waits. Borough Market, with its elegant grey exterior, bustles behind him. A man loads winter pansies onto a trolley, a woman leaves Konditor and Cook with posh bags, a man struggles under straggling limbs of eucalyptus and another man leans against the wall of The Market Porter pub, watching Jonathan watching him.

Jonathan walks over, hands in pockets. The man is in shirt sleeves, even though everyone else is wrapped up in scarves and puffa jackets. He crosses his arms and widens his stance, a subtle sign of aggression. He pulls his sleeves up further to show his muscle. Not so subtle.

'You all right, mate?' Jonathan asks. 'I was wondering if you were waiting for someone.'

'Not for you, mate.' He spits out the 'mate'. He walks off, muttering.

Great, he's managed to make someone think he was picking him up. The cheek. If he were actually picking someone up it would be much more clumsy than that. He wouldn't call them 'mate' though. Not that he has picked someone up in years. The last someone was Natalie.

Maria is standing outside the coffee shop, takeaway cups in hand. She holds one out to him even before he reaches her. 'I'll ask again. How do you do that?' he asks, taking the cup.

'Put the blindfold on again and I'll show you.'

He sighs. Why is he here? How could he justify this as work? He's here because it makes him one quarter of a teaspoon happy and that is more than he thought he could be again. Explain that to the DCI. 'Thank you for the kit,' he says. 'I'll use it, I promise.'

'Give it here and I'll keep it in my rucksack for now. You're going to need both hands.'

She's right. He hands her the kit and his coffee, then with the world black again, he instinctively holds out his arms. The ground has changed, there is a different feel to it underfoot, and it is echoing above and around them. They must have entered the market.

'Feel around you,' Maria says, letting go of his hand. 'It's the best way to get about by yourself.'

All Jonathan feels is panic. He has to bend to hear her and not just because of the sounds of stallholders bellowing and people buying and the echoes against a metal roof that make it sound like they're under a tin bath. It is as if taking away his sight has worsened his hearing.

He extends his arm and touches one of the iron columns that hold up this temple to fresh vegetables. London markets remind him of churches – from Smithfield's flesh cathedral and its wash of blood, the silver pews of fish at Billingsgate and the bright altar offerings of Colombia Road. The muttering and transactions are just like prayer, but with a more predictable result.

Two women stand nearby and he moves toward them, pulling his hand back into his pocket. He doesn't want to be up on an inadvertent sexual harassment charge. A strong, sharp smell of apples. 'Would you like to sample our apple and pear juice, madam?' a man asks one of them. 'The apples are local and freshly pressed.'

Jonathan moves on, his steps smaller as he checks the floor beneath him. This stall smells of vegetables and cardboard boxes. He reaches out a hand and feels carrots, knobbly broccoli and brains of cauliflower. 'Can I help you, sir?' a stallholder says. Jonathan can't tell if it's addressed to him or someone he can't see.

'I'm going to feed you something,' Maria says. 'Taste this and tell me what colour it tastes of,' she says.

He feels something against his lips. Cold, rounded. He takes a bite. It is fresh tasting. 'Green.'

Maria hands him the rest of the cool, tapered, occasionally haired carrot, then takes him down another aisle. They sample rich wine and herby olives, slices of nut breads and artichokes that are so vinegary that they make him sneeze. They go up every lane in the market, sniffing and touching and listening: Jonathan sniffs a trout like a piscine harmonica, making a fishmonger strangely happy; nibbles a chocolate truffle that tastes of a woman's neck and tries a tea so smoky that it could have been kept in a humidor. The mix of smells is a heady mess. Spices and fruit and fish and meat, like a tagine he had in Tangier.

'Are you taking all this in?' she asks. 'I know this place almost better than any other, it's one of the reasons I came to live in London.'

'You weren't born here?' Of course not. She uses long, taffy-pulled vowels that don't suggest London.

'I was born on the Kent marshes. My dad would bring me up to London for educational trips – to touch the exhibits at the Science Museum, go swimming in Hyde Park, take a journey round a market using my nose. He said I would know the world better than most and that I should never take it for granted.' She sounds breathless.

'Your dad sounds great,' he says.

'I was very lucky,' she replies.

When they leave the market, Maria asks, 'so what do you think? Were you making your own world in your head?'

'There were lots of images,' Jonathan said. 'But they were ones that I'd seen with my eyes. Even taking away my sight for an hour intensified everything but I can't get near your experience. You have no visual pictures to reference. I can't imagine how fascinating your world must be.'

Maria goes quiet. 'Can you at all understand why I might not want to give it up?'

'Of course,' he says, gently. 'I can see it is a gift, not a disability. Can *you* see that while we were depriving ourselves of sight, the stalker could have been following us, metres away?'

'No one was following us,' Maria says. 'I'd have heard them.' She doesn't sound certain. They walk on, side by side, stopping by a stall selling rolls of material. Jonathan touches the crêpe and silk and wool while sensing the growing agitation of the stallholder. Maria leans on his arm, reaching up. Something is placed on his head. It's a hat, a fedora by the feel of it.

'I've got one too,' she says. He touches it – it's a cloche hat, close to her head. She'll look great in that. Like an outspoken silent-movie star. Now he mentions it, he'll look great in that. He takes the hat from her head and swaps it with his. It probably covers her eyes and he laughs at the thought. She buys the hats and hands one to him.

Cars slug past on the A3. He feels out a wall on one side, a lamp-post, a shop window. The river calls on the shore; a clipper clips past.

Maria tuts. 'The clippers are eroding the river bank so quickly that no one can keep up. The Thames is too shallow and the clippers too deep – they scrape along the bottom and wash waves at the sides. If it weren't for mudlarks and the Museum of London then more history would be lost. Sorry, that's my soap box.'

'I like it,' he says. It is simple and true.

She laughs.

'Three lamp-posts in from the beginning of the street. Here we are,' Maria says as she dives into a doorway. Maria's map is such a different version of the same city. 'Every time a council decides to cut its spending and take away a street light I have to rethink the city again.'

'And the police receive more reports of crime. Which costs the council more in the long term. It is short-sighted.'

Maria laughs. 'You're not one to talk.'

'Where are we?'

'It's a café that uses herbs and vegetables from Kew. If you can guess what's in it from the smell then I'll buy you lunch.'

'Setting conditions for payment doesn't sound like a good date.'

'To me a good date involves chips and ice skating.' She stops as they enter the café. 'It's been nice, doing this. Helped distract me.'

Jonathan knows he hasn't helped in being here, in playing along with her game. He is lonely. He is fooling himself to think otherwise. 'I do what I can,' he says.

He goes straight home after. Sleep calls him upstairs without even opening the post. It is what he should have been doing all morning. The bed takes him into itself and, just as he touches the edges of unconsciousness, the door knocker falls.

Jonathan trudges down the stairs, wrestling a hand through his hair.

Frank stands in the doorway with a bag from the local bakery in his hands.

'Morning, Frank,' Jonathan says. 'Thanks for dealing with the electrician yesterday.'

Frank nods at the light on in the front room. 'They did the job then,' he says.

'It keeps coming and going. The trip switch must be faulty. Something's overloading the system,' Jonathan replies.

Frank glances over Jonathan's shoulder to the doorway to the kitchen. He smiles.

Jonathan looks round, sees nothing. He pulls his dressing gown tight. 'What can I do for you?'

'You're said you were a detective,' the big man says, refocusing on Jonathan. 'From Scotland Yard.'

Jonathan couldn't remember saying Scotland Yard. 'I'm in the homicide division. Why?'

Frank glances behind him. 'Can I please come in? I need some advice, but I can't go straight to the police.'

'Why not?' Jonathan thinks of the warm, comfortable sleeping bag he could be zipping into upstairs.

'I can't tell you on the doorstep.'

Jonathan thinks of all the things he could be doing other than talking about work. He needs sleep and a walk in which he can lose his week in the twists and old turnpikes of London.

'It's very important. It involves Finnegan Finch.' Frank is trembling, his big fingers tapping on the doorframe.

'Come in then,' Jonathan says.

They sit out the back on broken chairs. A pale sliver of sun cuts into the courtyard. After the muffins, Frank downs his coffee and breathes in deeply. 'This is going to sound ridiculous,' he says.

'Can't be more absurd than the alibis I hear on a daily basis,' Jonathan replies.

Frank raises his face to the sky. The light picks up the black and white hairs stubbling his head. 'I had a visitor at the parlour. He told me about a series of murders that has gone unnoticed.'

The desire for a cigarette is nearly overpowering. One wouldn't hurt, would it? Jonathan starts to roll. He nods for Frank to continue.

'In my line of work I often get people saying that someone is at fault for their loved one's death. It's part of the grieving process – anger and denial. If someone else is to blame then the mourner has a cause to champion.'

Jonathan nods. 'In mine as well.'

Frank puts his big feet up on an upturned flowerpot. A robin jumps from his perch on the warped fence. 'I thought that this was the same – a man livid about death, lashing out at anything and anyone. What he says is implausible. Until you begin to think about it.'

'And what does he say?'

Frank sucks in his cheeks and blows them out. 'He says that there are those high up, literally in the case of sky-rises, who help each other's businesses through corruption, cover-ups and murder.'

'Anything more specific? Such as a body or a suspect, or something tangible?'

'You have the body, there are lots of suspects but it is going to be very hard to grasp anything tangible.'

'I don't want to be rude to a neighbour, Frank, but could you please get to the bit that involves Finnegan Finch.'

'He was the man who came to me.'

'What?'

'He visited me.'

'So the body we found *isn't* Mr Finch.'

'Oh I'm sure it is. It ties up completely with what he says.'

Should he humour him? Call social services? 'If he's dead then how could he come and tell you?' Jonathan asks.

Frank fiddles with a button on his jacket. 'He's a ghost.'

'Excuse me?'

'I'm coming to you because you are my neighbour and I thought we might have some rapport and anyway my wife says you may have a way with them.'

'With what?'

'Ghosts. Seeing as you can stay the night when no one else has in the last ten years. Anyway, that's Barbara's notion and I trust Barbara's notions as much as I trust anyone's.'

'You're saying that Pedlar Cottage is haunted?' Jonathan asks. It is too early for this. He has barely rolled his first cigarette.

Frank eyebrows move up his big, bald head. 'You mean you hadn't noticed?'

'I don't believe in ghosts or anything else that goes bump in the night.'

'They go bump in the day as well.'

Jonathan stands up. 'This is my first whole weekend off in a month and I do not want to be working out what the fuck you are going on about.' He walks towards the back door and gestures for Frank to go ahead of him. 'Well this has been an immense pleasure. Be sure to call again.'

'Finnegan keeps going on about a ring.'

Jonathan stops in the doorway.

'He said the yellow diamond was given to prove that they are part of this circle. The Ring, he calls it.' Frank follows Jonathan through the house, talking quickly. 'He was murdered weeks ago, because he was caught up in something and wouldn't do as he was told. He wouldn't say more. We weren't best mates but I promised I would help.'

They're standing in the lounge, Frank's head bent under the ceiling. Jonathan's brain is hurtling. There has been nothing in the media naming Finch or mentioning the ring. He must have found out through contacts at the crematorium – he's an undertaker after all – or from the woman at DMD: they must all know each other, corpse-wranglers together. What is Frank's angle? What does he want? Is he one of those mediums who extract information from the police in order to extract money from the vulnerable? People like that make Jonathan's blood burn. When Gargie died, his aunt had paid out a small fortune on spiritualists and spirit guides and shamans, all of whom were happy to take her money and leave her knowing less.

Jonathan guides him out.

Frank steps onto the street. 'I know this must seem strange to you, and unwanted. Barbara had the notion that you weren't very happy and I trust Barbara's notions, but then I've told you that. Anyway, this must be difficult to hear and I'm sorry. But don't dismiss it. I'll be next door when you want to talk.'

He walks next door to the parlour. His huge bulk causes a shadow in the street.

Jonathan closes the door. He wishes that Natalie were here – if she were then he would burst out laughing, knowing that she would come from wherever she was in the house to ask what was funny. She would listen and then laugh with him, during the earlier, better times. Towards the end she would ask him to keep the noise down, that some people are trying to sleep/study/fuck other people. He's being unfair, he knows he is. Things are never that straightforward.

He picks up the post and sits down on the old armchair. One of them is from the Law Courts. The envelope is grey and grainy. He tears into it and there it is. The petition. She said she wasn't going to go this far. Masters is making her do it, he must be, there is no way she would do this herself.

She wants a divorce. He reads out loud the grounds for unreasonable behaviour

1) Jonathan is a workaholic and would never take a holiday or spend time with her
2) He sank into an irretrievable depression following the deaths of his colleague and father
3) He is a cross-dresser

The house doesn't say anything. It is silent for once, no creaks or self-closing doors. Maybe it is as shocked as he is.

He reads through the list again.

Reasons to be cheerful. 1, 2, 3.

And there are no more details about number three, as if that is all that needs saying instead of an inadequate word for something he once shared shyly with her as a sign of his trust, a gift.

He holds his head. He had kept all of Natalie's secrets, wrapped them up and secured them in a safety deposit box inside him, and she had promised to do the same for his. How could she betray him like this? Fear rushes over him – how public is this, is it read out in court? – and then anger. There is no fucking way he is going to agree to this. He is supposed to accept this crap? Well, fuck her, and her fuck, he will counter-petition and . . .

The anger can't hold, it's as if he is full of holes. How did he end up here? And why has he spent the last twenty-odd years pouring love into a sieve? He has nothing to show for it at all.

Jonathan shakes his head. A whiskey is looking good now. He'll go to a bar, later. Or maybe he should report the strange happenings – say that there is an intruder moving his things. Or maybe not. His team is, somehow, holding onto tenuous respect for him; if anyone thinks he's going mad then he'll be eased out. A chill runs through him. What if they find out what Natalie wrote on the petition? Or, worse, what if the press found out? Not that he is ashamed in any way, only of the way people act in response to something that is simply a part of him. Why should wearing clothes be taboo? He hears a dragging sound on the stairs, as if sacking is slowly descending. No one is there.

Frank's not helping.

Placing his feet on the footstool, he closes his eyes. Then opens them again. He stares at the footstool. The footstool that wasn't there when he sat down.

'You can stay as long as you like, you know that,' Simon says to Maria, putting his arm round Will. 'I was going to make green curry for dinner.'

'If I don't go now then I'll end up staying till we're all pensioners.'

'Sounds good to me,' Simon says. 'I'm worried about you. The police don't think you should leave, which I take as a personal victory. Either that or a complete failure – why don't they suspect me?'

She lightly punches his arm. 'You've both been vetted.'

'Yes, and they know you'll be safer here,' he says.

'Enough,' she says, pulling down his beardy face so she can kiss his cheek. Will hugs her. She can feel his reluctance to let her go. She picks up her overnight bag and walks over to the door.

Billy ruffs and paws at her hand.

'I'm going to miss you, Billy.' Simon gives him a big ruffle. 'Now make sure you take care of Maria. Don't go giving stalkers big snogs like you do with everyone else.'

Maria wishes she didn't have to go back, but she does. The police have finished with the flat, the locks have been changed and new ones added to doors and windows, and there is no way she's going to give in to fear. The thing she is most looking forward to is rummaging through her treasures. If she can't go to the shore alone then at least she can play with its secrets.

The doorbell rings. A huge bouquet of flowers is thrust into her arms. Roses and jasmine and lavender and thyme and rosemary.

She turns to Simon. 'You'll do anything to get me to stay,' she says. 'You are both lovely. How did you know I wanted these?'

'They're not from us,' Will says. Worry ripples his voice.

Simon takes the card before she can touch it. 'It's in Braille,' he says. She opens out her fingers but finds his there first, moving over the card, reading it as he taught himself when they were teenagers.

'What does it say?' she asks. Her fingers tremble on top of Simon's.

'I forgive you, Maria,' he reads out. His voice is barely more than a whisper. 'But you will have to pay the price.'

16

Her face when she received the flowers! She was so surprised and touched. Seeing her mouth drop open and her hands jump to her cheeks made everything worth it, especially after the week he has had, with the detectives making a mess of everything and getting in the way. He wanted to pick her up and spin her round and say, 'Now you know how I feel about you! Now you know who I really am.' He didn't though. He must not scare her – she is too delicious and delicate for that, like Darjeeling in bone china.

That is why she deserves the best. He has spent a fortune on this apartment, poured in all that the Ring has given him. It is the ultimate nest for her. She will be safe here; it isn't his official residence according to the police records. Everything and everyone can be hacked. All those hours spent in front of the screen constructing false trails and identities were worth it. It wouldn't be fair to be caught for what happened to Tanya. It was entirely her fault. If she had done what she had been told, what she had promised with her eyes, then everything would still be well between them. They would be married and the world would welcome them as lovers.

He picks up the knife and holds it up to one of the spotlights in the ceiling. Perfectly clean. He doesn't want to blemish it in any way, not even to cut cheese. That is another thing he has in common with Maria: cheese. Her online supermarket orders always contain Cheddar, Stilton, Brie and Gouda. One day he will take her to Alkmaar, the Dutch market where cheeses the size of cartwheels are displayed and sold.

But he will never use this knife. It is a replica of the one Tanya took out of her block and attacked him with. He likes women to be feisty but this was impertinent. Her scream had made him laugh. At that moment he knew that she wasn't the one. He wouldn't marry anyone who made that ugly sound. She had been fooling him all this time, with her illusion of perfection: her make-up and lipstick stayed flawless even when jogging. He was suckered in until that day, when his gloved hand grabbed the front of her face and dragged stripes into her foundation. All he could think of was how ugly she was.

He sharpens the knife. It is one of the few things, other than footage and memories, that remain from their relationship, now that Maria has Tanya's finger and ring. He likes the order and circularity that the ring represents. It was created out of his first fiancée; he gave it to his second and his second, he likes to think, presented it to his third. A beautiful sequence of events.

He places the knife back in the presentation box. There is no point throwing the baby out with the bath water. He could have taken the real one from her stomach, when the stars had gone out in her eyes and he had finished crying, but he would have had to pull the knife from her grasp and he was too considerate for that: while you can fall out of love with someone in an instant, you still care for them. He will never fall out of love with Maria.

Jonathan paces round the cottage. His Saturday of sleep is not going to happen. There must be another explanation for what happened with the stool. It is not moving now. He's been watching. Frank is playing some extravagant trick on him. This is supposed to convert him, make him believe in ghosts.

Sure, there are noises of something dragging over the floor in the night and he wakes up shivering.

Sure, there are times when everything of his is a jumble and others when everything is tidy, as if the house had never been touched by human hands.

And then there are the whispers that he puts down to the wind hurtling through the street, through floorboards, through him.

He runs up the stairs. He left the bathroom in a mess last night but now the toothpaste tube has been smoothed; towels folded; clothes rehung.

Jonathan goes through into the bedroom, sits on the bed and gets out his baccy tin. What is the most logical explanation for the changes?

1) He has become obsessively compulsive and amnesiac
2) Someone is breaking in and clearing up
3) The cottage is haunted

Reasons to be cheerful. 1. 2. 3.
'I'm getting out,' he says to the house.

The sergeant on duty doesn't even blink when Jonathan signs out the bike. It's a high speed special, deployed in chases and emergencies.

'It's Sigmund, isn't it?' Jonathan says to him.

'I've had all the jokes,' Sigmund says. The hollows under his eyes are so dark they look as if he slept in make-up.

'Not from me,' Jonathan says, 'and you won't either.'

Jonathan walks down to the garage. His thoughts stalk him, even walking here didn't shake them, wheeling from divorce to ghosts to every one of his professional failures. It's a vicious circle: he can't clearly see the case while his mind is murky with silt. Days off usually give perspective but not today. The only solution is to drive a motorbike at alarming speed and then consume such a vast quantity of spirits that some of his thoughts are lost forever. He starts the engine. The bike growls and rasps beneath him. He has to get away. Leave the cottage and London alone.

The motorbike roars, eating up the M4. The wind is behind him; he is chasing a buried memory. Rain dies against his visor. His phone is vibrating in his pocket and he does not care.

When he gets to Cardiff, he doesn't go immediately to his mother's house. Instead he stops at The Wharf in Cardiff Bay. No one else is stupid enough to drink outside by the lake's edge on a day like today. Raindrops spike his pint.

'You should have told me you were coming,' his mother says, ushering him in.

'I didn't want to put you out,' he says. Lies and passive aggression begin on the welcome mat.

Millie Dark, christened Millicent but call her that and feel her wrath, walks ahead of him down the hallway, picking up clothes from over the radiator. She is moving slowly, carefully. She has grown thin again – her shoulder blades show through her jumper.

'How have you been, Mum?' he asks.

'I went to the Millennium Centre yesterday to see a circus so I'm a bit tired today,' she says.

'Were you inspired to somersault down the stairs?'

'Not after last time.'

They laugh, falling into the old routine. Millie is a mistress of clipping the wings off honesty. When his dad had smoked, she didn't mention his wheezing, his mother's lung cancer, her concern that she could lose him: instead she hid his cigarettes. All over the house. Every night when dad came in, he gave them both a kiss and searched in silence behind paintings, under floorboards, in shoes, the breadbin, socks. He never found all of them – it had been the ideal time for fourteen-year-old Jonathan to take up smoking.

His mother lays out the kitchen table with tea and sandwiches and biscuits. The crocheted tea cosy was Gargie's – one of the few possessions of hers that weren't sold off or given away. He remembered the winter's day that Gargie, having lost her hat, went down to the shops wearing it on her head: 'It's called a cosy for a reason,' she said.

'Do you believe in ghosts, Mum?' Jonathan asks. He didn't intend to ask it but there it was, pulsing on the table between them.

Millie looks up from pouring the tea. 'What a thing to ask,' she says.

Jonathan waits. He drinks from the teacup and wishes there was whiskey in it.

'You haven't talked about ghosts since you were a boy.' She bites her lip.

'You weren't keen on me mentioning it then, either.'

'It isn't appropriate, little boys talking about such macabre things. You were much happier when you stopped pretending that you had dead friends.'

Memories surface, of the little boy by the river and the girl who sat by the school gates. Everyone had put it down to a vivid imagination.

'Is that why you came all this way to see me?' she says. 'To talk about spirits?'

Is it? Maybe. He doesn't know why he has come. 'I suppose death has been on my mind recently. I have been thinking of Gargie, Dad and Coleman.'

'Coleman?' she says.

'My colleague and friend, Jacob Coleman. He died last year.' The short version of a very long story. If ghosts exist then where is Coleman? It isn't like him to hide.

'It's only natural to mourn,' she says, patting his hand. 'Separating must make it worse for you. It makes you feel like you aren't rooted any more so you turn to those who ground you. You'd be better off thinking about those of us who are still alive. And visiting us more than once a year.'

Jonathan looks up, sharply. 'You know about Natalie and me?'

She laughs. 'Don't look so surprised. Did you think that your auntie wouldn't tell me? Neil let her know. He's a good boy. He's worried about you, you know. We all are. We know how you like to keep things in and not talk about them.'

'You are joking, aren't you? *I* like to keep things in?'

'Try not to dwell on dark things, Jonathan. It'll bring you down. It used to bring me down when your father and his mother went on about ghosts.'

'Dad used to see ghosts?'

His mother laughs, nervously. She swirls the tea leaves around the pot. 'Can we move on, darling? You know I don't like to talk about the past.'

Later, back in Spitalfields, the last dribble of whiskey in the bottle crawls onto the ice. It was a large bottle. The world is tipping like when he takes speedbikes round a bend, his knee on the ground and his head not far off. He hasn't eaten enough. Luckily, alcohol has enough calories to get him upstairs. Enough to crawl up the stairs, anyway. He can laugh at himself at least, there is no one around to do it for him, whatever Frank says.

His thoughts were lost to the road long enough to know that he is missing a vital one about the case. It is there somewhere, hidden in the shingle. Now, all he can think about is Natalie. The divorce petition was a cry for help, that's what it was. Of course it was. She's trying to get a reaction out of him. She must be hurting so much to do that. Natalie wasn't someone who would deliberately hurt him like that. She needs him, is asking for him. Why didn't he realise that when he got the form? He is so stupid. Call himself a detective.

He dials her number. It rings once, then is cut off.

He tries again.

'Listen, mate, you've got to leave her alone.' Masters' reasonable tones. Jonathan throws the phone across the floor.

Sss-cut.

There it is again, the strange dragging sound. It's in the room. There is an outline of something, of nothing, moving in jerks.

Sss-cut.

He is so tired. Every movement is an effort. He is pathetic, a forty-something worm whose life has been thrown back.

Sss-cut.

The pain in his chest pins him to the bed.

Why would Natalie want to hear from him? She made it clear how she felt. She wants him out of her life. He is worthless. Loathsome. She just took her time to come round and realise.

Sss-cut.

There is no point even trying. It could end so easily.

Sss-cut.

His heart beats whiskey-quick. There's a cut-throat razor lined up on the bed. A bath and two downward strokes would do it. He reaches.

Cut, it whispers.

A crash comes from downstairs. And another crash, then the sound of glass smashing.

He lurches out of bed, the phone dropping onto the sheets. Adrenalin whittles him into action.

Checking all doors and closing them after him, Jonathan slowly goes down the stairs. The lights are on. He hadn't left them on.

He steps down into the front room onto a floor dancing with light. The mirror over the fireplace wall has fallen from its hook and shattered. He steps through the shards into the kitchen where pots and pans sit in a pile on the floor. The gas stove is on, hissing like a cat.

The doors are still locked, the windows locked. No one is in the house apart from him.

It has been a long day's watching. She spent hours with him on the beach, then with Simon in a restaurant. Her smile is back and it hurts to see someone else be the source of her happiness. It was easy to see and hear everything – no surveillance team to fool, no office to go to and pretend he is working – but it is not enough any more. He has done humiliating things to be close to her and soon she will pay him back.

She has gone to bed now. He watched her on his phone, live from the unfound camera, and he can leave knowing she is safe asleep. He walks back to Hackney. Darkness wraps around him. London looks great at night, although it is at its best at dusk. It is a flattering light on any woman. When he and Maria get together at last he will take her on a crepuscular river trip. There will be a candlelit dinner and fairy lights, her favourite band. He has so many plans. He has a spreadsheet of activities they will undertake on their honeymoon.

He should not rush this though. There are three days to go, full of romance and fun. Time to put the trap into place. Nothing beats the chase. Very soon he will make himself known and she will never get to forget him again.

17

Day Five

Maria walks around her flat in new pyjamas. The stalker has not seen her in these, although that doesn't comfort her. What if they missed a camera? What if he found a way in during the night?

She calls Billy to her and thumps the edge of the sofa. He jumps up and they lie together, his big paws stretching either side of her neck. Sunday mornings at their best consist of croissant crumbs in crisp sheets followed by a trip to the foreshore. That's not going to happen today. She doesn't have any pastries, and surveillance isn't available to her on Saturday or Sundays due to budget restraints. The lesson is – don't get stalked at the weekend.

The doorbell rings. The hairs on her arms rise. Billy scrabbles to get up, scratching her face with his paw. He thuds towards the door but she calls him back to her side. They move slowly down the hallway. Her heart is so fast. This is what that coward is putting her through. She has never been scared of the world before or thought it meant her harm. She will not become a coward too.

She opens the door. She can smell rain on leaves and warm, buttery croissants.

Billy barks.

'I thought we could go to the beach,' Simon says.

'Yes, please,' she says. 'Where's Will?'

Simon shuffles on the doorstep. 'He's been called in to work, apparently. Last night too.'

'Again?'

He murmurs a 'yes'. She thought there was tension between them.

Maria gives him a hug. It's his turn to be looked after. 'Come on, then. Let's forget about the stalker for a day. You talk, I'll listen and buy muffins.'

Jonathan stands slowly. His shoulders ache, his head aches, his legs ache: everything aches from sleeping crunched up in the armchair. He didn't make it back upstairs last night. He had hoped that this would stop his nightmares. It didn't – he fell into them immediately. A voice, like his own but scratched, was talking and talking but he couldn't grasp the words. In his dream, the words had become birds made of bones, calling to him, taunting him. He ran after them but they turned into a wall of cawing, forming a circle around him, darting and swooping, wingless and outstretched, their bone beaks pecking at his ears.

A floorboard creaks above him. That's it. Off to work. There is little worse than being alone on a Sunday.

All crematoria look the same. It's as if one sadistic architect designed and built them all on one dreary day in 1977. They have all the depression of the end of the seventies with none of the punk or glamour. As it is, this low-rise yawn of a building throws up memories of a hearse in a low carport, of men in black suits resting his relatives' coffins on their shoulders and wobbling up to the front of a large beige room.

'Are you all right, Guv?' Rider asks as they get out of the car.

Jonathan nods. 'I'm fine. Heavy night last night.'

'Looks like it, if you don't mind me saying.'

'We can't all go out on a Saturday and wake up the next day looking like a bed that hasn't been slept in,' he says, taking in Rider's smug smile and annoyingly glowing skin.

'Funny places, crematoriums,' Rider says, walking up to the noticeboard. 'My grandpa was cremated here. I was only six. Cried my eyes out. I hated the thought of him in flames.'

There is no burning going on at the moment – do they stop on Sundays? Maybe there is a funeral coming up and they don't wish to smoke-signal death. He has never believed in the curtain that is pulled round the dead so that the living can walk away. Everyone knows that they are still there.

This may even have been where they took Gargie. Jonathan can't remember now. Strange what you forget and what is burned into the memory. He had followed her cab, converted into a hearse for the occasion. She would have been so pissed off with the driver – he didn't beep at anyone once. The vicar had bored his way through her potted life story, managed to mix up her children with her grand-children, her grandchildren with her various lovers and be the first clergy to be booed out of a memorial service. She would have loved that. She wasn't one for Christianity, was Gargie. She always talked of ghosts. He had too, then. If ghosts were real, then maybe she was there at her own funeral, whispering into his ear. What would she say to him now? *Tell them all to fuck off, darling,* she would say, her grin as wide as the Thames and as full of mercury. Jonathan shivers. He'll have to be careful today. Yesterday was too full of emotions, swinging from rage to a sadness that felt like it was going to drag him under. It is affecting his work. Again. Perhaps it is time to retire.

Michael Finch walks towards Jonathan and Rider. He looks barely out of his teens. He is wearing a dark suit that is too long in the arms and legs. He goes the long way, avoiding stepping on the grass and its small urns with carnations poking out. The wind tousles his hair like an affectionate aunt. 'Mr Finch. Thank you so much for agreeing to see us,' Jonathan says. 'I know this must be very difficult for you.'

Michael Finch nods. His face looks as if it has been grated. He has raw skin that is flaking off in places. There is no comprehension in his eyes. He must have seen that look every day during his short working life so far: the shock of loss, the holding on to anything that stays still for a moment. Quite an education for a young man.

Jonathan makes sure he looks right into Michael's eyes. 'We have no intention of intruding on your grief, but we need to talk to you about your father's death. You understand why, don't you?'

Michael nods. He still seems unable to speak, although his mouth opens and closes every now and again.

Rider walks over.

'Is there somewhere private that we can go?' Jonathan says. 'DC Rider here is going to interview the manager, Sandra, is it? Can you point him in the right direction?'

Michael leads them both round the back of the crematorium, walking next to the small strip of a garden where the flowers are laid out for the next service: 'MUM', one says in white blooms; 'To my only love', declares a card on a box of out-of-season tulips.

Unlocking a door in a wall patch worked with plaques dedicated to the dead, he nods at the next room along. 'Sandra's in there.'

Rider nods and knocks. A muffled voice can be heard inside.

'Is it normally this quiet at the crematorium on Sundays?' Jonathan asks.

Michael shrugs. 'It costs more on a Sunday but there are always a few who are willing to pay. We've got one in an hour.' He glances at his watch.

'We won't keep you long,' Jonathan says.

'This was my dad's office.' Michael lets Jonathan through and hovers in the doorway. It is a small, windowless box-room crammed with a desk, one huge chair, one small one and a wall of files. The opposite wall features a calendar full of cremations. Jonathan takes the smaller seat. 'I'll stand if you don't mind,' says Michael. He stares at his dad's chair.

'Do you have any questions for me, before I begin mine?' Jonathan asks.

Michael scratches at his already grated-looking face. He makes his hands into balled fists. 'I don't understand what's happening. We buried him two weeks ago in the memorial garden. There's a huge stone on it.'

'It wasn't your father's body that was cremated, Michael.'

'Whose was it?'

'We don't know. It's impossible to tell from the ashes.' Probably someone else that the Ring, if it existed, wished to dispose of – maybe Marc Bannister. It's going to be hard to prove one way or the other.

'I don't want them in the garden,' Michael says, his hand scratching at his neck. 'They don't belong here. It's the family plot.'

'Please don't distress yourself, sir.'

'Mum went to see him this time,' he says. 'She said he looked peaceful.'

Rosa Finch had not said the same thing to Jonathan when he had taken her to view and identify the body. Tears falling without end she said, 'He was everything I had. And someone threw him out like rubbish. He looks like a horrid waxwork.' She had stayed with him for an hour, talking. What made her cry the most was that he was so damaged that she couldn't hold his hand.

'Very peaceful,' Jonathan says. If Frank is telling the truth, Finnegan is anything but at peace.

'Do you think I should go and see him?' Michael asks.

'Remember him how you last saw him,' Jonathan suggests. 'That's what will stay with you, not his body.'

'Why did the police get it wrong the first time?' Michael says.

'We're trying to find out. Mistaken identification and other factors.' His aunt was mortified when Keisha talked to her earlier, apparently. She doesn't know how she will ever make it up to her sister. Kept saying, over and over, that it looked like Finnegan.

Michael's questions have died down, along with his anguish.

'Can you tell me if you noticed anything suspicious in the weeks running up to your father's death?' Jonathan asks.

'In what way?' Michael is distracted – still eyeing his father's chair. He probably feels it is disrespectful to sit in it. In fact, he probably sat in the one Jonathan is on for years. 'Would you feel more comfortable talking in this chair?' Jonathan asks.

Michael nods. There is the first sign of a relieved smile.

'And do you mind me sitting in your father's chair for now?'

A small shake of the head from Michael.

Jonathan sits on the edge of the chair, guessing from the way this comfortable, leather-covered office chair is set to tilting backwards that Finnegan reclined into it, feet most likely on the desk, yup – here are the black scuff marks from his heels.

'It's got a massage function, if you want that,' Michael says. He looks embarrassed. 'The chair, I mean. Dad said it was the best rub down he's had this side of Bangkok. He was joking, I'm sure,' Michael is quick to say. 'He's never even been to Thailand.'

Jonathan doesn't react. He meets enough men who make remarks like that. Most of the time the person saying it is a little prick pretending to be a big prick. 'We're looking for irregularities. Meetings that weren't in the diary, unusual or worrying behaviour. Anything would help. Please, in your own time.'

Michael sits upright and stares at his knees. He doesn't look more than twenty, but an inexperienced twenty. His grief fills the room, grey-washing the walls and everything in it. Jonathan sometimes wishes he could cut off his empathy, or give it away to someone whose own is faulty, like donating a kidney. His empathy absorbs people's emotions like charcoal. They burn up their feelings in him and leave feeling lighter while he is left with a pile of ash. Somehow, his empathy grows back, a phoenix heart.

'Dad's been stressed recently,' Michael says. He interlinks his fingers and touches his thumbs together to make a circle as if cradling a big invisible mug of tea. 'He's been busy, what with opening the new branches. He's been trying to train me up to manage one of them, but he didn't have much time for anything other than expanding the business. Mum's been on at him to get away all summer and he's been putting it off. She said he'd have a heart attack if he carried on the way he was.' He looks up from his knees. 'Is that what happened?' he says, his face pained but hopeful. 'Did he have a heart attack from all the stress?'

'The coroner's report is not out yet but I would expect it to confirm murder.'

'I suppose you wouldn't be here otherwise,' Michael says. 'I'll do anything I can to help.' He lifts up his chin. Jonathan wonders if he's been told that he will have to be the man of the house now.

'Were your mum and dad having any difficulties at all?' Jonathan asks. 'Have they had any rows?'

Michael shakes his head. 'They never rowed. It was embarrassing sometimes the way they carried on. "Canoodling" they called it. "Go away, me and your ma are canoodling".' He stops then and inclines his head. 'I did catch them having one argument recently,' he says, leaning forward.

Jonathan encourages him with a nod.

'I overheard them, a month or so back. They'd have stopped if I'd walked in – Mum is big on keeping up the performance for kids, she'll do it now with my little cousins and still does in front of me. She can't get beyond me being a child.' Michael's sad smile returns. Jonathan finds himself hoping it will stay. 'They were in the kitchen and I could hear them from outside. I was with Becky, my girlfriend, and needed to get something from my room.' He blushes again. So that'll be either condoms or drugs. 'We snuck in the front door. Mum was there with her hands on her hips, shouting at him and waving what looked like bank statements. She didn't notice us at all. We got out as soon as we could.'

'Did you speak to them about it?' Jonathan asks.

Michael shook his head. 'I was going to ask Mum at some point. Then I forgot. I didn't worry about it, they were completely in love.'

That can be exactly what it looks like until they leave you.

'You're training as an accountant, is that right?' Jonathan asks.

Michael nods and smiles shyly.

'And you've taken over the company's books? That's a huge responsibility. He must have trusted you completely.'

Michael's raw face twitches. It seems to wrestle with itself. 'He did,' he says. Tears fall.

'We're going to need to see your accounts across the business,' Jonathan says. 'Every crematorium or subsidiary enterprise.'

Michael nods. 'Do you think it could help find out who killed him?'

'All information combines to create a complete picture,' Jonathan says, standing to leave. Michael shuffles away, looks back to the chair. 'Your dad would be proud of you.'

Michael head nods up and down as he tries not to let the sob out. 'I'm going to finish what he started,' he says.

'I'm sure you will,' Jonathan replies. He resists the urge to pat him on the head.

'So many young blokes living with their parents now,' Jonathan says on their way out, feeling about ninety. 'It's a shame – stops them from growing up properly.'

Rider says nothing.

'You're living with your parents, aren't you,' Jonathan says. 'Shit, I didn't mean to—'

'What am I supposed to do?' Rider asks. 'I want to buy a house but even a tiny flat on the arse skirts of the city needs a huge deposit. I'm staying with my parents till I can save up enough, although prices are going up all the time, faster than I can save.'

'At this rate you'll be still at home when you get brought here in a box.'

'Tell me about it. It's not like a DS gets a great wage.'

'Is that a dig, young Rider? I don't blame you. Unfortunately it doesn't get much better till you've been in the job for years. So. What about Sandra? Did she have anything to add?'

'She seemed worried about telling me things. Some of what she was saying was gibberish. I've got it all recorded so everyone can hear it. It was difficult to break through,' Rider says. 'But I managed to get some things out of her. She said that for some time Finnegan had been freezing her out of some jobs. He oversaw the whole deal, from beginning to end.'

'And that was unusual?'

'Very, so she says. Usually she took in the bookings and dealt with the family and Finnegan oversaw things on the day. She said he saw himself as a "showman".' Jonathan thought of the big massaging chair. He saw himself as something important, definitely.

18

In the unusually quiet station, Jonathan sits with Rider and Keisha, going through a new pile of information and emails. He stops when he gets to one from IT. 'I can't believe this,' he says. A tiny black box was found attached to the wall in the coffee shop where Maria goes for lunch. It was stuck to the wall behind a plant pot. This device has been able to access many of the apps and sites she visited online, her passwords, emails, user IDs. It was only a matter of time before this happened, he just didn't expect it this soon. All areas of the Met have had sessions on internet identity theft and information leaked by smartphone use on public Wi-Fi, on creepyDOL and spy boxes either drone-dropped or placed in situ. Technology will have moved on since then. The stalker could have been finding out absolutely everything about Maria for months. And Tanya before her. And he would be surprised if there weren't others.

'Do IT have any hope of it helping us find out about him?'

'That would make it rubbish spyware,' Keisha says.

'You never know,' Jonathan says, 'the more footprints, the easier it is to find the shoe.'

'But we've found no footprints. From what I've seen today, I'm beginning to think he doesn't have any shoes. Or feet. Or a body.' She slumps into a chair.

'Don't say that. Not today. This is promising, though,' he says to Keisha, holding up a clump of papers. 'How did you break down the DMD accounts so quickly?'

'Came in yesterday on my day off, Guv,' she says. She doesn't even look up from her work. 'Been up most of the night.'

'Impressive. And you found . . .' He gestures for her to take over.

'Everything looks fine on one level, the DMD group has expanded rapidly and is using investment to offset profits legitimately but when I started exploring I found a fair amount was being siphoned into a tax haven, more into tax avoidance schemes that are knocking at the door of evasion. I then looked deeper still and found transactions that had no clear trail of money in and out.'

'What was the source of these transactions?' Jonathan asks. He smiles. Her enthusiasm is catching.

'Finch's Crematorium Group.'

'Brilliant, Keisha. I couldn't ask for more,' Jonathan says.

Rider huffs.

Jonathan laughs. 'And what do you have for me?'

'We've got a new Braille message from Maria's stalker, sent with a bunch of flowers that she had been looking at online. I've had it taken to forensics.'

'And yet you've given me more.'

'It's not just me. Celeste and Ed down from CCTV did most of the work. I've brought them down to get some of the praise you're dishing out.'

He hadn't even seen them, lurking in the kitchen area. They are as subtle as their surveillance cameras. Celeste looks even paler than ever. She has skin that looks like the sun only touched it once, and that was a mistake. Jonathan has never seen Ed wear anything except clothes the grey of the images he searches all day. Time codes must tumble through their dreams.

Celeste speaks first. 'I've been keeping an eye out for the girl who dropped off the box and placed the clay Braille on the wall. She was wearing gloves so we can't get those kinds of prints but I got thinking – the small dots she placed at the bottom – Kanga – didn't make sense as part of the message but what if it were a tag?'

Her eyes are shining.

'You think she may be a graffito?' Jonathan says.

'Ed then zoomed in tight on her open rucksack – there was at least one spray can in there.'

Ed gives a sheepish grin. 'I searched through graffiti stills and council records for the tag KANGA and found these,' he says. They have to lean in to hear his voice. He has a soft West Country lilt that reminds Jonathan of fudge and holidays, especially as he has the shaggy brown mop of a Dartmoor pony. He hands round printouts of striking graffiti. 'With a couple of exceptions, they're all around the South Bank and Southwark. This one is behind the old chocolate factory. You can see it from the train. And there's another one in an alleyway by the Old Vic. Her tags are all over the area. I wondered if she might live there.'

'How long did it take to go through that lot?' Rider asks.

'Twenty-five hours,' Ed says. 'Although I did eat twice during that time.' He looks at them as if fearing that he's said the wrong thing. When people laugh, he smiles. He looks round the office like a kid seeing Santa's grotto.

'Tell them the rest,' says Celeste. She is watching with glee. CCTV rarely gets this kind of glory.

'I thought I would wander round the area and see if I could find any more.'

'You thought you could catch her in the act, didn't you? Admit it, you'd love to be a vigilante,' Rider says, laughing.

Ed looks over at Celeste, confused as to how to respond.

'Carry on, Ed,' Jonathan says.

'I went down every street in a one-mile radius, originating from the central point of all the tags. I found four more pieces of graffiti tagged 'Kanga' and as I was going through Borough Market, I turned into an alleyway and found this.'

He holds up another sheet of paper. It is a photo of a yellow brick wall with more clay balls made into Braille. Keisha starts deciphering.

'Well done, Ed,' Jonathan says. 'You should be a detective.'

'Tell him the rest, Ed,' Celeste says. She looks like a proud, if patronising, mum.

'I found the fake IT engineer,' he says. 'He can't be seen on the way in, he must have kept out of the way, but there is just enough of him leaving for me to discern his direction and pick him up on another camera. Then another. I leapfrogged and followed him to a post office box.' He hands over another still. A man in a beanie hat entering the PO box office. This is something to go on.

'I have an incredible team,' Jonathan says.

Ed smiles, his eyes sparkling like the morning river.

Jonathan can't help grinning back. Now that's a man who loves his job. That used to be Jonathan – he had wanted to be a detective since he was twelve when he was given a 'First Detection Kit' for Christmas. It taught him to place a piece of string around his door, write letters in onion juice, place talcum powder on the floor to trap footprints and take fingerprints with poster paint. He was hooked. The first few years on the job had been great – to be on the beat in the middle of winter had left him feeling as if he was in love, with no need to eat or sleep. He would love to have that excitement back.

Keisha looks up. 'It says "ANSWER ME, MARIA!", with an exclamation mark at the end.'

There is something sinister about an exclamation mark. Like a clown: if you need to paint on a smile you have something to hide.

'I haven't managed to find any footage of her doing the graffiti,' he says. 'It doesn't make any sense. But there are hours and hours and hours to go through for each location, if they even have a camera in place.'

Jonathan pins up the tags and message. His pinboard looks like a mad man's scrapbook. 'Keep looking – you'll get there. And, remember, there may be more.' He stares at the board.

'Please tell me what's going on?' Frank says, sitting on the side of the bed. Even that makes her wince. 'You know there's nothing that you could tell me that would make me love you any less.'

She says nothing at all, just stares at the end of the bed.

He strokes her head as he used to. He hopes that she can feel it still or at least feel his love. He would do anything to get her back. If only he could love her enough to throw off the tiredness. They used to do so many things. She'd tickle his feet, even as a ghost, and he would be rendered powerless, his huge frame a long, wobbly giggle.

Barbara can now barely shake her head.

Frank wants to shake her out of it. Shout her down the stairs, say anything to provoke a reaction that would make her Barbara again.

'Leave me be, Frankie love,' she says. Her voice is as thin as a shroud. 'I just want to sleep. You go and have a good laugh with one of your mates.'

'I want to laugh with you,' he says. The tears are coming. 'You promised me you would never keep anything from me.'

She focuses her eyes on him. They are now the colour of a Limehouse canal. 'You wouldn't understand.'

That hurts. Drives coffin nails into him.

Anger knocks. 'You're being selfish, Barb,' he says. 'You're not trying. You're giving up on us without fighting. That's not the Barbara I married.'

She turns away from him towards the wall.

'You'd try it if you loved me.'

She cries out then, a high whimper that fades at the end. Her body is barely pulsing.

He wants to take back the words but they are there on the bed, slithering between them.

19

Jonathan stands at the door to the funeral parlour. The McNally sign is still, the wind has backed off. It is a suitably sober exterior – purple-grey paint with white borders to the windows. Box hedges squat on the sills like green Lego bricks.

He could turn away right now. There would be no recriminations; it's not as if he could go to DCI Allen and say that this bloke is on speaking terms with the dead, and one of them happens to be our floater. He would be placed on compassionate leave for his divorce and very kindly, very quietly, and very obviously to any other copper, condemned as a crackpot who has done his time. He would be an unfortunate example of what happens to a man of the Met. No one could blame him for walking the few steps back to the cottage and closing the door.

Jonathan knocks.

He can hear Frank talking to someone upstairs, his voice booming out of the top window. Jonathan knocks again.

Chains rattle, Chubbs unlock. Security around a funeral home is unsettling. Is it to stop the living getting in or the dead getting out?

'Jonathan Dark!' Frank says. He looks red-eyed, as if he's been crying.

Frank scrutinises Jonathan's own face. 'You'd better come in, I can see you've had a time of it.'

'Mr McNally,' Jonathan says. 'This isn't an official visit, exactly, but I will be recording our conversation. Is that clear?' He takes the digital recorder out of his pocket.

'Clear as a glass monkey's arse,' says Frank. He opens his arms and shows Jonathan into the funeral home. 'I'm so glad you came.' His blue eyes are bloodshot.

'This is a serious enquiry. You have given me information that only someone connected with the murder or murderers would know.'

'If it's a serious enquiry, why aren't we at the station? And why am I not under caution? So let's talk. There's so much to explain, not only about Finnegan.' With that, he turns and walks up the wide staircase, taking the stairs two or three at a time. 'You're just in time for Sunday tea. I'm terrible without tea.' His tone seems excessively cheery. He's putting on a front.

Frank shows him through into a large kitchen two floors up that runs the width of the house. From here he can see the top of Spitalfields Market. Frank busies himself in cupboards, pulling out cakes and biscuits. He sets to work buttering slices of bread.

'How many people are you expecting?'

'Other than you?' Frank replies, pulling out a chair for Jonathan. 'No one.'

'You knew I was coming? Oh. You must have seen the news.'

'The news?' Frank looks up from dolloping clotted cream into a bowl. 'Was Finnegan on the news? He will be pleased. He always wanted to be famous. No, I thought you'd be coming because I heard a storm kicking off in your cottage last night.'

Jonathan doesn't reply. He shakes his head to a slice of cake. His appetite is shrinking. So is he. He doesn't mind, it saves money. Although his clothes will need tying on if he carries on like this.

'What would you like to know?' Frank asks. He spreads his hands out wide. A gesture of openness and trust. Or one that tries to convince you of it. Jonathan has seen many a guilty man do exactly the same in an attempt to convince the police that he is innocent.

Where to start? 'You came to me stating that Finnegan appeared to you as a ghost.'

'Right so far.'

'And that he was murdered by members of some group or syndicate . . . the Ring.'

'Right again.'

'So who actually killed him?'

'This is where it gets complicated. He didn't see who murdered him, I think he was knocked unconscious from behind. I've been hearing whispers of it for years and years, but this is the first time I've known someone involved. I felt I had to say something.'

'What is Finnegan Finch's state of mind?' He can't believe he is saying this about a man who is dead.

'He's angry.'

'Understandably. I would be pissed off if I were dead.'

Frank laughs delightedly. 'Yes you would, wouldn't you! You'd be one of the ghosts who tears down the place.'

Jonathan shakes that statement away. 'I meant, do you trust his mental state?'

'No less than when he was alive. He has always been a bit unpredictable.'

Jonathan sighs and gets up to leave. 'You're wasting my time.'

Frank's eyes widen. 'I'm telling you the most important information you'll ever hear. The world isn't how you think it is, and you can help a ghost find his killer.' He slams his palm down on the table. 'I'll take you to meet him.'

Jonathan stares. 'Meet Finnegan Finch?'

'Yup.'

'The ghost.'

'You get to say I told you so if you don't,' Frank says, egging him on.

'If I don't, you get to stay in a police cell.'

Frank applauds. It sounds like two chops clapping. 'So I win either way. Good.' He checks his watch. 'I know where he'll be – we have some time for more of your juicy questions on the way.' He stands up. 'And I want to ask some of you – firstly, do you see anyone else in this kitchen?' Frank asks. His eyes are glinting.

The yellow walls of the kitchen are made warmer by the waning sunlight. The only sounds are the patient clock and those that drift up from the street. It doesn't look like a place of ghosts but Jonathan's heart is running too fast. Ghost stories have always done this to him.

Jonathan tilts his head. From the research he's done on the undertaker, he knows that Frank's wife died several years ago, and that he has become a recluse since then, emerging only to officiate at funerals. He is a well-known, well-liked figure and he is missed. Neville at Snow Hill Station said that 'Frank used to sing in my community choir. He would sing enough for ten of us, but he gave up when his wife died. Barbara was a beautiful alto.'

'Is Barbara here?' Jonathan asks, crossing his arms.

'No, she's in the lounge, watching telly. She likes a bit of comedy in the afternoon, why else would she put up with this face for thirty years straight.' Frank pokes his cheek and grins. There is something of a lie in that.

'Did she just . . . appear to you suddenly,' Jonathan asks, 'after she died?'

'No, it took me weeks to find her. I did actually pull my hair out at the roots because it hurt so much not knowing where she was. And even then she was only just there, pulsing like a firefly.'

Jonathan feels a spike of jealousy. 'So who else is in the kitchen?'

Frank puts his fingers to his lips and inclines his head. 'This is an old coaching inn. I often glimpse past punters stumbling up the stairs. There are the sweetest ghost horses in the yard. I take them carrots.' He catches Jonathan's cynical stare. 'You don't believe me. Fair enough. Look to the very corner of your eye. That's it. Then de-focus. Relax. Your perception will be thrown. Do you see any change in the light?'

'No.' Jonathan holds his breath. 'Wait. There is something strange over there in the hall.' He points to the doorway. A shadow is crawling under Barbara's door.

'I don't see it,' says Frank, frowning.

Jonathan shakes his head and the shadow is gone. 'I told you, I can't see ghosts.'

He didn't even say goodbye. He's showing himself in his true colours now.

The Whisperer is next to her. It strokes her face.

You don't have to live with this.
You are so tired. Close your eyes and rest.

It understands her. It is the only thing that does. And she is helping it, like Frank helps his ghosts. It is tiring, of course. But everyone deserves a chance. That's what it says.

Do you remember what it was like in the Gloaming? Like a heavy feather pillow pressing down

'I don't want to go to the Gloaming,' Barbara says. She sees her form coming through brighter, like a torch that has been shaken. But it's only temporary. The passion and denial fire her up but she can't maintain it. Her battery won't last.

Its nail points into the centre of Barbara's throat.

I'm doing this for your own good, Barbara. I'm your friend.

You're my friend

Someone like Frank will charge through when he dies. He'll be so present and palpable that no one will know he has gone. He won't know he has gone. You don't have it. You don't have the force of his personality. And you know that is true. I wouldn't lie to you.

The Whisperer is now engorged like a spider. Every word releases more of her pain, extinguishes more of her light.

Frank must love you so much to give up the real world. Just for you. To relinquish a chance of love with a woman who can give him what he wants.

Where do you think he is now? You joke about the way he looks at women on the television and how he wishes he had a woman with a body but you know, deep down, the truth. You can't satisfy him any more. Any living woman could give him what you can't. You'll never keep him. You're a selfish bitch.

The whispers fill the room like acrid smoke.

How much do you love Frank, Barbara? Letting him move on is the right thing to do, it's the kind thing. You're nothing but a burden now, as you are to your sons. Why don't they phone, Barbara? What did you do to them? They hate you. Frank will hate you soon.

Barbara crumples forward, rocking, crying ghost tears.

Sss-cut.

It digs its nails into Barbara. Covering her face with its caul, it drinks. There is not much more of her to go.

Ssss-h, it says.

20

'London is ghost-locked,' Frank says. People move out of the way, allowing him to pass: some nod; some veer; all look up to the feathers cresting his top hat. 'Every corner, alleyway, highway, high-rise, gym, café, canal, library or house is haunted in some way. Every window has a ghost looking out. Part of you sees, and it is this part which is screaming at all times inside.'

He glances at Jonathan. 'Don't tell me there isn't someone yelling in your brain.'

'I wouldn't dare,' Jonathan says. 'But I don't think it's shouting about ghosts.'

'It shouts about all the things that haunt you and that you are ignoring.'

Jonathan looks around. People are still out, enjoying the last of their weekend, the last of the sun as it turns into dusk. There is a feeling of urgency in the air. People are intent on their laptops, coffees, their conversations on the phone or in person. 'There wouldn't be room for all the ghosts of all the people that ever were,' he says.

'This isn't about space. Most ghosts are in a stage we call the Gloaming. They mill on the streets but take up little or no physical room. They are oblivious – listless spirits lacking the qualities that made them human, poor wights. They are Sleepers. You can walk straight through them without noticing. There are two in front of you.'

Jonathan stops. A man bumps into him from behind. A solid man, very much alive, muttering obscenities.

'Cities are difficult when you're in denial of ghosts. It is an unconscious stress to the body and mind. London is at once an old city heaving with history's spirits and a powerful, steely centre that attracts the young and driven. Its inhabitants breathe in ghost motes every day. Some thrive but many get overwhelmed and move away. The evidence of another reality fills their senses at all times and their brains can't cope. Self-delusion is tiring.'

'The whole world is ignoring ghosts?' Jonathan says, trying to keep the cynicism out of his voice.

'People are happy with binaries – one is dead or alive and that's it. Admitting more would mean looking at all the things that slip in between. The thing is, everyone can feel ghosts. Most people choose not to, consciously or unconsciously. We work very hard at deceiving ourselves.'

'You don't.' Jonathan watches Frank's face. He believes everything he says.

'There's always something we don't want to know.' His eyebrows twitch.

Jonathan knows that feeling – the stuffing down of what is obvious to all but you. Eating up ignorance till it eats you. He dismissed all the signs that she was having an affair.

'Look over there,' Frank says, nodding towards two people sat at an outdoor table. 'What do you see?'

'A couple having coffee but no conversation,' Jonathan says. 'They've gone beyond the point where they are interested in each other, but are not beyond staying with someone out of habit. I'd say neither wants the other to have anyone else but they don't want each other either.'

Frank laughs. 'You need some love in your life, Inspector Dark. Look closely. She could have put her bag on that chair, but it's on the table. The people on the other table are missing a chair, one is standing, but no one has taken it. Why?'

The empty chair seems occupied in a way it didn't a moment ago. Jonathan shivers, even though the sun is hot on the back of his neck.

'There's a ghost sitting on the other chair?' he says. He tries to dress his voice in sarcasm.

Frank nods. He stares at the chair with a sad smile. A woman with a buggy gives him the wide berth of those avoiding the mentally ill. Jonathan feels annoyed. Doesn't she know what's going on? Suddenly aware of what he is thinking, he stops. It is like changing a lens in his camera. Everything looks different. The butchers may have a ghost by the counter, the flower stalls a ghost who can't stop sniffing the produce.

'That's what I need to show you about ghosts,' Frank continues. 'Most ghosts are insubstantial, aimless and without consciousness; others, like wraiths, are balls of distilled emotion that can affect the living but rarer still and most interesting are those that have the same traits and personality, skills and flaws as when they were alive. They are a collection of their experiences taken out of the physical form. These few, however, especially if encouraged, can pull their memories and personalities into a tangible form and are able to converse with those that choose to hear them.'

Frank walks down the steps of Liverpool Street Underground Station.

'Where are we going?' Jonathan calls out.

'To meet your witness,' Frank replies, twinkling.

'I'd rather walk,' Jonathan says. He always prefers to walk, or take a taxi, anything that keeps the street near his feet and not layers above his head. 'Shame to take the tube on a day like this.'

'Do you want to talk to Finnegan?' Frank asks. Exasperation laces his voice.

Jonathan follows. He focuses on breathing in for six counts and out for six as people rush past. Take it easy. Breathe. There is nothing that can happen to you down here.

This is the only river in London that he doesn't love – the people that course underground. So many people, each one with their own destination and reasons for being the first onto the train and the first off again, flowing so quickly that there is no time to think.

The escalator cranks them down. Frank stands in front, looking straight ahead, seemingly oblivious to the stares.

'The trick is to not look back,' Frank says, craning his head to talk to Jonathan. 'No one wants to be clocked by an undertaker. They instinctively think that they might be next.'

Jonathan grips the edges of the rail. The ceiling is too close. The screens on the walls show rows of identical, smiling people, as if advertising a clone facility. The lines of people on the escalators do not smile. Ever. The underground people frightened him when he was a child. On a rainy day one summer holiday, Gargie took him on his first journey on the underground. She rode the escalator like it were a chariot, arms outstretched, head high. He became her page, lifting her purple skirts away from the metal teeth as she wobbled off at the bottom.

Gargie and he had got on a tube for South Kensington and she settled in for the journey, spilling over the seat. He climbed her, clambering onto her canopied lap. Four-year-old Jonathan looked around at all the people who stared into space or at their books or papers. 'Why isn't anyone speaking?' he asked.

The woman in the seat opposite smiled at him. But she didn't speak. That was weird.

'Hello!' he shouted into the carriage.

Papers were raised, some people tutted and glared at Gargie, which wasn't fair as Gargie hadn't said anything.

Jonathan scrambled off her lap and stood in the middle of people's knees. He rapped at the paper door of the man next door to Gargie. 'What are you reading?' he asked.

The man lowered the newspaper. He had eyebrows that were grey and like two fat slugs kissing. 'I'll be reading you the riot act if you don't shut up,' he said, which Jonathan thought was very rude. If Jonathan had said anything like that, Gargie would have put him straight to bed.

'Have you got a bike?' he asked the man. 'As you shouldn't be allowed to ride it this evening.' He said this very sternly.

The train juddered. Jonathan was pitched against a metal pole and banged his head.

The lights left him.

People screamed and stood on his hands as he tried to find Gargie. He could hear her calling for him but he couldn't find her. People panicked and stomped.

It was as dark as under the bed.

But scarier.

He curled up around the base of the pole and pretended that he was made of plasticine and that, even though people were kicking him, he couldn't be hurt. His hands covered his ears and, instead of the sea, which he had never seen, all he could hear was the rumbling of the underground.

'Are you with me, Jonathan?'

Jonathan looks up.

They are on the platform. Frank is holding him by the shoulders. 'I said, "are you with me?"'

Jonathan steps back towards the tiles. Pipes line the wall, wrapped in foil like seventies sci-fi. 'I'm here,' he says.

Frank looks utterly calm standing in a swell of tourists. He radiates peace like a bigger Buddha.

'Were you a special kid, then?' says Jonathan. 'Some kind of medium?'

'I simply didn't learn to dismiss it. Spirits were everywhere, right in front of me. The thing that *really* scared me was television. All those tiny people in a box in the front room, shouting at each other. Then they were in my friends' houses as well. They followed me. *That* was spooky.'

Gargie had told him stories of ghosts. They frightened Jonathan. If ghosts lived in his house then he was never alone, and they were watching him getting dressed and you weren't supposed to watch people getting dressed, he'd been smacked for that. It was confusing. Sometimes he thought he saw them. He was happy to say later that they had been his invisible friends but he remembered them. There was a girl outside his school that no one spoke to and a woman in Hamleys who wouldn't stop crying. She had slipped a box of Lego into his hand and Mum had refused to believe he hadn't stolen it. 'There was no one there,' she'd said.

Gargie believed him. She smelled of lily of the valley and was the woman other women came to. He wasn't sure for what, he just knew that whenever he went to her tiny house in Camden that another woman would be there too, crying. Gargie would not say why but he thought it must be about the ghosts. When they left she would go to the airing cupboard to feed her breathing bowl of friendship cake, a batter that she gave out to people who visited but it only grew, never diminished. Like her love. 'You have to put people's secrets somewhere, Jonathan: they're full of yeast and may rise up and spill over when you're not watching.'

Why is he thinking so much about Gargie?

'Tell me what you know about ghosts,' Frank says.

'Easy. A ghost is the soul of a person left behind when the body dies.'

'And what does a ghost do?'

'Rollerblading? Drag acts? The tarantella?'

'You're resisting. I understand. It's natural to spit sarcasm as a means of defence. Your idea of the world is falling about your feet. Now tell me what you think you know about ghosts. By the way – they can do all those things, given time.'

The train pulls in and they move to two seats, opposite each other. The carriages are nearly empty. Further down, two teenagers sit with their ears and eyes plugged into their phones; a woman fingers her Kindle; a man strokes his tablet. Frank has managed to find a place where they can talk without being overheard.

'Ghosts haunt places and people,' says Jonathan. 'They can't pass on until they have resolved some situation. They have to "let go".'

'Ah, the "unfinished business" myth. That's wishful thinking. There are stories about ghosts in every culture,' Frank says. 'And billions believe they are real, but very few accept that ghosts exist AND that this is the only world that exists. We can't face that.'

'There is nowhere for ghosts to go?' Jonathan says.

Frank nods. 'Ghosthood is not a limbo state – Earth is the only afterlife.'

Jonathan's head hurts. Occam's Razor would take its blade to the idea and cut it like a sheet on Halloween. Frank actually believes this stuff. And yet Jonathan is here. He looks around the carriage. More people have got on, several of whom are standing. 'Are those empty spaces made up of ghosts?' he asks.

'Some of them,' Frank replies. 'In one form or another. Did you notice how you were about to sit on that seat next to you, then changed your mind?'

Jonathan hadn't thought about it, he just did it.

'Well, in that seat is an attractive young woman. You did the gentlemanly thing and didn't sit on her.'

'You're joking.'

'I'm really not.' He turns to the seat next to Jonathan. 'Excuse me, young lady? My friend here, who is far richer than he is handsome, and as you can see he could be called a looker were he to get some sleep and food, would like to know your name.' Frank waits a second. He takes off his hat. 'Pleased to meet you, Emily. Have a splendid day now, won't you?

'That's Emily,' Frank says, taking out a handkerchief from his pocket. It is blue covered with white spots. He wipes his head and then replaces his hat. 'She says "hi".'

Jonathan doesn't know what to say. He had thought about signing up for the *Guardian* dating site, but this is taking it too far.

Frank carries on. 'Other than Emily, we have a chap in a bowler holding onto that middle handle, you see how it stands out further than the rest? That means a ghost is there. He just raised his hat to us. Did you know that ghosts change their livery as often as London does? They just have to regard themselves a certain way and they're wearing any clothing they can remember. It's one of the perks. Next to him is a Sleeper woman with the ghost of her Afghan hound. He's trying to lead her around.'

Jonathan feels a pang at the thought of his former pets wandering around as ghosts, looking for him. What would Maria feel about that?

'See there, between the two sets of doors? Ghosts from the Gloaming gather there. They're drawn down here and stick together, like cells. It's probably because the underground has a vegetative lull. You've probably seen Sleepers and not known. It's hard to tell the difference on the underground. No one responds to anyone else. Nobody is fully conscious.'

'They don't sound scary,' Jonathan says. 'Why are the living so scared of spirits if they're aimless or just carrying on with their lives without a body?'

'We're not supposed to talk about death,' Frank replies. 'People are superstitious – they think that if they talk about it, it will happen, whereas I still haven't won the lottery after talking about it for twenty-odd years.'

'You have to talk about death in my profession,' Jonathan says.

'And mine, but do you know what your wife wants to happen to

174

her body when she dies? Does she want to be embalmed? Buried? Cremated? What kind of memorial service does she want?'

Jonathan shakes his head. They had talked once before they were married, in his campervan on a rainy day in Rhyl, about how they would both play 'Starman' at the end of the service. They had hated the thought of the other one dead, even if, as they say, they are only in the next room. It doesn't matter if it's only the adjoining room if you can't unlock the door.

'Saying all that, people are right to fear some ghosts. The Feeders. They come in different forms to feast on pain and fear, to gain power instead of generating it themselves. Some scream. Some whisper.' Frank gives Jonathan a meaningful look.

Something Frank said snags. 'That woman. With the Afghan,' Jonathan says.

Frank nods.

'She's real. She's here in the carriage. Frank, you must be able to tell your delusions from your ghosts.'

'In some languages delusion and ghost are the same word. That woman is no more alive than the Hammers' hopes are in the Cup.'

Jonathan opens his mouth to protest but the woman and her dog aren't there.

The train slows. 'Do Not Alight at this Station, Marylebone Station is Closed for Repair,' the announcer clips. 'Do Not Alight at this Station. Marylebone is closed.'

The train slows. Frank grabs Jonathan's arm and strides along the carriage, weaving between people seen and not seen. The train stops. Frank presses the emergency button and the doors wheeze open.

Frank steps off the train, taking Jonathan with him.

Maria is on the Jubilee Line. She has just waved Simon off the train, him still insisting that she doesn't walk, that she gets a black cab from the station. She snuggles back and rests her elbows on the furry seat separators. The fabric covering the seat feels green, fresh green – the colour of the smell of roses. She still gets excited by trips on the tube. Maybe it's because she'll never be a true Londoner – the city was the place to escape to when she was a teenager on the south coast; or maybe it's simply that she's in her element when underground. Being within the earth brings her heartbeat down to something approaching normal.

She doesn't believe in reincarnation but if it *is* true, then she was probably once a badger. Or a mole. Or an apocalyptic type who liked to build bunkers. Something comfortable with the dark.

The voice comes out of the speakers. 'Waterloo.'

Maria has a girl crush on the voice of the underground. The way she says Buckhurst Hill is suggestive.

She sometimes takes a walk at half ten and treats the Jubilee Line as a lullaby. This line is one of the deeper ones, which makes her feel like she's communing with elder gods. It strides through the river like a ship; the list of stations said in that soothing voice is her shipping forecast: Waterloo, Westminster, Green Park, Bond Street, Baker Street, St John's Wood, Swiss Cottage . . . it's a list that elicits images of detectives, fairy tales and history. The ideal bedtime story.

Not that the other noises on the underground are always heartening. Right now there's an argument between a woman who's telling a young man to turn his hissing phone down. He's not keen. So much so that he's telling her to fuck off. What music does Inspector Dark like? Probably rock. Or indie folk like Ryan Adams. The train gives her random thoughts. It's the hypnotic rocking.

'Can I stroke your dog, please?' a man says. He is close. Too close. Standing above her, by the sound of it. She is used to proximity on the tube, everyone is, and everyone has learned how to zone out the surroundings and go wherever else they want to be, or whoever else they want to be with, but it doesn't feel like there's that many people on the train.

Billy stands. He snuffles the man's hand.

'He's very protective.' He is leaning over her. She's sure it isn't necessary. She's heard this voice before. It is muffled, as if speaking through a scarf, and altered, the strain showing it is not his natural voice, but she still recognises the tone.

Bond Street is coming up. She has no desire to go there; the only jewellery she likes is hundreds of years old and covered in mud. Change at Bond Street for the Central Line. She could then go over to Oxford Circus and get lost in a crowd.

She head butts her way up, hoping to get him on the way. 'We're getting off here,' she says, pushing through to the exit.

'Me too,' he says. He smells as if his clothes have been stuck in a lobster pot.

'Mind the gap,' her girl crush says as she rushes off the train. Maria wishes she gave other life advice.

She doesn't even know why she's doing this; people ask if they can pet Billy all the time.

Billy leads her through the platform crowd. She throws her awareness behind her but can't tell if that man is following. For the first time she feels more vulnerable with the blindfold on than off. She edges up one corner and turns back. A blur of moving. Seeing wouldn't help, she doesn't know what he looks like. Stupid, stupid. What would she say to the police? To Inspector Dark, who asked her to take it off for her own good? 'You're looking for a man with a muffled voice who smells like a fisherman's catch at the end of a hot day?' That will narrow it down.

Maria runs up the steps, feeling out in front with her free hand. Billy is trying to follow but he limps behind, picking up his left back leg. His arthritis is getting worse.

'Sorry,' a man says, knocking into her with the edge of something sharp and heavy. A suitcase. She holds onto the wall, gets her balance. But it is all wrong. She can't feel Billy's pull on his harness, his guidance. She cries out. The handle is in her hand but Billy is not at the end of it.

21

F rank waves to the departing carriage. 'Emily says goodbye,' he says. 'She liked you.' He winks.

'I have a wife,' Jonathan says. 'I'm not interested in anyone else. Especially women who aren't even there.'

Frank looks at him with pity. He'd love to sit down and have a heart-to-hurt-heart with him. Separation from Barbara would rip Frank up, like a prayer book in the hands of an atheist. His heart hurt enough when she died, and he knew he could bring her through. He had trained for years for that moment. Imagine if, after all the help he'd given people to come through the Gloaming, he couldn't do that for his own wife! But Jonathan's situation is different. His ex-wife has said and done things that she will never be able to take back, even if this was an attempt at attention-seeking. Sometimes people want you to fight for them, when they should fight for themselves. He'll keep quiet. Jonathan doesn't know how much Frank knows.

He leads Jonathan first to the driver's mess room. 'What are we doing here, Frank?' Jonathan asks. His jaw is clenching and un-clenching. He has the wild-eyed look of a ghost who doesn't know whether to live.

The room vibrates as a train passes underneath. 'That's the Jubilee Line,' Franks says, indicating to his feet. 'You'd think it would be the Bakerloo but that's the fun of the underground. You think you know where you are going, anticipate the twists but the map is misleading you. Nothing is at it seems.'

'That doesn't answer my question.'

Frank holds his top hat in his lap and jogs it on his knee. What if he is doing the wrong thing, involving the police? The police have been kept out of this for, well, ever. But this goes further than anything he's heard about – corruption soaking into the fabric of the city. He breathes in deeply. 'We are in this place because it's safe for the moment. Finnegan is lurking in the disused foot tunnels that used to connect the station to a building on Harewood Avenue.'

'Is this what ghosts do?' Jonathan asks. 'Haunt tube stations like old station masters?' He stands up and walks over to the sink in the corner. He turns on the tap, takes a mug from the drainer and fills it.

'Only now and again. He needs somewhere to stay. There are always ghost stations available for peace and quiet when new ghosts need to hide.'

Jonathan laughs and spits out a mouthful of tap water. There is no real joy or surprise in his laugh. 'I love that, a ghost in hiding. Ghosts make people hide under the bed, not the other way round. The worst has already happened to him, and whoever murdered him isn't going to see him now. He could make off with the crown jewels and people would just wonder why a sparkly hat was floating down Tower Hill. If ghosts did exist then it would make my job much, much more difficult.'

'It's not the living that he's hiding from. That's why this is difficult. These people, the Ring that he's told me about, there's every likelihood it has ghost informants and blackmailers as well as living. The city is not what you think it is.'

'But what—'

Frank stands and holds up his hand. He can hear Finnegan whispering to himself, getting nearer. 'He won't be long,' he tells Jonathan, stretching. This ceiling is not nearly tall enough. Do train drivers only come in small, or do they make them crawl in here like underground rats?

Finnegan appears in the doorway. He looks at Jonathan and narrows his eyes.

'We're going to have to trust him, Finnegan,' Franks says, attempting a tap on his shoulder. Sometimes you can almost feel a ghost. It's like a cobweb on your skin, only lighter.

'I'm trusting you, Frank. You've always been a friend. This bloke looks unhinged. I've seen cremains with more colour to them.'

'DI Dark is here to help you. He is investigating your death – he's as near as you can get to a doctor without a body to be doctored. Consider him your murder physician.'

Finnegan makes a sucking sound as if unsure. 'It's a tough ask to trust anyone in the Met. I know that the Ring has a number of officers working within it. I don't know any of them, which makes them all suspicious to me.'

'I will vouch for him,' Frank says. 'I believe he's one of the good ones.'

Jonathan stares at the space into which Frank is speaking. 'This is a joke, isn't it. I'm watching a man holding a conversation with an invisible friend.'

Frank feels for him. The person he trusted most in the world has fucked him over and up and over till he doesn't know which way is when. And here is Frank telling him that the world is one shared by ghosts.

'You came to see me, Jonathan,' Frank says. 'There must be something that you think Finnegan can help you with. Or me. If it's no use, then you can go back to the station none the wiser but none the more foolish either. Like any enquiry, you'd have ticked it off your list.'

Jonathan sits down and leans back in the plastic chair. 'I want to hear about his death. We withhold information so that, when a detail comes up that only a murderer could know, we have grounds to pursue the suspect. Give me a detail that only a victim would know.'

Finnegan also sits. He frowns. He is flicking between states – the Finnegan he was before joining the Ring, young, arrogant; and Finnegan at the end, nervous, paranoid, eyes shadowed and wrinkled. He seemed to age ten years in the months leading up to his death. 'Well, I was being chased, as I've told you, Frank. It's part of their ritual when they "exit" people from the Ring or if someone interferes with their work – they set you off with limited resources and have you pursued across the city. If you manage to cross beyond the M25 then you can keep your life. Of course no one has ever done it, that is known of anyway.'

'We need something concrete, Finnegan,' Frank says, watching Jonathan. 'I think Inspector Dark is five minutes away from walking out.'

Finnegan knocks Jonathan's hand. His mug tumbles onto the cracked lino. 'Is that concrete enough? Does he want me to put on a sheet and moan through the tunnels?'

Frank snorts.

'You can cut that out. I don't need theatrics,' Jonathan says, calmly picking up pieces of the mug. 'I need evidence.'

'Finnegan was saying the same thing, Jonathan. He was basically saying that he hoped you didn't need him to put on a sheet and go "wooo".'

Finnegan holds out his hands. 'WOOOOO!' he shouts in Jonathan's face.

It's probably best not to tell Jonathan about that. 'Incidentally,' Frank says, loudly to cover the sound of Finnegan's petulance, 'the cliché of ghosts wearing sheets has some truth to it – some can't quite summon themselves enough to appear to the living so they pop on something light. Most don't consider it flattering.'

Finnegan stares at his waving arms. 'Weird,' he says. 'Sometimes it looks as if my arms are barely there, others they look stronger than ever.'

Jonathan unsticks a work rota from the wall and looks behind it. 'So whenever I've seen someone in a sheet at a Halloween party then it could be a ghost?'

Frank shrugs. 'People don't lose their sense of humour when they die. Often it intensifies, like other aspects of their personalities. When you realise how absurd life is then everything can either become very serious or very silly, according to what kind of person you are. You can change after death too. People never stop moving on.'

'Don't I know it,' Jonathan says.

'How about this,' Finnegan says. 'For the last five years, my crematorium has been taking in unregistered bodies on the quiet and reducing them to ashes. Some of those are made into diamonds, some are scattered to the wind. Some coffins are empty. In return, I received a pleasant fee and help in securing planning permissions, finance and, let's say, helpful legislation. The organisation is never named but most of us call it the Ring'.

Franks relays this to Jonathan.

'So why did they kill him?' Jonathan asks. Frank can see him struggling to keep professional. His pallor looks even worse in this light.

Finnegan sits back down. The chair squeaks. Jonathan looks over and shakes his head. A man with a profession based on reason and evidence is not going to adjust well to this. Frank has been seeing ghosts since he was old enough to offer them his rattle. He remembers worrying that a ghost who sat in his room in a rocking chair would tell his mum that he hadn't slept. He became used to the behaviour of ghosts – how they come and go, how they comfort and chill the living, how they manage, through an effort of will, to thrive in the shadows of the physical world.

'I was fine going along with it for a while,' Finnegan says. 'Let's face it, it suited me, I was making a mint.'

Telling Jonathan everything as they go, Frank wonders if this is what it's like being a UN translator in one of the booths around a table of political heavyweights. Finnegan keeps going, standing up again. He stands inches from Jonathan's face and waves. Not a flicker from the detective.

'The problem came when I received a message telling me they wanted to involve my son, invite him into the Ring. And don't ask me for the fucking piece of paper, that's long gone. One of the advantages of owning a crematorium – saves on shredding. It's probably not unusual. There isn't an urn from Finch's that sits on top of a mantelpiece that doesn't have a piece of paperwork inside.'

He doesn't know whether to pass that on to Jonathan, but when he does it seems to wake the detective up. Jonathan laughs and begins taking notes, as if remembering what he's supposed to be doing.

'I knew it was only so that they had more of a grasp on me,' Finnegan says. 'They weren't after my son's skills, it was insulting really, to both of us. You've met him, I know you have – you'll know he's not the most dynamic of people. He was shy, a stay-in-his-room teen rather than a romancer like me. That isn't the world I want him in. I did all of this for him and Rosa and the family. I didn't make the decisions; I had to turn a blind eye to horrible things, I had to *do* horrible things. But you don't really want to know why they killed *me*, you want to know who to go after. I don't know exactly – I was hit from behind. But when you – or I – find them, I will haunt them for the rest of their lives. I don't know if you know what it is to love your soul mate and be parted from them before time. By the looks of you, you do; Frank does. He lives every day with the worry that Barbara cannot stay. So here we have it: I'll give you all the names I have, which isn't many. Nobody is given too much power or information till you get to the top. But I have some knowledge, otherwise they wouldn't have killed me. When I know you're taking me seriously, I'll help you in whatever way you like. That won't even be a favour, it'll be a pleasure.'

Jonathan looks up as Frank pauses in repeating Finnegan's words. 'Were you, I'm not sure how to put this, *around* when you were thrown in the river?'

Finnegan frowns. 'I don't remember the river. I have some memories of the van. I was in the back, my body that is. And then I was out of it. The engine failed in an industrial estate. Fear gave me strength enough to get out to the road and hail a cab,' he says. 'Next thing I know it's two weeks later and I'm off to Frank's in the same cab.'

'Hope the meter wasn't running,' Frank says.

'Can I have that list of names please?' Jonathan asks.

Both Jonathan and Finnegan sit down at the same time. They face each other across the room. They are mirroring each other's body language now. Frank studies them. Finnegan has just crossed his legs; Jonathan does the same. Finnegan leans forward, and so does Jonathan: Jonathan is moving to match Finnegan, suggesting that on some intuitive level he is aware of the ghost before him.

'The main problem with digging up the Ring is that I have no idea who is really running it. The people I can give you are new and low down in the pecking order, like me. One of them was the man who drove me to the river – Garry Harding. It was probably a van from his construction company, he's one of the Ring's newest recruits. He was next on the list to receive a ring so he could have been asked to kill me. I want that weaselly little shit chased. And there's Amyris Church, maker of the killing ring, as I call it. She's a piece of work. Quite the chameleon. We worked well as a team, but I can't say I care about protecting her or anyone else any more. It's the good thing about death. It gives you perspective. Beyond them and a few other low-level members, all I know is that it runs throughout the major institutions in London. The Met, government, business. It goes right to the top and bottom.'

Jonathan looks exhausted. He looks down at his notes. 'Why don't you haunt them into an admission?'

'He needs a translator,' Frank says. 'Although he doesn't need anyone else to scare the shit out of them.'

'Don't think I won't,' says Finnegan, 'but that's not enough. I want the Ring blown apart. Publicly. I want everybody who received one of those rings to be locked up for life.'

Jonathan's tongue appears at the edge of his mouth. 'Is there some sort of initiation into joining the ring?' he says. 'Seems like an organisation on such a wide, influential scale as this wouldn't give you membership just because you're useful.'

Finnegan shuffles in his seat. 'We all perform acts that you could call criminal for each other. We have to do things that cost us emotionally so that we are tied in—'

'Like insisting that your son is involved,' Jonathan says.

They are all but talking to each other now. Frank relays everything quickly and they face each other, hands in pockets, staring each other out. Both of them have things that they are hiding, Frank is sure of that.

'Exactly,' Finnegan says. He is lying, it is even easier to sense in the dead.

'But you already had the ring,' Jonathan says, moving forward. 'So what had you done that cost you emotionally? If you refused to get your son on board then how could you possibly be in possession of the ring?'

'I worked hard for them. It was in lieu of that,' Finnegan says. Jonathan can't tell that he is not meeting his eyes but Frank can. Finnegan's lying. Frank feels a sadness that spreads through him like a chill. Whatever comes out of this is only going to lead to more sadness.

Jonathan crosses his arms. He doesn't believe him either. 'I'm going to find the connections within the Ring and expose your murderer. Give me something in return. I want both of you to be on the lookout for the ghost of Tanya Baker. Ten months ago, she was brutally murdered by a man who had been stalking her. He has now passed a yellow diamond ring onto another woman. Can you track Tanya down? Would she, I don't know, haunt her house or her grave?'

'It would be a lot easier if they did,' Frank says. 'Although if spirits followed their bodies around I'd see the ghost of everybody that comes to be prepared for burial and while I did choose the job of psychopomp, I'd never have a day off. No, ghosts don't tend to care about their bodies. After all, I don't think about my rubbish after I've put it out on bin day. Often ghosts become conscious again in an entirely different place to that in which they pass. They might return to their place of birth, or where they got married, like my Barbara.'

'So if I gave you as much information on Tanya as possible, that could help?' Jonathan asks.

Frank nods. 'I'll get more details off you and ask around. If she is a ghost in London then we'll find her, although if she's a wraith or in the Gloaming then it will be harder.'

'Then this is where your role in consoling the dead is going to be useful,' says Jonathan. 'I'll need to see her by the end of the week. Tell her that we won't let her down again. Considering that I can't share this with my team,' he continued, 'I'm going to need physical, indisputable evidence of what you've told me, proof that will stand up in court and not dematerialise on the stand. Any mention of me in a train driver's retreat with an undertaker and a ghost would compromise the case, not to mention my reputation, which does lead me to ask why I'm doing it.'

'Why *are* you doing it?' Frank asks.

'The world as I knew it has altered. I can't go back. Imagine what the repercussions are for crime if someone could still be on the witness stand after they died. People wouldn't get away with their crimes by dying any more.'

'There are substances that can imprison even spirits, you know,' Frank says. 'And eternity is a long sentence.'

'I don't like the sound of that,' Finnegan says.

'Don't worry, Finnegan. I can't see the western world accepting the world as ghosted. The major religions would be shown up as card sharps.'

'It's true. There's too much invested in the world as it stands to let the shadows into the light. One whiff that I've taken on board the evidence of ghosts and the CPS will throw it out. Any decent barrister for the defence will give themselves a stroke through laughing so much.'

He stares through the empty doorway. 'Right. How do I get out of here?'

Maria's dog disgusts him. It is only a matter of time before it leaves a mess and he will have to clear it up. He is this close to slamming its head against the wall. He could leave its body outside her door. Maria would be very upset and it would work in his favour, he would declare himself there for her and it would drive her into his arms. And it would be so very easy to do away with the dribbling fool of a pet. Dogs are so stupid. It would even come trotting and panting to its own death considering how easily it went with him. That is a reflection of all the time he put in, all that hard work and foresight. He is so good to her, such a good person. He doesn't like dogs at all and here he is looking after her dog just to teach her how to behave. Now that really is love. *Not* killing it will be his wedding gift. No, here is the gift – if she shows that she has learned from his patient teaching and doesn't go to that detective again, *then* he will never lay a hand on the creature. As if it can read his thoughts, the dog trots to its makeshift bed, whining.

He hums as he makes the omelette. He was going to have kippers but he dropped them in the crush when taking the handle from her hand. Cheese and ham will have to do. It must be right. Fold it over too soon and it will be runny in the middle, wet eggs make him retch. Leave it too long and the omelette has no shake, no wobble. It is like a woman who has been to the gym so much her bottom no longer undulates when he fucks her from behind.

What would making love be like for Maria? She certainly is interested in sex. She gets her computer to read erotic stories at night, bedtime stories indeed. Maybe it doesn't matter that she's blind. Women aren't supposed to be as visual as men. Maybe it wouldn't matter. He's also heard that they have better imaginations but that is not good. When they close their eyes you don't know who they are thinking of.

He tips the frying pan. The omelette slides onto the plate. He places it on the small table.

Maybe she feels more as a result, maybe she will orgasm from him touching her skin, from kissing her prominent collarbones.

The dog looks up from his bed and yawns. Lazy animal. Does it know how hard he works for him? For her?

Picking up his cutlery, he looks down at the omelette. It is already cooling, congealing. He doesn't want it any more.

The dog lifts a paw. He has no choice but to lift the spoon and bring it down hard against its spine.

22

J onathan is nearly back to the house when his phone goes.

'All right, Guv,' Keisha says. The rustling of papers and her chirpy tone tells him that she is column-deep in a spreadsheet.

'You sound like you're nearing a conclusion on the Finch accounts.' He feels dizzy. His head is too full of things few other people know. 'Where have you got to?'

'The Finch Crematorium Group is doing very well indeed, even with an expansion that is spreading their private crematoria out into the country. He has received the rights to every new crematorium built in the country in the last five years. While that's not many, it begins to look like—'

'A monopoly,' Rider shouts out. He seems pleased to know the word.

'Anyway,' she continues. Jonathan can imagine her glare at Rider. 'Hiding under an innocuous account that led to another account that went the way of things you shouldn't ask about, I found that he was receiving ten grand every month from a catering company called Zeta Holdings. Zeta Holdings is a subsidiary of a large scale catering company that provides meals for airlines around the world. They have a large factory outside Three Bridges, close to Gatwick.'

'Any idea why Zeta Holdings would be giving money to a crematorium? Or crematoria?' Jonathan asks.

'Not yet,' Keisha says. 'Here's where it gets interesting, though, Zeta Holdings' sister company, or more like second cousin twice-removed company, is one of the regular purchasers of DMD's stock. Particularly the yellow diamonds. I haven't managed to officially get hold of the Zeta accounts so I'm not officially able to tell you that they make regular, almost untraceable, monthly payments of ten thousand pounds to hundreds of companies and individuals. It's harder to refine it further at the moment. You get to a certain point and it's like trying to pick salt out of the sea.'

'How did you find all that lot out?'

'Denver from IT.'

'Amazing – that man could hack a diamond with an egg whisk. Tell Denver that he's a genius and I owe him a pint.'

Keisha doesn't reply.

'What is it?' Jonathan asks.

'I need to talk with you. Not over the phone.' She is whispering.

'Tonight?' he asks. He had been hoping to go straight to sleep. And then he remembers the dreams that come strapped to it. 'Okay. I'll come to the office. See you in half an hour.'

'Not in the station. Somewhere no one could overhear us.'

'Come to mine,' he says, unable to think of anywhere that would be guaranteed bug-free. 'Bring a jumper – the heating's gone again but it'll be private. There'll be no one to hear us but ghosts.'

Jonathan stares at the flat-pack cupboards in the kitchen. He is knackered but he should start on them. Constructing them will help him stop thinking about Maria's dog, lost on the under-ground, and he needs to pay Neil back for his generosity and make this place decent – it should be a London crime to keep a house unlived in.

He is laying out the panels when Keisha arrives, bottle in hand, her satchel packed with papers. She walks through into the kitchen and nods. 'It suits you,' she says.

'Crumbling, past its best and haunted?'

She laughs. 'Still standing, though. Have you heard about Billy?' she asks, arranging her notes on the living room floor, the case laid out like the Giant's Causeway.

He nods. Maria had sent him a short, heartbroken message. Part of him wants to head out right now and search the streets. He'll do that tomorrow, he has already promised her. 'I told them not to drop weekend surveillance.'

'It may have happened anyway,' Keisha says. 'I'm hoping it is a coincidence.' They look at each other. Silence fills the kitchen. 'No, maybe not.'

'Your big secret had better be good news.'

'It is. Sort of. I'll get your demands out of the way first.'

'Polite requests. From your superior officer.'

'Either way, here is the sobering list you asked for, of women killed in the last ten years.'

'I should also have asked for women who are missing presumed—'

Keisha points to another list on the floor.

She is bouncing from foot to foot.

'Come on then, out with it. You realise you've built it into a big mystery,' Jonathan says. He opens the bottle and pours her a glass. 'This had better be good.'

'I didn't want to talk over the phone,' she says. 'I've become paranoid about who might be listening.'

'That's sense, not paranoia.'

'I don't know who to trust any more.' She tilts her head as if wondering if she could trust Jonathan. It needs thinking about, he's not sure that *he* trusts Jonathan at the moment.

'You could go straight to DCI Allen, if you want. Or maybe above her, I'm not sure whether I would trust her.'

Keisha pauses for a second, drinks some wine. 'It's not you I don't trust, just everybody else.'

'Why?' Jonathan asks.

'I've been following up the lead on the fake computer engineer. The manager of the PO box was quite receptive once I had explained that as a murder investigation was under way, I was within my rights to search every locker.'

'You do know that you're standing so far outside of your rights that you can't see them any more?' Jonathan says. He pours himself some of the wine and settles into the armchair. It is good to have company in the cottage. Visible company. The cottage seems cosy for once, friendly. As if nightmares could never happen.

'Oh yes,' Keisha replies. She grins at him. Drinks more. 'I gave him Foister's meagre description and a still of the CCTV footage. For once we got lucky. It rang a bell.'

Jonathan frowned. 'Seems unlikely.'

'I know,' she says. 'It was the hat – he remembered thinking it strange that a man wear a hat all through a hot summer. He dropped something off last week so it was still on their own CCTV system.' She pulls a still out of her papers and holds it out.

Jonathan takes it. The man in the hat is slotting something into the open PO box. 'Did you get a look inside?'

'Sure did.' Her grin gets wider.

'Then could you tell me, please?'

She shows him another picture. 'Don't worry, I haven't touched anything or compromised evidence, just taken pictures in case things mysteriously disappear. I've declared it a potential crime scene and had it locked up till the SOCOs are sent down.' The picture is of, among other things, a glove, a necklace and a clay pipe. Most match the description of items Maria has reported missing.

'Why all the secrecy? You could have told me in front of everyone and got all the glory.'

'I told you I didn't know who to trust for a reason.'

'Go on.'

'I thought I would do some initial digging into who rented the box.'

'That's either showing great initiative or criminal tendencies.'

'Both,' she says. 'Anyway, I traced the account back. It took a while but I got there. It's someone on the team.'

'Who?'

'Denver.'

23

Day Six

Pudding Lane is bollard-grey and straight out of the seventies yet Jonathan shivers, imagining the ghosts of the Great Fire walking beside him. He nods to them, just in case, out of respect.

Blake Merry's Private Crime Museum is in the upstairs of a shabby-looking house off Pudding Lane. Like Maria, Blake Merry is a sifter of secrets but in his case the mud he is raking through is murder. Many officers in the Met consult with him on criminal history but Jonathan is sure that there is more to Merry than that. He has been here several times in his career and he is still not sure where Merry stands on crime.

Blake Merry opens the door and leads Jonathan up the thick-carpeted stairs. 'Come through into the study,' he says, offering him a sherry. A fire tickles the coals in the hearth. Jonathan stands in front of it, taking some comfort in its warmth.

'Please, sit down,' Blake says, pointing to the armchair next to Jonathan. He is thin and bent over, like a scythe. He sweeps round, tending to his collection as if it were a zoo. He feeds leather-bound books with neatsfoot and lanolin, turning them over in his hands to nurse them with oil; grooms the collection of dolls found at crime scenes; talks to Crippen's door handle, the lost Ripper letter, the acid bath itself, as if they would at any minute talk back to him and wish him a very good day.

Jonathan settles back into the armchair and sips the ash-dry sherry. Merry hands him a porcelain hot water bottle, warmed to blood temperature. 'You look a little cold. I like to place it behind my back in that chair. It was a gift from my father,' Merry explains. 'He bought this for me at an auction. The provenance said it belonged to Amelia Dyer.'

'The "angel-maker".'

'Exactly so, Jonathan.' Blake blinks. 'Yes, I can see from your face that you're not keen. Me neither.'

He is not merry about crime. He takes it very seriously, but every now and again he smiles when he talks about a favourite murder or misdemeanour, like a candle flaring up when a window opens.

'I need your help on a confidential case, Blake.'

'That is why I am here.'

'I can't say where I got the information but I believe that there is a network, a ring in London and maybe beyond, that is connected in some way by a yellow diamond ring, made out of human cremains. The members of the ring seem to be well-connected or rich or useful, preferably all three.'

Blake blinks. He steadies himself against a bookshelf. 'I think I need more sherry,' he says, pouring it into his half-empty glass.

'Are you all right?' Jonathan asks.

'Perfectly. I don't think I can help, I'm afraid. It was a delight to see you, though.' He walks to the door as if to show Jonathan out.

'Two people have been killed, a woman is in danger and I don't know how far this organisation flows. Help me, please.'

Blake stares at him for at least a minute, tapping his fingers on the shelf. He then nods and moves across the room to his notorious filing system. He has no computer, no database, just his brain and thousands of notes on every crime committed in London, written on postcards in tiny handwriting, decipherable only by Merry and kept in an apothecary's cabinet. It would be a great loss to crime investigation if there were to be a fire. And, indeed, when he dies. Then Jonathan remembers. If ghosts exist then Blake will barely notice dying, marking the passing from life to death with only a note filed under 'G' for ghosts, although he'd probably prefer the term 'revenant'. If Merry knew about the ghost world then he would devote the rest of his life to finding dead murderers and getting down their accounts. Perhaps he is already. What if Jack the Ripper is living on as a ghost? Imagine the offers he would get.

'Here we are.' Merry holds up a file marked, barely legibly, as 'Crime rings – cross-institutional'. It is thick. Very thick.

'Any chance that I can have a look through that?' Jonathan asks.

'None whatsoever,' Blake says, merrily. His long fingers sort through the cards and clippings, tutting at some, muttering to himself. 'Here we are,' he says, retrieving a note card and handing it to Jonathan.

'You're going to have to translate for me, Blake. I forgot my glasses.'

'You don't wear glasses, Jonathan.'

'No wonder I forgot them, then. Please, read out your shorthand otherwise I'll have to admit I can't.'

Blake pushes his own pebble glasses down his nose to read his notes. His eyes are the colour of his sherry. He nods once. 'This is a rumour, you understand, if one added to over many years. The details were passed on to me by an officer at New Scotland Yard. He had been involved in the Ring for years but was dying and felt that the knowledge was corroding him from the inside. He asked me to keep it confidential, and only to let on if someone honest came looking.'

'You think I'm honest?' Jonathan asks.

'I believe you are looking for the right reasons,' Merry replies.

'Has anyone else come looking other than me?' Jonathan asks.

'A few,' Blake says. He then turns his hawk-like head away – the gentleman's way of telling another gentleman to desist with the line of questioning. Another gentleman would comply.

'Who?' Jonathan asks.

Blake looks at him with reproach. He folds his arms.

'So what is this rumour?' Jonathan resists looking at his watch. Blake can't be hurried. He'll sulk and curl away into the corners of his shelves.

'The yellow ring was first talked about in some circles in the nineteenth century. The city was emerging from the industrial revolution into empire building. Some people thought that capitalism functioned best when there were influential people underpinning it, making sure that vital businesses never collapsed. Such an event would leave the country and the elite vulnerable. As a result, wealthy people pledged to support each other, and to seal the deal, as they say, there was an initiation ceremony that involved winning their trust. On completion of this rite, a mourning ring was given to the new initiate.'

'A mourning ring?'

'Mourning jewellery was popular in the period. It was usual to wear a ring, locket or bracelet that contained a lock of a beloved's hair. Obsessed with death, the Victorians. Such a shame the world has changed. It is quite for the worse.' He thinks on that for a moment then shakes his head. 'I've got the one that he gave me, if you want to see it.' Blake sails through into the next room where he has shelves of boxes, big and small, in which to keep his exhibits. He brings one back into the study then, spinning through an enormous tangle of keys, chooses one by sight and opens the box. Inside, in a smaller box, is a beautiful topaz ring. He lifts a hidden lid in the top of the ring. A coil of hair sits in the centre and in tiny letters on the lid is written 'forever kept'.

'The horrible twist is that, according to the rumour, the hair was from a victim, killed to show that the murderer was loyal to the ring.'

Jonathan had known Finnegan was lying. Who had he killed to get hold of the ring?

'It gets worse, although this may be embellishment. The person killed had to be a family member or close friend. That way they knew they were committed before they got the ring.'

Jonathan looks at the ring. The hair is soft and blonde. Child's hair. He won't touch it. 'Anything that could point to the use of the yellow diamond ring in modern times?' he asks.

Blake Merry hesitates. For the first time since Jonathan has known him, he looks frightened. 'Be careful,' he says. 'One of the reasons it's called the Ring is the circles in which you have to turn to break it. Dossiers and people get lost down the middle.'

'You're saying you don't want to get involved.'

Merry looks away. Some dismiss Merry as a peddler of paranoia and superstition, selling posh Penny Dreadfuls to the Met and collectors, but he digs things up in the grey wastelands between crime and the law that put him in danger.

'You're not being threatened, are you?'

'All I know is whispers, Jonathan.' He is lying. Everyone lies.

'I've had enough of whispers. Anything could help – people are being killed.'

'I prefer to stay in the past,' Blake says. 'I do not dirty myself with the present.' He returns to polishing his books.

Jonathan emerges onto Pudding Lane. The imagined ghosts have increased in number. He stuffs his hands into his pockets. He still doesn't have any gloves. The meeting with Merry has done little to make him feel more positive. Once again, the streets have shifted under his feet. The world is not as he thought a day, a week, a year ago. It is cold and full of spirits. Everything he thought he could rely on has changed. He is being divorced, he has no home, no family, no love, no evidence that can support what Frank and Finch have told him – he can't even control his tins or toothpaste tube. But ghosts and personal disaster are nothing compared with corruption on such a scale.

He takes out his phone and calls Keisha. She answers immediately. 'Where have you been, Guv, it's all going on here.'

'I need you to look something up for me,' he says. 'Find out if there have been any deaths in Finnegan's extended family or friendship circle in the last few years.'

'Why?'

'Tell you later.'

'Anything else you want me to do?'

'Yes. Cut the sarcastic tone. I presume Denver has been taken in?' he asks.

'Yes, Guv. He's in custody. He wasn't very happy by the sound of it.'

'I bet he wasn't.'

'SOCOs are on their way to search his flat in Hackney. We've got problems here, though, sir. The IT team is pissed off that we're opening an investigation, say that he is being framed. They went straight to DCI Allen who told them that she had OK'd it. She was great, actually, seemed keen to know everything.'

'Did she now? I'll be in to interview him as soon as possible. Do you want to join me? He wouldn't be there without you.'

'I need to do something first but I'd love to. The thought of him doing this under our noses makes me feel sick. Can't wait to see his face when we tell him what we've got on him. There's more coming, as well. Ed is in the middle of tracing the graffito girl's tracks from the point where she made the first Braille wall. He has called in tapes from across the city to find out where she lives. Celeste says he looks like he's been up for days but then lots of single guys look like that, it's all that . . .' She stops. Silence. 'Sorry, Guv, I—'

'Let's move on, shall we?' Jonathan says.

Keisha makes a noise that he'll take for assent. 'Anyway, both lead to the same place. She's sharing a flat in New Cross. We checked out the tenancy agreement – in terms of age, she's most likely to be Aggie Wright. I put the name through SWAAG and, guess what, she's had community service for vandalism.'

'And you're off there now, right?'

'I'm standing outside,' Keisha replies. 'With Rider.'

'Good. Tell Ed to have the day off, although that's probably a punishment to him. Any word on Billy?'

'I've checked with the RSPCA, Battersea, Missing Pets Bureau, rehoming charities, vets . . .' Keisha says. She's going above and beyond, as usual. 'Nothing at all. The positive is that we also haven't heard from the stalker. I'd expect him to gloat in some way. It's still possible that Billy ran off into the crowd. He's chipped so he still may be handed in, you never . . .' She trails off.

'I hope so,' Jonathan says. He doesn't want to think of what the stalker would do with the dog.

Maria shuts the window on the salt-rich smell of the Thames. She'd hoped to sink her thoughts into the archaeological dig at St Barts but the city ditch, fascinating as it is, is no match for the moment that keeps playing over and over in her mind – the second when she lost her physical connection with Billy. She feels his absence like a strong presence. It tugs at her like a new moon.

'Should haves' whisper in her head: she should have stayed with Simon; she should have listened to Jonathan and Keisha; she should have held Billy close at all times.

Hugh's heavy steps command the hallway. They stop near her

door. 'You coming out with us tonight?' he asks. 'We've booked a table for seven-thirty.'

'I don't fancy it, thanks,' she says. She's not going to tell him that she has plans with Jonathan tonight.

'You don't seem your usual self,' he says, several metres away.

'I haven't been sleeping well,' she replies.

'No. I know.' His voice fills the room. 'No Billy today?' he asks. There is something briny in his tone.

'Not today.' She manages to keep back the tears until he leaves.

'I absolutely love you and, were I not a lesbian through and through, I would do all that is unholy with you,' Keisha shouts down the phone. She punches the air as she walks up the street.

'A thank you is all that's needed,' Ed says. She can feel the blush on his skin from here.

'You'll have all the thank yous you can manage, you gorgeous hunk of genius. I can't believe how much you've found. Are you all like that, you pixellated pixies? We should get your brains put in jars.'

'Can we finish using them first?' he asks.

'Let the poor bloke off the phone,' Rider says from the pub bench over the road.

She carries on talking to Ed. 'The Guv says you can have the day off, by the way. Up to you, though. You deserve it.'

'That's harassment, you know, talking to him like that,' Rider calls out when she rings off. 'If I did that I'd be up on a charge.' He's always trying to stop Keisha having any fun. Both of them will be angling for the DI spot when the boss gets promoted, or removed. Unless he can pull this case around, it looks like he's tumbling head first into whatever is worse than a desk job. Such a shame – he used to be brilliant.

Rider comes over, smelling of knock-off aftershave and swagger. He'd be a halfway decent detective if he lost a third of the attitude, and a handful of the gunk on his hair. He rings the bell.

A bed-headed young man opens the door, rubbing his eyes. He's wearing trunks and nothing else.

'I'm DS Baxter, this is DS Rider. Is Aggie in?' Keisha asks, brightly. She's wearing jeans and a hoodie, similar to Aggie's uniform.

He nods and yawns. His breath smells of tooth decay. Walking two steps down the hall, he bangs on a door. 'Aggie,' he calls. 'Got some people saying they're the police for you.' Even that seems to be an effort. He'll probably go for a lie-down, now.

The door opens and a tall girl comes out wearing pyjamas. Don't these young people have jobs to go to? 'What is it?' she says to him. Then sees Keisha. Her eyes dart to a gap in the doorway, just as Rider steps forward to fill it.

'DS's Baxter and Rider here, we'd like to ask you some questions,' Rider says.

'Come in,' she says, sullenly.

She takes them into the kitchen and sits them round a pine table covered with box files, books and memory sticks stashed in cereal bowls. On the wall is a selection of watercolours, 'Kanga' scrawled at the bottom.

'So you're a fine artist as well as a graffiti artist,' Keisha says, standing up to look closer at the pictures.

'I don't see the distinction,' Aggie says. She has bright teeth and hair that has been wrestled into plaits.

Rider lays down stills of Aggie placing the clay dots on the walls. He clears his throat. 'This is an informal interview but if you give us any trouble at all then we will arrest you for vandalism and aiding and abetting a serious crime.'

'What crime?' she says, her voice rising. 'I only did some guerrilla sculpture.'

'That's a new way to describe harassment,' Keisha says.

'I don't understand,' Aggie says. 'I was sponsored as part of my Project Starter. You know, you set up an account and people donate money in return for a bespoke artwork. I get to eat; they get some art. This was by far the coolest commission so far.' She looks at the pictures with sparkling eyes. 'It looks all right, doesn't it? I'm going to use it for my portfolio. I love the idea that it's a message only a few people can read, and then only with their hands. It's so direct and personal.'

'It's part of a murder enquiry,' Keisha replies. Her voice is low, accusatory.

'Whoah,' says Aggie. 'That's where you're wrong. It's a love story.'

'How did you come to that conclusion?' Rider asks. He is staring at her as if she is an alien, albeit a beautiful one.

'I deliver messages to a mystery woman all round London. I see them as love letters to the city,' Aggie says.

Keisha shakes her head. Artists.

'I've got three more to do. Get this: tomorrow I'm spelling out a wedding vow in pebbled Braille alongside St Bride's church.' Aggie smiles. 'Isn't that cute?'

'Get this,' Keisha says, wanting to take the girl's head and scream into her ear. 'The engagement ring you delivered was made of human remains, wrapped around a severed finger. Still think that's romantic?'

Keisha bursts into Jonathan's office, fuming. 'She told us about two messages that even Ed hasn't found,' she says, '"I love you" in bottle tops and "Come to me" in Smarties lids, both on the route that Maria takes to the Bermondsey foreshore.'

Jonathan tenses his fist. She would have passed them today, her hand trailing centimetres beneath the Braille.

'You were right about the weddings – the banns are to be made against the walls of St Bride's church.'

He pictures the walk by the church on Fleet Street, towards St Paul's, passing the forbidding doors of the Inns of Court. 'That's the journalist's church, isn't it?' he asks. Perhaps the stalker was telling her something, revealing something intimate about himself. 'It's possible that he's a journalist. Look into it, would you?' Something is tickling the back of his mind. His instinct is trying to speak but can't be heard above the others' whispers. Anyway, he can't trust his instinct. 'What else?'

'The SOCOs found Maria's perfume in Denver's bathroom cabinet.' She pauses. 'And Tanya's.' One of the items that Tanya had first reported missing.

He mustn't jump to conclusions. Or let the urge to punch Denver take over. Both Jonathan and Keisha need to calm down. 'What are the results on Finnegan's relatives?'

'Are we really going to do this now?' Keisha says.

'Just tell me. Slowly.'

She sighs. 'OK. There were two results for Finnegan – his brother-in-law died in a boating accident and a close friend of his was killed while they were on a jolly to Holland.'

'Any investigation into Finnegan's involvement?'

'The records show that he had very strong alibis at the time of both.' Keisha's breath has slowed.

'I'm sure they do. Right. I think we're ready now. Let's see what Denver has to say, shall we?'

Denver is on a chair in the centre of the interview room. There is no table to hide behind. He is ashen. His solicitor sits next to him, briefcase between his knees.

Jonathan breathes out the anger that is streaming through him. It gives him strength but will not help.

Keisha takes Denver through the tape etiquette and repeats the charge. Jonathan positions his chair in front of him.

'This is wrong,' Denver says. He reaches for Jonathan's shoulder. Jonathan pulls away. 'Let me look at the account, I can trace who hacked me. It's too easy, don't you see? I'm being framed.'

His solicitor whispers in his ear.

'You're wasting time,' Denver says to Jonathan. 'Don't stop looking. He's still out there. It's Day Six.'

He hasn't sat down with Margery Dark in years, not properly. Usually she appears at his door at some point in the month, a confused ghost in tow, and then leaves to ferry the living and the dead around London. Today she's sitting in the mourning room with a Scotch on the table next to her. She inhales the fumes like a Delphic oracle. He would say it was a bit early for that, not even ten in the morning, but what does it matter to a spirit?

'To what do I owe this tremendous pleasure, Frank?' Margery asks, picking up the glass to catch another whiff of whiskey. 'I've been on since six and had some nightmare customers in already, only one of them a ghost. Now he had a legitimate beef with the world. The living ones natter on about traffic and house prices and I want to slap them, I really do.' She turns her attention to him, looking at him with eyes that spook him with their perception. 'You're worried, Frank. What's going on?'

Tears are forming already. He can't let himself be taken over with what's happened to Barbara. Other people need him. 'I need your help. Do you remember giving a lift to a Finnegan Finch a few days ago?'

Margery nods. 'He was in a state. It wasn't the first time I saw him. I picked him up in Barking of all places. He ran out of energy within minutes and disappeared. The other day he seemed almost fully realised although he had no idea that he was dead. I don't know who I feel for most, sometimes: those that know they're ghosts and have to deal with it or those in denial. I still take one woman around to work every day just as I did before her car crash. She does her make-up in the back. It's amazing to watch: no face to make up but, right in front of the mirror, her features becomes more pronounced, her lips get redder. Amazing thing, an act of will.'

Frank takes off his hat and plays with the feathers. 'Your Jonathan is keen to help. He was investigating a murder last year . . .'

Margery puts down the whiskey glass. 'Johnny would help a nit onto his scalp. He has a heart you could stow away in.'

'Did you know that he was living next door?'

Margery sits with her legs wide, her paisley skirt spread across her knees. Her white hair is in a candyfloss puff around her face. Her grin shows off teeth that rarely got a glimpse of a dentist. 'I might have heard tell. It's better than him sleeping in his office or in the bed of that wife of his.'

'You didn't like her then?' Frank asks.

'Lovely girl, but she'll never stop looking. Happiness for her is always in the next street, only it turns out to be a cul-de-sac without a sufficient turning circle. She'll leave this new one within a year or, worse still, she'll go back a street, like a penalty in Monopoly, and try to take up with Jonathan again.'

'You don't lose interest in anything, do you?' he says.

'Why would I, when there's so much to marvel, grumble and wonder at? Of course I look in on my family every now and again. Although there's not much I can do when they don't know I'm still here.'

'What if Jonathan does know?' Frank says.

'You haven't told him, have you?' Margery says, stomping down her stick. 'He pushed his ability away when he was a child, it will be a shock to find it again. His job would become infinitely more complex if he knew about ghosts.'

'He knows about ghosts,' Frank says.

'Thanks to you, I suppose?' Margery says. 'Judging from the look on your face. Well that's scuppered his year, as if he doesn't have enough to think about. Honestly, Frank, you don't think.'

'It could help him prevent another murder,' Frank says. 'So yes, I told him the bare minimum about the ghost world. Not about you, of course.'

Margery settles her chin onto her hand. 'Oh blow it,' she says. 'He won't know which way is up any more.'

'Will you go to him?' Frank asks.

'I don't know if it's right,' she says. She looks like a young version of herself now, unsure. 'I don't know how useful it would be for a grown man to have his Gargie back, that's if he ever gets used to seeing ghosts again. I've given him all the advice he needs and more.'

Frank shrugs. 'I think he could do with some help at the moment. He seems lost.'

Margery rarely looks this sad. 'I'll think on it.' She lets out a long breath and gets up with a heave and a sigh. She moves to the hard chair nearest Frank. 'How can I help him in a roundabout way, for now?'

'He's asked me to look out for a young woman, a newly departed, who could be a key witness for a murder case. Her own murder.'

Margery laughs. 'They'd have a job getting the jury to believe her testimony.'

'The person who stalked and murdered her has a new obsession. A young woman who, if I'm reading between the staves right, is something of an interest to young Jonathan.'

'He never liked to keep things simple.'

'Can you help me find Tanya Baker?' Frank asks. 'She lived in a flat above Shoreditch High Street, number sixty-three, and worked at a swanky gym round the corner. You know everyone, Margery, I know you can winkle her out. She might not even be in London,' Frank says. 'She may be a traumatised mess but we've got to try. There isn't much time.'

'Tanya, that rings a bell.' Frank looks to the stairs, biting his lip. 'What's behind this, Frank? You're not telling me something, I can tell. You're making me nervous.'

He shuffles, nervously.

'How's Barbara?' Margery asks. 'I haven't seen her about. Someone told me she was ailing.'

'She's not doing well.' The tears are coming now. Her kind, big, worried face has set him off. Tears drip off his chin onto his pressed white shirt.

'Where is she? Upstairs?' Margery says. She takes the form of her younger, more athletic self and sprints up the stairs. She does enjoy being able to be at once young and old and in-between.

'She's through here.' Margery pretends she doesn't see Frank's tears. She enters the darkened room.

Barbara is on the floor, her body curled like a monkey's paw.

Margery crouches next to her. Barbara is barely there. Her outline has a drawn-out pulse, becoming more vivid for one second out of every five. Not a good sign.

'She didn't have enough resistance to stop falling through the bed,' Frank says. His face looks like a guilty dog's. Big Frank is blaming himself. Barbara will be worried about worrying him. And so it goes on.

Margery stamps on the floor. 'The floorboards are oak?' she asks. Oak is a blocker of ghosts: one of the few substances that they cannot pass through easily.

Frank nods. Without the oak, who knows where Barbara would fall. His hand covers his heart as if stopping it from falling out.

'Can you talk, sweetheart?' she asks Barbara.

Barbara does not reply. She doesn't even turn her head towards the sound.

'She wants to leave me,' Frank says. He sits down on the bed and holds a pillow to his stomach. 'I'm keeping her here.'

Margery feels a charge in the room. Something has woken up. She walks around the room, listening.

'If I wasn't so selfish she'd be able to go. I haven't once considered her—'

'Shut up, Frank,' Margery says. She sees herself at her largest and

tallest. When she's like this, her voice alone could send errant punters running from her cab. 'You're feeding it. Drawing it in with pain
and negativity. Once she has nothing left, it will start on you.'

'What will?' Frank says. He paces the room, glaring at the walls as
if he could stop his house falling down around him.

'Barbara isn't wishing herself out of existence. Can't you see she's
fighting the urge to go with everything she has? It must be a terrible
tug upon her, poor love.'

'What is? What's using her up?' Frank asks. His eyes are desperate.

'A Whisperer. You haven't heard it rustling and talking?

Frank shakes his head. 'No. I wish I had.'

'Maybe you're too robust to see or hear it.'

'What can I do?' His voice splinters.

'It keeps low to the floor so this is just making her worse. Raise her
up, on oak, if you can. Counteract the poison – whisper how much
you love her, tell her of her worth. Most importantly, if you can, get
her to see it as a parasite, a separate entity. If she can externalise it
she may stand a chance.'

Hope fireworks in his eyes. 'It's outside of you, Barbara,' he says.
She gives a low moan.

'Tell yourself the opposite of what it whispers,' Margery tells her.
'It runs from that. It hates to be contradicted. Do not give it compas-
sion, tell it to fuck right off and be done with you.'

Margery bends to stroke Barbara's forehead. Tiredness falls on her
like night. This is a sick room. She turns for the door and beckons
for Frank to follow.

'I have never encountered one of the Few before,' he says at the
top of the stairs. The Whisperers were just one of the Few – the tiny
percentage that feed off the majority.

'I wish they were few,' Margery replies. 'I would say there was one
in every other house. If it isn't already whispering, or splintering or
possessing then it's waiting for an opportunity to strike.' Margery
turns to him. 'You need to look out for yourself as well as Barbara.
She can't stay present if you've already left.'

'It can't kill me, though, can it?'

'It can stopper up your heart with hatred until it breaks.'

'And Barbara?'

'Unless it can be turned around she will be gone. There will be nothing of her left. I'm sorry, Frank.'

He sees her to the door. 'Thank you, Margery. What can I do for you?'

'You can keep an eye on Jonathan. My Johnny Darkling. I hear whisperings around him too.'

It fed so well it overslept.

Its belly is empty again. It is never full for long.

Ss-cut.

It scissors the air with its tongue. The house remains full of pain. The bald man, the living one, is ready to be tasted. He will not last long.

His heart has not the muscle to withstand the hurt.

That will come when she is gone.

Ss-cut
You are not wanted
Ss-cut

It will take just one more slice
of her soul. One last

cut.

24

Jonathan stands on a table and holds out a hand. The meeting room fills up with silence. A mutter bubbles up, then pops to a stop. 'Thank you all for staying on,' he says. 'You've already given up much of your spare time in the last five days. I am proud of every single one of you.' Jumping down, he looks as many of his team in the eye as he can.

Rider and Keisha stand at opposite sides of the room, bookending the team; Sally is here as the sole representative from IT as the others are supporting Denver, denying that he could be the stalker; Celeste and Ed are standing together, blinking as if their contact lenses have dried out from the life-force-sucking images they watch. The forensics team who are in the building and working on the case are there; Mike Reynolds and the SOCOs . . . they are all looking at him and each other with suspicion.

'We have a rift in the team. A long tear down the centre because we suspect one of our own. I haven't done enough to hold the team together so far and I am sorry. I've been distracted, chasing other leads while everyone else has been doing the work to drive it all forward. Thank you all. The work you do often goes unthanked and unseen but you are the stars behind London's sky.'

The silence feels clearer this time. Ed starts clapping, followed by Keisha and then others join in.

Mike doesn't. He stands with his arms folded. 'That's all very well, Guv, but some of us feel excluded from the investigation. We know that theories aren't being shared with the team. If there isn't cohesion, then the team fails by default.' Supportive murmurs criss-cross the room.

'I apologise for being distracted; I ask forgiveness for being unavailable; I tell you straight up that I have been a dick at times but I am in no way sorry for the decisions I have made as a DI. This rift has been caused by evidence pointing to one of our own, by aspects that I still cannot tell you. It is possible Denver has been framed just as it is possible that Denver has used information he received from the team to harass, stalk and kill. I stand by my decisions and if you want out then by all means transfer or leave. Is that clear?'

Jonathan's last word sings around the room followed by a welling of 'Yes, Guvs'.

'Right, then,' he says. 'I reckon we should all go down the pub where I shall buy everyone a quick pint. You coming, Mike?'

Margery sticks her head out the window. She feels the rush of air passing through her. That's cleared out whatever was trying to stick to her at Frank's. It was one of the most powerful Whisperer scents she had encountered. She hopes Jonathan can resist it.

It would help him if she could find Tanya. She's been back to the station where she picked her up in case she had a connection with it. There are plenty of ghosts who hang out at King's Cross and Charing Cross and St Pancras. Tanya wasn't one of them.

Margery eases her cab into Shoreditch. Tanya died young, maybe she liked to go to the bars. She scouts for smashed shop windows and checks each sign – they often buckle or fall when a wraith cries. People think that hooligans and drunkards cause broken shop windows. Not necessarily so. Much is blamed on booze that ghosts get away with.

Margery parks round the corner on a double yellow and wanders up to Tanya's old flat. It is now rented by a lovely couple with a very friendly Maine Coon. There is no sign of a squatter. You can always tell if a ghost is sharing a home with the living because there is the strange sensation of being squashed into a room that should be big enough. It will also smell of burned out candles, hard to tell in a student flat. Poltergeists and teenagers are linked for a reason.

No one looks round in Goodwin's Gym when the automatic door opens but nobody enters. Two girls with implausible eyebrows stand behind the desk, nattering about their abs. Margery must have had abdominal muscles once otherwise she couldn't have marshalled her motorbike round London, but they were modest and liked to stay swathed. She certainly never saw them but that never bothered her or any of her men. The living are so concerned about making their bodies smaller or bigger, maybe because they won't be in them for long.

Margery scans the room. Bike pedals spin, trainers thud on running machines. There is no sign of a furious dervish of a ghost. As she moves towards the weights area, she notices an open door, leading out the back. Ah, there are the candles and the low electrical buzz. Ghosts vary in their tone: wraiths like Tanya vibrate in G minor, and those in the gloaming in A minor. Not that she knows what all that means in music terms, the Gloaming just sounds sad.

She follows the corridor round to a storeroom filled with toilet rolls, hand soap, hand lotion and towels. On the floor, in a shimmering pile, is Tanya Baker.

Jonathan rushes up the stairs of Pedlar Cottage. He stayed longer than he thought at the pub and now has just over an hour before he meets Maria. What to wear though? The usual man-in-mid-forties uniform of jeans, T-shirt, jacket? Whatever he chooses, it won't be the tie that was laid out on his bed when he got up this morning. It's time to leave. He'll ring Neil and tell him to try another tenant. The ghost has won.

Maria won't care what he's wearing, not because she cannot see, but because it won't occur to her to mind. They are going to hand out flyers on the Jubilee Line, asking for information on Billy's disappearance. He's had it authorised as part of the investigation and, who knows, it may even help but it's a stretch, even for him, to have Maria there. He has been justifying it to himself on the way home, telling himself it's not a date.

Jonathan opens the wardrobe and takes out his Paul Smith suit, the dark grey one with a purple map of the underground on the lining. He lays it out on the bed, angling the limbs of the jacket and trousers so that it looks like a crime scene outline. That's about as much fun as he can have with men's clothes, if you don't count kilts. There is so little variety: do you want skinny cut or regular with your jean? He should have lived in the eighteenth century when men wore heels, wigs and astounding hats and no one thought anything of it. Now men don't get to play peacocks, just cocks in identikit feathers.

He'd *like* to wear his long black jersey dress. It's comfortable but close-fitting, flattering. He hasn't wanted to wear it, or any other 'women's' clothing, for nearly a year – the thought made him sad and shut down. Many things came to a halt when his marriage stopped – he no longer listened to music, avoided his favourite fish restaurant in Clapham. All these reminded him of life with Natalie, for better and for worse.

He takes the Donna Karan dress out of the plastic shroud and places it next to the suit on the bed. Joining the sleeve of the suit to the sleeve of the dress, he sets them dancing across his sleeping bag.

He checks his watch. He's got time, just. He strips down to his trunks then pulls on the dress. It has a wide neckline and follows the V of his torso down to his waist then clings to his legs right down to the knee. He straightens his shoulders back then looks at himself in the dresser mirror. There – there it is. The twinkle in his eye he thought had gone for good. What would Maria think? She'd be unable to see him in the dress but she'd feel it. Would she accept it? Accept him?

He'd do his nails red if he had time for them to dry, and the bravery to walk into the night as a DI wearing a dress and nail polish. It would be in the *Daily Mail* within minutes. He'd be 'The Transvestite Detective', the puns would come running – a complex human being reduced to a by-line and a lifetime of justifying himself to strangers about why he likes clothes. It's a misleading description – *trans*-vestite, *cross*-dresser – as if gender were two opposing riverbanks: if that is to be the way, for now, he would rather swim between them.

Both his work and his personal phones are ringing. One is Frank and the other is Natalie. And he has to leave if he is to get to Maria on time.

Margery pulls up outside the funeral parlour just as Frank arrives in a hearse. He parks round the back then runs out. 'I got here as soon as I could.' He looks into the cab. Tanya is flailing in the back, raging in between tears. 'I've tried to call Jonathan but he's not answering.'

Tries again but again there is no answer. 'What are we going to do with her?' he asks.

Margery has no bloody idea. She's a broken one. That stalker should be stopped before he ruins someone else's eternity.

'Listen, sweetheart,' Margery says, gathering as much of the wraith to her as she can. It's like trying to herd a rain cloud. 'I can't keep singing to you all night.' It had been the only way to get her into the taxi, soothing her with snatches of songs and strokes to her constantly changing hair. Margery sings 'Hushabye Mountain' as they walk up to the front door of the funeral parlour. Frank joins in. His rich baritone gives it solidity. He is looking around the parlour as if something is wrong. Soothing Tanya through into the mourning room, they lock the doors and stare at each other.

'We could talk to her before he gets here,' Margery says. 'Lay the groundwork. You go first, you know more than me about the case.'

'You're better at this than me.'

'I've never taken that excuse from anybody – you only get good by doing. So do, Frank.'

Tanya howls as if her soul is being hoovered up.

'It's OK,' Frank says, approaching her from the side, keeping his arms wide and in view. He smiles to show he is not a threat.

Tanya flinches and shrinks away, knocking books from shelves. She crawls into the corner of the room and tries to slink into the cupboard, as if getting out of their eye-line will save her. Margery's rescue pets behaved like this, all teeth, claws and hisses, but beneath that was a need to be held and touched and shown that everything would be OK.

'I know this is very hard for you, darlin',' Margery says, squatting down beside her. 'But there is someone who needs your help.'

Tanya looks at her with eyes every bit as suspicious as they have a right to be.

'You've had a horrible time, both before you died and after. You must be a very brave woman to be here at all, not curled up in a ball in the Gloaming. I need you to show some of that courage tonight.'

Tanya is listening, not responding yet, but definitely listening.

'The man who attacked you and took your old life away has targeted another young woman. She is in great danger. That bastard will attack her if she does not do exactly as he says. You know what he is like far better than me. If you could help to find and arrest this man then this young lady won't have to suffer as you did. The detective on the case is my grandson, as it happens, whom I would trust with anyone's secrets, sorrows or heart.'

Tanya has coalesced into a face, not an emotion. She is trying to move her mouth again.

'That's it, love, hold onto the meaning of the words and force them through.'

Tanya wrangles her mouth. 'Why?' she says. The word comes out long and arching in the air.

'Why did it happen to you?' Frank says. 'Is that what you're asking?'

Tanya snarls at him. She fixes on Margery. 'Why should she get away,' she says, pausing to gather the words into a rope, 'and I didn't?'

'It's not fair, is it?' Margery says.

The wraith moves closer to Margery, leans into her.

'Not fair at all. But it is right, however hard that is,' Margery says.

Tanya whimpers. 'He will come after me,' she says, clutching onto Margery. Her eyes are unseeing. 'I watch him. I've been in his apartment. It's as if he's still holding me to one spot.'

'He can't touch you now, love. You're already dead.'

Tanya shakes her head. 'He stood over me after he killed me and said that when he died he would find me, and I would never be able to shake his ghost. He has it all on camera. He watches it over and over.' The words pour like a tap left to run out standing water. 'Those same words, repeating – he'll find me and haunt me always. I can't risk that.' Her voice is so quiet they both have to lean in close.

'But he is going to die one day ... What harm does it do to help this poor young woman now?' Frank asks.

Tanya turns her wild eyes to him. 'Because if I stay away, he'll go after her and not me. She'll be his perfect one.' Tanya's arms snake round her own body. She strokes the sides of her arms.

'You could make a real difference in someone's life,' Frank says. Margery holds up a hand to stop him but he carries on. 'Believe me, you don't want to pass up any chance to help.' He keeps looking upstairs. He's worried about Barbara.

'Who helped me?' she spits. She is becoming more substantial, pulled through by emotion. 'I went to that policeman, Tony. Did as I was told and logged every time I was followed. Every email. Every troll online. And he did nothing. No one did. Not your grandson, not Tony, not the papers.' Her face melts into fury and she twists away from Margery. 'He wishes he did now. Every night as I watch him sleep.' She dashes across to the door and out and onto the street, crying into Spitalfields' lilac sky.

Frank sees Margery out then turns back into the parlour. It is unsettlingly quiet. No comforting murmur of television from upstairs, no cooking smells, none of the subtle changes in the atmosphere that speak of a ghost's presence. Not even the telltale smell of candles.

'Barbara,' he calls out. 'Honey.' No reply.

Panic seizes him. He runs up the stairs, willing her to be sitting up in bed, smiling at him. Guilt is making him worry, that's all this is. He has been distracted by Finnegan's appearance. He should have been paying her more attention. It will be different from now on. He checks in the kitchen, the spare room, the bathroom, up to the attic room and closet. Silence fills the house like earth. 'Where are you hiding, baby?' he calls to the walls. An echo of his voice is his only answer.

He stands outside the bedroom door, his hand on the doorframe. He's saved this room till last, hoping. Maybe she is so weak she is barely touching the world and that is why he cannot feel her pulsing.

He pushes the door and it swings away from him. The curtains are closed, the room absorbing light from the doorway and turning it to dark. He turns on the lights. For a second he thinks he sees her lying on the bed, but it is only the bedsheets, rumpled into an empty shroud. Five long rips run down its centre and though to the mattress. The headboard is covered in ugly scrapes. And the floor. In one board, at the end of a deep scratch, stands an iron, pointed nail.

His raw keen as he drops to the floor could wake the wight that walks his halls.

'Hello,' Jonathan says, as if talking to her was the most expected and commonplace of events. 'I'm returning your call. How are you?'

'I've been better,' she says.

213

Hearing Natalie's voice is like beer after a ban, a cigarette after seven years of abstinence.

'You got the papers then?' she says. He takes it as a good sign that she can't even say the word divorce.

'I did.' He is going to let her come to him this time. Anything else and she'll run.

'I need to speak to you,' she says. 'Will you come over?'

'Is he there?' Jonathan asks. He manages to keep the jealousy out of his voice. Again, first aim is to not push her away.

'I've sent him away.'

A stone of hope. Something nags at him. Something isn't right.

But so much *is* right – this is his *wife*. The woman he climbed a tree for in Donegal and stayed there during a thunderstorm singing 'There is a Light That Never Goes Out.' The woman he sat with in bed, holding her in a hedgehog ball as they bawled for babies they would never hold. The woman who wrapped her arms around him and told him that she loved everything about him. Everything, she had said.

A couple of years of difficulty is nothing compared with all of that history. It makes it more special. Their love can withstand anything, like Frank and Barbara's.

Forty minutes later, he stands outside the house. Their house. Pressing the doorbell, he has all the nerves of a boy meeting a girl for the first time.

The curtain flicks open and falls back again.

His heart had better behave itself.

He takes off his hat – it is the one Maria bought him. She'll probably be wearing hers. He should have rung her to explain. She'd understand if she knew.

The door opens slowly. Natalie looks thinner, as does he, but is stunning. She is wearing a black dress that sticks as close to her as he used to and the necklace he gave her five years ago on the boat across to Ireland. For one moment he thinks they are going to embrace and then she steps back into the hallway.

He follows her into the living room, a guest in his own home. He stops himself asking if he should take off his shoes. This is the moment he has been waiting for. All those months on the sofa, then the camp bed in the shed, then the office, they would mean nothing soon, that man would mean nothing soon.

Natalie nods for him to sit down. They bought this sofa together in the sale, lolled on it in a shop window, pretending to be catalogue models. The house holds a rabbit hole of memories: there's the mirror in which they sat next to each other and put on Halloween make-up; next to him is the table that they bought in a junk shop in Pimlico; on the floor is the rug that they chose together to replace the one that they ruined with a New Year's Eve party for just the two of them.

There have been changes, though. The cushions are now bright red, with apples on them. A new vase sits on the coffee table. He had expected that their wedding photo would have gone from the mantelpiece but not how much it hurts.

'I'm really glad you called, Natalie. Why did you want to talk?' he asks.

She pours two large glasses of Merlot and sits down in the rocking chair that Gargie had left him. She had also left him the motorbike and sidecar in which she had learned the Knowledge, but that had been sold to pay for their honeymoon. 'I kicked Justin out,' she says. 'He has another woman, I'm sure of it. I've seen pictures on his phone. He doesn't come home till late. I think he may even have a flat somewhere else, I saw a mortgage statement.'

Jonathan shakes his head. He can't stop himself. 'It's a difficult job, Nat. You know the hours.'

'I know,' Natalie says, eyes to the floor. 'But he's not you.'

That silence between them. It used to end in an argument or with him kissing her.

She is crying, waiting for his response. What has passed between them is as heavy as water but harder to hold in the hand.

Kneeling down on the carpet in front of her, he takes her wine glass from her hand. The world folds back to where it belongs.

Maria checks her watch again. Ninety minutes late. But it's not a date, it's not a sign of absolute thoughtlessness, he is probably caught up in something for the case and hasn't been able to get in touch. That'll be it.

She has already called Jonathan twice. Three times would be

humiliating. She wipes off some of her blusher. Simon showed her how and she trusts him enough to know that he wouldn't let her loose on rouge if she made herself look like a clown.

'Let's go out,' she calls to Billy. No drumming of paws in the hall. The remembering is terrible. Every time she forgets that he is missing, guilt geysers inside her, along with grief. It is bone deep, this loss. It leaves her brittle. She finds herself wobbling as she walks along the street, even though she would go out without him with no problems before. She fears her steps, has no confidence that the ground will be there. Worst of all is knowing that Billy is in the hands of a man who would hurt the person he claimed to love.

She walks to her chair and picks up Billy's collar. She holds it to her nose. It is distilled Billy, warm hay and dirt. She found it earlier, on her front step. Along with it came a letter, punched with a Braille machine and a fifty pound note:

'You are not helping yourself, my love, I told you to stay away from the police. I took Billy so that you could see your error but it is my fault that I was not clear enough. Forgive me, Maria. My job is to instruct you, make you the woman you want to be. We have both failed. Maybe we both need to lose something to teach ourselves the right way. Use the money to buy yourself something to wear tonight, that tells me it is you and me against the world. I will know what you buy and know that you love me. Do this for me and you won't lose anything else, I promise. In fact, you will gain even more of my heart. In love, x'

She called Jonathan when she got the message and tries again now. Still no answer. He'll get in touch soon. He has to.

Maria picks up the phone. Simon answers quickly. There is a slight pause as he walk away from his television. She can still hear the telly – a dog is barking in the background. It makes her stomach twist to hear it.

'What's wrong?' he says immediately. He can hear when something is not right. He can locate and interrogate a problem within minutes. She tells him everything. 'Shall I come round?' he asks and gets an earful of sobs in response.

Simon is at her door half an hour later with their time honoured emergency kit of hummus, crusty bread, crisps, chocolate and wine.

'I also have the works of Benedict Cumberbatch on Blu-ray. I thought you might be in need of another detective,' he says. His voice has a giggle in it that she catches despite herself. 'It's going to be OK,' he says, wrapping her up in a hug. 'You don't need anyone. Not even me. You are strong and resilient and no one can touch you.' He kisses the top of her head.

25

Day Seven

Jonathan wakes in his old bed. His right arm has gone numb from holding Natalie all night. She sleeps on, her hand tucked under her chin as it always is when she sleeps. He doesn't move. This is love, that overwhelming, breath-stopping sense that even when it is wrong, it is right. And there *is* a sense that this is wrong, but his wedding ring says they'll get over it.

He wants to stay forever under this duvet. It rustles with feathers and rests heavy on his body. Love and bed are the best anaesthetics. Easing his arm out, he shakes off the pins and needles prickling his arm. Natalie turns over and mutters, then falls back into soft snores.

He sits up in bed and looks around the bedroom. It is like a Spot the Difference competition. The candles have been half-burned since he was last here, leaving flame shadows on the wall. That's a new mirror. The trousers of another man hang over the door of the wardrobe.

He gets out of bed. It is the seventh day. What is he doing here? He checks his phone, finds missed messages and texts from last night. Frank and Maria, both desperate to talk to him. And he hadn't been there for them. Natalie stirs. She opens her eyes and smiles. She looks like she did when they first met.

'I'm really sorry but I've got to go,' he says, stroking her leg down to her toes. 'If you'd like to meet up later, then maybe you could come to my new place.'

She sits up straight and pulls the duvet up to her chin. 'I thought you'd be home for good,' she says.

'Let's talk everything through later,' he says, looking about for his shirt. It is hardly the Walk of Shame when it is from your own house.

'Can't you take the day off?' she asks.

'I can't. Someone is in real danger,' he says. 'I should have been on my way there last night, but came to you when you called.'

'Have you been seeing someone, Jonathan? Is that what it is?' Natalie's voice is small and crawls up the walls.

'No! I have to make sure that this woman is safe, that's all. You can phone anyone on my team if you don't believe me.'

'Your team thinks the world of you. They would do anything for you, even cover up your lies.'

'I'm not lying. A stalker is planning something for today.'

'That's right up your street – stalking. We've seen you, walking past the house at night. Spying on your wife, how sad is that? Although not for much longer.' She swings her legs out of bed, holding a pillow to her chest. Her face is contorted.

'You're right, I won't need to skulk around any more.' He reaches for her hand. 'Let's not do this. We don't have to fight. I was thinking of bringing back a bed picnic when I finish work.' Maybe memories of bed crumbs past in their student halls and hotel rooms, on the futon in their first flat, can appease her.

She pulls away. 'I meant I wouldn't be your wife for much longer.'

That lands so hard he has to hold onto the wall.

The look on her face is one of absolute triumph and total pain. This is the Central Line of their relationship. They go through the same stops, unable to step off.

Sss-cut.

The sound of hissing is in the room with them, playing under their conversation. In the corner of his eye he sees something pulling itself under the bed.

'Who's Maria King?' she asks. Bitterness breaks up the beauty in her face. This isn't really her. She wants to be held, reassured, just as he does.

'She's the victim of stalking. Her life is under threat. I told you I needed to go to work.' He stumbles over the words as he tries to work out why he feels guilty.

'Is that why she's calling you? No? I thought not.'

'We don't have to do this, Natalie,' he says, gently. 'We can get off now.'

His phone goes again. Another text. From Frank. 'Come now. Mine. Tanya is here.'

'Just leave,' she says, turning away.

Garry Harding's office in Soho is just round the corner from his new skyscraper, the Fizz. Jonathan hurries past the pavement cafés packed with people. He has messed everything up. He has let Frank down and missed the opportunity to interview Tanya and as for Maria – he tries her phone again. It rings twice then the call is cancelled. She doesn't want to speak to him. He doesn't blame her. He has no faith in himself, why should anyone else?

'Thank God,' Keisha says when he rings her. 'I didn't know what to do. The DCI stormed in and said that she's been told to let Denver out on bail.'

'What?' Jonathan stops in the street. People tut as they pass.

'He's already gone. All that evidence and he's got bail. I don't understand.'

'That's the power of influence,' Jonathan says.

'Excuse me, Guv?'

'I suspect our stalker is very well connected indeed.'

'What can we do?' she asks. There is a desperation he recognises in her voice. He is teaching her all the wrong things.

'We've got to keep going,' he says, for her benefit. 'There is a witness that could tie everything down.'

'Should I bring her in?' Keisha asks.

'I don't know where she is. She would be a key witness if I could get her to stay in one place.' And if he could get the whole of society to admit the existence of ghosts. Nothing difficult, then.

'She's flighty, huh?'

'That's one way of putting it.'

'We also have another lead. Sally and the IT team have found a chink in the chain of email proxies that the stalker sent the footage.'

'That seems so long ago but it was only six days.'

'Well,' she continues, 'it leads back to one of our first suspects.'

'Martin Crow?'

'Spot on, Guv.'

He enters the offices and sits in the plush waiting room, waiting to be fetched by Harding's secretary. The reading materials are mainly about yachts and country living and, as he distrusts how the countryside leaves your fluvials running clear, he scans through the names of women murdered or missing in London. He will go through them all later, put in the spade work that will get the rest of the team onside. One of the names is familiar – Sian Van Hausen. He met a Sian Van Hausen once – though he can't remember where. It is as if there is a barrier up against the memory. Something is stopping him seeing.

'Detective Inspector Dark? Garry is ready to see you now.' The woman shows him the way to Harding's office.

Garry is standing by the door, his hands on his hips. 'Always willing to help the police in their enquiries,' he says. 'Would you like coffee?' His eyes scoot around his office as he pours out the filter coffee as if working out if he has anything to hide. He almost certainly does, and he doesn't look like the type that is good at hiding.

They sit at the back of the office on two sofas pushed into an L shape. 'What can I do for you, Inspector?' he says. He takes a mouthful of coffee. No yellow ring.

'This is an unofficial visit at this stage. A courtesy call, if you like. Your name has come up in connection with a Mr Finnegan Finch who is believed to have been murdered. Does that name sound familiar?'

Another mouthful of coffee before Garry shakes his head. 'Sorry. I don't think I've heard of him. Maybe he's one of the contractors on the new build? I could look up the men I've got working on it if you like?' He stands up and walks to a filing cabinet, most likely to get away from Jonathan's gaze. Garry Harding is lying. Badly.

'Do you have a yellow diamond ring, Mr Harding?'

'That's a strange question,' he replies, laughing nervously.

'How about anyone in your acquaintance or employ?'

'Odd line in small talk you've got. Or are you missing a ring, DI Dark, is that why you're asking? Because there are some excellent diamond merchants in Hatton Gardens.' Harding can't keep still, moving about the office, glancing at the phone on the desk.

'We have information that Finnegan Finch was killed near the Tate Modern and that his body was driven away and dumped in the river.'

Harding stares at him. A sheen of sweat appears on his forehead.

'That isn't ringing any bells? How about that a witness has stated that you were the driver of the van? No? Then you won't mind telling me where you were on the last Saturday in September.'

'I don't need to answer these questions,' he replies. 'Now leave before I get my solicitor or your superior.'

'Did you assist in the disposal of Finch's body?'

Harding crosses his arms and refuses to speak.

Jonathan moves closer to Harding. He towers over him. 'Do you know of any members of an organisation called the Ring? Have you made deals with high-ranking government officials? How did you get permission to build this monstrosity? Do you think you have any chance at all of getting out of this alive?' He fires the questions one after another.

'Shut up,' says Harding. His upholstered face is as slick as leather in the rain.

'Did you murder Finnegan Finch?'

'No!' Harding cries out. 'I didn't kill anyone.'

'Yet.'

Harding covers his eyes with his hand.

'Look,' Jonathan says, leaning forward. 'We both know you're in this over your head. That's why your office is on the ground floor, I bet. You're not comfortable in high-rise, high-stakes games. I understand completely. You feel that you can't breathe, that this was a way to get ahead in business and now, well, it's got out of hand, hasn't it? If you're to keep on receiving money for this construction from the Ring, as I suspect you are, then you will have to kill. I can't see you excelling at that, can you? Do you know what happens to bad assassins?'

Harding is transfixed by Jonathan. 'They end up in the river,' he replies. Got him.

'Bring me some evidence of the Ring and I will get you out,' Jonathan says.

'I don't know anything,' he says. His eyes plead, though. It won't take much for him to turn witness. He longs to speak.

'Bring me genetic material that can be linked with a crime. Failing that, a paper trail or even a taped confession.'

Harding's eyes go first to his mobile phone and then to a picture of a woman on the table.

'Is that your wife?' Jonathan says, picking it up.

Harding nods.

'Then do what you can to hold onto her.'

Garry shakes as he picks up the phone. 'I need to speak to the woman, the one who came here.'

'You can speak to me,' her bodyguard says.

'I've had a visit from Inspector Dark. He knows that I was involved in—'

'Not over the phone.'

Garry wipes his forehead with his sleeve. 'How can he know about the van?' he says.

'Would you shut the fuck up? We'll have someone round to you soon.'

'I need to talk to her now.'

Muffled voices. The heavy returns. 'Hold on. I'll get her.'

Garry waits, hearing the heavy talk in a low voice. It sounds like the woman is replying.

'Looks like you'll get to prove yourself earlier than expected,' the man says, 'without a heavy penalty. Unless you fail, of course.'

'What do I have to do?' Garry asks. He feels cold, like his blood is being replaced with iced water.

The phone goes dead. He takes that to mean he should wait for further instructions.

He is outside Aggie Wright's house. Two of her flatmates are in there with her but they're all going out before too long. He will get inside and leave a message, show her how it's done. In language that *she* will understand.

He sits in the car, eye on her front door. He does not have time for this but he will have to make it. If she had done what he asked, everything would be OK, but she has talked to the police and sent him a PM saying that she was disgusted, that she hopes the police catch him for what he's done. She did not see the plan through to completion. No vision. No patience. What kind of artist is she?

He is good at waiting. He was taught as a child that you have to wait for what you want and earn it. He has earned Maria's love. His romantic plans for tonight are in place, his flat readied for her arrival. This pathetic 'artist' has not even earned her right to live. He will be the one to decide if she does.

'I don't know anything about computers,' Martin Crow tells Keisha, his voice lifting in frustration. 'How would I arrange something like that? I'm useless with technology. Can't you do something?' he asks his solicitor.

His solicitor whispers in his ear.

'But I've done nothing wrong, why should I be silent? There's nothing to worry about if I've done nothing wrong.'

Ah, the call of the privileged idiot everywhere. It's a cruel day when you find out that that's not true. For Keisha, it was being searched when she was thirteen. She was carrying two CDs and one of those candy necklaces that you can chew while you're wearing it. None of them had been nicked. There had been no reason for them to stop her. But they did. And her brother. Again and again.

'Why don't you look at the other men she knows? Her friend, Simon, could be the stalker for all you know. Or his partner, Will: he seems pretty devious. He's said horrible things to me on nights out. She's got a shrink, and work colleagues. How many times do I have to say that I love Maria – I wouldn't do anything to hurt her.'

'The stalker we're after said similar things many times over. It didn't stop him killing his previous victim.'

'When did unrequited love turn into stalking?' he asks.

Since Facebook, Keisha wants to reply but manages to rein it in.

'How about when that person puts someone under surveillance, taps their phone calls, monitors emails, checks which websites they visit and what they download?' Rider says. There is a touch of smugness in his answer. He'd like to take Martin down, be the one to crack the case and get a confession but Keisha knows instinctively that this one is innocent. Of this crime at least.

'I didn't know that the government loved us that much,' Martin says. 'Look, if the stalker is that tech savvy, couldn't they have routed the IP to me? I have no idea how all that works but isn't it possible?'

'Sounds like you know a fair amount,' Rider says.

Two loud knocks on the door. Rider gets up and whispers in the corridor. 'Interview suspended at eleven fifty-three a.m.,' Keisha says. 'We'll be back later.'

Keisha follows Rider out into the corridor. 'What's happened?' she says, seeing his face fall. 'Oh no. Has Maria—'

'It's not Maria. Aggie Wright. She went home and found her house had been trashed. Her paintings have been sliced into pieces. Some of them have been stuck on the kitchen table and arranged into this.' He hands her his phone.

The pieces had been meticulously arranged into letters that said 'TIME'S UP, MARIA.'

'Do we know where Denver is?' Keisha asks.

Rider shakes his head. 'If he's behind this, and we sent him home . . . anyway. The forensic team is on the way,' says Rider. 'I've told Richard to make any prints a priority although I'm sure he will have been careful as usual. He's working on Billy's collar and the letter.'

'Look how all those pieces fit together. It must have taken the stalker ages,' Keisha says.

'Aggie and her mates were out – at a film they booked online.' They exchange glances.

'We should have kept her in.'

'This isn't the place to lock people up for their own protection, Keisha,' Rider says. His tone is more gentle than usual.

26

Jonathan takes out his earpiece. Now Aggie is under attack. Bad news after bad news. The traffic is even worse than usual. He is on his way to see Natalie over lunch with enough flowers to fill Frank's funeral parlour. Still that voice is saying that something isn't right. He tries to block it, along with the other whispers, but he knows that there is a gap between him and Natalie that he cannot ignore any more.

He needs to concentrate on work. He is in free fall. The interview with Harding was a dead end or, worse, he has just alerted the whole of the Ring to his enquiries. He's not thinking. Once again he has been distracted and the job has suffered, as has those he is supposed to protect.

Maria sits in her normal chair in Iain's therapy room, waiting while he takes another booking on the phone.

'How are you coping without Billy?' Iain says, getting right in there.

She won't cry. Not any more. She waits for the tears to retreat. 'I miss him so much and feel more vulnerable. Wobbly. I think that's also because everything has been rocked. This stalker makes me feel eyes on me at all times. Of course if there had been a surveillance team watching and following me in the underground then I might not have lost Billy at all.'

'You make it sound like they're punishing you instead of protecting you.'

'I know. I should be doing my lists of things that I should be grateful for, like you taught me.'

'But you're not?'

'Billy used to be top of the list. All I can think about is him not being here. Simon is brilliant; I couldn't do this without him and Will. They're the ones who have made everything OK since my operation.'

'Simon. That's your friend, isn't it?' His tone is strange. She can't decipher it. She's irritated that he didn't remember who Simon was, given that she's been coming for months.

'Yes. I hate the thought of losing him. I shouldn't rely on him so much. I hope I'm as good a friend to him as he is to me.'

'And there's no more to it, your relationship?'

'Why does that matter?'

Iain says nothing.

'I love him, not in a sexual way at all. I don't have that "if only you weren't gay I'd jump you" thing.'

Iain sloshes water into a glass. She hears him take a sip. 'I want you to see that you still have much to be grateful for.'

'Oh.' Maria crosses her legs. She feels anxious and does what he's suggested: rub her arms to comfort herself and tap her collarbone.

'That's good, Maria,' he says.

For the first time, it feels weird that he is watching her.

'Let's find a way that you can approach the situation with some power. What makes you feel out of control?'

'Going to the police.' Inspector Dark, really. Jonathan is erratic, and challenging. Each time she takes something to the police, something else is taken away from her. 'If something else arrives, I don't want to tell them. I wish I hadn't given them his collar. I have nothing of Billy left.'

'You have disobeyed the stalker at every turn by going to the police.'

'That's right.' The room feels charged with something she can't put her finger on.

'I know you are not supposed to give advice,' Maria says, leaning forward. 'But what would you do?'

'I can't give you advice, you're right. All I know is that I wish for you to feel like you have power in your own life.'

A door slams in the hallway outside.

'I thought I was the only therapist in today,' he says.

Tanya Baker races down Straightsmouth, anger fuelling her through the DLR and out the other side. She streaks through Greenwich, passing time before Maria comes out from seeing that useless therapist. She's not going to leave Maria's side from now on. The psychologist is pathetic, the police worse than useless, none of them can stop a knife from taking away Maria's life.

Maria is as scared as she was. As scared as she *is*. They are of a similar age, only Maria will be able to get older, have a family, achieve in her career, wear purple. If she is lucky. No. He will not let her go. There is only one ending to this, if he is not stopped. If he kills Maria then they would be as sisters and could— No, she won't even think about that. There must be something Tanya can do. She can't inform on him, she knows that he always keeps his word and he has said that he will haunt her forever. But there's got to be something else that she can do with her death.

He rings the doorbell, flowers almost covering his face. There is no answer. Lights are on upstairs, curtains still drawn from earlier. Maybe she's waiting there for him. In bed.

He gets out his key, hesitates, then puts it in the lock. It doesn't fit. They probably changed all the locks months ago. The back gate is also locked. He could climb over and try the back door but that would really break one of her boundaries.

He rings her phone and then the door one more time and steps back to see if there's any movement upstairs. There is. Justin Masters stands at the window.

'DCI Allen wants to see you immediately,' Lindsey says as he enters reception. 'She seemed livid. Good luck.'

Jonathan grimaces. 'Thanks, mate,' he says. He walks up the stairs, making up a rollie. The smell of tobacco calms him.

DCI Allen is at her desk, papers laid out. She is cross-referencing them with a file on her computer.

'You wanted to see me, ma'am,' he says. He stands up straight, ready to take one of her famous blasts.

'Sit down, Jonathan,' she says. She sounds tired rather than angry.

Sighing, she stands up and walks over to her coffee machine. 'You look as if you need this as much as I do,' she says, handing him a cup. 'Actually, you look like you could do with reanimation.'

Jonathan smiles. 'This case may be getting to me.'

'Well, you're not alone there.' She sits back down and gestures to her screen. 'I've had an order from the superintendent to call off all surveillance on Maria King.' She grinds her teeth. He has never seen her so invested in a case.

'Why?' Jonathan asks.

'Budgetary reasons were the only grounds given,' she says. Her eyes carry irony well. 'I've tried to find money elsewhere but I am blocked at every turn. It's so frustrating.'

His brain races to wherever Maria will be. It is Day Seven in the stalker's countdown. He won't be resting. Time's up, he said. 'I'll go and park outside her flat,' Jonathan says, slipping his coat back on. 'Keep watch on her overnight.'

'You're showing how much the case is affecting you – you know how inappropriate that is. Normally you would just go and do it, not say it out loud. Anyway, he targeted you to send the footage to. It could make him angry if he sees you,' she says. 'It was at this stage that Tanya was killed, we need to make sure Maria isn't. I've talked to her myself. She's going to her friend's house tonight. Simon, is it? He'll be a safer bet.' It's true. And Maria probably wouldn't want to see Jonathan. And he wouldn't blame her at all.

'What about Denver? The attack on Aggie's flat came right after he was released. Can we bring him in or have him under surveillance? I'll do it if no one else will. Rider and Keisha will help.'

'Releasing Denver was another order from the office of Superintendent Bernson, overruling mine. They will not let me authorise further surveillance, unofficially or otherwise.'

'Why?' he asks.

'Denver is protected,' she says.

'Or he is a distraction to cover up for someone else,' Jonathan says.

Keisha comes in. 'I've been going through all the IT investigations, ma'am, as you asked.'

Allen looks from one to the other. 'Shut the door, please, Keisha.'

Keisha stands behind Jonathan's chair. They both wait for DCI Allen to speak.

'I'm going to go out on a limb,' she says. 'As you said in your rousing speech yesterday, Jonathan, there has been enough suspicion in this case.'

How did she know about the speech? Jonathan hadn't even known she was in the building.

'Oh, I keep an eye on everything,' she says. He must have shown surprise. 'I understand why you've kept information from the team: I've kept information from you because I didn't know if you could be trusted.'

'And now you do?'

Allen laughs. 'As much as this job allows. I don't trust anyone any more.'

'What have you been holding back?' Jonathan says, leaning forward on his chair.

'The yellow diamond ring. It was what alerted me to this case. I'm investigating corruption in the Met and, every now and then, I hear mention of the Ring – a syndicate that crosses business and government.'

'The old boys' network,' Keisha says. 'Nothing new about that.'

'Only now women can join,' Allen replies.

'And murder is the entry qualification,' Jonathan says.

Allen stares at him, eyes narrowed. 'How did you find that out?'

'Blake Merry.' Jonathan can't say that he found out from a ghost.

'Ah,' Allen says. They hold each other's gaze. A river of the unsaid passes between them.

'I don't know how this Ring relates to it,' Keisha says, 'but our systems have been hacked, data played with. I haven't the IT skills to trace exactly what has happened but we're being manipulated.'

'By whom?' Allen says. She looks at Jonathan, her head on one side.

'Could be anyone,' Jonathan replies.

He does not like the amount of time that Maria spends with Simon. He doesn't even believe that men and women *can* be friends, even if one of them is gay. Anyone can play gay. There are women at work that he can go and have a drink with when they've finished up, but there is always the suspicion of sex in the air. You shouldn't mix work and pleasure. He hasn't felt the same way about the Ring since that woman took over operations. Her orders demean him.

Maria is trying to make him jealous. It is one of her little games. Like when she blindfolded Dark. She knew that he would be watching. She is taunting him so that he reveals himself. She wanted to move his timeline forward, well that is a dangerous game, little one. She thinks she's playing with the big boys but she has no idea. She doesn't yet know what he can do. Time is up, she'll know within hours.

Her dog barks from its cage. He throws it some dry food and it lands inches away from the wire. It sniffs and sends out its tongue but cannot reach. He wants to see the beast's ribs. Maria will learn what happens when she insists on disobeying him. The dog whimpers. It seems to know what he is thinking. It licks at the burn on its foot. It had to be taught. Maria will also have a lesson burned into her. Tonight.

27

Maria wanders through the flat, missing Billy with every step. He is usually there beside her. Her footsteps sound lonely.

She takes out the coin that Jonathan found. It is highly corroded and covered in mud. Plugging in her home-made electrolysis kit of a mobile adapter split into two wires, she attaches one crocodile clip to the coin, the other to a spoon coated with the residue of old coins, and places the spoon in the beaker of salted water. It is magic, this bit. The saline changes into a thick brown soup, bubbling away like a witch's brew, ridding the coins of their centuries, transferring them to the spoon, and leaving the pennies shiny and new.

She leaves the coin for half an hour and gets ready, choosing jeans and a woollen jumper that makes her think of the way sand feels under her feet.

Eight o'clock. Simon should be here by now. He said he would pick her up at seven for their trip to the cinema. She's been stood up too many times recently.

There is no answer when she rings. She'll go to his flat, that's what she'll do, and stand all woebegone at his door before laughing. The protection team left earlier, very apologetic, claiming that they'll miss her cups of tea. It feels strange to not have one of them out there. She feels exposed, as if the tide is out.

Cabs sound different to cars and it isn't long into her walk that she hears one coming up behind her. It slows down and she gets in. She can't face the underground any more and if she takes the bus it'll be ages before she gets to Shoreditch.

She gives the road name but the driver doesn't reply, just drives off. Maria leans into the seat. London streams past her, all sirens and electricity and laughter and tears. This cab doesn't smell of the usual fake pine freshener, instead it's like a church at a wedding – candles and incense and flowers. It is strangely relaxing, like getting into a bath. The cabbie still says nothing, there's only the sound of Heart FM playing its love songs.

'How much?' Maria says when the taxi pulls up. Some of the cabs have signs that tell you and give change but she doesn't have an app on her that can read and translate.

'Hello?' she says, getting out and knocking on the window. It winds down. 'How much is the fare?' The cab driver says nothing but Maria can hear them moving in the seat. 'I've got money and I'm keen to pay you.'

Still nothing. Very strange. What if her stalker is a cabby? What if he is there in front of her right now? Something tells her that he isn't.

She slips ten pounds onto the passenger's seat. The window winds back up and the taxi pulls away.

Standing at Simon's door, she can hear music playing inside. She rings the doorbell. No Simon. She still has her key in her bag, she'll surprise him. She lets herself in. 'Where are you, you lazy bugger?' she shouts.

Her words echo round the flat. 'If you're both hiding in the bedroom then you should probably say before we all get embarrassed.'

The door to the living room can only open halfway. She pushes harder. Something is blocking it. Slipping through the gap, she smells coins and iron mixed with the salt of the foreshore and something horribly sweet. The scent makes her heart follow fast on the heel of its beats. She walks into something on the floor. Crouching down, she reaches out. Her fingers find hair. Simon's hair. It is matted and wet. 'Simon,' she says, fumbling for his hand. It is cool and there is no pulse. His blood has stopped running. Simon has stopped.

Maria cries out. She wants to hold him and rock his big body, get into his big bear arms and not move again. But she cannot move him any more, she knows that much.

This is because of her. There is only one way this will end if she doesn't do something. Take control, Iain says. Bringing up Facebook on her phone, she accesses the message from the stalker. She sends a reply to his account with clear instructions and copies the text into all the email addresses he's connected with. He will be looking out for her messages.

Taking her new necklace, bought today with his fifty pounds, she slips it round her neck.

'I'm going now,' she says to Simon. 'I'll get someone to come and look after you. I love you. And as for you,' she says to her stalker, whoever and wherever he is, she holds up the necklace and the charm on it says 'FUCK YOU'.

Garry answers the door on the third knock. It is the woman, standing there with her shoulders back. Two men stand behind her. One of them holds a baseball bat in his gloved hands.

'It's time, Garry,' the woman says. 'We're playing the game. We're going after Dark.'

Jonathan is so tired that his eyes are going to roll out of their sockets.

'You should go home, Guv,' Keisha says. 'You look banjaxed.'

'I'm taking that as a compliment. You did great work there, unravelling the IT trail. You should leave too. Get some rest before tomorrow. I'll be playing a game of stalk the stalker whether the DCI likes it or not.'

Keisha hasn't taken her eyes from her screen. 'Not yet. I've got a lead on Finnegan Finch and I want to keep pulling it till I find the dog.'

'You need to stop sometime. Sleep is good for results, believe me.'

'I won't be long, Guv, I've got an inkling.'

'Follow your inkling, then, but get some sleep.'

Keisha waves her hand to dismiss him. He smiles. She is going to make a great DI one day. If she doesn't take too much from him.

Turning the corner, Jonathan starts rolling another cigarette. He is too anxious to eat. He'd give anything to crave chips again. He is barely out of the building when his phone goes.

'You've got to come back, Guv,' Keisha says. She is panicked, her voice clipped. 'Simon is dead, he's been stabbed with a replica knife to the one used on Tanya. There are also knives missing from the knife block.'

'What about Maria?' he asks, feeling sick. 'Wasn't she supposed to be with him? Has her flat been checked?'

'She was the one who called it in, Guv. She said that she'd had enough and is going alone to make him to join her world. She said you would know what she meant.'

'Jonathan Dark?' a male voice says from the alleyway.

The phone is knocked away.

Jonathan is grabbed from behind, his arms held. A man walks towards him, whistling. Jonathan calls out for help but the man just smiles. A van pulls up and both men force Jonathan inside. He is pushed down onto a seat. Two men sit on either side of him, their faces covered. His pockets are turned out, his jacket removed and the lining searched. His wallet, his keys, everything is taken. A woman sits in the passenger seat. She doesn't turn round and he can only see the side of her face. It is familiar, though. Fuck, where has he seen it before? Amyris Church has hair that colour but then so do lots of women.

'You've been flying too near to the sun, Mr Dark,' one of the men says. He recognises the voice from somewhere. 'There is a status quo that needs to be preserved and we are out of balance. To correct this, we like to play a game. We've been playing it for over a hundred years. You'd think it would be easy to leave the city but it's not. It has walls and gates that go far beyond the Roman ones. This is our homage to the city. You can tell him the rules, Garry.'

One of the men takes off his balaclava: it is Garry Harding, his face red. 'You will only have what we give you: your Oyster card, small change, watch and one of these cigarettes.' He takes one from Jonathan's cigarette case and shares out the rest with the men.

'Can I at least have a lighter or a match?' he asks.

Garry looks over to the woman in front. She shakes her head. 'Sorry,' Garry says. 'And there's another thing.' He closes his eyes, as if reciting the words by rote. 'You have one hour's head start and then we will be coming after you. That is our only promise. We won't try to find you until your sixty minutes is up. If you manage to escape past the M25 then you get to leave the country and not come back.'

'Tell him why we're not worried about letting a detective go,' says the woman. The voice is muffled behind a scarf. It is familiar, though. 'Seeing as he could turn straight back to Scotland Yard.'

'We will hurt your wife,' Garry says. 'Your cosy time last night will be your last memory of her.' He looks as scared by that as Jonathan. They have probably threatened Garry's wife too.

'Leave the city. Your time starts now,' the woman says.

The men surge and he is pushed out of the side of the van. It drives off, number plates covered. Jonathan looks around. He is in Birdcage Walk. He runs, his mind wired, racing through possibilities like electricity through the city. Contacting his team will put Natalie in danger, going to her will lead to his death and hers; he could hide in a ghost station until the spotlight was off him. Frank must know ghosts who could help him escape; if not, his cousin has contacts in another underworld; maybe this is the way out of the mess he has made: he could leave London and never look back, lose himself in another life. He pictures himself in Berlin, starting again. Alone. Keisha's words echo back. Maria is in danger. What did Maria mean by making the stalker join her world and that Jonathan would know? Her world. She offered Jonathan her world.

He hails a cab but it drives straight past, and the second. The third stops and the door opens. 'Thank you,' he says. 'Borough Market, please.'

Keisha thumps the table. Got him. She calls the Guv but it goes straight to voicemail. It'll have to be Rider.

'What do you want?' Rider answers.

'I need you to come with me to arrest Michael Finch. I went through the accounts again – he's there, getting a cut. He was in on it.'

'On his dad being murdered?' Rider doesn't sound convinced.

'It's our biggest lead so far.'

'Can't it wait till tomorrow? I'm at home about to go to sleep,' says Rider.

'I bet you look cute in your nightie and bed socks but I can't sleep with Maria in danger and at least we can interview Finch to-night, then the Guv will be chuffed. He needs cheering up. I have never seen him so depressed. I can't just sit here. Are you coming then, or are you going to sit and seethe when I get all the glory?'

'I'll be there in fifteen minutes,' Rider says.

The cabbie drops Maria off on Stoney Street. Drinkers clink their bottles and laugh. She is surprisingly calm, she is in control for the first time this week.

In her messages to all of the stalker's accounts she said that she would meet him by the entrance on Bedale Street, and that he should be wearing a blindfold. He may or may not wear it but at least she will be face to face with him. Either way, she has a knife in her coat pocket.

Rowouff. Rowouff.

Billy.

She runs towards his bark, calling his name. The barks get louder and more urgent. She bumps into someone, 'Sorry, love' they say and move on knowing nothing. She could tell them everything or run away but that would bring others into danger. The stalker is not going to stop. Neither will she.

Billy bundles into her, whimpering and barking and licking her. She buries her face in his fur and remembers Simon doing the same. She pats him down to check for injuries. He is holding one paw up. She touches it and he whines.

'Sorry, baby, I'm so sorry.'

'Maria.' A man's voice, quiet.

Maria stops, frozen against Billy. It is him. The one from the underground. And before, she knows she has heard him before.

'I am so glad you asked to meet me. I was worried that my punishment would put you off me.' He sounds shy, as if opening himself to her.

Vomit burns through her throat. She sobs once and anger comes. 'What, killing my friend? Why would that put me off you?'

'I am so glad,' he says, not picking up her sarcasm. 'I have done what you asked. You can check if you like.'

Grimacing, every part of her wanting to pull away, she reaches out and touches his face. He is wearing a large eye-mask, it feels the same as hers. Then she remembers the one that went missing from her house when she was being filmed.

'You said that you wanted to show me your world. I would very much like that.'

'Let's go,' she says. He believes they are in synch. She hopes Jonathan is following.

The cab races through the streets, beeping other cars and people out of the way. The driver, though silent, seems to know Jonathan is in a hurry and revs hard every time they get out of traffic. He wishes he or she would turn the radio off.

It has been seventeen minutes already but he won't need the hour that they've given him. He just needs to get to Maria. She is drawing the stalker out, like pouring salt on a red wine stain. She will know what to do, she has a practical streak, unlike Natalie.

Sian Van Hausen's name keeps turning over in his thoughts. Why now? What is he missing? He used to trust this part of his brain, chasing the connections, the lines that ran underneath a case. He thought he had lost it, maybe he has and this is all that remains, like the remnants of a cocktail cabinet after a party. A party. That's where he met her. He closes his eyes and plays back what he can recall, no detail too small. It was a birthday party in Romford. The semi-detached house was packed with people who spilled out into the back garden. There was Pimm's with mouthfuls of mint and talk about cricket and he had wanted to either get pissed or go home but couldn't do either because he was with colleagues and had to stay reasonably sober for the team. He had wished Natalie were there, she'd have a witty comment to make about everything and everyone but she was having dinner with her mother. He had probably got the better deal.

He wandered over to the table of unopened presents and saw a woman standing by the fence. She was wearing a long black coat on the hottest day of the year and was very pale. 'Are you all right?' he asked.

She looked right through him. They stood in silence for a while.

'Do you want a drink? I'm going to get one. Sorry, I don't know your name.'

'Sian,' she said, turning to him. Her perfume was strange, like candle wax. 'Sian Van Hausen.'

'What can I get you?' he asked.

Her smile struck him. It was so sad. 'It's up to you,' she replied.

'I'll see what there is,' he said and walked into the kitchen. When he came back out, two G & Ts in his hands, she had gone. When he got home that night he found his wife with Justin. That was only this summer, though it feels like longer ago. Sian Van Hausen, according to that list, had already been missing, presumed dead, for a year. And then Jonathan remembers. It strikes him like a mug falling to the floor. Sian had stared at the person whose birthday it was as if he were her murderer.

Tanya twirls her hair round her finger as she did when she had lived. Her hair seems to get longer and longer the more worried she gets.

She follows them into the dark market. Maria has a tight grip on the dog's leash and holds on to the stalker's arm. She is talking to him, telling him to smell the cinnamon still in the air, the ghosts of fruit in the empty boxes.

Why is she doing this? Why is she inviting this freak of a man, this thin, nasty invader into her life?

The dog limps along beside her, his eyes never leave her face.

The market stalls are not as empty as Maria imagines. There are more ghosts here than Tanya has seen in any one place. The market is teeming with spirits haggling over energy. Spectres hold hands and one becomes stronger, as if siphoning off petrol from a tank. Money is exchanged, small metal coins. 'What can I get you, love?' a stallholder asks her, holding out her hand. Tanya wants to stay, see everything they've got, to listen to the shouts and cries. For the first time since her death she feels alive. She will come back but she cannot lose Maria.

Maria leads him out of the indoor area and onto the main road. Someone must notice them, two blind people and a dog walking up the A3. It's amazing what people refuse to stop and see.

'I've been wanting to do this with you,' she says, taking his hand.

'You did it with Jonathan first,' he says. Jealousy spits through his tone. She is going to have to play this carefully.

'I knew you would be watching. In my mind, it was you,' she says. Bile burns her throat as she says the words.

'That is good to hear,' he says. His voice is smooth again. He squeezes her hand and she has to resist the impulse to pull it out of his clammy grip. She needs to gain his trust, throw him off his guard.

'There's so much I've been wanting to talk with you about,' she says. 'I want to tell you everything. Things I have never shared with anyone.'

'I don't need to tell you anything,' he replies. 'You already know me so well. I know everything about you. The way you dance by yourself. The way you henna your hair and leave it to dry like mud.' He lowers his voice. 'The way you touch yourself.' She swallows the vomit in her mouth.

The river is calling her; she can hear it running towards her. It is low tide but it turns for her. The perfect time for mudlarks. Especially blind ones. Most sighted mudlarks leave dark larking alone, but to her it is no different.

'I want to show you something. Down here,' she says, placing his hand on the rails beside the steps.

'You first,' he replies.

Jonathan shouts his thanks to the driver and, cursing the traffic, steps onto Park Street. He runs into the empty market, scanning the stalls, aware of the lingering smell of the goods – vinegar, spices, incense. He runs down one aisle, thinking he sees them, but it is only the dance of shadows from a passing car. There are no footsteps, only his own. There is the faintest suggestion of a whisper. He stops, listens. Nothing. Adrenalin is coursing, stopping him from feeling the bruises that are developing on his face.

He knows who it is. How has he missed it? What if he is wrong about where Maria is, too?

Where else would a mudlark go?

'I got traffic to keep an eye on Michael Finch's favoured clubs. He's often there in the evening. One of them saw him leave Soho House about half an hour ago.' Keisha gets into one of the high speed cars. 'What?' she says to Rider's disapproving look.

'Where do you intend to go?' Rider asks. 'Bomb it around Soho till we kill someone?'

'Can you find out if Ed's on CCTV tonight? We'll need someone we trust to find Finch and keep him tracked. He'll be able to track anyone if we give him a starting point.'

Rider gets on the phone and asks for Ed. 'If he's not there, then ask Celeste. We need to know where Michael Finch went after leaving Old Compton Street and keep us informed of every step he takes.'

'Take Billy,' the stalker says when she's standing on the beach.

'I thought you could tie him up. There's a bollard three steps to your right.'

'None of us is going to leave the other again. Is that clear?' he says.

'You're absolutely right. I'm sorry. Here,' she comes up a few steps, 'lower him down to me.'

Billy lands with a thump in her arms and she staggers back on to the stones, landing on her side.

'Are you all right, darling?' he asks, anxiously hurrying down. The metal steps sound like a warning bell.

She forces herself to stay where she is as he stumbles the last step and reaches for her. 'This isn't far from where you proposed,' Maria says.

He laughs gently. 'That must have been a surprise.' There is hardly any other sound down here at this time of night. The traffic is muffled, the river listening its hardest.

'Just a bit, but a good one,' she says. 'It would be lovely to know your name, at least. Seeing as you know so much about me.'

'I've got to keep some mystery left. I was thinking of letting you feel my face, later,' he says, shyly.

'What about your job?' She is searching for the knife. It must have fallen out when she broke Billy's fall.

'It's boring; you wouldn't want to hear about it. What are you looking for?' he asks. 'I can hear you moving the stones.'

'A foreshore find to commemorate our first meeting. You have given me so many presents. It's time I gave one to you.'

'That's a lovely thought. And there I was thinking you were looking for this knife.' There is no smile left in his voice.

'I've picked Finch up, Keisha,' Celeste says, triumph in her voice. 'He's on the move. But there's something else—'

'Give me street names,' Keisha says. There is no time for chatter – barking at her is going to be the only way.

'You need to hear this, Sergeant. I logged onto the other computer so I could follow as many cameras as possible. I knew Ed would be working, he can't stop. He's got an office in his pocket. There is a live feed – and it's really weird but . . .'

'What?'

'It's the DI. I can pick up at least three cameras following him up to London Bridge. And Michael Finch is heading that way.'

'Keep looking,' says Keisha. She turns to Rider. 'The Guv's in trouble.'

'You didn't ask me to come here because you loved me,' he says. 'You wanted to hurt me. I've never wanted to attack you. I wanted to love you. Make you smile and make you mine.'

She is held against the wall. He opens up her coat and holds the knife against her stomach.

'You stalked me, scared me, took my dog and killed my friend. How is that loving?'

'You had to be shown, Maria. You had the potential to be perfect. I see people all the time who are flawed. That's my job. I listen to them when I can be bothered, and I see every one of their vices. You can afford to live behind your mask. I can't. I wish I could.' He snaps off the silk mask. It hits her face. 'That was probably why I was stupid enough to fall for a cunt like you.' He spits out that word. 'How could I have been so stupid? I thought you were different. One out of the millions. When you bought a necklace with my money, I thought you'd accepted me for me, just as I would accept you for you.' He pauses, the pressure on the knife lessens but he still holds her hard by the shoulder. The wall is sharp against her back. 'Show me the necklace,' he says. 'Show me that you accept me.'

Very slowly, she moves her hand towards her neck. She lifts up the motto.

He gasps and she shoves him but it isn't enough. He pushes her down and tries to wrestle her hands to the ground. The knife cuts her palm.

Billy barks, jumping up at them.

He yells and turns to shove Billy away. Billy yelps. And is silent.

The barking has stopped. Jonathan runs quicker. He can see the steps, only a hundred metres ahead, next to the bollard and a bench. Two men rise from it.

Garry Harding walks over. He is holding a baseball bat against one leg as if that will conceal it. His hand is shaking.

Jonathan runs up to him. 'Where's Maria?' he asks, grabbing Garry by the collar.

'Who's Maria?' the other man says. It's Michael Finch. He grins at Jonathan and, with Garry's help, loops his arms so that they are pressed behind his back. 'Time's up, Inspector,' he says. 'It's the shortest distance that anyone in the game has ever travelled. You have that record at least.' He has lost all of the shy teen and now has all the hallmarks of the arrogant, untouchable twenty-something.

The sound of a struggle comes from the beach. 'Someone's getting lucky,' Michael says. Jonathan struggles and gets one hand free, grasping hold of Finch's shirt.

The van screeches up behind them.

Tanya watches as Maria rolls away from him and stumbles towards the shoreline.

He lurches for her and catches her calf. The waves whisper nearby. 'Come here, you stupid bitch. You know that no one is going to help you, don't you? Your precious detective is otherwise engaged and will soon be as dead as your friend.'

Rage burns in Tanya at every word. He said them to her too. The anger is alive, twisting in what was once her guts and allowing her to blaze. She rides it towards him, her silent screams the negative of Maria's and, summoning every element of energy she has, slams into him.

The river rushes in and reaches for his legs. Tanya's arms wrap around him and he is pinned down onto the wet stones. His mouth is wide open in a shout but, as he said, no one is coming to help.

The Thames closes in around him, fills his throat, taking him for its own, taking him on his own journey. And wherever that is, she will be there.

'Get down on the ground with your hands above your head,' Keisha yells from behind Jonathan, jumping out of the van. 'Get down on the ground. Now.'

Michael kneels with his hands up and then falls to the ground. Jonathan runs down to the steps.

'Guv,' shouts Keisha. 'Where are you going?'

Her voice fades as he steps down to the shoreline. It takes a while to see Maria in the dark. She lies near the wall, shadows covering her like a blanket, her head on a rock. Next to her, a furry shape is slumped on the stones.

'Maria,' he says, feeling for a pulse in her neck. Nothing. He moves his fingers. They tremble on her pulse point. There. It is there – faint but steady. Her coat is open and blood has soaked through her shirt. It's coming from her stomach. He presses down to stop the bleeding. 'Help,' he calls out. 'We need help. Call an ambulance.' Moving her as little as possible, he rests her head on his lap, still pressing into the wound. 'Stay with me, wherever you are now, it's better to be here. I'm here.'

She moves a little. That might even be a laugh.

On the street above, sirens close in. Billy lets out a sigh. 'You'll be all right,' he says. He's talking to himself as well.

It's only when Maria and Billy have been carried up the steps that he sees the shoes sticking out of the water. And, attached to them, as the river slides back, is Ed.

28

Michael Finch sits in the interview room with his arms crossed, grinning. 'You have no evidence against me,' he says. 'There is no proof that any of your allegations took place.'

'What about the money coming into your account from the holding company?' Jonathan asks.

'Simply a tax efficient way of my father giving me an allowance. They paid me instead of him for the cremation services of any deaths that took place in the nursing homes they run. It worked. Anything else you've got? Anyone speak out against me? No? I thought not.'

'How about assaulting me while I was in the line of duty?'

'I thought you were launching an attack, as did my friend Garry. Anything I did was in self-defence and, if you remember, all I did was restrain you.'

Jonathan puffs in irritation. 'There's nothing we can hold him for,' he says to Keisha.

'That's right, Inspector, glad we got that sorted.' Finch stands and holds his hand out to Jonathan. Jonathan does not take it.

'Now, there is never an excuse for bad manners. Goodbye, Inspector.'

They wait for Finch and his solicitor to leave. 'Do you think this is going to work, Guv?' Keisha asks.

'We may have enough from Garry Harding but this would help. Anything could help. We're in for a fight, whatever happens,' Jonathan replies.

Keisha watches Finch walk out to his waiting car. He slips something from his glove box onto his finger. The car glides away. 'I'll give it five seconds,' she says, 'that should be enough.' She counts down in her head, then pulls out after him in the unmarked car.

Rider winds down the window. Cold air blasts through the car. 'It's three cars in front. Finch is in the back.'

'He's probably opened the champagne already.' She can't wait to see Finch's smug face fall.

'What makes you think that he won't go straight home and put his feet up?' Rider asks.

Keisha shrugs. 'The Guv reckons that he'll want to crow. He thinks he's got away with it.'

'He probably has, if this Ring actually exists. The thought that we're carrying out our lives and living by the law while the people that make and uphold those laws are pissing all over them . . .' Rider stops. He puts his chin on his hand and looks like a little boy. Keisha wants to ruffle his hair and hand him a yo-yo. 'I don't know what the point of my job is any more.'

'Who else is going to watch out for them?'

'But how? It's like smog. We don't know how high it goes up or how wide.'

Keisha nods. 'You could be part of it for all I know. Anyone could that has a position of power or influence.'

'Look at Ed. You'd never have thought he was capable of any of this. Or Finch.'

Keisha nods but doesn't speak. She dropped the ball on Ed. The DI asked her to follow up the journalist link, and she had on suspects, but not on the whole team. Ed's first job was in IT on Fleet Street.

'Do you really think I could be part of the Ring?' Rider asks.

Keisha glances at him, then back to the road. 'No way,' she says. 'Your shoes are too cheap.'

Rider flicks through the radio stations. He settles on Heart FM. That's all she needs.

Finch's car eventually stops in front of a large house on the edge of Greenwich. They slow down, watching as he enters the house before parking several hundred metres away.

They walk up to the front gate. A security light goes on. 'Ready?' says Keisha.

Rider nods and they stride up the shingle to the house. Keisha raps the heavy door knocker. Michael opens the door, sees them and sneers. 'What are you two doing here?'

Keisha holds up the warrant and barges past Michael, through a plush hallway into a huge kitchen diner, with windows that look out onto the night. Rosa Finch sits at a table in the adjoining conservatory, wearing silk pyjamas, drinking wine and eating home-made biscuits. A vase casts a shadow that looks like Alfred Hitchcock. 'What's going on?' she asks, her eyes wide.

Finch comes in, on the phone. 'We need you here. Yes, you've got to come right now. That's what you signed up for, isn't it?' He ends the call. 'My solicitor,' he says. 'You must really like me to follow me home.'

Keisha reads them their rights. 'I thought you said you didn't know anything about a yellow ring?' Rider says, looking at Finch's hand. 'And now there are two.' He points to Rosa who is attempting to pull the glinting yellow diamond ring from her finger. 'Our boss only caught a glimpse of her face in the van with Garry Harding but when he saw Michael in the station it clicked. We thought you could lead us to both rings.' Rider's smile would find a place on a shark.

'I'm sorry, Mum,' Michael says. He looks more like a wheedly boy than a businessman. That's all it takes.

'We don't know what he's talking about,' Rosa says, staring at Michael. 'They have nothing on us. They won't find any, either.'

'Nothing, Mrs Finch, aside from CCTV footage of you getting into the van in which Inspector Dark was kidnapped. We also have you recorded on Garry Harding's phone, at various times. Threatening him. Colluding to commit murder. Not to mention his testimony against you.'

Keisha reads them both their rights. Rosa's eyes narrow. Her demeanour has shifted from icing sugar to glass.

'Turns out Garry wasn't as stupid as you thought.' Or perhaps he was even more stupid than she thought, making evidence that will end up convicting him.

'There is no way you can have CCTV footage,' Rosa says, smirking.

'Why's that then?' Keisha asks. 'Know something that you think we don't?'

Rosa and Michael look at each other.

'Not at all,' Rosa says. 'I was simply saying that you can't have footage if it didn't happen.'

'Nice slide there, Mrs Finch,' Keisha says. 'There I was thinking it was because you knew about our CCTV department and how Ed wiped all incriminating evidence on behalf of certain people. Only you trusted the wrong person. Not only did his actions call attention to the Ring, but he didn't sufficiently destroy the evidence. We have thousands of hours of footage. Nothing and no one can ever be deleted.'

'You've charged me with murder, what evidence do you have for that?' Michael says.

'Footage of you, Mr Michael Finch, approaching your father, Mr Finnegan Finch, on the South Bank and hitting him over the head with a baseball bat. If we're lucky, the same baseball bat that Garry Harding has in his possession, given to him with orders to kill Detective Inspector Dark.'

'It wasn't that blow that killed him, it was later, in the warehouse,' Michael says.

'Shut the fuck up now, darling,' Rosa says.

'Is that any way to talk to your child?' Keisha says. 'Time to separate you two. You'll both be going to the station so we need another car.' Rider escorts Michael out. He tries to look at Rosa but she turns away. 'Wait in here,' Keisha says to Rosa, pointing to the orangery and checking that all the doors and windows are locked. 'I'll be right here, watching you. You'll know what that's like. Now, if you don't mind, I have to make a phone call.' She can't wait to tell Jonathan.

Finnegan follows Rosa into the orangery. He watches her pacing. She is angry. Magnificent. Part of him longs to leave with her, sit next to her in the back seat, in the cell, in the court so that when she denies it all and is proved innocent, he'll be there. But she isn't innocent. He knows that now. He thought *he* was the one taking too many evenings out and weekends off, so much so that he was relieved when he would come back late and find that she was still out 'with the girls'. All that time spent in the office or out talking with clients, he just thought she was thorough. They had underestimated

248

each other. He should have believed her when she said, crying in his arms after Seamus died, that she would kill her brother's murderer.

'Hello, Finnegan,' Rosa says.

Finnegan flinches. She is talking to him as if he were still alive.

'You might look more happy to have the family together again,' she says. 'If only for five minutes.' She is looking straight at him.

'You can see me?'

'Whether you're a pathetic, mooning ghost or a pathetic, unfaithful husband, I can always see right through you.'

'You had me murdered, Rosa.'

'And I'd do it again.'

If he had a heart it would have turned to avocado stone. 'They've got everything they need, you know.'

'It will be lost. That's the beauty of the institution, Finnegan, and if you had been clever about it you'd know. Whatever mess Ed has caused, we'll cover it up. These recordings by Harding? They'll disappear. The Ring is too big to be taken down, it circles everything.'

Finnegan whirls around and out of the orangery. Rosa tries to follow but Keisha Baxter is behind the locked door. Keisha puts her phone down. He takes a non-breath, grabs her phone and returns to Rosa, hoping she did not see him place it by the vase.

He moves as close to her as he can. Her look of hate and disdain makes him step away. 'Why did Michael do it, Rosa? Why were you involved and not tell me? Was it because I was unfaithful?'

She laughs. 'I'm not a hypocrite, darlin'.'

'Then, why?'

'That ring you gave me. The one you said was made out of my hair. How did you really get it exactly?'

'I killed someone,' Finnegan says, quietly.

'Speak up.'

'I killed someone.'

'Which someone was that?' There is no love left for him in those eyes. Nothing.

'Seamus.'

'You killed my brother to join a gang. They came to me when you started creaming money off the top and talking about leaving. They told me what you had done to my baby brother. I may have understood if your life was under threat but you didn't even need to kill him. They would have chosen a victim for you.'

Finnegan sinks into a wicker chair. 'I'm sorry, Rosa. I'm so sorry.'

'It wasn't even a hard choice. I jumped at the chance. All those years helping you run the crematorium, bringing up our son, they meant nothing to you.'

'Did you have to involve Michael?' Finnegan says. He can hardly get the words out.

'Michael was the one who told me.'

Finnegan stares at her.

The door is unlocked. Keisha Baxter holds it open and escorts Rosa out. Rosa looks over her shoulder briefly, then walks away. Her face, the one he kissed so many times, is snarled up, jaw clenched.

He watches through the living room window as she gets into the police car. He never really saw *her* before, only the Rosa he wanted to see – the beautiful, homely wife and mother with a head for the family business. Not that it's not true, only that truth has many faces and he picked the one he liked best.

Back in the orangery, he takes out Keisha's phone from behind the vase. The question is, what will he do with the recording? It will have value to DI Dark, or that man Blake Merry. There must also be ghosts in the Ring – all rings have shadows. There is always money to be made and he has evidence in his hand: Rosa's confession and, in between her answers, the susurrations of an Irish spectre.

He wanders through the house, placing all the photos he passes face down. Rooms tug him into them, netting him with memories. This is how houses become haunted: when you have no body, memories are the driftwood you cling to. He will not get stuck here. He doesn't know where he will go or whether he will have the energy to stay Present but it's not every day you get a new life. He's coming for death, ready or not.

29

DCI Allen holds out her hand. 'Congratulations, Jonathan,' she says.

'Thank you, ma'am. That means a lot. Congratulations to you, too, I've hear you've been promoted.'

'I'm not going to take the job. If they think they're buying me off with promotion then they'll have to think again. I want to investigate the Ring.'

'You'll have to do a Snowden,' he says.

'If I have to.'

'It will unravel almost everything.'

'If I do my job right it will,' she says. 'If I get that far.'

'I hope you will, ma'am. I'll do what I can to help.'

The voice of Superintendent Bernson snakes down the hallway. The only time he makes an appearance is for the press or after a successful case. 'We might be able to avoid him if we tiptoe out now,' says DCI Allen.

Too late. 'Ah, the inspectors of the hour,' he says, slapping the door-frame. He holds a bottle of Glenmorangie in the other hand. 'What can I say? Congratulations to everyone on the team. The media is going crazy for the story. Internationally as well. The murder of Tanya Baker has been cleared from our books and consciences and you, personally, stopped Maria King from suffering the same fate. A mother and son murder team will be on trial. The press love it that it was revenge for Finnegan Finch's adultery. Sex and murder. Great stuff.'

'There's no sign of a confession from the Finches,' Jonathan says. 'Rosa claims that her ring was a present from Finnegan, a leftover from a batch at DMD. Michael says it's a drinking club that has initiation rituals supposed to look like murder. Any footage will be contaminated because of Ed's involvement.'

'Well, the unfortunate business of Ed Castor aside, the Metropolitan Police shines once again.' Nothing seems to trouble his forehead. It is as if life is a jolly game, an Oxford romp.

'We have uncovered large-scale corruption in our own system, sir,' DCI Allen says, her voice exasperated. 'That is hardly a triumph. Everyone in the Met should be investigated.'

'Absolutely,' says Bernson, his pale eyebrows wiggling. 'We'll uproot it, weed out the canker. Meanwhile, give this to the team on me. He laughs again, white hair flopping.

Jonathan shares the bottle of whiskey out with the team, pouring it into their glasses. Their faces are without any sign of celebration. Tony leans against the wall, his head in his hands. 'Thank you all for coming in,' Jonathan says. 'You've all been working hard. I know this is hard to consider a celebration but Maria is alive and a killer has been stopped. You'll see that soon. It's difficult to come to terms with having had poison in our midst. It will take a while to trust again, but we will. It's not our fault that we assume humanity in those next to us. Celeste can't face coming in, knowing what she was sitting in the same room with all this time, but the alternative is to be suspicious of everyone. To be always on watch. No one can live like that all the time.'

Denver looks over at Keisha. 'Sorry,' she whispers.

'Ed set up innocent people so that we would suspect each other and doubt ourselves, all the time paying no attention to him,' Jonathan tells the team. 'He fooled us for years. I don't think I will ever forget searching his flat and realising that I never knew him.' One memory in particular will surface time and again – opening up the cupboard and, finding buried in cremains, footage of Sian and Tanya's deaths. He thinks of meeting her ghost in the garden at Ed's birthday party, the one where Jonathan gave him the West Ham mug.

'What happens now, Guv?'

'What do you mean?'

'It's only just started, hasn't it?' Keisha says.

'That's right,' Rider says. Keisha nearly forgets to swallow her whiskey in surprise at Rider agreeing with her. 'Michael could go down for murder, Harding, and maybe Rosa, for a reduced sentence in abetting, Amyris Church will probably get away with having trafficked murder victims into diamonds because so little ties her to criminal activity. The problem is everybody else. Who did Rosa report to? Who has infiltrated the Met, the media, the government? We wouldn't even know about the Ring if Ed hadn't thought he was better than everyone and gone rogue. It lassoes London. How the fuck do you begin loosening that?'

'I don't know, Rider,' Jonathan says. 'I suppose we begin to build a case a diamond at a time. Unless the evidence disappears, of course.'

'Like ghosts,' Rider says.

Jonathan leans back in his office chair and closes his eyes. It is very nearly midnight. The day needs to finish. This week needs to roll over and be done. It has been the worst of his life. His back hurts from being manhandled, his brain hurts from holding on and Natalie has battered his heart again. Enough.

His phone goes. 'What is it, Natalie?' he says.

'I wanted to apologise for not being in earlier. I had to sort something out and didn't get round to calling. I'm sorry.' She has her sweet voice on.

'You don't need to lie. I know he was there.'

'I didn't want to hurt you,' she says at last.

He laughs louder than he means to.

'Whatever happens. It was nice to see you again.' He can almost hear her say 'for the last time'.

'Right.'

Her silence doesn't stay long. 'Me, Justin and Mum have been talking. Do you own that house in Spitalfields? Because if you do that will definitely factor in the divorce.'

The cells of what they had finally break down.

'You know what, Natalie? Thank you,' he says. 'That's exactly what I needed to hear.'

30

The brass knocker falls on the door of Pedlar Cottage. He puts down his glass of Mount Gay, the last of the night, he promises.

Upstairs, something falls. Tomorrow he will pack his few things up and leave. He'll sofa surf for a while. Find a house that won't breathe nightmares.

Jonathan opens the door. Frank stands on Folgate Street, holding a heavy-looking plastic bag. He seems to have shrunk in the wash.

'Come in,' Jonathan says, showing him into the living room. 'Do you want one of these?' he asks, waving the glass.

Frank shakes his head. 'I'm trying not to.' His eyes are red.

'What's happened?' Jonathan asks. 'Is Barbara OK?'

Frank's mouth pulls down at the edges. 'She's gone. It got in, attacked her. I didn't even notice.'

'What attacked her?' Jonathan says. He settles Frank into the armchair.

'Do you need to ask?' Frank asks.

Jonathan leans forward, confused.

'It's been growing strong on you, my Barbara, on anyone with a crack in them who has been in this row of houses. The robust can shrug it off, the sensible don't stay. It leaches others like a virus. A fatal one.'

'I'm sorry about Barbara, I really am. I can't imagine how much of a loss that must be.'

'I think you can. The worst part is losing her again. I'm a funeral director and I have nothing of her to bury.' His chest heaves.

'Can you get her back from the Gloaming? You did before.'

'Whisperers consume until there is nothing left. It is the only way to kill a ghost. As far as I know, there is nothing of Barbara left.' Tears flow into his mouth.

'I'm so sorry. Maybe we could have a ceremony?'

Frank nods. 'I'm here to warn you, though. With Barbara gone, it will move fully on to you.'

'I'm fine. Alive and, well, not kicking, but at least on my feet.'

'So you've been eating and sleeping?'

'No one sleeps well in the Met.'

'Forgive me for asking but I could not live with myself if I didn't. Have you thought of stopping it all this week?' Frank says.

'Who hasn't?' Jonathan tries to smile.

'How near did you get?'

Jonathan does not answer.

'I am worried about you.'

'It can't kill off the living, whatever it is.'

'It can break them. Make their lives into a gloaming. Those are the true ghosts,' Frank says. 'The ones who were never really alive when living.'

'Aren't you at risk, too?'

Frank shrugs. 'It's hard to care at the moment but I will keep in mind, for Barbara's sake, that the thoughts are not mine. Do the same, won't you, mate? Externalise the words it whispers. Know that they only have the shadow of truth and they will not last in the light. Trust yourself. Don't let doubt win out.'

'Consider it done.'

'Don't brush this off. You can do it. I know you have been destroyed by loss but your instinct is still there, if you'll listen to it. Your family was called Darkling for a reason.'

Jonathan knows he is giving another blank stare. 'What do you mean?' he says. He has never known so little in his life.

'Darklings are those who can see and speak to ghosts. It's where your name came from.'

'I can't see ghosts, I've never—' he stops. Sian Van Hausen. The woman on the tube. The Whisperer. The visible friends of childhood. How many others has he spoken with?

'It takes as much practice to communicate with ghosts as it does to be one. You just need to see.'

Jonathan stands up to indicate that Frank should leave. He will deal with all this later. 'I'd like to find Tanya and tell her that Ed is dead. She might be worried that he'll stalk her.'

'She knows,' Frank says, putting a hand on his shoulder. 'She was there at the time. How do you think Maria survived?'

'She fell onto a rock fighting with Ed. He must have fallen too, only he had the misfortune to black out and drown in the river.'

'Not so much misfortune,' Frank says.

'What do you mean?'

'Tanya was there,' he says, squeezing Jonathan's shoulder and letting go. 'She held him under the water.'

'*She* killed him? I thought she was worried about being stalked again?'

'Ed is the one who should be afraid – Tanya has all the makings of a Sgath – a ghost who haunts ghosts. Rough justice in the afterlife.'

'Are there other kinds?'

'I know you meant that rhetorically but yes, there are. That's a conversation for another time. Tanya told me to say goodbye to you, and to thank both you and Margery.' Frank's eyes twinkle, just a little.

'Margery?'

He smiles. 'Margery Dark.'

Jonathan's legs are going to buckle under him. 'You know her?'

Frank nods, his grin widening. 'How do you think I know about your name? I've worked with Margery for years. She brought Finnegan to me and helped us find Tanya.'

So many thoughts. Too many questions. 'Can I see her?'

'She says she loves you, will always be there when you need a cab but that you have everything you need, if you can trust yourself. Except for this. She's been saving up her cab money.' He points to the window.

Jonathan walks unsteadily over. On the dark street sits a Honda CB550. Attached to it is a shiny silver sidecar.

'That's for me?' he says.

Frank nods. 'She's proud of you. And this is from me.' He opens the plastic bag, takes out a covered box and hands it over. Jonathan slides off the cover. It's a Ouija board. 'I thought you might like to learn how to communicate,' Frank says. 'You could meet your flatmate, the one who's been playing housekeeper, and ask him how he saved your life.' He walks onto the street, looks up to the sky and its yellow threat of rain. 'Be careful, OK?' He is hunched as he walks back to the parlour.

Jonathan places the Ouija board on the table, places the planchette next to the word 'GOODBYE'. The last time he used one was when he was fourteen at Vanessa Turner's birthday party. She had dared him, while lighting a candle, to join her and three others round the table. Vanessa asked if any spirits were present. There was nothing at first, and then—

SS-cut.

He looks to the stairs.

SSS-cut.

The Whisperer is coming.

SS-cut.

SS-cut.

It drags itself off the last stair. Jonathan can see it fully now. It is the colour of split milk and scrapes along the floorboards towards him.

The Whisperer stops inches away.

> *Natalie never loved you.*
> *You drive everyone away, in the end.*

Sadness slips over him like an overcoat.

> *You repel everyone who cares about you.*

There is too much truth in the words to externalise them. Of course he repels them. It explains everything. He is the poison in his loved ones' lives, he is the common denominator. He does not deserve love or pity or worry. He needs to feed the Whisperer his heart, stop the pain.

Ss-cut

On the table, the heart-shaped planchette spins on the spirit board. It stops, pointing to the word 'NO'.

The Whisperer lifts a nail to his chest.

You deserve nothing.

The planchette pivots, agitated. The motorbike keys fly from the table onto the floor by his feet. For one moment, he can smell Gargie's perfume, Dad's cigarettes, Mr Sheen and real ale. They are here. They never left. They have faith.

Jonathan grasps the Whisperer's cold hard nail and, trusting his instincts, twists it back and jams it into its swollen thorax. 'Goodbye,' he says. The caul bursts and out flows the sound of stoppered rage.

The room smells of boiling milk and burnt hair. Jonathan sits with the Whisperer's words circling him. But they are no longer inside.

An hour later, Jonathan places the motorbike keys in his pocket. The Whisperer has not fully gone. The words never leave but they are now in the sidecar, not in control. He sits down next to the Ouija board and places his forefingers on the planchette. 'Hello,' says Jonathan. 'I know you're there. Thank you – I know you've been looking after me. I'm Jonathan Dark: defective, detective. What's your name?'

The planchette wobbles under his fingers. It jerks across the orange board.

Epilogue

It has been weeks. London is lit with Christmas pageantry and the streets heave with workers, shoppers and tourists; the scurrying and the shuffling; the lovers and the lost ones; the ghosts and the not-yet-gone. The Thames winks at Jonathan. Jonathan winks back and the river blushes with dusk.

Maria is on the bench where they first met. Hearing his steps, she smiles and stands. She's wearing a new purple trench coat. He can't wait to ask her what colour it tastes like. Her hair is now cropped to the nape of her neck, the place where it was slashed is no longer noticeable. She stuns him. He tries not to show it, but if he were allowed he would spin her round and round just so that he would be dizzy for a while and not be able to speak.

They sit down on the bench, the bronze statue of a benevolent-looking man next to them. 'Who's your friend?' he asks.

Maria grins. 'Dr Salter. The titled prince of the Thames is back and *all* of his family is here this time.' She points in the direction of three sculptures depicting a woman, a young woman and a cat.

Jonathan defocuses and looks into the far corner of his eyes. A blurred outline of distilled emotion is in his peripheral vision. It has the feeling of smiling. Jonathan whispers in her ear. 'He never went away.'

She looks puzzled. Soon he will tell her about the ghosts that he knows walk and float and bellow in front of people's noses. Of living with Coleman, an obsessive compulsive ghost and former colleague, who saved his life by making a mess. It will take careful introduction, although his instinct says she already knows. He wants to harness his own Darkling sense first, get back his own instinct, and work out how to live in ghost-locked London.

'I missed you,' she says.

His breath gets caught in his throat. It is amazing what the heart can do. The connections grow back. Slowly.

Billy leans against him. His leg is still bandaged but he no longer holds it up in the air when he sits. He flinches, though, when people walk past.

'I thought we'd get some chips,' Jonathan says. 'Then go to the ice rink at Hyde Park. I warn you now, my balance is terrible. I'll be holding onto you.'

'That sounds perfect,' she says. She lifts her hand and touches his face for the first time, reading his nose and the bump on it, the smooth skin behind his ear, touching his chin as if he were a love letter.

'I'm so sorry,' he says. 'About Simon. How are you doing?'

She hesitates.

'Only talk about it if you want to,' he says.

'Everyone is being so supportive. The Amellos bring me more cake than I can eat, I see Will all the time and we get on better than before. I have even got back in touch with my mum, but . . .'

'None of that takes the pain away for long?' he suggests.

She nods. 'Exactly. I keep thinking of things to tell him but can't. I've rung his phone over and over to hear his message. The strange thing is that I can feel him around sometimes or hear him talking to me. Stupid, really.'

'Not at all. He hasn't left you. I promise.'

They sit in silence for a while. Billy rests his head against Jonathan's knee.

'I brought you something,' Jonathan says at last, digging in his pocket. 'I went mudlarking this morning.'

'You didn't,' she says. She is smiling now.

'I took the bucket you gave me. I've been a few times in the last month. You're right, it does help you think.'

'Did you find anything?' she asks.

'I discovered that finds are like relationships – I was grateful for the first few: the Victorian coins, pins and pipes, then I found that the rare, unusual ones became more precious. This was my last find.' He places it in her hand.

She feels out the carvings: the face; the set of scales in perfect balance.

'It's a pilgrims' badge,' she says. Her mouth is slightly open as she turns the badge over in her hands. She laughs. 'I can't believe you've been doing this for a month and found something I've been wishing for. You're a lucky bastard.'

'Well that's true,' says Jonathan. 'But I also have access to eBay.'

She pretends to punch his shoulder, then feels for his hand. 'Thank you, however you found it. That's very thoughtful.' Her thumb is stroking his, down to the nail. She feels the smooth surface. 'What colour is it?' she asks.

'What do you mean?' His heart beats quicker.

'What colour is your nail varnish?'

Jonathan breathes deeply. 'Dark blue,' he replies.

She is quiet. Jonathan takes his hand away. She reaches for it and holds it tightly while, with the other hand, lifting up one corner of her eye mask.

'You don't need to,' he says.

'You've been inside my world. Now I want to see what you see,' she says.

She opens her exposed eye. 'The shade suits you,' she says. She's trembling against his arm. She looks up at him.

He smiles at her. 'You iris is beautiful,' he says. 'Just as I imagined – the green of the taste of raw carrots.'

Her laugh is a rising fire lantern.

Outside the chip shop, Jonathan bends to scratch behind Billy's ear. They both strain to see Maria through the fugged-up windows. Billy's breath huffs up the glass. 'She'll be back soon,' he says. Billy's tail thumps against the door.

Maria comes out, blindfold back in place, and hands Jonathan his sausage and chips. She waves half a pickled gherkin. 'I couldn't wait. Never pass up the chance of a pickle,' she says. She reaches for his hand. It feels right in hers. Like home. And trust. They walk away with bags of chips to take the place of gloves.

*

Ed runs towards Maria and Jonathan. Tanya is behind him. She is always behind him. She walks slowly yet never more than a few metres away. As Ed passes them on the pavement, Jonathan looks straight at him. He can't help Ed now, even if he wanted to. No one can help, nowhere is safe. Even the river runs the other way. Ed wishes the Thames would take him far from Tanya; from what he has done; from this city of unseen steps. It won't. He can't get away. Death has no sequel.

Acknowledgments

Thank you so much to Genevieve Pegg, Eleanor Dryden and Laura Gerrard for editorial guidance, support and loveliness, professional Whooper Angela McMahon, Sarah Bauer, Katie Seaman, Juliet Ewers, Sophie Painter, Julia Pidduck, Graeme Williams, Jon Wood, Sophie Calder, Jen McMenemy, Marcus Gipps and all at Orion/ Gollancz, Rupert Heath, Diana Beaumont and Meg Davis for agenting wonders, Alice Jakubeit, brilliant bloggers everywhere, libraries and bookshops, the Cockblankets, the WFTV mentees, Rob and Rod, Peter Mould, Patrick Knowles, Laura Lockington, Steph, Jock, Helen, Rob, Mark, Johnny, Guy, James, Sarah, Kevin, Marie, Paul and all in the crime, horror and fantasy families for making a straddler feel so welcome. Huge thanks also to the excellent London Mudlark for the advice and pipes, the Museum of London, Martin Ellis, Jacqui, Oliver Sacks, the Beaumont Society, Death Salon, St Barts Pathology Museum, the Order of the Good Death, Black Phoenix Alchemy Lab, those who wish to remain anonymous and my amazing friends and family including my gorgeous Matt, Dame Margaret Rutherford, Mum and Dad, Gran Gran, David, Carolina, Karen, Michelle, Zo, Marcie, Roz, Sam H, Judith, Sam K, Della, Nigel, Lou, Steve, Caroline, Kirsty, Ben, Emilia, Dom, Heidi, Jonny, Nim, Nickey, Matt, Bertie, Rob, Laurie, Kitty, Leon, Ceejay, Erol, James, Liz, Peter, Danny, Nicky, Lita, Gene, Keith, Lin, John and all at the Stables Theatre. Lastly, thank you to St Leonards, the London foreshore and ghosts of all kinds.

A serial killer with all the time in the world . . .

THE BEAUTY OF MURDER

Stephen Killigan has been cold since the day he arrived in Cambridge.

Seven hundred years of history staining the stones of the university have given him a chill he can't shake. Then he stumbles across the body of a missing beauty queen – a body which disappears before the police arrive . . .

Out Now